Fear The Hunted
By: Jinn Nelson
ISBN: 978-1-927134-81-8

Bluewood Publishing Ltd
Christchurch, 8441, New Zealand
www.bluewoodpublishing.com

Other titles by Jinn Nelson

Coming soon

Pirated

Due in 2013

For news of, or to purchase this or other books, please visit:

www.bluewoodpublishing.com

Fear The Hunted

by

Jinn Nelson

To Matt, Desiree, Sofia and John -
Enjoy! Never forget who you are. Isaiah 43:1
Jinn

Dedication

To Tristan, who first inspired me, to Aria, my dear lioness, and to all my family, whom I love so deeply.

A story not about you, but for you.

A few people who deserve recognition:

Jeremy Nelson, anam cara, my Tegid Tathal. You endured the most and the worst, and told me to keep going. Without you, this book would not be.

Thanks to my dad, the Lion Heart. Though proud of my writing, you never pushed me beyond what I was ready for. I am ever grateful.

Mom, who taught me everything from kindergarten to 12th grade, and then some. You are glorious.

Lauren L., who got me started, and her husband Eddie, who doesn't usually like books but said he liked this one. So I didn't throw it away.

Lisa G. and Sam, my support team. Every writer should be so lucky to have friends like you.

Casey, a truly good writer never satisfied with his work, and a constant inspiration. You've reached one person already, and you can reach many more. Don't ever stop writing.

Thanks to the writers who got me writing again: Jeremy L., Echo, Misty, Dewey and Crystal.

And to the writers who, though we've never met in person, keep me going: James Scott Bell, Stephen Lawhead, Robert Jordan, Kaisey, Kokubyaku, Nicole and Mikayla.

This book is because of you.

I thank you.

Pronunciation Key

All unmarked vowels are short or soft
S is soft as in 'sea'
Vowel sound always comes after apostrophe:
l'e \luh\
l'a \lah\
y' \yuh\

Vowels
ie \ee•ay\
ae \ay\
ai \ay´eh\
ei \â\ ex: eir \air\

Aenti EirNin \ay•EN•tee âr•NIN\
Aleph \AY•lef\
Anithe \AN•i•thuh\
Anrac \AN•rak\
Cail \kay´el\
Camil Askanda \kuh•MEEL as•KAN•duh\
Carmul \kar•MOOL\
Core \cōr\
Daehexa \dey•HEX•ah\
Derrh \dur\
Dnae \din•AY\
D'tanesse \dah•TAHN•is\
Elaa, elaa \AY•lah\
Esobir \es•oh•BEER\
Estimal Glor \ES•tĭm•ol glōr\
Eulba \YOOL•bah\
Grano \GRAH•no\
Imra \EEM•rah\
Inatru \in•A•troo\
Kcen \kuh•SEN\
Kilar \kil•AR´\
Klenit \klen•IT\
Kmoch \kim•OCK\
L'abri Glor \lah•BREE glōr\
Laic \LAY•ek\
L'estim Glor \luh•STEEM glōr\
Llyna \LIN•uh\
Llynx \leen´ks\
Maanx \mayn´ks\
Machaun \MAH•shon\
Maon \MAY•on\
Mytch \mich\
Natug \NĂ•toog\
Natami \NA•ta•mee\
Nier \NEE•air\
Raelcun \ray•EL•coon\
Sema \SEH•mah\
Seya Wul \SEY•uh wool\
Siegra \see•ĀY•grah\
Sienna \see•EN•ah\
Tarrom \tar•ROM\
Teyeda \teh•YEH•duh\
Telracs \TEL•racks\
Terra \TER•rah\
Yettmis \YET•mis\
Yessac \yeh•SOK\

Prologue

Troy

My memories are…erratic. I remember how the ocean sounded, breaking against the cliff face. I remember dirt and chalky rocks crumbling away beneath my toes and spinning through the air, making white dots on the surface of the water. Staring down, I lost my balance and began to fall. My mother caught my wrist just in time, pulling me safely against herself. I cried, terrified of the horrible thought: death in the water.

"The ocean is not evil," she murmured in my ear, caging me in her warm arms. I smelled salt essence, tinged with rose oil. It was the smell of home. "It can be very dangerous, but it is not evil."

"I don't like it," I sniffed, burying my face in the soft crook of her elbow. "Can we leave?"

"Avoid falling into it, but do not run from its glory. Look."

I looked, and saw fearsome beauty in the glittering waters, painted pearl and jade and scarlet by the glowing sun just above the horizon. We sat in the long grass on top of the cliff and watched the sun disappear behind the rim of the world. We saw the elusive flash of green that was the sun's last light shining through the water. We watched the stars appear in a clear twilight.

"The dawn always comes," she said when I lamented the dark. "You will live to welcome the morning."

I have lived through many nights since then. I have faced terrors more horrible than the ocean. I have faced the terror of love. The terror of destiny. The terror of loss. I have been conquered.

When I stood on the cliff edge the second time, my mother was not there to catch me.

When I fell, I didn't even remember her.

I didn't remember anything.

Part One

The Outcast

Chapter One

It was early evening. A girl who did not belong in the forest sat in the dirt beneath the grandfather tree at the edge of a potato field.

"Sienna, who is that?" Ten-year-old Terra of Kcen brushed hair out of his eyes with the back of a grubby hand, smearing dirt on his forehead.

His sister Sienna, arms bare to the elbows, turned from her pile of freshly dug potatoes. "Terra, how many times must I tell you to keep your eyes on your work? They're going to eat without us if we don't hurry."

"But Sienna," he whispered loudly over the leafy tops of the withered plants between them, "it's a girl!"

That much was readily apparent.

Sienna turned back to the pile of potatoes she was separating by size and stowing in burlap sacks, to be delivered to Michel the trapper tomorrow evening. She would never admit that she also snuck glances at the girl, even though Terra had seen her doing it.

He frowned, exasperated. No one was curious when they ought to be, especially dutiful Sienna. Terra tugged a large potato from the roots of its mother plant and tossed it in her general direction. It bounced off her shoulder and rolled away over straw and dirt.

"What if she's lost?" he asked when she spun around again to glare at him. Her headscarf slipped down over her puckered forehead, a crimson slash above her eyes. "The wolves will get her if she stays out here alone."

After a full day of harvesting and bundling oats, their biggest crop, she was not excited about digging up potatoes as well, but it couldn't be helped. Sienna adjusted the scarf, pushing it back so the line of her yellow hair showed and tightened the knot at the back of her neck. "Just finish, Terra. Worry about it later."

Terra sighed. Sienna always talked like this when she didn't know what else to do. She didn't know what to do when the girl first wandered onto the field twenty minutes ago. She didn't know what to do when the girl did not wander away again. So, as most people in their village would, Sienna ignored her. Terra might have ignored an adult, maybe, but he could not pretend against a girl his own age. Might as well ignore starvation.

The girl in question sat, not quite touching the shagbark trunk, with her knees pulled close to her chest, drawing in the dirt with her toes. Tattered lines of green silk, the remains of a fine gown, draped over her legs. The silk disappeared beneath a rough-looking tunic wrapped around her torso.

Reddish stains dominated the once-white fabric. Her dark hair was matted in an angry snarl to her shoulders.

In light of there being a mysterious girl in his field, Terra decided his work was finished enough. Michel would surely understand. He set his potato rake upright in the dirt, prongs buried firmly in the damp soil. He made his way toward the strange girl, staying low lest Sienna see and interrupt him, crawling on his hands and knees to the edge of the row. He came close enough to see deep scratches on the girl's forearms, too many to count, and halted.

"Are you lost, Llyna?" he asked, using the formal address for a young girl.

She ignored him, or didn't hear. Terra scooted closer and crouched next to her, burrowing his toes in the dirt.

"Are you lost, Llyna?" he repeated a little louder, hoping Sienna wouldn't hear him. The girl barely raised her head to reply. Terra leaned closer to catch her answer and wrinkled his nose. She smelled of salt and old blood.

"I don't know."

"Then, who are you?"

"I don't know." The girl shifted and rested her head on her knees.

"Terra!" Sienna spotted him and marched over. Her faded red skirt swished above her ankles, dirt and straw drifting to the ground.

Terra took a deep breath and stood. "Sienna, this girl is hurt. We have to take her home with us." He hesitated, faltering beneath Sienna's level gaze. "Please? If we don't get her out of here before dark, the wolves might eat her."

At this, the girl raised her head. Her dark eyes, bloodshot, locked with Sienna's. Hair mingled with dried blood stuck to the left side of her face where a long, vertical gash was scabbing over. Terra and Sienna stared at it, silently recognizing but not wanting to believe it was what they thought it was.

"You'd help if it were me, or Imra…" Terra searched for further convincers but came up short. For a dreadful moment they were all silent. A yellow leaf, the first of its kind, broke from its branch overhead, fluttering down to rest on the girl's head.

Sienna knelt, bringing her eyes level with the girl's. She reached out and carefully freed the leaf before it became part of the black snarl. She smiled at last in the way Terra loved, that made people comfortable without needing words. "Come with us, Llyna, yes? We will help you."

With further coaxing, the girl followed Sienna and her brother through the forest, her steps halting and painful. Sienna led the way. Her burlap sack, hastily filled with the rest of the potatoes they'd gathered, hung heavy over her right shoulder. Terra carried a smaller one, leading the girl by the hand. His heart pounded. He'd dreamed of having adventures, but now he was having one. It was wonderful.

"I like this adventure," he said.

"Finding a lost servant is an adventure?" Sienna's backward glance was incredulous.

"Well, and she's hurt," he defended. Though bringing home a lost servant girl hardly compared to, say, fighting off wolves using only his belt knife (and becoming the village hero for life), it was the biggest adventure he'd had in ten years of life.

"Bringing in the harvest without Father is enough adventure for me," she answered.

That's because you're boring, Terra thought. To be polite in front of the girl, he said, "That's an adventure, I suppose. This one is more fun though."

Sienna shook her head and walked on.

Golden hickory leaves glimmered above them, catching the last of the sunlight. Terra hoped the wolves weren't hungry enough yet to approach the village through their fields. Wildlife wasn't scarce yet, but during the cold months when the forest population dwindled, roaming wolf packs came for Kcen's livestock. They were worst at the end of the season, when snow drifted up against the houses. The villagers took turns at night, sleeping and watching in shifts. Those were long nights for everyone. Terra spent them lying awake under a pile of bear skins, wondering when—if—his father would return from night guard.

The moon showed through a screen of branches when the siblings and their charge arrived at the edge of the fields. Dark shapes of houses—the rest of the village—could be seen beyond their own small house and barn.

Terra glanced back at the girl. "Do you…know this place?" He gestured toward the scattered houses with his potato rake.

"If she knew this place we would know her," Sienna pointed out, still ahead of them.

The girl's dark eyes reflected the candlelight shining from the windows as she shook her head slowly.

"This is Kcen," Terra told her gently. "One of the forest villages."

The girl mouthed his last words, staring ahead, then asked, "Where is that?" Her voice faltered, as if she had not spoken for days.

"Kcen is part of Cathylon. That's our island," Terra added, in case she didn't know what Cathylon was.

They stopped to deposit their potatoes in the big root cellar by the barn and hang up their potato rakes, and in the entry they left their dirty shoes by the outside door before opening the inside door to the house. Terra took the girl's hand again and led her into the welcoming candlelight.

"Mother! Father! We're back," Sienna called. The workroom was empty except for their mother's spinning wheel, a polished hickory worktable and a row of shelves with assorted family treasures.

"And guess who we brought home!" Terra piped up, stopping beside her. "A servant girl!"

"Terra!" Sienna whispered fiercely, too late. "Let me tell them—"

"What?" Their mother, a thin woman with a crimson headscarf like Sienna's covering her pale hair, hurried from the hearthroom. Wet smudges stained her sage-green apron.

Behind her, Terra's other sister, Imra, hung back in the broad doorway. Only half of her white headscarf, one wide gray eye and one pearl-white braid were visible; the rest of her was blocked from sight behind the wood casing.

"A girl?" Core, Terra's only brother, emerged shirtless from the bedroom. A gray tunic dangled from his long fingers. His thin, furrowed eyebrows matched his incredulous frown. "That's no servant. That's a savage."

"You're as much a savage as she is," Sienna returned primly, raising her chin.

"I am not!"

"Core," said his mother, "Dress yourself, please."

Core murmured an apology, slipping the tunic over his head. At twelve, he was nearing adulthood, though in Terra's opinion he still had quite a ways to go.

Imra glided forward, along the wall between the hearthroom and the entry, until she came to the corner beside the door where she stood, watching. Terra nodded to her, encouraging what for her was a bold move. Even though she was eleven years old, she wasn't as confident as her siblings.

"Where did you find her?" Terra's father, Harok, stood in the doorway to the other bedroom, supporting himself with a pale hand on the frame. He caught his breath before approaching to kneel before the girl.

"By the field, beneath the grandfather tree." Sienna stepped aside for him.

The girl's nostrils expanded, inhaling his scent, and she shrank against

Terra's side, gripping her tunic closed at her chest and stomach in tight fists.

"It's okay," Terra murmured, squeezing the girl's hand gently. "He won't hurt you…don't be scared."

Sienna also saw the girl's fear and stepped close again. "Perhaps if we tell her our names…" She smiled at Harok and then at the girl, reassuring. "This is my father, Harok. I am Sienna, the oldest. That's Terra—"

"I'm Core, second oldest."

"That's our mother, Cail—"

"One moment, Sienna." Harok sighed, squinting at the girl. The dark circles forming under his eyes matched hers. "What is your name, Llyna?"

"I—I don't know," she whispered as her eyes flickered over his face.

"It's alright, Harok. I'll take care of her." Cail swept them all aside. "You should keep resting. Sienna, would you prepare a bath? And Terra, bring the kettle, please."

While she encouraged the girl across the workroom to the sisters' shared bedroom, Terra dashed into the hearthroom and retrieved the iron kettle warming in the coals. He carried it, full and steaming, back to the bedroom, treading carefully across the pinewood floor. To his disappointment, Cail met him at the door and took it.

"She is going to bathe now, Terra. You can come in when she is done."

* * * *

"Father will take her to Tarrom, won't he?" Sienna mixed hot and cold water in the tub to bring the temperature down for bathing while Cail coaxed the girl out of the stained, oversized tunic. "If she is Inatru's property, the Inatru should take care of—" Sienna turned at her mother's gasp.

Cail dropped the tunic and put her hand over her mouth, staring at the girl's back. Sienna hurried over to look, then wished she hadn't. Narrow, scabbed cuts slanted every which way over the girl's shoulder blades, across her upper back, down her spine and ribs to the top of her hips. The remains of a green silk dress showed here and there, embedded in the dark brown scabs.

Cail lowered her hand from her mouth and breathed in slowly, then reached into her apron pocket for her shears. "Sienna, bring a wet cloth."

Sienna's lips moved without words before her voice finally returned. "Either she was dragged on her back through thorn bushes, or someone—"

"Sienna." Cail's voice was forced calm. "A wet cloth, please."

Sienna closed her mouth and turned away. She pulled the rag box from underneath the bed and dragged it beside the tub, shaking her head.

"I'm going to help you out of your dress," Cail told the girl, showing her the shears. "I'm not going to hurt you." The green bodice was mostly intact on the girl's front. The skirt was torn to shreds all around. Cail snipped the material free from the waist to the ragged neckline, going carefully around her back where bloodied silk stuck to the girl's skin. The girl shuddered, squeezing her eyes shut. After the last remnants of the dress came free, Cail picked a soft rag from the scraps of cloth inside, dipped it in the water, then gently pressed it against the girl's back. Pink rivulets ran down her legs, staining the clean water.

Sienna laid a nightshirt on the bed, then took the kettle and a pail for more clean water.

"We will need to make an infusion for her," said Cail. "Some of the cuts are looking bad."

"I will start it."

For the next hour, Sienna and her mother were busy boiling a medicinal infusion for the girl's wounds to stop infection, making bandages out of rags to wrap around her back, and coaxing her to eat some soup, while the rest of the family ate supper without them.

Terra was sitting on the floor beside the door, waiting for them when they finally came out. "Is she okay?" he asked, worry clouding his bright brown eyes.

Sienna made her smile warm, trying not to think about the cuts scoring the girl's back that were now hidden beneath bandages. "She will be fine." She brushed the top of Terra's head with her palm.

Cail came out, closing the door behind her. She gave Terra a tight smile and walked quickly into the hearthroom. Sienna followed. The room was empty save for Imra, who was putting away the last of the dishes from supper on shelves lining the far side of the room. Core thumped around in the workroom, stacking wood, keeping busy. Cail stooped to stir the tureen of stew now cooling on the hearth. Two bowls and spoons waited for them nearby. She picked one up and ladled soup into it.

"Whips," Sienna said finally, keeping her voice low. "Somebody whipped her."

She had seen that pattern of cuts before, when the chieftain's son Mytch used a new whip on a pig's carcass. He had laughed, delighted as each stroke opened a new red fissure in its fragile flesh. Sienna had not cared much for him after that. Even on dead things, cruelty was not funny.

"Whoever it was will not get her back," Cail murmured. "Inatru property or no."

Sienna looked up, surprised. Her mother simply frowned at the tureen, face flushed with rare anger.

"Say nothing of this to your siblings, Sienna. Imra and Terra especially. I don't want them to have nightmares."

"Yes, mother." Sienna took the bowl, suddenly exhausted. It had already been a long, tiring day of harvesting, worrying about her father who shouldn't be ill so long from a simple chest cold. Now they had a strange, injured girl on their hands.

"And say nothing to the neighbors, or your friends, until your father and I take her to Tarrom. We'll find out where she is from and what happened." The last part sounded like a promise.

Terra slipped into the room and stood beside Cail, leaning against her skirts. "Mother, can I go to her now?"

"Let her be alone for a few minutes." Cail smiled for his sake. "It will take time for her to adjust to being around us. Try not to frighten her."

Terra glanced over his shoulder, lowering his voice. "Mother, has she been whipped?"

Sienna blinked. She'd forgotten that Terra was there for the incident with the pig.

"What makes you think that?" Cail asked calmly.

"I saw cuts on her arms, like—"

Cail bent down and hugged him, one arm around his shoulders and one hand on his head. "She has been through something terrible, I think. What she needs now is a friend, not an interrogation. Can you be her friend, Terra?"

Terra nodded solemnly, brown eyes wide. Sienna almost smiled. He probably considered making friends with mysterious girls quite an adventure.

"Good. Help Imra clean up, and then you can see the girl. I'm going to talk to your father. Everything will be alright." Cail set her spoon on the hearth and turned to leave the hearthroom. She glanced back as she went through the doorway, and Sienna caught the worry in her eyes.

Chapter Two

Terra sat on the floor at the girl's feet, trying to talk to her. It wasn't easy. She sat as though condemned to death, hands in her lap, staring at her bare feet. Her hair was combed and parted in the middle. It framed her face, two long sheets of black that joined to cover her neck and shoulders. One of Imra's nightshirts replaced the girl's oversized tunic and filthy dress. In it, the girl seemed more tangible, yet at the same time, even more foreign.

The right side of her face was the least injured, just a bruise above her eyebrow and another on her cheekbone. And the long, scabbed gash that curved from her temple almost to her chin. Her eyes were intelligent, wide with apprehension. The left one was rose-colored around its black iris.

"Are you hungry?" He tried to ignore his own swollen stomach. He had all but inhaled his soup at supper, he was so impatient to speak to her again.

The girl shrugged. Terra noticed a wooden bowl Sienna had brought sitting beside her on the bed, scraped clean except for a bit of potato residue on the sides. He rolled his eyes at himself and changed the subject. "Do you like knives?"

She drew her bare toes further beneath the hem of her nightshirt.

Terra pulled his knife out of the sheath on his belt, shining and sharp. He gazed at it a moment: his greatest treasure. "My father gave me this on my tenth Eulba." He gave her the leather sheath to examine. "I made this sheath myself."

She fingered it delicately. A flicker of interest crossed her face. Encouraged, he took the knife back and grinned at her. "Watch this."

He stood, the knife's blade grasped gently but firmly in hand. Taking careful aim, he hurled it at the log wall. The knife flashed in the flickering candlelight, digging into the wood with a thunk. The girl's eyes followed Terra's knife, then lifted to his face. She wasn't scared or unsettled, he noticed with delight. His sisters were put off by knives or wrestling, or anything rough or challenging. Not this girl.

"You like it, don't you?" he asked, touching her forearm lightly.

She nodded slowly, as if thinking, 'Do I? Yes, I do…'

Sienna entered at that moment. "Terra, what would Mother say if she caught you doing that?"

Terra knew exactly what she would say. He grabbed the knife from the wall and returned it to its sheath—not a moment too soon. Cail opened the door and stepped in. She had removed her apron, and her red skirt was vibrant.

"Your father and I are going to take the girl to the chieftain."

"Now?" Terra asked, eyes widening. The girl turned away, staring at the hole left by his knife, perhaps listening, perhaps not.

"Yes. Obey Sienna while we're gone."

Terra grimaced. "Might I come?"

"No." Her usually mellow tone held an edge of controlled anger or anxiety.

Terra knew better than to argue and stepped back with a meek, "Alright, mother…"

Cail nodded, crossed the room to the girl and knelt before her. "How are you feeling, dear? Better?"

The girl reluctantly pulled her eyes away from the wall to Cail's face. Cail reached for her limp hand, and the girl allowed it to be held, warm in Cail's fingers.

"Would you come walk with me? Harok and I have someone we'd like you to meet."

The girl looked uncertain, but Cail smiled and helped her stand. "I'll be with you the whole time, don't worry. That's right…on your feet, now. You'll be safe with us."

"What will he say about her face?" Terra hovered beside the girl. "Will he let her stay here?"

"No more questions now, Terra. We will be back soon." Cail nodded to Sienna and led the girl out of the bedroom.

* * * *

The girl went as directed, not sure if she were dreaming again or not. Usually she was afraid in dreams. She was afraid now, but the voices that spoke to her were kind. A boy with friendly brown eyes kept coming to her and smiling. A woman had bathed her and put bandages around her back and ribs. That hurt, but it didn't frighten her. A stinging burn across her spine and shoulders replaced the horrible itching, which was actually a relief. She had eaten something but couldn't remember the taste. The boy had come again and thrown a knife at the wall. That wasn't frightening either. The hole left by the blade held her attention. Some distant feeling like a remnant dream called to her through the little black mark.

Then the woman had returned and taken her hand, asking her to walk somewhere. The dreamlike feeling fled.

Now the woman led her outside, into a dark world. The serious-looking man, Harok, waited for them, and when they came out the three of them walked down a packed dirt road. This was familiar. She had walked in the dark for some time, before she found the field and the boy found her. However, this time the kind woman led her through it.

Bright gold, glowing rectangles floated past, lit by hearth fires on the inside. They belonged to houses, windows, but to the girl they were disembodied burning shards, doorways to a nightmare. She turned and pressed her face into the woman's' side, hiding from the sight. After a few more steps down the road, the woman bent and picked her up. The girl leaned against her chest and put her arms around the woman's—Cail's—neck. The warm hand pressed gently against her head, and they moved on.

After some minutes of footsteps crunching dirt, a gruff voice spoke out, stopping them.

"Harok? What brings you at this hour?"

The girl kept her face hidden against Cail's soft neck, finding comfort in her warmth and clean smell, while Harok, standing beside them, answered.

"I apologize for disturbing the chieftain, but it can't wait."

"You don't look well. Who do you have there?"

"I don't know. She is lost and badly wounded. We think she's a servant."

"Tarrom doesn't have any—"

"I know."

A pause. Then, "Come in."

The girl opened her eyes and saw a smear of light behind Cail that widened, casting weird shadows on the ground. She shut her eyes again as they moved forward. Cail's arms shook as she set the girl on her feet, on a smooth wood floor. The girl leaned into her, trying to merge with her skirts and disappear.

"Well, this is unusual." A man's voice, deep and confident, rose in volume as someone approached.

The girl dared not turn her head to look.

Cail bowed, bending at the waist. "M'lord."

"M'lord," echoed Harok.

"Harok, I hope this unexpected visit means you're feeling better. Who is this?"

"I am surviving alright." Harok sounded tired. "Sienna and Terra found this girl near our field when they were harvesting. We don't know her name or where she's from."

"Did you try asking?"

"She can't remember. M'lord—she has a servant's mark."

Cail gently turned the girl around so the owner of the voice—Tarrom—could inspect her. He had a red beard and red hair. His eyes were the same strange blue as Sienna and Cail's. He squinted at her as if trying to solve some puzzle. His tunic was a much brighter white than Harok's, and he wore a dark green cloak over his broad shoulders. She knew that made him important, but the knowledge was fleeting, like fading dreams.

Cail knelt behind her and carefully brushed her hair behind her ear, revealing the cut on the left side of her face.

"It's new." Tarrom sounded surprised. "Inatru servants are marked when they are much younger."

"She was also whipped," Cail said. She was trembling with anger. "At the same time she was marked, it looks like."

The girl looked past Tarrom, where a young man sat at a long table, watching them. He too had red hair, but no beard. He seemed confident. Did she like confidence? Yes, she did. She liked kindness better, though.

"Once marked, a servant becomes property of the Inatru who marks them. One can do what they want with their property but—" He glanced at Cail as she tensed "—abuse is almost unheard of. They are more valuable when strong and healthy."

"It could have been…someone else," Harok suggested. "Considering the turmoil caused by the High King's death, perhaps it was Seawolves."

"Then her presence could mean the Seawolves have made it further inland than we thought. Or wanted to believe." The chieftain frowned deeper.

"The mark could be incidental."

"That is unlikely…"

Their voices faded to the girl's ears as she focused on the brown lines on Harok's hands. They disappeared beneath his sleeves. She stared hard, trying to remember why she knew them.

Why, why, why...

She felt eyes on her and looked around. The young man at the table frowned at her. She returned the frown quizzically, tipping her head to one side.

Cail rested a hand on her head just then, bringing her back into the continuing discussion. The young man leaned forward with his forearms on his knees, also listening.

"Chieftains in smaller villages rarely need servants. They're more commonly sent to growing cities like Camil Askanda," said Tarrom. "But there has not been a Lady in this Hall since my wife passed away. There is probably extra work to be found for the girl."

The young man frowned deeper at this. Sadness as well as anger, at the mention of the Lady's death.

"Might the cook appreciate some help?" Cail offered.

"She might. I cannot promise the girl will be accepted, in any case, by the other villagers. Especially right now."

"We will accept her," Harok said quietly, and Cail patted the girl's shoulder.

"You have always been soft when it comes to children," Tarrom answered, arching his eyebrows. "Both of you."

"As you said, things are uncertain for everyone right now. Especially for children," was Cail's level reply. "Harok's illness has put us behind on the harvest. All the children are working in the field so we don't lose our crop, so I have no one to help me in the kitchen or with deliveries. She will not be a burden to us."

Tarrom stood, squaring his shoulders. "I will not say she can stay yet. It is twelve days until the change of the seasons. If no one claims her before then, and she is no threat to our village, I will let her be my servant and Kcen will become her home."

The girl held his gaze as Cail and Harok bowed. He seemed to be waiting for something. The girl stood straight with her shoulders back, pondering the lines on Harok's hands again. A memory tickled her mind, fluttering in a void. Something important. Time running out…but why?

Tarrom grunted. "When she's recovered, send her to the wayfaring house. Mytch will teach her what to do."

The young man straightened, his frown turning into a smirk. Cail took the girl's hand again and led her back outside, into the dark.

* * * *

The next morning Terra sped through his chores, earning a few laughs from Core and a raised eyebrow from Sienna, who was helping with chores in their father's place. Nevertheless, Terra was the first one back in the house and ready to eat, conveniently seated beside the girl. She was clothed in a sleeveless brown dress and white headscarf, borrowed from Imra. The dress was slightly large, even with the back lacing pulled snugly as possible without hurting her. The front sagged with extra material; the armholes gaped. The scarf covered her hair completely, gathering the length of it in a bulky knot wider than her neck. Her palms rested flat on either side of her plate, elbows bent at right angles, to avoid scraping her cuts. Most of them scored her shoulders, but a few laced her elbows and forearms. Her knuckles were bruised but the backs of her hands at least were not cut.

She watched his father enter the hearthroom, following his movements with actual interest. Terra touched her left hand, the one nearest to him, and smiled when that brought her eyes to his. When she came back from seeing the chieftain last night, she'd seemed more dazed than frightened, which Terra considered an improvement emotionally. His parents related the news to him and his siblings, with mixed responses. Core was skeptical. Sienna was worried. Imra was silent, watching. Terra was elated. His new friend could stay!

"Did you sleep well?" He hoped she would be more inclined to talk after a night's rest. He had hardly slept at all. He was too excited.

She shook her head, no, but patted his hand in return.

He grinned and held it gently. "Me either."

"She was clinging to Imra this morning in bed," Cail said, leaning between them to set a bowl of porridge before each. "I think your kindness is starting to help her. She's starting to trust us."

Terra grinned, kicking his feet back and forth under the table.

Cail finished filling bowls with porridge as the rest of the family seated themselves. A mound of pork sausage and fried potatoes waited on Terra's plate, sending savory steam twining into the air. His stomach twisted. When they were all finally ready, he dug in with a will.

"What will you do with the girl today?" Sienna, sitting across from Terra, blew gently on a spoonful of porridge before tasting it.

"She'll stay with me in the kitchen," Cail answered. "It will be a few days until she's well enough to work in the chieftain's hall. I could use some help here, besides."

"If she does have an Inatru master, won't they come looking for her?" Sienna asked, still worried.

"Maybe not, if their village is far away," said Harok. He looked more tired this morning, despite sleeping. He glanced at his bowl but did not eat one bite. "They'd send word through one of the merchants, and have him bring her back."

"The merchants are apparently collectors of people now, as well as village contributions," his mother murmured, barely audible.

Terra was fairly certain 'the girl' didn't appreciate being talked about like she were a stray dog. "She has a name. We should find out her name."

"We won't know that until she feels like talking," Core returned. "If she can."

"Well until then we should call her something," Terra said hotly.

"I think her name is Aspen," said Imra, seated on the girl's right. She spent most of her free time in the forest gazing at the trees, and collecting bits of moss and plants she found interesting. Today she wore her headscarf folded so it only covered a little of her hair, with the ends weaved in her pale braid. "It's a pretty name."

The girl was staring once again at Harok, eyebrows puckered in deep thought.

"I'm sure she has a name already. Llyna ought to do for now." Sienna finished eating first and stood. "Right now the harvest is more important than names, if we want to eat when it snows."

Terra grimaced. He couldn't deny this was true, but they could think of a name and harvest potatoes at the same time. If it were up to him, Terra would have named his oldest sister 'one who cares too much about work', if such a name existed.

Core, sitting beside Sienna, caught Terra's eye and grinned. "We could call her Sadie."

"We're not going to name her after the cow."

"We named you after the pig…"

Harok coughed, a harsh, painful spasm. The children glanced at him, then at each other, and quickly finished eating. Every minute wasted meant risking the crops. When Terra left the house, Cail was bending over his father, her hand on his broad back. He was nearly doubled over in his seat, coughing uncontrollably.

Terra worked fast just so he could finish sooner and visit the girl again. He followed Core, bundling sheaves as big as he could hold, as fast as he could.

While he worked, he talked, thinking aloud.

Father's sickness was definitely getting worse; he should be getting better. They were waiting for Ecallaw (who knew everything about diseases) to return from delivering remedies to another village, but what if he didn't return in time and Father died? At least Mother had some help in the kitchen while Sienna and Imra were needed to finish the harvest. Didn't it seem that the girl was more alert this morning? Imra had told him before breakfast that the girl was clinging to her in bed; the girl had smiled at Terra several times; she was becoming as attached to the family as they were to her—

"You're just saying that because you like her." Core finally broke in, sounding weary. "Hurry up, we're falling behind."

"I am hurrying. And she is responding to everyone. I'm just saying she smiled at me."

"She won't stay with us, even if Tarrom accepts her. She'll be his servant."

"What does that matter? She'd still be our friend…"

By midday Terra's words dried up. He worked silently behind Core, mechanically gathering stalks, tying them, carrying them to the wagon and gathering some more. He was about to ask if they could stop and eat when Core looked toward the dirt track that led past their house to the road and muttered, "Look who's coming."

Terra turned to look and groaned. "What is he doing here?"

A solid young man with harsh blue eyes and a permanent smirk approached, striding through their field as if he owned it. Pinpoints of light filtered through the trees, shining on his ruddy hair. "Is that scythe sharp enough? You haven't made much progress."

"We know what we're doing, Mytch." Core shoved his scythe into the oats, his jaw set in resignation.

"Are you sure?" Mytch folded his arms and appraised the field. "It looks like the girls are beating you. Did they take a break to let you catch up?"

"Not everything is a contest, Mytch."

"No, just most things."

"Then why don't you get a scythe and try keeping up with us?" Terra grunted, bundling a sheaf and hefting it in his arms. He hurried to the dirt track and dropped his load where the cart usually waited. His sisters had taken it to the barn to unload it. Terra hoped they would hurry. Mytch usually behaved himself around Sienna. She was fifteen years old, an adult by village standards, while Mytch was only fourteen.

"I came to ask about the girl," Mytch was saying when Terra came back to gather another sheaf.

"What about her?" Terra stiffened, squinting up at the older boy.

Core shook his head and kept swinging the scythe.

"What has she told you about herself?" Mytch asked.

"Nothing. She doesn't remember anything."

"She must remember some detail," Mytch scoffed.

"If she did, she'd have told us," Terra retorted.

"What makes you think that?" Mytch narrowed his eyes.

"You're just looking for trouble, aren't you," muttered Core, swinging away.

"It's amazing to me that no one considers the path of their own thoughts." Mytch folded his arms. "I just want to know why she's here. Our village is closest to a main travel route. You do know that, right?" His tone implied that he doubted they knew where their own village was.

Terra bristled. "Go home, Mytch."

"Don't disrespect me. I'm making a point. The nearest route travels north and south. The Seawolves invaded the northern coast just days ago."

"She's a refugee, obviously." Terra picked up an armful of fallen stalks.

"Not from the coast, though. She arrived too quickly, an injured girl on foot. She must have come from a larger town, where chieftains keep servants. The Seawolves probably destroyed it. She's been here a whole day now. They probably weren't far behind her."

"Don't be stupid." Terra gathered more stalks, making a sheaf he could barely get his arms around. "We would have heard of something like that happening."

"You know less than half of what happens in Cathylon." Mytch sneered. "Anyway, if the Seawolves haven't arrived in the forest yet, they will soon. That girl might be here to spy, or kill my father."

"She's cut to pieces right now. How could she hurt anyone?" Core shook his head again.

"That got her in, sure," Mytch persisted. "My father hardly stopped to think, when your parents showed her to him. One look, and they all pitied her too much to ask the obvious questions."

Core finally turned to face Mytch. Terra hoped he would to engage and help win the discussion. Instead, Core looked past both of them and his brow crinkled in concern. "Mother's coming."

Terra spun to see his mother running toward them, skirts hiked above her shins.

"Mytch, please take me to your father. Please—" Cail panted. Except for faint redness in her cheeks, her face was white. "We've been giving Harok the wrong medicine."

Core dropped his scythe and hurried to her side. Cail put a hand on his shoulder, looking at Mytch. "It's not malaise. It's white fever."

Mytch almost bumped Terra's shoulder, hurrying past to take Cail's arm. His sneer had vanished. White fever started slowly, but when death came, it came quick. Mytch knew that better than all of them; his own mother had died of it. Terra's stomach clenched.

"Go to the house until I get back!" Cail called over her shoulder to her sons. Terra prayed it wouldn't take long to explain things to the chieftain and find the right medicine.

Core and Terra ran to the house, feet pounding and throwing up dirt behind them. When they burst inside, they found the girl sitting beside the fire, watching a pile of dough rising on the hearthstones.

She looked up when they entered. "I remembered something," she said.

"His hands made me remember first, but then his cough…"

Core ran to his parents' bedroom. Harok was coughing inside. Had he been coughing all the time they were gone? Terra swallowed down anxiety and stepped into the hearthroom, toward the girl. "What happened?"

"I saw the red lines on his hands and I saw they went up his arms. And he was coughing out white foam, and then I remembered. It's white fever." She smiled, proud of herself. Terra's return smile was shaky. He dared not go into the bedroom to see his father. What he could hear was bad enough.

Core came out of the bedroom, pale and shaken. "Hopefully it's not too late. Once the phlegm turns red it will be. That's how it was with Tarrom's wife."

Terra leaned against the doorway to the hearthroom. "If Ecallaw were here, he would have known."

"Apparently, the girl knew." Core laid a hand on Terra's shoulder and gestured to the girl. Newfound respect crept into his voice. "Father says she told them what it was. She probably saved his life."

Terra's smile steadied and grew. He turned and knelt before her, taking both her hands in his. "Do you know what you've done?"

Her eyes widened, uncertain.

"You saved my father's life!" He leaned in to kiss her cheek gently. Her eyes were even wider when he looked into her face again. Her fingers tightened on his.

"I'm glad," she whispered—a revelation more than a response. "I'm glad I helped."

"You did help." Terra laughed breathlessly. "He's going to get better, thanks to you!" He wanted to say her name, but she still didn't have one, so he smiled more and squeezed her fingers.

"There's a problem, though," Core said.

"What problem?" Terra glanced back at his brother, smile fading.

"Father said she told mother the recipe for making the medicine."

"So?"

"The recipes are from the sacred writings. Only the Inatru know them."

Terra shook his head. "She's not Inatru. Her skin is too dark. And she has the servant mark…"

"I know," Core said, frowning at the floor. "But this girl is no servant."

Chapter Three

The house was filled with the pungent scent of garlic. The girl, having just set the table for the evening meal, sat down there on the middle of a bench to rest. Harok, already sitting at the table, smiled at her. Cail also smiled as she moved around the hearthroom, preparing the meal. Harok was improving on the new medicine, and after four days his cough was nearly gone. The girl noted that the whole family seemed quite pleased with her because of this.

She gazed past the tabletop. Her vision blurred, unfocused. Colorless memories trickled through her mind: a wagon on a forest road, disappearing in the muddy light of dawn, the edge of Terra's field at sunset. The time between those memories was blank. She might have walked for days, but she only remembered one sunrise, so perhaps she had only walked for hours. She had moments of awareness, when Cail carried her through the dark to the chieftain, or when Terra threw his knife at the wall, or when she recovered a scrap of memory about illness. However, that awareness soon receded, more time passed in a muddle of colors and sounds, and her struggle to wake began anew.

At length the family gathered in the hearthroom, coming in from the barn, the fields, the bedrooms. Their voices, conversation, rose and fell in her ears. Imra set a small bundle of purple flowers on the table beside the girl's hand. The girl struggled to rouse herself and respond, but she was too slow. Imra moved away again. The girl rocked slightly on the bench, staring at the string binding the feathery bundle together.

The family sat down to the evening meal, scraping the benches eagerly forward. Their hands tapped the board, politely impatient while Cail dipped into the tureen over the coals and brought each a bowl of stew. Harok was served first, and his rough palm caressed Cail's hand as she set the bowl before him. She lingered, obliging, and then was gone again to the hearth. Sienna moved around the table, stopping to pour water into each cup, smoothly tipping the jug. Terra and Core, on either side of the girl, contained their fidgets while Sienna poured for them. They reached for their cups after she was done, touching the rims to their lips and splashing liquid into their mouths.

The girl watched, passive, scraping her thumb back and forth over the board in front of her. Her notched thumbnail caught against the horizontal wood grain, bumping and snagging until she turned the thumb, pressing lightly with the supple pad. The rest of her fingers crept up beside her thumb, and the sensation increased through each fingertip. She pressed her hand down on the board, imprinting the fine lines across her palm.

Harok asked about the harvest, and Core reported they would be finished the next day. He swelled his chest when Harok complemented their hard work.

Terra set his cup down. A small impact shuddered through wood to the girl's hand. Core scooted forward on her other side, rocking the bench, making a tremor when he did that touched her feet. She rubbed one foot over the other beneath the table, pressing her big toe against the high ridge bone of her arch. Comfortable heat from the fire brushed her bare ankles below the hem of her dress. A wooden spoon rested between her hand and Terra's on the tabletop, pointing toward her cup. She picked it up with her fingertips and turned her hand so the spoon lay across them. Invisible pulp follicles stood up against her skin when she rubbed the belly of the spoon with her thumb.

Sienna inquired how much longer until the girl was recovered. A few more days, Cail answered from beside the hearth. Terra spoke up quickly, suggesting she be allowed to live with them and then work in the Hall, since Tarrom had no rooms set aside for servants. Words came and went that meant nothing to the girl: Inatru. Wayfaring house. Seawolves.

Cail set a bowl of stew before her. Cubed potatoes and stringy meat swam in a brown, salty broth.

Tarrom would decide what was best, Cail reminded her children gently. If he decided she could live in the village, they would still see her. And perhaps she would be allowed to share at least a few meals with them each week—here the girl glanced up, realizing the 'she' was herself—if she did not get to live in the same house with them.

The girl breathed in, leaning over her bowl. The scent of stew was joined by others, smells she knew existed but now gained meaning. There was the friendly drift of smoke from the hearth fire, and hot candles melting beneath lesser flames. Streams of clear wax flowed over the darkwood bases onto the table. There was the good earth scent clinging to Harok in spite of his washed hands, and the sweeter dusty smell of straw that had followed Core and Terra in from the stable. Finally there was the subtle spice of hickory in the walls, and the faint, sharp tang of frost pushing against the window shutters.

"If she did get to live with us, we could take care of her," Core suggested. "Better than Mytch would, at least."

"She could share our room," Sienna added, earning a grin of approval from Terra.

The girl felt a tiny smile starting in the corners of her mouth. Terra's grin made her feel lighter. Happy, even.

"Perhaps." Harok wiped a hunk of brown bread around his bowl, sopping up the last of his broth. "I could mention the idea to Tarrom. That is, if she wants to stay with us."

The girl swallowed and nodded, her throat tightening. She could become family. She could live here, in the forest. She could live.

The hopeful conversation continued. The girl breathed deep between quickening mouthfuls of savory broth, mealy potatoes and saturated meat, aware of the shift in her being like a slow light rising and wishing more than anything that she could stay.

* * * *

Terra slept well, deeply happy. The evening meal had turned into a celebration, and his elation rose as he watched the girl's eyes grow brighter than ever. By the end of the night, she was even talking in whole sentences, whispering and smiling with Imra, and meeting all of their eyes with confidence. She had lived with them for almost a week; in his mind, she was now part of the family.

Terra ate quickly the next morning, racing Core to finish first. Core won by mere bites. It was the last day of harvesting, which added to the light mood that carried over from last night. Terra paused to smile at the girl and pat her hand before rushing to the entry room. Core was already there, pulling on his boots. Terra flicked his foot at one, spinning it away from Core's reaching hand.

"Oh. Accidental." Terra reached for his own boots. Core stepped forward and scattered them with a kick. Terra dove for one, but Core was faster. They collided and landed wrestling. Dried green leaves and grit crunched beneath them. His palm pressing Core's face, Terra craned to find a boot. He saw one resting just above their heads on its side. He reached, snagged it, then pushed away from Core, rolling to his feet.

Imra stood in the entry doorway, trying not to laugh. "May I get past?" The girl stood behind her, peeking around at them.

The boys faced them, quieting hard bursts of laughter with effort. A leaf wagged above Core's ear, snarled in his hair. The girl covered her mouth to hide her laughter. Terra shoved his foot the rest of the way into the boot. It was loose. Too big. Core lifted Terra's boots, one in each hand: victory. He offered the boots to Terra, withdrawing at the last moment. Terra lunged forward. Core allowed the boots to be snatched while he rubbed the remains of a leaf through Terra's hair. Terra pretended not to notice, retreating to the corner beside the outer door to put them on. He launched Core's boot off his foot with a forceful kick. It sailed heel over toe and bounced off the opposite wall. Core dodged the missile easily, shouting a laugh.

Imra giggled and slipped past them through the entry, going out into daylight. Grinning, Terra waved to the girl and followed. The sun's first rays glimmered through green branches edging the long meadow that cradled the village, and shadows stretched along the ground toward houses that dotted the soft grass. Terra skipped along the wide trail that ran between the house and the barn, toward the fields where Sienna was already at work with a scythe.

The day flew by. It felt like minutes after Terra began gathering and tying sheaves that he looked toward the house and saw his father leading the girl by the hand, walking toward them. Terra grinned and waved. They waved back, a tall figure in a worn gray shirt and brown trousers, and a short one in a brown dress, stepping out, side by side on the wide trail. A rainfall of gold and orange leaves flickered behind them.

"We came to see how you are doing," Harok explained when they stopped beside Terra.

The girl held up a clay cup. "We have water from the well."

Terra and Core downed several cups each, and then Core and Harok walked into the field, inspecting their progress. Terra and the girl sat down beside the bucket to rest.

"Do you do this every day?" she asked.

"No. We do lots of other things."

"Like what?" The girl leaned forward with her elbows on her knees.

"We feed the animals and plough and plant, and we deliver food to other families here."

"I bet all the families like you."

Terra smiled modestly. "We're not the only farm in Kcen."

"Well, I like you."

Terra wanted to put his arm around her, but that might hurt her shoulders. He shrugged and handed her the cup instead. "Would you like some?"

She shook her head. "It's for you, because you're working hard."

"Aren't you working too, in the kitchen?"

"Yes, but it's not hard."

"You can have some anyway," he said, filling the cup and putting it into her hands.

Core and Harok came back with Imra and Sienna, who had been

harvesting in another part of the field. After the sisters drank, Harok took the bucket to refill it at the village well. To Terra's delight, the girl stayed in the field with him and his siblings.

They showed her how to gather bundles of grain and bind them, and then Terra led her to the wagon to deposit the sheaves. She was out of breath after a few trips, but smiling. Harok returned to the house after bringing another bucket of water, but allowed the girl to stay and watch them work.

Core laughed at Terra, who began working faster and trying to gather sheaves too big to hold.

Terra ignored this; he had an idea. "You know, if we finish soon we may have time to throw knives." He glanced back at the girl. She was watching them, one elbow resting on her knee, head resting on her fist.

"So that's why you're working so hard," Core laughed.

"You want to as well, I know it! And, we could bring the girl. She might like to try."

"That's unlikely," Core scoffed, but Terra noticed his pace also increased. They moved along quickly, and when Terra looked back at the girl a while later, she was many yards away.

Mytch was standing over her.

Terra dropped his bundle of grain and hurried over to them.

Mytch frowned down at the girl; she glared up at him.

"I am not hiding," she was saying.

"You're clearly well enough to work in a field," Mytch answered. "If you can work, you are recovered and you're to come be my servant."

"Is your name Tarrom?" the girl asked.

"My name is Mytch. I'm his son."

"If I am a servant, I am his servant. Not yours."

Mytch blinked. His frown deepened. "But I am in charge of you. I'm going to teach you how to serve in our Hall."

"What are you doing here, Mytch?" Terra stopped beside them, close to the girl.

"He is bothering me," the girl said flatly.

"You are disrespectful!" Mytch retorted. "If you speak that way again, I'll have my father send you back to the Seawolves."

"Don't pay attention to what he says," Terra told the girl. "He just lives to bother people."

Mytch turned on him. "I helped your father too. Don't forget that."

Terra frowned, gnawing his lower lip. He couldn't deny that. Mytch had taken Cail to Tarrom and then ran with the medicine back to Terra's house to give it to Harok. He even apologized to Terra and Core while he was there for insulting them earlier. It seemed the only time Mytch acted reasonable was during a crisis.

"What is a Seawolf?" the girl asked. She pronounced it slurred: *Seya-wul.*

"They're killers," Mytch answered before Terra could. "They're probably the ones who hurt you. You probably ran away before they could kill you, but your master wasn't so fortunate."

"That's enough, Mytch!" Terra stepped forward.

"It's the truth," Mytch muttered. "No one here wants to know the truth, except me."

"You don't know what happened. Stop scaring her." Terra reached for the girl's hands. They trembled in his grasp.

Mytch folded his arms and shook his head, disgusted. "She hasn't even told you her name yet, has she?"

"She doesn't remember it!"

"Yet she remembers an obscure remedy for your father. Do you really believe she remembers nothing else?"

"You don't care what I remember." The girl scowled at Mytch. "You are angry because Harok lived and your mother didn't."

"You don't know anything." Mytch stepped toward her, fists clenched.

The girl stood. "You are angry. And sad. But you can't send me away for that."

Mytch pushed Terra aside and leaned down, his face close to the girl's. "I can send you away because you're dangerous. The Seawolves are probably following you. They'll hurt everyone because of you."

He glanced up and straightened. Sienna was approaching with Imra, both carrying sheaves.

Terra bristled, every muscle tight. He surged forward, grabbing the girl's hand again. "We already have a troublemaker. His name is Mytch of the Inatru!"

"I am only looking out for my village." Mytch's tone became deceptively light. "Hello, Sienna…"

"Is everything alright?"

Terra heard Sienna's question but did not look back. The girl kept pace beside him, gliding on the balls of her feet so she stalked rather than walked. Terra soon veered off the trail, treading through native grass and winding around sprawls of blackberry brambles, leading the girl behind the barn. The cluster of aspens between their house and the village grew larger as they came close, and Terra went straight to it.

"This place is where Core and I play," he told her, stopping at the edge where the close-growing trees formed a screen with trunks and branches. “Mytch won’t follow you here.”

Core caught up to them, out of breath. “Sienna asked Mytch to leave. Is she alright?” He nodded to the girl.

“No. Mytch upset her. She’s shaking.” Terra forged ahead, thrusting branches aside and holding them for the girl to pass through. Waist-high grass grew inside the ring of trees. The light was dimmed by overhead branches. Terra let go of the girl’s hand and dragged a thick severed trunk into the center of the ring with Core’s eventual help.

Terra took out his knife, tested the edge needlessly with his thumb, and then set his feet. Core stood by the girl in silent knowing, watching Terra’s arm cock back and then hurl the knife at the target. A furious throw. The blade dug into the wood, shivering on impact.

The girl glided forward to examine the target, her eyes lit with rare interest.

“Don’t pay attention to Mytch.” Core took his own knife from his belt and stepped up beside Terra. “He only talks like that because he knows you’ll respond.”

Terra felt a little better. “He’s stupid. He doesn’t know what he’s talking about.”

The girl turned to face them, standing before the target. “I want to try.”

Terra looked at her, surprised, then at Core. Core shifted from one foot to the other, shaking his head.

Terra shrugged. “Do you think you can?”

The girl raised her eyebrows, offended. “Of course I can. I’ve watched you.”

Terra retrieved his knife and handed it to her, handle first. “Throw hard, or it won’t stick in the target.”

The girl nodded. She examined the weapon carefully, grasping the blade between the length of her thumb and forefinger. Biting her lip in concentration, she set her feet in the tall grass. The hem of her brown dress brushed her calves, swirling subtly with her movement. Her hand drew back to her ear. Her eyes narrowed, focusing on the target. Then she stepped forward, throwing with her whole arm, and sent the knife deep into the target. Terra almost laughed out loud, seeing her face light up at her success.

Core whistled appreciation. “Wow.” His voice held a note of respect that he didn’t use with his sisters or any of the village girls. “Have you ever thrown a knife before?”

She shook her head slowly. Some hair escaped the headscarf on one side, covering the ugly purple scab that ran down her cheek. “Maybe?”

Core retrieved the knife and handed it to Terra before taking his turn. The girl's next throw was too high, and they searched a while before they finally found the knife in a sapling trunk beyond the target.

Core eyed her as they resumed throwing. "Are you sure you don't remember your name?"

The girl shook her head, watching Terra take a throw. "No." There was a slight hint of desperation in her voice.

Core sighted along the blade of his knife before throwing it. "Do you remember anything before you came here?"

The girl squinted into the golden canopy overhead. "I remember a fire. And water. Lots of water..." She closed her eyes, swaying slightly. Perspiration appeared on her forehead above her tense brow. "I remember standing in this forest, and a wagon driving on the road. Driving away in the dark. The sun came up, and I walked until I was too tired. And then I saw your field, and I sat down, and then you talked to me."

Terra touched her shoulder lightly. "Why didn't you tell us that before?"

"You didn't ask." She opened her eyes and took the offered knife. The blade flashed through the air, easily reaching the target. They watched in silence as she retrieved it and Core's.

"Well," Terra said when she returned and handed Core's knife to him, "what do we call you until you remember your name?"

The girl pondered a moment, turning Terra's blade over in her hands. "Something strong. I am strong."

"I don't know if there are any strong names for girls," Core said. "We should just call her Llyna. It's safer."

"Llyna isn't a name!" Terra protested. "It just means Girl."

Core moved to the next obvious choice, aiming and then throwing his knife. "Call her Lady."

"She is not a woman either!"

"I'm not?" The girl touched her white headscarf. "Imra said women must wear these."

"You are a woman," Core said, "but a young woman, which means we call you Llyna. Older women are called Lady."

"When a girl is old enough to wear a red scarf in her hair, she is sometimes called Lady because..." Terra squirmed, unsure of himself. "Soon she will be married."

"Do you get to do that?"

"I don't," he scoffed, amused at the idea of himself with a scarf wrapped around his head. "Only girls do. My sisters do. When a girl is five years old, she must wear a white scarf in her hair. She wears it until she is old enough to be married, and then she can put on a red one."

"Why?"

"I don't know. It's tradition. Our village has always done it."

The girl gave him a sideways glance as if to say, *how strange*, tugging unconsciously at her white scarf. "What is old enough?"

"Old enough…is…old enough."

Core began to laugh. Terra shot him a look, his face heated.

"Old enough to have children," Core told the girl, then added when she opened her mouth, "You'll know when you know. Ask Sienna—she can tell you how it works."

"Yeah," Terra echoed, studying his feet with unwarranted interest.

"Terra got in trouble when he asked about it," Core confided, and dodged his brother's wild fist, laughing.

"It's only something for girls to know about," Terra told her, eying Core who stepped, grinning, out of arm's range. "We just marry the ones with red scarves and tease the other ones when they make us nervous."

"You should be nervous," Core said.

"You should keep moving." Terra's next throw missed the target, and he spent several minutes digging through the ferns to find it. He came back with a new thought. "We could give her a boy's name."

They stared at Terra for a moment—the girl looking intrigued as she took the knife from him, and Core taken aback.

"Is that allowed?" She threw the knife.

Terra shrugged, looking at Core for an answer.

Core bit his lip, crossing and uncrossing his arms. "It's never been done, Terra. Anyway, we should go back to the field. Sienna will be mad if we make her and Imra finish."

The girl retrieved the knives while Terra considered. A new idea came to him—brilliant. "What about Troy?"

Core's fingers jerked as the girl handed his knife to him. He yelped and jumped back. It dropped, point first, into the grass near his foot.

"It's a girl's name," Terra said quickly.

Core snatched the knife up. "Only one! And only because she was the only female warrior, ever, in history!"

"She wasn't the only one. I heard the queen probably was. Really, Core, you're overreacting."

"Who was Troy?" the girl asked.

"She was a hero, in the days when Kcen was first settled," Terra told her. "The island was in chaos. Everyone came from different nations, they spoke different languages, and there was constant war until the Inatru established our laws. No one remembers Troy's real name, because when she began to be known as a warrior, people hailed her as Troy."

"What did she do? Troy?" The last was added quietly, as the girl tried the name out for herself.

"A man died fighting in battle when Kcen was being established. His wife took his spear and learned to use it. For ten years she protected the village in her husband's place. It was the first time in decades that someone broke tradition and was actually praised for it. You could be the next Troy!"

Core protested, "Terra—"

"She can throw a knife as well as we can, and I would bet my spear she can use that as well."

"You don't even have a spear," Core muttered.

"She deserves the name, Core."

Core looked up, searching the boughs overhead for patience. "Tarrom can name her. That's not our responsibility."

"How can you say that? She's not a lost cow." Terra ripped up a sheaf of grass and threw it at him. The stalks scattered, wafting down. "She has the right to a name of her own. She wants to have it!" He might be assuming more than he ought, but Terra figured if he were a girl, he would want to be named after a hero.

Core looked at the girl. She looked back at him, a smile lifting the corners of her mouth. Terra took her hands, leading her to the center of the ring of trees.

"This is a sight." Core crossed his arms. "A boy of ten acting lord of a girl older than him. She was alive at least two years before you were born. Think of that."

Terra rolled his eyes. He turned his back to Core and solemnly bade the girl to kneel. "I hereby bestow upon you the name Troy. Rise, Warrior. Live a life worthy of the name."

Troy looked up at Terra, fully meeting his eyes. The sun glinted through the leaves overhead, throwing light down on her hair and face.

"I will." She stood slowly, grasping his fingers for support, shoulders straight in spite of pain that made her grimace. "I will."

"If the ceremony is now concluded," Core said dryly, "can we please return to the field? Sienna is calling us."

Chapter Four

Terra's eyes flew open. The house was silent, save for the wind hissing in the trees outside. He didn't know how long he'd been sleeping. He had stumbled to bed almost as soon as he finished eating. The last four days had been a flurry of work, finishing the harvest and making late deliveries to families in Kcen, but the grain was in now. That was one less thing to worry about. Harok and Troy were steadily recovering. Tomorrow Cail would prepare a feast, celebrating both of them. Not only that—the day after tomorrow marked the beginning of Derrh, the snowy season. Troy would be taken to Tarrom for his final decision whether she could stay or not. No one had come to claim her, and no news of a runaway servant had reached Kcen. She almost certainly would be allowed to stay.

Despite his excitement about a feast, which happened rarely, Terra had fallen asleep instantly, sleeping without even dreams, until something woke him.

There it was again: faint scraping, then a muffled thump like something hitting the floor. Terra slid out of the bed, glad he slept on the edge so he would not wake Core. He padded over the cold floor to the door and pulled the leather handle, tugging it open. He tiptoed to the girls' bedroom and pushed the door open just enough to see inside. He expected to see three bodies—his sisters and the girl sharing the large bed—but there were only two. The girl was not there.

Terra's breath caught. He turned and searched the workroom with his eyes. Nothing. Perhaps he was dreaming. He glanced at the windows along the hearthroom wall, in case some face might be peering in. No…but someone was there.

Terra squinted at the hearthroom door.

Troy stood in the doorway, swaying on her feet. Her hair reflected blue-black in the watery light. Terra sighed, relieved, and started toward her. Her eyes were half closed. She was asleep, but standing up.

Terra crept closer, his heart pounding. Cold air brushed the skin on his chest, a reminder of his half-dressed state. "…Troy, wake up."

No response to his voice. Instead, Troy raised her arms, swinging languidly at some invisible presence.

"Let me go…let me go…" Tears slid from her closed eyes. Her head turned toward her shoulder, jerking as if trying to avoid blows or a blade.

Terra's stomach lurched. Was she dreaming about the person who marked her? Dreaming about a Seawolf? He reached out, touching her shoulder. Troy flinched, crumbling to her knees.

Terra panicked. He caught one of her hands as she lifted it to shield her face. "Wake up!"

Troy curled over her knees, flinching as if she were being struck from behind. Terra grabbed her shoulders, trying to shake her awake, make her alright again. She moaned and rolled onto her back. Terra bent over her, as her eyes opened wide. She shrieked, tucked her feet to her chest and kicked Terra in the stomach with both heels.

"Oof!" He doubled over as air left his lungs, clutching his ribs.

She kicked again. Her heel connected with his chin and he stumbled backwards, eyes watering from the blow, groaning as he breathed.

Cail came, almost running, clutching her nightclothes to her chest. She grabbed one of Troy's hands, and then the other.

"Mother! Moth—" Troy finally saw where she was and went still, darting glances around the room and at Cail's face. Sweat glistened on her forehead.

Terra stood back, hugging his stomach. Blood ringed his mouth. He licked his lips and tasted it.

"Shh," Cail soothed, drawing Troy to her. "It is all over now. You were dreaming."

Troy's trembling shook them both. Her face tightened as the nightmare came back to her, and she began to cry.

"I am here," Cail murmured, rocking her. "Don't be afraid. I am with you."

The bedroom door stood open. Terra's siblings hovered in the doorway. Imra came forward and knelt beside her mother, her face close to Troy's.

"Don't cry, Troy." Imra patted Troy's hair, then combed her white fingertips through it, ever gentle. "Don't cry."

Sienna went to Terra and put an arm around his shoulders. "Are you alright?"

Terra nodded. His lungs took their time filling back with air. "I was trying to help…" he croaked.

"She's just scared, Terra," his mother said. "She didn't mean to hurt you."

"I know." Terra ventured near and took Troy's hand in his, no longer caring if his chest was bare and his mouth bleeding.

"Did I hurt you?" she whispered, seeing Terra's lip. Her palm was coated with sweat, but the shaking had lessened.

He shook his head. "I wanted to help, that's all. It doesn't hurt." It did, actually. It throbbed.

"Why am I out here?"

"I don't know," said Terra. "I woke up and you were out here."

Cail looked at Troy closely. "Do you remember your dream?"

She shuddered, burying her head again on Cail's chest. "Only the water. I was…drowning. Someone was pushing me under…"

Terra leaned closer to catch her whisper. She smelled of sweat and blood, again. She shuddered and pressed against Cail's chest. Imra stroked her head and then kissed it. Terra stared at Troy's back below the line of her thick hair. Small spots of blood seeped through the cloth.

Core brought Troy a blanket from the bedroom, but the wool scratched at her cuts and she shrugged it off with a look of apology. Sienna found soft rags in the rag box, and Cail tended the few bleeding scratches. Harok built a fire in the hearthroom from last night's coals. The family sat with Troy around its gathering warmth, sipping sweetflower tea from clay cups, talking quietly and watching the window shutters grow lighter with the shifting shades of dawn.

* * * *

Breakfast was subdued. After cleaning up, Troy waited by the boys' bedroom door, picking at a loose thread in her brown skirt until they came out after dressing.

"Your mother says Core is to watch out for me today while she helps with deliveries. Where will you be?" She tucked stray hairs back into her white headscarf. Cail had wrapped the length of her hair with the headscarf and bound it in a wide knot covering the back of her neck, to keep it off her shoulders.

"He will be helping her. We all must do our work." Core smiled kindly.

"I'll be back before sundown. Here." Terra fumbled at his belt, unfastening his dagger and sheath. "You can use this in the copse today, if you like. When my work is finished I'll come for you."

She ran dark fingers over the leather, remembering their last time there. She had a name now, and a home. A small smile crept over her lips. "Thank you."

Terra, obviously proud of himself for making her smile, hopped away with a happy, "You're welcome!"

Core shook his head and led Troy outside, heading down the main road to the well.

"What do you do in the morning?" Troy looked for a place to stow

Terra's dagger, but had no belt or waistband.

"What do you mean?" Core asked. He carried two buckets, swinging them at his sides as he walked.

Troy wondered if she should offer to carry one, but maybe that wasn't acceptable. There was a lot she still didn't know. "You leave in the morning, then come back to eat. Where do you go?"

Core looked puzzled. They turned off the road and walked to the well, situated between the chieftain's Hall and a smaller building. Harok had told her on previous trips to the well that it was called a wayfaring house, where villagers brought contributions for merchants to take to the bigger cities.

"You mean when we feed the animals?" He set his bucket down by the stone rim of the well.

"Yes, I suppose." Troy tugged at the knot against her neck until it came loose. She shook her hair free, letting it settle about her shoulders. It didn't hurt too bad, she decided, and tied the headscarf around her waist. "Could I go with you?"

Core gave her a skeptical glance. "You could ask my father. I don't think he'll let you until your cuts are completely healed. Though, by then you'll probably be working in the Hall." He fastened the bucket to a hook attached to a coiled rope and lowered it down.

Troy nodded, satisfied with his answer. She tucked Terra's sheathed dagger into her new 'belt' and patted it, proud of her innovation.

They waited until the rope was taut with the weight at the other end, then Core strained to pull the full bucket up.

"Can I help?"

"Sure," he grunted.

Troy grasped the rope ahead of him. Together they hauled the bucket up and lowered the next. A musty smell rose up as the rope scraped against the stones.

"Cutting the morning peace to ribbons already, I see. Sienna threw you out early today."

Core cringed. "Mytch. Are you here for water?"

"I'm here to see her." Mytch pointed at Troy as he crossed the last yards from the Hall to where they stood.

Troy caught the bucket and pulled it to the edge of the well before turning. Her jaw tightened as she met his eyes.

"Where did you come from? Tell me now." Mytch stepped closer. Behind him stood a boy with a round face, who looked about Terra's age. He watched Mytch with an adoring expression, the same way Terra sometimes looked at Harok.

Troy's heart began to pound, and she breathed deeply to calm herself. She turned back to her bucket, pulling it up over the edge of the well, spilling some on her hands.

Mytch grabbed it from her and set it on the ground behind him. "Why are you here?"

"I didn't come to trade words with the village idiot," Troy snapped, wiping her hands on her skirt.

Mytch's blue eyes darkened to gray. "You'd best watch your tongue—"

"You—" Troy stepped forward "—had best leave."

"Don't threaten m—"

She knocked the words away with her fist, a fast crack against his chin, surprising herself as well as the boys. "I don't make threats."

Mytch closed his eyes, and when he opened them again they were back to their carefree blue. He smiled, touching his jaw. "Ki, you have a spine. Too bad you haven't a name to go with it."

Core scowled, bristling as Terra had the day before. The round-faced boy's mouth hung open, horrified.

"That is a sacred word," Troy said, and blinked. It was sacred, and ancient. But no one had told her that… "And I have a name. It's Troy."

"He thinks he can say anything because he's the chieftain's son," Core muttered. "Just ignore him."

Mytch smiled wider. On his face it was as menacing as a frown. "Troy? The Troy? Surely you jest!"

"I don't." Troy walked past Mytch, deliberately exposing her back. She picked up her bucket and walked to Core's side.

"We have to go." Core turned away, and Troy followed.

Mytch continued to mock. "Where's your spear, Troy? You wouldn't go anywhere without that, would you?"

"I can see why Sienna doesn't like to talk to you, if this is the way you treat people," Troy said without looking back.

Core groaned quietly beside her, but it was too late.

"This is how I treat pretenders!" Mytch retorted, following them. "You abandoned your master, didn't you? You pretend to remember nothing so that you can hide here."

Troy dropped the bucket, ignoring the bit of water that splashed against her leg, darkening the hem of her dress. Her head turned slowly. "I am not hiding."

"Why don't you just admit it? You are."

Troy stood stiffly, grinding her teeth.

"See? You don't belong here," Mytch shouted. "You don't belong anywhere!"

Troy felt Core's hand brush her arm, but he was too slow. With blurring speed, she spun and flew back toward Mytch. The top of her head rammed his stomach, and they went down.

Core's shout was distant in her ears.

They rolled over in the dirt, a tangle of red and black hair, and slammed into the well with Troy on top. She hammered him with her fists until he caught her wrists, his heels scraping lines in the dirt as they struggled. Troy used her knees, her elbows, even her head to pummel him.

Core jumped forward and grabbed at her arms, trying to pull her away to end the fight. The boy ran up and hit Troy squarely on the jaw.

Troy's head snapped back, slamming Core in the mouth. They both staggered back. Core stepped in front of Troy with his fists raised, but Mytch backed away, wiping his nose. Blood dripped onto his gray tunic. The boy stood at Mytch's side, trying to look bigger than he was by swelling his chest.

"Don't you hit Mytch!" he yelled. "That's your chieftain's son!"

"Erif ki, girl!" Mytch snuffled through swelling lips, elaborating on his previous expletive. "Erif al ki! You're a savage! You'll be repaid for this!" He turned and stomped back to the Hall, holding his hand over his nose.

People left their yards, coming to see the trouble and perhaps aid the chieftain's son. Core put an arm around Troy's shoulder. "Are you alright?"

She nodded, staring at the ground. Core grabbed both buckets from beside the well and began walking home. Troy followed a few paces behind, feeling dizzy. Her jaw and head throbbed. Something tickled her neck, trickling down. She touched it, and her fingers came away wet with blood: her skin had split where the boy hit her.

Core veered Troy off the road when they came to the copse. She breathed easier when she reached the grassy circle inside the trees. Here she was safe, away from eyes and words condemning her.

Core set his buckets down and reached for her shoulders to make her face him. "Are you really alright?"

Troy nodded. "Yes, but your mother will be upset if she sees me bleeding again."

Core wiped at the blood on her neck with his fingers. "I'd be surprised if Mytch ever hit a girl. His cousin Aleph was trying to impress him, probably. He's always trying to be like Mytch. Do you want to go to the house and rest? I'll explain things to mother when she comes back."

Troy shook her head. "No…I want to stay here and be alone. Just for a little while."

She wanted to run and hide herself away as quickly as possible. Mytch's words made her feel exposed, though to what she wasn't sure. Exposed as a terrible person, maybe. She did not want to be a terrible person. She wanted to be like Terra. Like his family. Innocent.

Core frowned, worried, but eventually nodded. "I'll take the water to the house. I'll be back in a few minutes."

After he left, Troy looked around the copse at the wall of trunks and branches. Her fingers stopped trembling when she touched the hilt of Terra's dagger. She drew it out, comforted by its weight in her grip. Then she lowered herself to the ground near the chipped target log and settled on her side with one arm stretched out, supporting her head, the least painful position she could find. Terra would surely be done with his work soon, and then he would come here to find her.

Troy closed her eyes. The tall yellow grasses surrounded her with soothing rustles. The wind sounded like water: a constant rush, with an ebb and flow, never fully ceasing, like waves rolling onto a sandy shore. The sound lulled her, covering her. Her eyelids stayed closed, and her head listed to one side, lips parted.

She dreamed.

Rhythmic waves rolled onto a shore scattered with jagged white stones. They were sharp and cold beneath her feet. Blood seeped from her heels and toes, staining the rocks. It ran down her arms and tickled her back. The cuts had come open again. She ought to stop the bleeding. The hiss and slur of waves droned insistently, resonating in her skull. Strips of cloth fluttered, trapped beneath the stones. She pulled one up and wrapped it around her arm.

The cloth hissed. It opened slitted yellow eyes as it soaked up her blood, turning from white to red, and burrowed into one of the deeper scratches. She grabbed at its tail too late—the snake went inside her.

Her eyes opened, sluggish. Grass rustled, disturbed by the wind, sounding like footsteps. She closed her eyes, but still saw the grass. She looked down on herself, a brown-clad girl curled up in the green sea of grass. Little red snakes emerged from her open cuts and slithered over her body. She grabbed at them frantically, crushing their thin bodies. They oozed red between her fingers.

It was a dream. She must wake—

Hands clamped down on her arms. A man's flat, damp voice filled her ears.

Let the snakes in. It will be over soon.

She screamed, and made futile slashes with her knife. More men stood over her. They were pushing snakes into her body—

Troy woke, screaming. A figure loomed over her, hands reaching. A boy. He was real. He groaned, small eyes bulging in a round, freckled face, as the knife—the knife in her hand—slid into his stomach.

The nightmare was supposed to end when she woke. Her lungs pulled in extra air. The rest of her would not move.

"Aleph!" Someone else was in the copse. That voice was familiar.

"Mytch…" The boy croaked, and fell onto his back.

Mytch shoved Troy aside, crashing to his knees beside Aleph. Troy rolled over gingerly to her hands and knees, arching her stinging back off the ground. It throbbed, throwing her stomach into a fit of queasiness. Blood was slick on her skin, warm and wet on her fingers. Her throat burned, and her breakfast came up.

Mytch was screaming for help.

Troy heaved one last time. "I didn't see him—"

"We were trying to scare you, not—" Mytch gasped and grabbed a fistful of her hair, pulling it aside to bare her neck. "Ki—you are one!"

Coughing, Troy beat against his forearm with her fist. He backed away, mouth open.

"Who is screaming?" A man thrashed into the copse. His strides slowed for the barest second at the sight of blood, and then he sprang forward, running in earnest. "Aleph!"

"We didn't know she had a knife—"

"My son! Aleph!" The man cradled Aleph in his arms, his shoulders heaving.

Mytch eased back, arms hanging aghast at his sides. "Kmoch, we didn't know…"

Kmoch turned to glare, first at Mytch, then at Troy. His eyes bulged, their whites stark against the flushed red of his skin. His neck was a mass of tendons, tight and pulsing with building fury. "Who is this?"

Troy's throat burned, choked with acid. Her skin throbbed. She rubbed her palms against the grass, smearing it red.

"Who is this?" His bare snarl startled her to her feet.

Mytch told him.

Kmoch lunged at her. Troy sprang away, tearing up dirt and grass, sprinting on her toes. He went after her, bellowing.

"Seawolf! Someone! A Seawolf has killed my son!"

Chapter Five

"It was an accident."

"She is a Seawolf, and the chieftain's relative is dead."

Angry tears burned Terra's eyes. He stared at his house growing nearer through the trees where Troy waited for them. Their news was not good.

At the sound of screaming, Terra had dropped his spading fork and sprinted from the potato field, arriving outside his house in time to watch a hysterical, unbelievable scene unfold: Troy clinging to Harok, her face hidden in his tunic. Kmoch, shouting that a Seawolf had killed his son. Men armed with spears, coming for Troy. Mytch, sitting on the ground by the stable, ashen cheeks streaked with tears.

Cail came rushing from the house and hurried Troy inside. Harok planted himself before the door, defending his wife and the frantic girl from angry retribution.

The issue was taken to the Chieftain, Tarrom. For the next hour, Terra and Core stood with their father in the Hall of Kcen, beneath the vaulted ceiling that soared on grand wooden wings, in defense of the Seawolf—Troy was no longer considered a servant—who had just killed the chieftain's nephew.

Kmoch and Mytch bore personal witness to the charges. Mytch described the tattoo he discovered on her neck: a compass star in black ink, the four points piercing a thin outer circle like knife blades—the mark of the Seawolves. He stared hard at the floor as he spoke, avoiding eye contact with Terra or Harok. The mention of Seawolves set the villagers present into fits of conversation, the ladies' lips moving in rapid speculation, the men muttering oaths from the sides of their mouths.

Unfortunate Aleph died within minutes from his wound. Troy had delivered the stroke with a stolen knife—

"The knife was mine," Terra had spoken up, on hearing this.

"I am told you found this girl." Tarrom searched Terra's face.

"Yes, m'lord."

"Are you the owner of the stolen knife?"

Terra had to breathe deeply to control his voice. "I own it, m'lord, but she did not steal it. I…gave it to her."

"And were you there when she killed Aleph with the weapon you gave her?"

"No, m'lord."

"Were you not aware this girl is one of the Seawolf traitors?"

"No, m'lord."

"Why not?"

"I…I never saw the back of her neck."

One hour of discussion was all it took for a verdict to be reached: outcast. One hour, and Troy was lost for good. Kmoch, the most injured party, wanted the death penalty, but Mytch of all people argued against it.

"It was my idea to sneak up on her," he admitted, "and I encouraged Aleph to approach her because…I didn't want her to hit me again. She should not be killed because of our choice."

"Indeed, you had a hand in my son's death, but I must forgive you because you are my brother's son," Kmoch growled. "Otherwise I would have you exiled."

"He will be punished, Kmoch," said Tarrom from his chair. "He will never forget this day or the part he played in his cousin's death. If he is smart, he will make choices in light of the incident—" He gave a slanted look at Mytch "—starting with finding a sufficient way to restore himself in our eyes."

Mytch seemed to shrink where he stood while Tarrom and Kmoch continued talking. For several moments he did not raise his eyes from his feet.

In the end, Kmoch relented. "Send her away," he said, before he left with his wife to bury his son. "And if Mytch feels so responsible for this tragedy, perhaps he should leave with her."

The chieftain's eyes were blue chips of stone in his somber face as he ordered Harok to send the girl away immediately. Two spearsmen would be sent to make sure the command was obeyed.

Terra, Core and Harok walked home in silence. Harok stared ahead, eyebrows drawn together above his eyes. Core was dazed. Terra was outraged.

Mytch had followed them as they left the hall. His eyes were haunted and bloodshot, the skin surrounding his mouth pallid. "I am sorry—"

Terra turned on him, fists raised. His father caught his arms before he could land a blow, pulling him away.

"Not sorry enough!" Terra snapped. "She'll die out there, alone! Did you think of that? Did you ever think of anything besides yourself?!"

His own voice rang in his ears the rest of the way home.

"But it was an accident," he said again. "Mytch should be punished as well!"

"His cousin is dead. That is quite enough punishment for now."

Harok's sharp glance silenced Terra, who stared at the ground again, seething.

Cail was on her knees in the entry, scrubbing the floor with a weathered rag. Her movements were steady, but one look at her eyes revealed her trembling thoughts, and she was on her feet in a moment.

Terra did not stop as her questions began. He hurried past Sienna, who stood against the wall listening to her father's recount of the proceedings with both hands covering her mouth, and went into the bedroom.

Imra knelt with Troy on the floor, huddled with her arms around her neck. Troy raised her face from Imra's shoulder as Terra entered. He joined them on the floor, completing the triangle with one arm around Imra's shoulders and one around Troy's. He kept his weight light, finding a space of whole skin on her opposite shoulder to touch.

"I told her it's okay—we're still her family," Imra whispered.

Troy's head sank again, bowing to her chest. "I killed him…" Her shoulder shook beneath Terra's hand. Imra kissed her hair, and Terra rested his forehead on Troy's warm temple.

"It wasn't your fault, Troy. We know that."

"I had another dream—"

"When she woke up, Aleph was standing over her," Imra finished, when Troy's voice descended into quiet sobs. "She did the same as before, when you stood over her, only this time…"

"You would never use my knife for something bad," Terra reassured softly into her ear. Troy's tears dripped on her clenched hands. Terra reached down and covered her hand with his, shielding it. He felt suddenly grown up, protective of the fragile girl weeping her fright out on his bedroom floor. "Aleph didn't know about the dreams, or he never would have done what he did."

He should have included Mytch in that statement, but he didn't. Mytch didn't deserve such an excuse.

* * * *

The sun glared red through the trees as Troy left the only family she knew. Cail led the way down the dirt track to the barn, where Harok waited with a black, saddled horse. Imra held one of Troy's hands, and Terra clutched the other.

"Is he for me?" Troy stared up at the black gelding.

"Yes." Harok held out the reins. "His name is Laic."

Troy reluctantly released Imra and Terra's hands to take the reins.

Harok cleared his throat and rested a hand on her head. Cail handed him a sturdy burlap sack filled with bread and salted venison. He tied it behind Laic's saddle, already laden with a bedroll, hatchet, rope and other small tools he'd scavenged from their barn that Troy might need. Sienna came forward with a cloth bundle containing two dresses, one from each of the girls. Harok found a place for it, beside the hatchet. Sienna hugged Troy, her smile tremulous. Core's smile was also shaky as he gripped Troy's hands in farewell.

After they had all said goodbye, Terra stepped forward with his knife. Troy started to refuse but he took her hand and drew it toward him. "My father says knives are tools, not weapons. You should take it." His voice was steady, but his eyes begged her.

She nodded, and he hugged her. "Please come back to us," he said, low in her ear, "even if just for an hour."

"I promise, Terra. You've done more for me than anyone. I will repay you."

Terra's eyes clouded his vision as Harok lifted Troy into the saddle, then adjusted her stirrups. Their eyes met a final time.

"Farewell, my friend," he choked.

Troy nodded, turning Laic toward the forest.

"Ride west," Harok called a final instruction. "Follow the sun as it sets. You may reach the next village before dark."

Laic broke into a trot, and Troy did not look back.

Terra watched her until he could no longer see her among the trees, then sank down to the grass. His mother knelt behind him, gathering him into her arms. He turned and pressed his face against her shoulder to hide his tears.

* * * *

Night came. The trees filled with shadows, deep places seeming to stare, retreating as Troy rode toward them. The forest was unending, empty. Even Laic was indifferent, ambling beneath her as if he walked alone. Her last hours in Kcen, starting with her nightmare and ending with a worse one, played over and over in her mind.

Finally Laic stopped and began to graze, snapping plants between his teeth. The reins slipped from Troy's fingers, slithering to the ground.

Troy swung one leg over the saddle and, hanging onto it, lowered herself down. Her arms and back stung, burning. Leaves crunched under her feet, shriveling into the ground. She sank to her knees—at least the earth stayed solid beneath her. She clenched handfuls of leaves while her tears splashed down. Her throat closed on itself, squeezed by sobs.

The forest ignored her. Laic continued to chew and snip his meal. Troy's teeth clashed together as she began to shiver with cold. Her jaw began to ache.

A crackle of footsteps—not Laic's—brought her head up with a jerk. Her heart began to pound, sending blood in a tingling rush to her fingers and toes.

She looked up. A slouched form stood beside her. He was tall, with reddish hair.

"You!" Troy was on her feet, driving into him as hard as she could. They thudded to the ground.

Mytch grunted something, but she obliterated the words with her fists.

"I almost had a family! You ruined it! I'm going to die out here, you…" She began to sob again. Talking was too hard. Hitting was easier.

Mytch's teeth were stained red, glistening a little in the moonlight. He did not fight back. "I came to help you…"

"I don't need your help!" Her fists slowed, faltered, then went slack at her sides. She crawled off his chest and withdrew to crouch with her back beside a fallen tree trunk. "You've done enough."

Mytch sat up and slid his arms out of the straps that held something to his back. It was a bundle wrapped in gray wool, much like the bedroll on Laic's saddle. He set it beside him. "If there were any way to undo what I've done, I would. This is all I—" He sounded about to cry.

Strangely, this made her own tears evaporate. There was no way to undo what was done. There was only regret. They both must do what they could with it.

"I do not need you." Her whisper was automatic. A few of her cuts had split open again, now a burning ache.

Mytch's scoff was faint. "You were going to give up. Not even trying to direct your horse. You need me. Where you go, I will go. You will not wander alone."

Troy was silent, not wanting to move and send further pain through her body. Chills crept over her as wind passed overhead. Mytch got to his feet and went to Laic. He returned with Troy's bedroll, unrolled it and draped it over her shoulders. Her shudders immediately calmed.

He went away again, then returned a while later with an armful of sticks which he dropped on the ground before her. Taking a stone and flint from a pouch at his side, he struck a spark and then nursed the spark into a flame. He added more sticks to the growing fire until the heat reached Troy and she was comfortable. He sat opposite her, one leg folded beneath him, resting his wrist on his other raised knee, saying nothing.

Finally she whispered, “Do as you wish. I will not stop you.”

Chapter Six

Two years passed, then three.

News came to Kcen, brought by the merchants: villages raided by Seawolves. Daehexa's chieftain, killed by Seawolves. The new High King sent warriors to engage them, and Inatru warriors even went to the Seawolves' island to fight them on their own ground.

Terra's family did not speak of Troy, amongst themselves or to anyone else. In silence they labored through the rest of that season and then the relentless snow. Derrh died and Grano emerged with its flowers and budding leaves. Eulba's hot days waxed and waned. Nier brought the next harvest. Derrh was reborn in flurries of frigid snow and sheets of ice covering the ground.

The empty feeling of Troy's absence slowly faded, but Terra did not forget her. He didn't know if Core or Sienna—or any of them—still thought of her, but it didn't matter. Terra thought of her. Harok had made him a new knife to replace the one she took, and whenever he used it he was reminded.

Another year came and went. Derrh came again, excessively cold. After the wolves scoured the forest for food, they approached Kcen. Every man, young and old, must take his turn on the night guard, even troublemakers, and in his thirteenth year, Terra spent his first night on watch with four other men. They stood around an open fire, made both for warmth and to warn the wolves away. Their forms wavered in the fire's heat. Terra, however, walked to warm his blood. Conversations with the other villagers were awkward, still, and he was tired of their looks. He had not so much as sneezed in the wrong direction since the incident with Troy—The Seawolf, they called her—and still they expected his next antic was just about to happen. He had done nothing wrong then, and nothing wrong now, besides keep his distance and his own counsel.

The dark watched him, brooding in the trees. He gripped his spear, brooding back at the dark and hoping he was only imagining those shadows moving close to the ground. Terra fought down a shudder and turned to walk toward the fire.

One of the men shouted.

There was a rush behind him, a slurred run, heavy panting. Terra whirled and jabbed with his spear. Too late. The wolf dodged and leaped onto Terra's chest, knocking him onto his back. He lost hold of his spear. The wolf stood over him, teeth clicking together when its jaws snapped, snarling for his flesh. He thrust both hands against the beast's neck, fingers sinking into matted gray fur, to push the huge head away. The others were shouting, running toward him.

The wolf's head came down, its breath coal-hot on Terra's face, warm saliva dripping on his cheek—

Suddenly a soft whiz, like a bat's wings beating the air, whooshed past Terra's head. The wolf yelped and shied back, pawing at its neck. Terra rolled to his feet and ran for his spear. He drove it into the wolf's side with all his might. It whined, then was still.

The others were there, fanning out in case the wolf was with a pack, but it was alone. Terra leaned on the spear shaft, panting. Snow clung to his back and pants, melting against his skin. He shivered, staring down at the dead animal in disbelief.

Embedded in the wolf's bloodied fur, just below its jaw, was the slim shaft of an arrow.

* * * *

He sat alone in the copse the next day, studying the arrow. No one in Kcen owned a bow, much less could use one. The use of weapons was strictly regulated by the Inatru, as was everything. Kcen was allowed spears only, and small knives like the one he owned.

Keeping the arrow was against law, but Terra could not part with it yet. His fingers touched the chiseled flint head, then ran up the shaft to brush the gray goose fletching. It was lovely.

A rustling in the snow and cracking twigs brought his head up with a jerk. He dropped the arrow behind the log target and leaned against the bark, pulling his knife and a short branch from his belt. He slid the blade along the branch, as if he had been standing there whittling all along, watching the curl shavings grow then fall at his feet.

Something flew over his head and thunked into a tree behind him.

Terra ducked. Looking over his shoulder he saw it was a dagger, standing out of the trunk like a misfit branch.

"Amazing." Two cloaked figures, one taller than the other, stepped into the copse.

Terra gripped his knife with a shaking hand and scrambled to his feet.

"I knew this would be interesting, but I hadn't counted on entertaining," the smaller of the two said.

"Shortsighted of you."

"Apparently."

Terra's mouth hung open. "You—you—"

The smaller stranger who had spoken first was cloaked in black from head to foot, head covered with a coarse wool cowl. Terra couldn't make out the features, but the voice was unmistakably female. The other, a head taller than the first, was equally as shrouded, but Terra glimpsed a ruddy beard. "Who are—?"

"Pardon us for disturbing you." The woman spoke over him. "I misplaced a possession of mine. My companion was helping me look for it."

The other figure produced an arrow from the folds of his cloak. She took it from him and held it out. "It looks like this. Have you seen it?"

Terra squinted in disbelief. "Where did you get that?"

"It is mine."

Terra felt faint. He inhaled deeply to clear his mind. It didn't help much. "Who are you?"

"You once said I am a warrior by nature."

It cannot be...

"Troy?"

"His power of comprehension is staggering," the bearded one observed.

Troy pulled back her cowl. Her eyes were dark and cool as ever. Her hair was long and hung down over her shoulder in a thick braid. She wore no headscarf. Her face, though still youthful, showed maturity in the tilt of her chin, the firmness of her lips, as she studied him. Her left eyelid was slightly stretched toward her temple, pulled by a vertical scar.

"You're back?" Terra could hardly contain himself. His fingers trembled as he slid his knife into its sheath. "I never thought—I mean, I hoped you weren't—"

"You knew I would come back, as promised, and could not wait to hear of my travels," she finished for him, tilting an eyebrow.

Terra remembered the knife embedded in the tree behind him. He reached up—she'd thrown it a good two feet above his head—and pulled the blade free. Examining it closely, he saw the hilt was inscribed with his name. It had been his knife once, before he gave it to Troy. "You kept this?"

"To remember you by."

He stared at it in wonder, then raised his eyes to hers. "You were the one who saved my life."

"I promised to repay your kindness to me."

"Why didn't you show yourself?"

"We weren't intending to stay."

"But you'll stay now, won't you?"

Troy breathed deeply. "I do not think it would be wise."

"Please. For a day, even."

Her brows drew together, and a flicker of pain—or regret—registered in her eyes before she nodded. "Alright. But we should not stay long."

"Your companion is welcome as well," Terra offered generously, hoping his mother would not care. Troy gave the man a sidewise look, and he pulled his hood back. Red hair fell in thick, tight braids over his shoulders, and bright blue eyes glittered out of a stone-hard face.

"My thanks, Terra. I…am afraid showing myself here would betray Troy's presence. She was outcast once on my account, and I would rather it not happen again."

Terra's eyes widened. "Mytch?"

Mytch's expression did not change, but it softened a little. His eyes were, at least, obviously alive. "Is my father well? Ki, I have heard so little of Kcen since I left."

Terra stared at him a moment, trying to collect his thoughts. "I thought—we thought—you were killed by wolves, after you ran away." Terra had been selfishly glad to hear it then. It was a small justice for his part in Troy's exile. Now, face to face with Mytch, he was briefly ashamed. The bully had gone, and a man returned instead.

"I found Troy not far from here and have been traveling with her since," Mytch said simply.

Troy nodded. "He has more than repaid his fault, Terra. I have forgiven him."

A pang of jealousy corkscrewed through Terra's shame. He swallowed both down and offered his hand. Mytch took it in a tight, calloused grip, still with that constant detached smile.

"Welcome, Mytch," Terra said. "Both of you, welcome home."

* * * *

"Oh, there you are." Cail was crouched at the hearth, spooning broth over a side of venison on a spit over the flames. She turned as Terra poked his head through the open doorway to the hearthroom. "Could you bring some—?"

Troy stepped up behind Terra. Cail dropped her spoon. It clattered loudly in the surprised silence. Imra saw them and stopped mid-stride in the middle of the hearthroom, holding a fistful of table knives before her like a bouquet. Quick, knowing tears filled her eyes.

Troy removed her cloak and passed it to Mytch, then walked into the hearthroom. She wore a sleeveless tunic and travel-stained breeches. Thin white scars laced her bare arms, dipping into the hollows of her biceps and curving around her shoulders, long fingers from her past refusing to release their grip.

She stepped forward and put her arms around Imra. Imra returned the embrace, gripping Troy's shoulders. When she pulled away and smiled at last, two tears dropped onto Troy's fawn-colored tunic.

"Troy?" Core pushed between Terra and Mytch, knocking Terra on the shoulder in passing. "How did you get here? Where's Terra been hiding you?"

Troy released Imra, turning in time to catch Core's full weight in her arms.

"You look like a warrior—"

"A huntress—"

"My goodness, children, let her breathe!" Cail exclaimed. "Core, don't choke the life from her. Are you hungry, Troy?"

"I'm hungry!"

"You're always hungry, Terra," Core laughed.

"Where's Sienna? Go get her."

"Have you been living in the wild, Troy? You look it."

"She's a forest girl, remember?"

Troy was unable to answer any question before another was asked. She turned to Mytch and shrugged, still smiling. He winked at her, and she shook her head. Her smile moved to Terra, who was mirroring Mytch's posture, arms folded, one shoulder resting on the door frame.

Just for a moment, they were alone in the room, their looks the only words either heard.

You're beautiful, Lady.

I'm no Lady. She spread her hands at her sides, as if her appearance could prove it.

His eyes perused her figure: booted feet set apart on the narrow pine floor planks, her travel-stained charcoal breeches, the weather-worn quiver hugging her right thigh, calloused dusty palms smelling of woodsmoke and oiled leather, the narrow leather belt cinched about her hips, her tapered waist. Her dark braid. The unshakable line of her lips. The scar tracing her face from temple to jaw. Her dark eyes, untamed between a sable fringe of lashes.

She was more a Lady than any Terra had known, or would know. He was suddenly grateful for the solid door casing to hold him up. His legs wanted to fold beneath him.

The front door opened and shut, and Sienna gasped behind him.

"Hello, Sienna." Troy's smile changed, still fond, but without the weight that weakened Terra where he stood.

He watched their reunion, light-headed with joy. Sienna hugged her, then Imra again, then Cail. They barraged her with questions: where had she been, what had she done, and—goodness—were those arrows?

"Your horse is still outside, Troy," Mytch said at length from the doorway.

Imra gasped. "Laic? Is it Laic?"

"Thank you, Mytch," said Troy. "Yes, it's Laic—"

"Mytch?" It was Core's turn to gasp.

"He has been looking after Troy," Terra slipped in an explanation, of sorts.

"May I stable him? The horse?" Troy asked.

"Core will show you where to put him," Cail said, "and then we will hear your story over supper."

* * * *

"So he's a war horse now, eh?" Core, about the same age as Troy, had changed as well. His hair was rust-colored and curlier since she had last seen him. He stood a little taller than she, and his shoulders and arms had filled out.

Laic stood patiently in the aspen copse where Troy had left him, still saddled. A rolled-up bundle secured by leather straps rested just behind the saddle. Troy put her hand into the woolen folds as if to check for something stashed inside.

"He hasn't seen a war yet. Where should I put him?"

"His old stall is empty. Doesn't Mytch have a horse?" Core asked.

"Not recently."

"Why not?"

"It died."

Laic's ears lifted when they entered the stable and his nostrils flared, recognizing familiar scents. He went straight to the unoccupied stall, sniffing the corners and the walls. Core forked clean straw onto the dirt floor for bedding.

"What happened?"

"Wolves. Do you have grain? A handful will do." Troy dropped an armful of grass hay in the square manger. Her answers were becoming terse, and Core let the subject alone.

"A little in that sack, over there."

When they'd finished feeding and brushing Laic, Troy stowed her saddle and pack bags upright against the far wall.

"Is that a sword?" Core glimpsed a length of bluish blade before it disappeared inside her cloak.

Troy's glance was wary. "I've learned many things since I left." She pulled her cloak closer around her body, against his curiosity and the chill of evening.

Core shook his head and smiled wistfully. "I wish I had could learn them as well."

"Knowledge comes at a cost. I would not want any of the things I know weighing on you."

"Why?" Core turned and led the way from the stable. "You only seem stronger."

"Strength is an illusion. To gain these skills, I have had to kill men. I have seen them…" She hesitated. "Destroyed by a stroke of my sword. This is not an adventure. It is merely a way to survive." Troy's eyes gleamed with a strange light, sharp and deadly.

"But…can't you even show me a little of what you know?" he asked. "It may come in handy when I watch for wolves at night." He didn't mean to upset her, but the thought of handling a real sword excited him in spite of her warning.

Troy pressed her lips together. "I suppose I could. Some of the basic techniques. Maybe."

Core grinned and led the way back to the house.

Chapter Seven

"Mytch and I rode through the first night to the nearest village." Troy told her story during supper, between bites of roast venison and brown bread. "That was at his insistence—"

"Wisely, with your cuts half healed at the time."

"We spent the night in a barn and left again before dawn. Mytch showed me how to build a fire, how to use a spear, somewhat—"

"Somewhat," Mytch scoffed around the meat in his mouth.

"Terra, pass the bread," Sienna prompted quietly.

"—and we rode north, to leave the forest as quickly as possible. Mytch was sure we would be able to hide for a while in Daehexa, since it is so large."

"Did you meet anyone on the way?" Terra passed the basket of steaming rolls to Sienna.

"Did they discover your…?" Imra hesitated to say it.

"We stayed away from the merchant roads at first. Mytch knew they would be collecting contributions from the other villages until Derrh brought the snow." Troy tapped the wide leather cuff circling her neck. The ends touched at her trachea, crisscrossed with thin brown laces to hold the cuff in place. "Mytch received this in exchange for labor at a farm on the edge of the forest. The cuff is hardly visible when I put my cowl up. Most often people assume from my scar that I am Mytch's servant, and don't give me a second look."

"Does it chafe?" Sienna touched her own neck, trying to imagine such an unforgiving accessory.

"I don't mind it."

"It saved her life, on several occasions," said Mytch, with a prolonged glance at Sienna. "Daehexa was attacked by a large group of Seawolves days before we arrived, and Daehexa's chieftain was killed in the skirmish. It was all we could do to keep from being drawn into the upheaval. If Kilar had not befriended us…"

Terra looked up from his second helping of venison in time to catch the sharp, warning look that passed from Troy to Mytch, before she continued.

They found work, she told them, at a stable run by a man named Kilar. Troy spoke of him fondly: a man with a bushy chestnut beard and friendly blue eyes, as spry and spirited as the horses he trained. She described landscape stretching beneath blue sky, miles of grass covering humps of hills, with incredibly few trees. Horses ran there in wild herds. The rich lived in houses built of rare cottonwood; the poor lived in huts of sod.

"We worked in the stables and lived with Kilar and his wife. Kilar was also a warrior, greatly respected in Daehexa, and was the chieftain's close adviser. He became the new chieftain soon after the former's death. The decision could not have been more fortunate for us. He is a good man and our close friend, despite being Inatru."

"Don't forget that I am Inatru, and would have been a chieftain too." Mytch turned to Troy, one eyebrow tilted. "We are not all evil miscreants."

"But you are a miscreant," she returned, and when he chuckled she turned back to their story. "He offered to train Mytch in Anrac, the lowest level of warrior skill. The Inatru established four ranks of warrior training among themselves – Anrac, Noclaf, Retinaw and Magellan," she explained.

"Then the Inatru not only placed themselves in control of every village," Terra realized out loud, "they control the entire scope of combat and defense." This was a vaguely disturbing concept. Suddenly the Inatru were no longer a natural presence in his mind, but a shrewd force to be reckoned with.

"Many who train as warriors never reach Magellan—"

"Troy has." Mytch pretended not to notice her irate glances at his interjections. Apparently he received them often. "Even Kilar had to acknowledge her prowess."

"Mytch taught me in secret at first."

"Then she surpassed me." Mytch was enjoying himself, and not entirely at Troy's expense. He seemed proud of her.

"Kilar was certain I had previous training—"

"Which you may or may not—"

"Would someone please put some meat in his mouth, so I may finish before dawn?"

Mytch laughed and accepted another slice of venison from Sienna, which she offered with a demure smile. It was the first time Terra had seen Sienna actually smile at Mytch in his life.

They learned to ride with their hands free, using their legs to guide a mount, while defending with shield and spear. Terra imagined Troy atop Laic, brandishing her weapons as Laic charged through knee-high grasses, defending against bow and sword and spear.

"After months of rigorous training, Kilar was pleased to give us our first shields and spears as tokens of completion."

Mytch swallowed and added, "Everyone present thought she was a man, except Kilar who already knew, and of course myself."

"It was Kilar's idea, so that I could stop training in secret. I cut my hair and tied it back, wore no scarf, and bound my chest. With the cuff around my neck, and as long as I kept silent, no one was the wiser. Thank you, Sienna." Troy held her cup as Sienna filled it from a steaming jug.

"It's an infusion with honey. Imra made it." Sienna smiled toward her younger sister, who bowed her head to hide her blush as she cleared dishes from the table.

No one voiced a note of displeasure at Troy's story, though she was breaking law—repeatedly—and knew it, and intended to continue. Terra thought the living she made was completely justified, even if it was backwards to tradition.

"Then where did you go?"

Troy tasted the infusion, delaying her answer.

"This is very good, Imra. How did you make it?" Mytch asked when the silence sustained.

"With mint leaves and caddy."

"I haven't heard of caddy."

"It's a name she made up," Sienna said, setting the jug on the board and sitting down again. "No one in the village could tell her what it was."

"Those who still speak to us."

Troy lowered her cup at Terra's words. He shook his head at her weighted look, dismissing the statement.

"After Daehexa we went to Engar by a lake called Redllew," she said slowly, picking up the story once more. "Kilar had already sent word of us to the chieftain through some traveling merchants. He was impressed that we were recommended by Kilar himself. At Engar we trained in Noclaf, the second warrior rank. We learned to use a bow and arrow in combat—"

Terra grinned, and Core exclaimed quietly. Both earned a glance of disapproval from Cail. Troy noticed this, and steered her descriptions toward the scenery: Lake Redllew shimmering beneath a hot sun with the ridge of blue mountains looming in the east. The people there lived in plank houses painted bright green around the windows and doors. At night there were rows of fishing boats on the lake shore, rocking in the shallow waves. In the day they bobbed like corks scattered over the mouth of the lake, nets sunk deep to catch fish lurking in its throat. There was a feast of battered silvertail when Troy and Mytch earned their bows with the other Noclaf warriors.

In Telracs, a village near the northern mountains, they learned the level of Retinaw: to fight with no weapons at all.

"You used nothing?" Terra was incredulous that such a way of fighting could exist. His world, village life in the forest, was rapidly shrinking in his mind, while images of Troy's experience expanded to fill the void.

"Sometimes we would use staves, but most often had only our bodies to defend ourselves. There we learned to turn ourselves into weapons that could not be taken from us. This knowledge served us well when—if—someone should attack on the road, and there was no time to draw weapons."

"Then we traveled south, to Camil Askanda, the home of the Inatru and now also of the new High King, Estimal Glor. Troy earned her sword there and became Magellan," Mytch said, interrupting yet again. Troy's glance this time was a threat of pain. He smiled. "She is very modest of it. I was not skilled enough to earn that level."

"Perhaps you should tell the story."

"Nonsense, I'm not good with details. Haven't the patience." He seemed to be sorely trying hers.

"The home of the Inatru?" Sienna's eyes widened, and she leaned forward over the board. "They are so fierce there, from the stories…"

"Every bit the truth." Troy nodded. "The sword is the sign of a Magellan, but the Inatru warriors in Camil Askanda also use a special type of spearhead that has four blades instead of two, that come to a point at the tip. The star-shaped head maims as well as punctures. The Inatru who use them take great pride in their invention. We left there as soon as I earned my sword."

"They let you train even though you're a woman?" Core asked.

"They did not know." Troy tipped her cup to see the liquid inside, then downed it. Mytch said nothing.

"Where did you go from there?" Terra asked, and conversation turned once more to their adventures. They shared stories of travel, crossing the island through sun-baked grasses buffeted by a warm wind, hiking up rocky hills dotted with sparse green bushes, breathing chill mountain air while traversing rocky ravines, where waterfalls roared behind clouds of white mist.

Through their words Terra saw midnight stars above their campfires, their feasts of fresh roasted game and cold spring water flowing from fat leather flasks into their parched mouths. They were always moving, always wary, shrouded in mystery.

It was long dark by the time they finished. Sienna was yawning, Imra asleep with her face buried in her folded arms on the tabletop.

"We have bedrolls," Troy said when Cail mentioned blankets for them. "Mytch will sleep outside, and I can lie by the hearth. You've done more than enough for us."

Terra went to bed reluctantly and lay for a long time beneath the blankets, staring into shadows. Visions still clung to his imagination: Daehexa nestled in the grassy plains, Engar sprawling on the shores of a silver lake, Camil Askanda bristling with Inatru warriors, Telracs hidden in the mountains.

And yet, there was more. More than she would say. He knew it. Perhaps Troy was trying to shield them. She was breaking law by becoming a warrior, after all, and now they were accomplices. But her silences at certain questions, and Mytch's interjections, were like signs pointing to everything she was not saying.

Didn't she trust them enough to tell them the truth? Did she think they would betray her? And to whom, the chieftain? The villagers? Kcen was a minuscule threat to her, with her warrior prowess, as Mytch called it.

Whatever the reason for Troy's silence, Terra was determined to draw the whole story from her.

* * * *

When Terra woke the next morning, Core was already gone. Troy was sitting on the floor when Terra walked barefoot into the workroom, pulling his tunic over his head.

She sat facing the doorway leading to the entry, clothed as she had been the day before, with her legs folded beneath her. Her cloak was draped over her left shoulder only, leaving her right arm bare. A sword lay on the floor beside her hand, unsheathed. The long straight blade was dull blue in the feeble light. Two handguards of silvery metal split from the pommel, flower-like, arching over the grip.

Terra slowed, blinking. "Did you sleep?"

Troy's look was inscrutable, working over his face, his tunic, his patched chore breeches. She seemed to find whatever she was looking for because her eyes were soft when they returned to his face.

She stood and pulled her cloak over her right shoulder, fastened it at her throat with a wood toggle, then picked up her sword. "Come with me."

She led him outside into a gray dawn. Their steps crunched over patches of snow, following tracks that led past the stable to the copse.

Core and Mytch were already there, wrapping rags around bundles of long sticks.

"We do not have much time," Troy said. Her voice sank into the air, absorbed by the lingering stillness of night. "I will teach you what I can, but do not think you are ready to use a live blade after this. You will only hurt yourselves. And do not tell your mother."

"I knew it was a sword!" Core jumped to his feet, coming forward to inspect it. She steadied it, point resting in the grass, with one hand around the leather-wrapped grip. The pommel nearly reached her hip. "How do you carry that thing around?"

"A baldric, strapped to my back."

The blade was indeed blue and, when Terra touched it, had a porous texture like stone. Yet, it was polished like steel. The handguards felt the same, but they were silver-white.

"What about the bow and arrows?" Terra wanted to know. "Can we learn to use those as well?"

"Yes, and a staff?" Core asked.

Mytch brought the cloth-wrapped bundles, which would serve as practice swords, and handed one to each of the boys. "We cannot stay long, but we will show you a little of each."

* * * *

In the evening, while Terra hurried through his chores, he caught sight of Mytch walking alone toward the potato field. Troy had disappeared a little earlier, while Terra and Core were obliged to chop wood and tend the animals before the evening meal.

Terra lingered by the door of the stable, slapping the empty milk pail against his leg. Mytch was going to meet her, no doubt. They would discuss their secret business standing close together, heads leaning in, their breath mingling—

"Here's the milk pail." Terra dropped it beside the stall Core was raking. It hit the dirt floor with a hollow clang and tipped over.

Core's face peered around the post a moment later. "I'm busy—"

"I'll help finish when I come back!" Terra closed the stable door on any further protest, jogging along the dirt path to the field.

Mytch was alone, pacing around the grandfather tree with his head bowed. Red braids swayed on either side of his face, shielding it and his mood from sight. Terra's feet carried him along regardless, and before he knew what he was going to say to explain his forceful arrival, he and Mytch were facing each other. Mytch stopped in mid-pace, arching his eyebrows while Terra groped for words.

"I think…we will eat soon. Is Troy…?"

"She is in that clearing." Mytch gestured behind them to a patchwork of snow and grass visible beyond the trees. "It smells good, even from here."

"What?"

"The evening meal." Mytch's eyebrows hovered above laughing blue eyes, while his mouth remained stoic.

"Oh. Yes." Terra tried to regain his composure and only lost his skill of conversation. "She's been making mushrooms and...honeycomb with it all day."

"Will you do something for me?"

"Yes?"

Mytch took a thick bundle from inside his cloak and held it out. Terra took it and turned it over in his hands. The bundle was wrapped in a worn rectangle piece of leather. At either open side, he could see thin sheets of a pale yellow-brown something, a stack almost as wide as his palm. The leather cover was tied with a crumbling leather string, tucked into itself to keep the whole package together. The short tail hung just off center of some black stitching on the flat surface: a compass star. The sign of the Seawolves. Terra gaped at it, then at Mytch.

"It's called a book. Will you give it to Troy? It...sort of belongs to her."

Terra held the parcel—the book—in both hands like a slab of crumbling bread. Its weight was that of a heavy stone, and so old he thought it might soon disintegrate. "Yes. Why can't you give it to her?"

"I already know what it is, and what it means."

"What it means?"

"Go ask her." Mytch stepped around him to walk back to the house, his arms disappearing behind his cloak signaling some purpose fulfilled.

Terra was left standing with the bequeathed object, looking after him. The sudden turn of whatever he had expected going into this exchange made him lightheaded. He traversed the few yards past the grandfather tree to the clearing. Troy sat on a hill in its center; the hill was a glorified mound usually covered in grass, now streaked with snow remains. She sat cross-legged, cloak pulled around her. Her head was bowed slightly and the last rays of cooling light played over her dark hair. Terra took a deep breath before climbing the hill. He moved quietly but she whirled around before he had taken ten steps, one arm snaking out of the cloak to brace against the ground. Her lips twisted in a threatening snarl, which faded so fast when she saw him that Terra thought he might have imagined it. Her face softened, and she graced him with a small smile. She might be glad to see him. Terra decided to believe she was.

"Come to watch the sun set?" She nodded him forward.

He sat down next to her. The sun was already behind the trees which ringed the sky above them. The usual blue was an inferno of new color. Red, orange, pink and gold smeared together as the sun went to its rest.

"Mytch said this is yours."

"I'm only carrying it. He knows that."

"Did he give it to you?" Terra hadn't considered the book might be a gift from Mytch until he asked. Immediately he felt cold inside, waiting for the answer.

Troy let out a short sigh. "No. We were both given it by someone else. We're taking it…" She narrowed her eyes at the beauty overhead, leaving the sentence unfinished.

"To Camil Askanda? Are you afraid to go back?"

"I've never been to Camil Askanda." A hard edge creased her forehead, making her words sharp. "I've become something more than a warrior, Terra. And not everything we told you was true. Don't tell your family." She lowered her head at the last words, and the edge corroded away.

Terra frowned. "Where did you go?"

Troy moved her hand along the top of the snow, brushing it with her fingertips. Terra had a flash of memory: Troy, the young girl, drawing in the dirt with her toes, afraid to look up. He balanced the book on his lap and took her hand. Icy water warmed between their palms, but her fingers continued to shiver.

"Troy?"

"We did live in Daehexa for almost a year, and Kilar trained us in Anrac, the first warrior level. That was the truth. But we earned the next two levels, Noclaf and Retinaw, in the south. In a hidden city called Yettmis." Her eyes widened and she breathed deeply, as if to hold in apprehension. "Neither of us have reached Magellan yet. We stayed overnight in Engar, but we never lived there. We rode to the mountains on an errand for…someone in Yettmis…but we have not been past the foothills. We never saw Telracs, or Camil Askanda. We're on our way back to Yettmis from the mountains. Some men from Klenit on the coast—warriors, you could call them, but they are more than that—met us in the foothills. They gave us the book."

"Isn't it yours though? Mytch said the book—"

"Mytch and I don't always agree." She drew her hand away from his and took the book, holding it against her ribs as she pulled her cloak closed against the chill breeze.

Terra lapsed into silence, searching the ground beside him.

"The Seawolves found us in the foothills after the Klenit—warriors—" She stumbled again over the word, "—left to return home. They are days behind us. If we keep going, the Seawolves will pass Kcen without touching it. It's us they want, not you."

Terra squinted to see her eyes in the fading light. She averted them, tightening her brow. Her mouth was tight, her jaw set, all of her skin a stern mask concealing what her eyes could not. A shimmer hovered on the rim of her eyelid. "I didn't want to come here, but Mytch insisted. We have already endangered you with our presence."

"It will be okay, Troy."

She slammed a fist onto the half-frozen ground. The treacherous tear gleamed—a thin line of red materialized beneath it. "You have not seen what I have! Nothing is safe with me here."

A chill shook Terra's spine. The tremor seemed to sweep through him into the ground, speeding outward over the frozen grass, the forest, the plains, the lakes, the mountains. Out there, terrible men roamed. Troy's tears showed what she couldn't bring herself to speak. She needed him.

He was ready. "I will help you. I promise, wherever you go I will find you. We will face those who hunt you together."

"You can't promise that—"

He reached for her shoulder. "Yes, I can. I will train, I will learn whatever I have to. Take your book to Yettmis, take it anywhere in Cathylon. I will find you. I promise it."

Her chest rose and fell sharply and finally she looked at him. Terra's fingers tightened on her shoulder. He leaned forward into the beckoning white vapors, leaving her lips and their breath mingled. Seconds passed and neither looked away. Before he knew it, his lips were touching hers.

Chapter Eight

Darkness fell. Troy and Terra walked back to the house for the evening meal. Troy left her cloak open and walked close enough to Terra that their knuckles touched. The book was lightweight in her other hand.

Snow, swept from branches by eddies of wind, caught the yellow candlelight shining between the slats of the shutters covering the bedroom windows, frozen sparks floating, swirling. Their breaths puffed white from their mouths, dissipating as they passed through. Terra was smiling. Their steps crunched in tandem, carrying them alongside the house on their left, past the stable on their right. The stable door stood open. Shadows hurtled about inside, back and forth across the rectangle of lantern light outlined on the muddy snow.

"Oh!" Terra stopped short. "I left Core in the stable. I should help him finish. I'm sorry."

He had nothing to apologize for, but his disappointment was for missing the rest of their walk.

"Go. I will see you in the house."

"Don't leave before eating."

Her mouth tightened, the beginning of a smile. "We'll eat together, and then I must go."

"I will come for you."

"I know."

She continued alone to the house, a lightness hovering in her stomach, lifting her from the inside. At the entry door she stopped to collect her breath, her fingers touching the frosted latch. Long had she felt uneasy with herself, as if she harbored a surging terror in her body with only her skin keeping it contained. But for a moment all that would be forgotten. She would walk into a warm room and see her beloved friends. She would eat with them, wonderful hot broth and mealy seasoned potatoes, and talk of anything but danger. She would tell Imra about the kiss, and maybe learn to blush. Maybe remember how to laugh.

Smiling, Troy opened the door.

Sienna stood crying in the entry.

Mytch was with her, outlined by a slash of yellow light let in by the gaping inner door. He turned his head when Troy opened the outer door and withdrew his arm from around Sienna's shoulders. "The Seawolves attacked a village not far from here. Harok just received word. He went to get Core and Terra in the stable."

Sienna had turned her face to the wall when Troy stepped in. Now she gathered her composure and wiped her face with both hands. A sliver of light crossed her nose and cheekbones; her skin and eyes glistened. "Tarrom has called for every man to ride with him, to avenge them. They killed Tarrom's brother, and—"

Troy's glance veered sharply back at Mytch. He nodded.

"I advised Harok not to go. These may be the ones who chase us or they may not be. Harok was told they also took several young women captive."

Sienna hugged her middle, shivering. Troy closed the outside door, shutting them in together with the blade of light from the next room. "They will be overpowered. They cannot go."

"His standing among the others is not favorable," Sienna said, trying not to sniffle. "Tarrom's brother was Kmoch, the same man whose son, Aleph, was killed…"

"Also by a Seawolf," Troy murmured. Aleph's death was accidental, but that was beside the point. She recalled Terra's comment the night before. The other villagers probably blamed Terra's family for that death as well, since they had taken responsibility for her.

"If my father stays behind, it will be the same to them as condoning the attack and the traitors," Sienna finished.

"The others won't care who stayed behind. They'll be dead." The room felt too cold. Troy felt for the door behind her to pull it closed, then remembered it already was. "Where is Cail?"

"In the hearthroom with Imra. Still cooking, I think. She's bent the law as far as she can without breaking—we all have."

This time Mytch's hand made it to Sienna's shoulder, resting there with a gentleness that surprised Troy. His fingers brushed the red tail of her headscarf, unconsciously twining it in his grip. "We will bring them back. In the meantime, you will all be safer if you hide. After we leave, put out the candles and hearth fire, then take your mother and sister to the copse. No one will see you unless they go inside. We will bring your brothers and father to you there."

Sienna nodded, the last of her tears drying on her lashes. "I'll do whatever you think is best."

"May I borrow a dress?" Troy asked. "I might be recognized in these clothes."

Sienna took her to the bedroom and showed Troy her small wardrobe. Troy chose a brown wool skirt and pulled it on over her breeches.

Imra slipped into the room after them, closed the door soundlessly and crossed to the bed where she knelt down. She pulled a small leather pouch from under the mattress, opened it and drew out a crimson thread tied to an arrowhead. She held it up, turning to show Troy the simple necklace.

"Terra gave me the arrow you saved him with." She slipped the red loop over Troy's head, then stepped back with her hands folded in front of her. "I dulled the edges," she added, one side of her mouth lifting in a ghost of a smile.

Troy touched the arrowhead and tried to smile back. She looked down at herself. The hem of the dress stopped at her shins, showing her breeches. She bent and rolled them up past her knees.

"It will do. No one will notice." She hoped it was true, but really she had no alternative. A few minutes ago she was convinced her pursuers were only interested in chasing her, not sacking villages. Was this the same warband or another? If they wanted the book, why take women and slaughter chieftains instead? In any case, she was more worried about the ones who knew her than those who might try to capture her. Besides, she had her weapons, and Mytch to watch her back.

She embraced Sienna and Imra a final time, then left the house with Mytch, tucking the necklace underneath her vest where it pressed against her sternum, slowly warming.

A raiding party, even of Seawolves, was not so concerning as those who wanted the book. And the sword, she remembered grimly.

They walked to the stable, followed by Sienna. Inside it was dark—Terra and Core and their father were already gone. Troy and Sienna set their saddles in an empty stall. Mytch broke open a bale of hay and piled it over top. Sienna found empty burlap sacks for their travel packs and helped Mytch put his in while Troy looked around for a place to hide the book.

"Leave it," she grunted when she turned and saw Mytch pull out her sword, bundled in her bedroll. "I can't afford to be recognized with it, if the Seawolves we clashed with are nearby."

"What of the book?"

"I'll keep it," Sienna offered.

Troy frowned, shaking her head.

"Mytch told me what it is," Sienna informed her. "I won't let anything happen to it."

Troy turned her frown on Mytch.

"We don't want anything happening to you if they do find it," Mytch said gently, avoiding Troy's eyes and laying his hands on Sienna's shoulders.

Sienna raised her face toward his, straightening. "I'll be careful."

"I know you will, Sienna."

His eyes were softer than Troy had ever seen. It was unnerving. Troy turned away from them, tightening her grip on the book. She finally tucked the book into the bedroll with her sword, closed the top of the burlap sack and pushed the bundle deep under the bale of hay. Then she did the same with Mytch's gear in the second sack. Mytch dragged another hay bale over and the three of them scattered it on top, obscuring the whole thing to a pile of loose straw.

* * * *

Terra rode on his father's left and kept his eyes forward, on Tarrom's broad shoulders wrapped in black bearskin. The fur shook with miniature waves, swaying in time to his mount's trotting steps. The horse was Inatru bred, lithe and leggy, a vigorous animal never used to plowed fields. Terra's mount like all the others was stout forest breed, but she stepped eagerly, strong and alert.

Terra shifted his spear to one hand and rubbed her neck beneath her milk-white mane, relishing the heat through stiffening fingers.

"There now, Makala. You will do well." It was her first hunt—and Terra's first battle—but they were only Seawolves, after all.

"No need to fear," said Michel, the trapper, who rode on Terra's other side, near enough to hear him. "Their strength is in surprise. They never attack directly, but sneak in the shadows and strike at every turned back. If we face them bravely, they will run before us, surely. Never fear."

The chieftain's plan was to surround the Seawolves' camp then rush in and take them by surprise. They would be exhausted so soon after fighting in the other village, too tired to defend themselves.

"Easy prey for us, the men of Kcen," Tarrom had assured them when they gathered in front of the Hall at his summons. "We will teach these traitors not to trifle with our neighbors and kinsmen!"

Terra was among the last to appear with Core and Harok, still absorbing the abrupt turn of events. Instead of scolding him for leaving Core to do the chores alone, Harok handed Terra a spear and told the terrible news: the chieftain's brother—and almost a whole village—was slaughtered by Seawolves, and vengeance was now duty. Terra went without protest.

They rode through a half-mile of still trees toward the neighboring village. The scouts sent ahead by Tarrom reported that the Seawolves had made camp in a clearing not very far from Kcen. Clearly an attack was imminent. Best if Kcen struck first.

The moon was a melted smudge of light behind clouds that blanched trunks and skeleton bushes, luminesced spots of scattered snow on the ground. The men moved together in a tight group, each darting sidelong glances to make sure his neighbor's pace matched his, and his own matched everyone else. They thumped over frozen ground, crunched through dead plants, in line and step and rhythm with Tarrom in the lead.

Their furs were different colors, black, brown, gray and mottled, but all fit the same, covering the hunched forms plunging forward in wholehearted pursuit of their chieftain. Terra went as well, but his heart was for Troy. He was ready to face those villains, the Seawolves who terrorized her. Determined to protect her, he now had a chance to act. Perhaps she wouldn't have to leave if he could triumph tonight. Everything she had told him on the hill crystallized into a single line: the Seawolves hunted her, they made her afraid, they hurt her. Now he—Terra of Kcen—would end her conflict.

At a place where the ground dipped and the trees thinned, they found the Seawolf camp, a muddy hollow scattered with sleeping forms. The trees cast shadows across them, lacing legs, torsos, backs and shoulders with arabesque patterns. Their hair was blacker than the shadows, their limbs long and thin like Tarrom's desert horse. The Seawolves apparently lay down wherever they happened to stop, like dogs waiting for a master.

Tarrom turned his horse, stopping a few yards from the camp, and the little warband gathered close around him. He looked like Mytch, Terra thought as Tarrom quietly gave them orders, like a ruddy rock, but aged. He wanted to say something to him about Mytch, that his son was well—even heroic in spite of his younger mischief. Tarrom would be proud to know it, Terra thought. Tarrom and his brother Kmoch had both lost sons, and now Tarrom had lost his brother to these Seawolves. Terra stared at Tarrom, hoping to catch the chieftain's eye, but Tarrom did not turn his way. The moment passed and they dispersed into position.

Terra was separated from his father and brother, and at first he was worried. Then he saw Core not far down the line curving around the hollow and felt better. He looked forward and copied his brother's focused appraisal of the camp within. Every man was silent, deciding where to run in among the sleeping forms, who to engage first. They waited for Tarrom's resounding bellow that would signal the charge and begin the retribution. Wind blew, frosted with the scent of coming snow. Blurry moonlight enveloped them.

The shout came.

Terra was caught up in the sweep of men and horses charging into the camp while, as one, the Seawolves jumped up with spears in hand. They had been waiting. Terra's chest pinched with cold dread as Makala carried him into the thick of them.

A man jumped at him, thrusting his spear upward at Terra's throat. Terra twisted aside and snapped back with his own spear. Shock made him quick—or else his attacker lost heart—for the spearhead rushed into the warrior's soft belly. Terra felt tissue and bowel give way. His fingers went numb. His mind froze, capturing the keen anguish of the pierced man: black eyes wide and watering, thin cheeks quivering, a groan pushed through slackened lips. His hands groped at the haft, and Terra at the same time jerked back, horrified. The spearhead reemerged, coated red. The warrior couldn't scream, but Terra did instead. Makala jumped forward, the man fell behind them and Terra was surrounded by a churning press of bodies. He thrust his spear about desperately, but each Seawolf seemed to be everywhere at once. Three village men closed in on one warrior; all of them fell dead within seconds.

Hot blood sprinkled Terra's face, stinging his eyes, smearing the scene crimson. He didn't know whose blood it was. He swiped a hand across his eyes, stupidly searching the ground. It was already carpeted with bodies, many of whom he recognized. The shouting around him turned from wild war cries to terrified screams. Terra had never heard a man scream before. Now they were all screaming, high woman-like squeals. Everywhere he turned there were more Seawolves, and another of his kinsmen fell dead. There was a neighbor. A friend's father. A friend. Hot tears escaped Terra's eyes, mingling with blood and washing it away.

A warrior grabbed Makala's reins. Terra tried to push him away, but the spear was too unwieldy for such a close space. The man's eyes burned into his, lifting a knife to throw.

Something hummed past—an arrow—and plunged into the man's chest, knocking him down. Terra was yanked off his horse. The air left his lungs as he landed hard on his side. His spear was wrenched from his hand. Someone loomed behind him. He spun around, fists his last resort.

It was Troy.

"What are you doing here?" A sob grew in Terra's throat. He took the spear she held out to him.

"Saving you," she panted, shouldering her bow and picking up a discarded spear.

"You—" Terra ducked, diving to the side as another spear sliced the air between them. Troy whirled her own spear and thrust it behind her. A charging warrior buckled over the shaft. Troy wrenched it free and grabbed Terra's hand, running.

"Where is Core?" She pulled him along, bounding up an incline, stopping behind a large tree well away from the battle.

"I don't know! He went with my father."

Troy glanced around the tree trunk. "I'll find them. Stay here."

Terra gratefully obeyed, sliding down to sit against the trunk, resting his head on the bark. His whole body throbbed, shaking with adrenaline. A few moments later Mytch emerged from the darkness with Core, who was cradling his left arm with his right hand. Blood dripped between his fingers.

Terra dropped his spear and ran to them, grasping Core by the shoulders. "Core, where is Father?"

Core's face was streaked with dirt and sweat. Tears washed half circles beneath his eyes and made lines down his cheeks. He seized Terra with one arm around the neck, pulling him tight against his chest. "He was fighting. Two of them…"

Terra couldn't speak, trapped in his brother's shaky embrace. Core's left arm was folded between their bodies. A mouth-shaped laceration gaped on his forearm in front of Terra's eyes.

"Stop the bleeding, Terra. Core, you'll be alright. The cut is not fatal." Mytch took them each by a shoulder as he spoke, then turned and sprinted down the shallow slope, back to the battle.

Core released Terra and they stared after him, breathless. Terra finally reached for the hem of his shirt, tearing off a long strip to bind Core's arm.

"She was right." Core stared at him as if that would keep him from disappearing. "Killing men is not strong. I hate it."

Terra nodded vaguely, seeing his own killing stroke again in his mind. Seeing his father—

No. No. Don't think of it.

Troy reappeared. She was visibly shaken, glancing over her shoulder every other moment. Her skirt—when did she put on a skirt?—was blotched with gleaming wet stains. Terra's stomach lurched.

"Troy, did you find my Father?"

She turned toward them, her face tight, saying nothing.

Terra scrunched his eyes closed and inhaled deeply. He was going to be sick. He clawed a handful of snow and rubbed it on his face. Dead. Harok was dead. His father, dead.

A crackle and snap of sticks behind them brought Troy whirling around, spear extended. Mytch stumbled toward them, an arrow buried in his shoulder.

Troy rushed to catch him as he fell forward.

"I'm alright," he gasped, struggling upright. His face gleamed gray-white. "We must leave. I saw four-bladed spears, and now arrows…there are Inatru with these Seawolves."

Now it was Troy who looked sick. She closed her mouth, breathing heavily through her nose. Her eyes darted over his face, wide in the shadows made by her brow. Coarse threads of hair clung to her temple, obscuring the scar that distorted her left eyelid. "They've seen us—"

"We must go." Mytch returned her look and amplified it, his lesser red mane standing out unnatural against his grayed skin. "The book is unprotected."

Troy pulled at the shaft in his arm and they both winced when it came free. Quickly she tore a shred from her skirt and wound it around his bleeding arm, then pulled his arm around her shoulders as he stood. "Terra, Core. Stay close to us."

They broke into a shuffling run, stumbling in the darkness over logs and bushes, leaping up and running, retracing their path back to Kcen. Terra's muscles bunched into knots, tighter with each leaping step. He gritted his teeth and pushed on. He would not stop running until he reached his house, his sisters, his mother—

"Torches!" Core yelped beside him. His face was stained orange by the flickering glow.

"Too bright for that," Troy grunted through clenched teeth. She gripped Mytch's wrist, bearing his partial weight. It was too bright, even for a hundred torches. Heat rolled past them in surges, and the air stank with smoke. Mytch pulled his arm from her shoulder, running now on his own. They came to the edge of the trees and passed into the clearing where Kcen lay.

To their right the chieftain's Hall, taller than the other houses, blackened beneath groping fire coming through the windows. The roof of the wayhouse collapsed, spewing sparks upward. Every house along the main road was burning.

Terra yelled this time, to no one and everyone as they burst into the meadow. "Mother! They're in the house!"

Troy grabbed his arm, yanking him along, staying close to the trees. "They went to the copse. Come on!"

They ran past houses wrapped in flames, past dead fields beginning to smolder. Steam and smoke filled the air. Here and there, between the haze, they saw spears—some with four-bladed spearheads—bouncing, swinging, flying. Women screamed as they were struck. Warriors dragged hysterical young girls, tying them or subduing them with fists.

"What are they doing? We have to stop them! Stop it!" Terra veered toward the village.

Troy's fingers latched tighter around his arm. "We can't stop them."

Terra lunged again, trying to tear free. "We have to! We have—"

"We can't!" Emotion shredded her voice. "Just run, Terra!"

They passed the last house and sprinted in a tight group toward the copse. It was lined with a backdrop of smoky, hot light that pushed shadows toward the runners. Terra's house was also burning.

"The stable," Troy gasped. "Mytch!"

"I'll go. Get them inside. Core, help your brother." Mytch ran on, past the copse toward Terra's house.

Core was already disappearing in the deeper shadows of the trees. Terra stumbled after him, leaning against Troy, his breath coming in hard half-sobs. The trees surrounded him with safety, blocking out the horrid sights and sounds of the massacre. The grass rose to meet him, welcoming him.

Their mother came forward, her arm around Imra. Core told them what had happened in a choked whisper. Cail's face crumbled and she succumbed to her knees.

Troy looked around the copse. "Where is Sienna?"

"She sent us ahead…" Imra answered, staring at her mother's shaking back.

Terra turned to run out of the copse, to find his sister, but Troy stepped in front of him and caught his shoulders. Terra twisted, straining to tear away. "Let me go! Sienna's out there!"

Troy put her hand on Terra's face, making him look at her. "Mytch is getting her. Any chance of surviving this night lies in this copse and in your silence." Her eyes were reddened, while her mouth spoke the hard truth to him, saving him. "Your death will not help anyone."

At some point—Terra did not know how long—Mytch materialized through the trees. His face was white. Soot ringed his eyes and powdered the tips of his hair black. A corner of his cloak smoldered beneath a rising thread of smoke. He seemed unaware. In his arms he carried a limp form. Sienna.

Soot blackened her headscarf, and clung to her hair and clothes. Blood dripped from her back onto the snow between Mytch's boots, making a puddle in the slush beneath her.

Terra ran to her, in lockstep with Core. Her dress was torn at the waist, her abdomen punctured with a wide, ragged hole. It was too wide and ragged to be made by an arrow or even a normal spearhead. Terra remembered the four edges on the Inatru spearheads and shuddered. "Sienna? Can you hear me? Sienna!"

Mytch sank to the ground, holding her against himself. His face was white, spotted with blood. Terra crashed to his knees beside them and touched Sienna's limp head with trembling hands, turning it toward him. She seemed to stare at him, unblinking. Her skin was too cold…

Troy was beside him, focusing her attention on Mytch. "What happened?"

Terra tore his eyes away from Sienna's face to look at Mytch, who was also staring at Sienna.

"She went back for the book…"

Troy's head dropped onto Mytch's shoulder. "Al ki, mi elaa…"

"They saw her. She fought, but…" Tears made shining trails down Mytch's cheeks and dropped onto Sienna's neck. "I didn't reach her in time."

Cail cried out suddenly, making Terra jump. Troy backed away as she stumbled toward them and took Sienna's body from Mytch, cradling her daughter against her chest. Mytch remained on his knees, arms hanging limp at his sides. Cail curled over her, rocking and moaning. It was another sound Terra had never heard before, a horrible guttural dirge, especially from his own mother. Core and Imra huddled with her, but Terra could not move. Mytch stood suddenly and walked away, standing alone in the shadows.

Troy stood also and picked up a charred object that had dropped to the ground when Sienna's body was transferred to Cail. It disintegrated to ash, crumbling in her hands. She hurried away to stand beside Mytch. Terra focused on their conversation to escape from his mother's weeping.

"Is this the book?" Troy asked.

"The stable was burning when I reached it," Mytch answered. "Everything was burning. Sienna had found the bag and dragged it out, but they were outside… It burned while she struggled and died."

Troy turned her hands over, staring at the ash that sprinkled onto the dead grass and snow.

Mytch's hand went to his chest, unfastening the baldric strap and handing the sword to her. "This survived."

"Elaa ki…" She breathed the words like a prayer as she took it. "The book is gone."

"I killed the ones who…attacked Sienna. But I was seen by others." Mytch pointed at something moving outside the trees. "I think I was followed."

As he watched them, Terra dug into the stiff grass with his fingers, clenching it hard. *So wrong.* They had all been deceived, yet what else could they do? His heart split in his chest, aching. He curled over his knees until his forehead rested on them. *We were so wrong...*

Suddenly Troy was there, kneeling beside him. He released his grip on the grass to reach gratefully for her hands. Instead, she pressed the hilt of her sword into his palms.

"Take this."

He fingered the curved, chill handguards in a stupor.

"No matter what happens, do not come out."

Suddenly the metal was burning his skin. He jerked, dropping it.

"Troy—"

She thrust the hilt back into his hands, along with her bow and quiver. "Do not follow me."

Mytch hissed an oath, then scattered the remains of their book, obscuring it with a swipe of his boot. "They're coming, Troy."

"Troy, don't go out there—" Terra's throat seized and he couldn't finish.

Her warm hand rested on his shoulder. "Do not follow me, Terra." Her hand lifted, and he was cold again except for the hot tears leaking from his eyes.

"Troy—"

"Troy, they are here!" Mytch's voice rose a note toward the end.

Her spear rested beside them on the dead grass. She picked it up and spun on her heel toward Mytch. Terra hung his head again and sobbed.

* * * *

Mytch's hand found her shoulder for an instant as they strode toward the group of Seawolves rushing toward them. Troy breathed in, exhaled, and then her hands moved automatically, spinning the spear in front of her.

There were too many already. She thrust the thought away and swung out, connecting with the nearest warrior's skull. Her fingers absorbed the shock and he sank to the grass. Every breath steadied her, and she saw clearly. The onrush broke around them and became a swarm. Troy made every stroke count. By every fallen warrior the family hidden in the copse was made safer. Warriors were thrown back and returned stronger, a frenzy growing to down these two who resisted.

Troy put her back to Mytch's, together infallible. Sweat stung her eyes. Her hair came loose from its binding and floated around her face, a tangled frame. She stabbed forward again—and was shoved from behind by a heavy weight. She spun, leading with her spear. Mytch sank into her even as she stumbled back. Troy caught him, lowering his body the rest of the way to the ground. His eyes stared at nothing. His chest caved in at the center, mutilated by a star-shaped spearhead. Blood spilled from his mouth, streaming over his chin and onto her wrists.

A scream tore from her throat, unearthly, like the groaning of tree roots being torn from the ground. Hands closed in from all sides, pulling at her arms, her hair, her clothes. Her spear was jerked away. She had only her hands to fight with now, her hands and her body, and the terrible scream that wouldn't stop pouring from her chest.

* * * *

Terra, pressed tightly into the sheltering branches of the trees, watched in silent horror. A rope snaked around Troy's head, settling on her shoulders, then snapped taut. Her scream choked into silence. More ropes were wound around her wrists. Troy lunged, fighting against her bonds, until a warrior knocked her on the head with the pommel of his sword. Terra's eyes shut involuntarily, and he had to pry them open again. Troy sagged to her knees. Her captors hauled her up and pushed her, stumbling, past the copse.

"Any chance of surviving this night lies in that copse and in your silence," she had said, and she was right. He could not stop them. He could only watch.

Terra stared after her stumbling form until the leafy branches hid her from sight, and then he could only listen to thumping hooves and wagon wheels creaking as the Seawolves made their way south.

Chapter Nine

Snow began to fall, lacing the ground with white. It melted and turned into mud beneath dragging feet and wagon wheels. It coated the ropes binding Troy's wrists, melting then freezing against her skin, mingling with her blood when the skin rubbed away.

Young women wept in line behind her, dragging their feet over bare plants and frozen dirt. The wagon in front of her bumped forward, pulling the rope taut, stretching her arms and shoulders ahead, straining to pull them out of joint. Wood rattled, axle against wheel, a hollow sound clattering constantly in her ears. Sweat froze on her face, cracking when she bunched her cheeks in a grimace. Her lips split into sharp fissures of pain when she licked them. A cold ache crept into her skull, pushed by the wind into her ears and nose and mouth, gnawing as it settled in her forehead. Her steps became monotonous: one, then another, followed by yet another, for hours on end.

Troy raised her head when the wagon finally stopped, peering through her frosted hair to search for signs of an approaching enemy warrior. The rope tugged, jerking her arms at the wrists as the captives behind her sank to the ground, huddling together for warmth as much as the ropes would allow.

If she remained the only one standing, someone may mark her, making it that much harder to escape if the chance came. Troy bent a knee, leaning against the back of the wagon for support, and what small shelter it could give her from the wind. One leg of her breeches was beginning to unroll, and she fumbled with it until it was hidden again beneath her skirt.

Sienna's skirt.

Her hands clenched.

Troy heard the footsteps before she saw the warrior approach: a thin, wire-muscled man with a stiff leather satchel slung over his shoulder. He crouched beside her, dipping into the bag and offering her a fistful of jerky. A thin, curly beard clung to his lower face. Cold reddish skin rose above it, blushing darkly along his high cheekbones.

"Tone down your look, woman," he muttered at her narrow stare, "or you will fast find yourself Machaun's target."

The jerky gave off no smell, but her stomach remembered its taste. She forced her fingers to uncurl and put out her bound hands, watching as he dropped bits of meat onto her upturned palms. She felt nothing.

Machaun, the king's right hand, they had told her in Yettmis. Machaun, who guards the book of Inatru for the king. The king, who seeks to possess the book of Esobir.

Secrets lay within the books, some known only to the Inatru, others closely guarded by the Esobir. Precious few Esobir lived in Cathylon, hunted by the Inatru nearly to extinction in recent years—a hunt sanctioned by the king and led by Machaun.

And now the book of Esobir was destroyed. Burned. Burned because of her.

"Let him come."

The warrior regarded her, forearms resting across his knees. His long-boned hands drooped from his wrists, weighted and tired. His eyes had once been gentle, without the swollen resignation clinging to his heavily fringed eyelids. "He hunts a certain warrior, an Esobir. Desperately."

"He slaughters children and farmers in his desperation. Let him come," she said again, snipping the words between her teeth. Caution had died in a burning village, left stiff in the grass, staring through sightless blue eyes at the midnight sky. The Esobir, the Inatru…all were nothing now.

"We are all of us desperate." The warrior stood and ambled past her, down the line of captives. Three points of a compass star tattoo showed at his nape, the fourth point hidden beneath stiff waves of black hair.

Troy ate the jerky slowly, picking dried shreds of meat from her cupped hands, chewing carefully and thoroughly before swallowing. This warning from a Seawolf was unexpected, like cracking open a walnut and finding honey inside. It was wrong, yet there was no lie in his frank words or his haunted eyes.

She shut her own eyes, letting her head rest against the edge of the wagon. There was no way to soothe the throbbing headache from the cold, or the bruise aching on the back of her skull, so she let the pain be a part of her. One did not consider their own digits, or focus on breathing; pain was simply another piece of her body.

A heavy garment dropped over her shoulders, and Troy looked up into the face of a slight young woman, her tawny hair bound with a black and white cord instead of a scarf. She handed Troy a tin of water before adjusting the cloak around Troy's shoulders, tying it beneath her chin. "The Seawolves are tending their wounded, and then we will continue southwest. Best sleep while you can. Morning won't come soon enough for Machaun."

"Where is he taking us?" Troy balanced the cup carefully in her numb hands. Little waves of water escaped the cup through a V-shaped chip in the rim, dripping down the outside.

The girl crouched in front of her. A strand of hair hovered in front of her left eye. She brushed it back. "Camil Askanda."

Troy took a long swallow. The sweet water slipped down her parched throat, a cascade of cool relief. She handed back the cup awkwardly with tied hands. The water spilling over her fingers felt warm only for a moment. "To Estimal Glor."

"Yes. The High King," the servant murmured. Her lips twisted, making the title a mockery, while her wide-set gray eyes took inventory of Troy's face. They lingered on her scar. "You think, perhaps, that walking into a cage of starving wolves would be a safer journey. The wolves are only dogs on leashes."

"And you?"

"An indentured servant."

"You have my pity," Troy said, and meant it. The girl's eyes were sickened, tense at the corners, slurring an otherwise fine face. She would have been more suited to hold a fine instrument instead of the cracked cup, drawing her tapered fingers over silken strings in soft firelight, seated before a chieftain's hearth instead of shivering beside a train of captives.

"It is not usually so…brutal," the servant allowed.

"They've left some alive in the past."

"Machaun was not with them in the past. He is the king's second in command, chieftain of Camil Askanda before Estimal Glor settled there four years ago. He has their families at his mercy."

Someone would have suffered this night, then, whether she and Mytch had moved on in time or not. Machaun was desperate to find the book of Esobir, the Seawolves were desperate enough to kill for him, and the High King benefited from their hunt, safe from blame in his grand Hall.

"Dogs on leashes, indeed," Troy muttered.

"Be careful you don't wake their master, with your hands thus tied."

"It seems someone already has."

"The one he's looking for threatens his power."

"Do you mean the king, or Machaun?"

The servant's eyes widened, looking past Troy. "Put your head down," she breathed, barely moving her lips, reaching for Troy's hood.

Troy ducked her head instinctively, gasping through parted lips as snow filtered from the folds of cloth, powdering her ears and neck, sifting down her tunic. Through the cloth muffling sight and sound, and stifling her breath with the heavy odor of sour milk, Troy heard the servant's voice close by her head.

"M'lord." Her one word told Troy that Machaun was standing over them.

He was not pleased. "Where is Maon? What are you doing?"

"Seeing to the captives who are still alive, m'lord. This one has frostbite already."

"They have that Esobir to thank for it, wherever she is." His voice was deep, but hoarse from shouting and breathing smoke. "If she cares for their lives at all, she will show herself and surrender. If they all die before we reach Camil, I will find another town and start again. We have fooled around long enough."

The servant said nothing. Her hand rested against Troy's knee with a slight downward pressure, a silent command not to move while Machaun's vicious shadow loomed over them. Troy bowed her shoulders, tucking her arms and elbows into her ribs, to appear as small and contrite as possible. Angry as she was, desperation also drove her. She must choose her battles, and this was not the road she wished to die on. She would face him—there was no doubt of that—but not here. Not on her knees.

Boots shifted, obliterating snow and soggy dead leaves beneath Machaun's weight. "Finish and move on."

"Yes, m'lord." The servant's hand remained on Troy's knee until the sound of Machaun's boots and the threat of his presence were gone. She lifted the hood a fraction, and cold fresh air rushed against Troy's face. She sucked it into her lungs, cleansing away the mildew stench.

The servant's whisper was adamant and full of command. "You left Kcen alive because you are a woman and appear to be a certain age, but that does not ensure your survival. Do not let him see your face." She pulled the edges of the cloak around Troy's body, closing out the frigid air, before hurrying away.

* * * *

They walked from dawn until dusk the next day, hardly stopping even to swallow a piece of jerky and a cupful of water. The strain on Troy's wrists grew into a twisting knot, traveling up her shoulders and into her back. When the wagons rested for a few hours, the captives dropped where they stood without a word and fell asleep, too exhausted even to sit up.

Troy was grateful to lie down and let the knots in her shoulders untie themselves. The muddy ground was cool on her burning skin, lulling her to sleep each night with its soothing comfort. Snow turned to rain, and they slogged through mud slime until finally they came to the end of the forest and the river Aganus.

The Aganus was the border separating the desert from the rest of

Cathylon, it flowed in a nearly straight line through the whole island, fed by high mountain springs in the northwest and emptying into the ocean in the south. Several rafts, used by the merchants who traveled this road to collect from the villages in the forest, rested on the near shore. The Seawolves went to work, herding captives and wagons onto the floating platforms. Troy's feet hit the hard wood, which swayed and rocked beneath her sore feet, and suddenly she realized it was familiar: the men calling to each other as they heaved at the tow ropes, the hollow stamping of the horses' hooves on the wooden planks—even the water lapping at the shore.

She closed her eyes tightly, trying to shut out the feeling, but it was too strong to be ignored. Images flashed through her mind: swelling white sails…fishes jumping in silver-tipped water…and black, choking waves.

Troy's head began to throb. She was aware of her knees hitting the wood planks, of her own unnaturally loud gasping. Desperately she fought her own memory, fought for emptiness, and the images dissolved into the recesses of her consciousness.

"Can you stand?"

Taking a slow breath, Troy opened her eyes and raised her head. The servant girl bent over her, holding the coiled rope with one hand. Her eyebrows puckered, filling the wide space between her eyes with tiny wrinkles. She cast a glance immediately behind them, and Troy turned to see what she was looking at.

Machaun stood on the edge of the second raft, long legs spread to steady himself against the rock and splash of water beneath his boots. His close-cut, ruddy red hair tufted in the wind, revealing a wide forehead beneath. A cape of red fox skin wrapped around his muscular bulk, covering his leather scale tunic with deceptive softness.

Troy ducked her head when their eyes met, the folds of her mildewed cloak falling across her face. Her skin prickled, imagining him watching her still, marking her.

They reached the other shore, moving quickly against the rushing waters, and pressed on into the desert toward Camil Askanda. Grasses and trees eventually disappeared, as did the snow. Sand became the dominant feature of the land: deep, white, gritty sand, which made walking even more torturous, travel even slower. Troy became accustomed to the daily regime of endless walking in the warming weather until the sun set, eating a mouthful of food and water, sleeping for a few hours, then walking some more. She noticed, however, that the Seawolves ate no more than their captives, and were treated no better by the Inatru except that they weren't tied to wagons.

Troy's hood became stifling, insulating her breath and its own sour perfume around her face. Sweat dripped into her eyes and mouth and nose, and her stomach clenched into a perpetual fist of nausea. Finally, after the second day of sweltering beneath her hood, the servant girl took mercy on her. She removed the hood during a nighttime rest and tied a faded red scarf around her hair. "I have something for your face," she said as she twisted Troy's braid into a knot and tucked the ends of the scarf around it, so none of her hair showed. She spread mud over Troy's left cheekbone and jaw, adding to what was already there, covering her scar. "Machaun has no interest in these girls, other than vicious bait, but the scar sets you apart. Once he sees it, he would not let you out of his sight."

That meant there was a chance to escape, somehow. Troy did not mind the mud, since her clothes and limbs were already crusted with it. A little more made no difference. "What does the scar tell him, besides setting me apart?"

"That you are the king's property."

A tremor of sickness worked across Troy's middle, and she suddenly wished for the hood again.

Thirteen days after leaving Kcen, the great city of Camil Askanda was visible on the horizon. Thick walls of stone, cornered by needle spires like giant bedposts, guarded the Inatru's city. The king's Hall was a tall, flat tower blushing red above the walls. In the deep orange shine of sunrise and the bloody glow of sunset the Hall looked even darker, sometimes sparkling crimson, sometimes paler desert rose, with the milky outer walls below like small young petals giving birth to the richer colors within.

"It was structured after blueprints found in the Inatru's book," the servant girl told Troy one evening, sitting beside her for a moment in the sand as Troy drank her ration of water. "In honor of their heritage. Apparently the Inatru hail from a branch of the Ancient race, but accuracy is difficult to find in a half-translated manuscript. Then again, they have been here the longest. Who are we to question?"

Her name was Sema, she said, and didn't seem to mind that Troy did not return the courtesy by giving her own name.

"Do you know him?" Troy gestured with her tied hands at the curly-haired warrior who had given her jerky and a warning the first night.

He lounged against the lead wagon, just in her line of sight, popping dried meat into his mouth. They had not spoken again since that night but he studied her face when he brought her ration, as if he thought it might tell him something he needed to know.

"I have traveled with his raiding party, but we rarely speak," Sema said quickly.

"He is odd." Troy squinted into the wind, which was trying its best to throw grit in her eyes.

"His name is Maon. He was among the first Seawolves brought to Camil Askanda in chains after the attack on Carmul. The other Seawolves trust him, many are influenced by him."

Maon pretended not to see them watching him, pinching fingerfuls of food and chewing thoughtfully, staring at the red line of sunset separating sky and sand.

"If he is such a warrior, he could walk away from Machaun and the king right now, if he chose."

"He could, but his family cannot, and they are in Camil Askanda still. I believe he has a wife and daughter." Sema picked up her flask and cup, preparing to move on. "It is said the Seawolves aligned themselves with the king. He does not release his possessions easily, if at all."

Troy lowered herself to the ground using her elbows and rolled onto her back in the sand. It was warm from the sun and somewhat comfortable. She rocked her head back and forth, hollowing out a headrest, and closed her eyes. "You mean the High King? The Seawolves betrayed him when they attacked Carmul."

"That is what the rest of Cathylon was told. Some of us know better." Sema's steps slushed away through the sand, leaving Troy to contemplate her cryptic words.

Yettmis—the city she should be at now with the book and Mytch—lay behind them, underground and unreachable as far as she was concerned. Even if she could escape right now and miraculously slip away without being caught or killed she was not about to lead the Inatru to the hidden city. And what did it matter if she escaped or not? Her purpose was gone, her brother in arms dead, and Terra…

She never should have gone to Kcen.

Now she was bound for Camil Askanda, and how was she to explain herself there, to a king she didn't know and already hated? To a king who had already put his mark on her, possibly with his own hands. She grimaced, knowing how quickly a conversation between them would doom her:

Where do you come from?

Does my lord refer to my city of residence, or the city of my origin?

Where were you born?

I don't know.

What is your name?

Troy had been considering an answer to that question. She'd settled on something succinct and ironic, unrecognizable unless one could speak the

Ancient language. Still, the further she let the imagined conversation ramble, deeper went the grave she would be digging herself, or worse.

Prepare a room for this one. Her answers interest me. I would question her further...

She could not let him have her.

Troy heard bones grinding. It was her teeth. She worked her jaw open and shut, forcing calm through her taut muscles. She counted her breaths, focusing on the rise and fall of her chest, until sleep tugged her into oblivion.

She woke as Maon pressed a blade against her throat.

"Not a word, woman." His head and shoulders blotted out the stars directly above her.

Troy didn't know who she would shout to, if she did.

"Sit up." He pushed her upright with one hand behind her shoulders, settling his arm around her neck. The cold blade nudged beneath her jaw. "You may not be the one they are searching for, but you'll do well enough."

She stared ahead. "If you kill me, you will solve my problems and compound your own."

"Machaun wants a body. The king wants a renegade servant, and they will pay a fine reward."

"Machaun did not come to Kcen just for a body." What he did want had burned to ashes in the village he had ransacked. It was the only small justice born of this tragedy. "Was it a promise of reward that put their collar around your throat in the first place?"

"Loyalty," his breath hissed through tight lips, "to our queen, who we believed was in danger."

"Why should I believe that?"

"Why should I believe you are not a runaway piece of property? You certainly look it." His arm tightened around her neck.

"I am no more property than you." For the first time in her life, the cuff around her neck was not saving it. "Look at my neck."

"You are one to speak of collars..."

Troy lifted her chin as he tugged at the laces and loosened the cuff, then bent her head forward as he tugged it free. His muttering stopped. Except for his tight breathing, he could have been a statue behind her. Quickly he replaced the cuff, drawing the laces tight with shaking hands.

"That chokes—"

He loosened them. "What is your name?"

"Llynx."

He came around to face her, balancing on one knee. "Llynx? That is not—"

"It is my name." She leaned forward, eyes hard, forcing the lie to be truth. Troy was no more. "Now, what are you so desperate to trade me for?"

Chapter Ten

She entered Camil Askanda on a wagon bed, buried under what hay was left to feed the cart horses. A heavy oiled cloth stretched over the hay, shielding it from inclement weather and keeping it in place.

Maon had shoved her, minus the smelly cloak, beneath the hay after cutting her free. "Don't move," he grunted, "or you're dead."

The last leg of her journey, less than two days before entering the city, was the most miserable yet. The hay shuddered musty pieces of itself over her prone form. It crept into the crevices of her clothes, around her waist, at her neck, past her armpits and shoulders. It sifted into every rip and tear, sticking and spreading against her damp skin, until her entire body became a constant itch. Moving made the discomfort worse, so Troy tucked her head between her folded arms, pressed her mouth against a crack between floorboards where breathable air seeped through, and tried to sleep.

She dreamed of suffocation. She dreamed of insects devouring her skin. She dreamed until the rumble of wheels bumping over sand changed to the clatter of cobblestones. Somewhere outside the wagon, voices rose and fell in discordant harmonies, bartering their trades. Then the voices faded away as the wagons proceeded over an endless cobble road to the Hall of Camil Askanda.

There was a long time of waiting, and Troy pressed her forehead into the hollow of her arms, descending into a tortured stupor. The wagon jerked, moving again, then came to a stop as it crossed a dim shadow. She opened her eyes and saw dirt beneath her through the crack. Dirt, and more hay.

A shadow flickered past on the ground, with the sound of light footsteps, and then the hay above her redoubled its downpour as the oiled cloth was dragged off the cart. Troy squeezed her eyes shut as grass dust coated her face and lashes, even with her head down, burying her in misery. A moan left her mouth, followed by a convulsing cough when she breathed in clouds of the stuff.

"Llynx." Sema's voice was soothing outside the wagon boards, by her head. Maon had shared Troy's new name. Apparently the servant and the Seawolf spoke to each other after all. "We are in the king's barn. You can come out."

Easier said than done.

Troy ground her teeth, shut her eyes, and slithered from under the hay, scooting backwards. Sema pulled at her waist to help her, driving the prickly hay further into her skin. Troy would have slapped her hands away, if her own arms were not busy pushing herself out of the wagon as fast as possible.

The misery continued, clouding her vision and perception, as Sema guided her from the long barn, up shaded stone steps, through a narrow damp corridor and finally into a small bedroom. Troy stopped in the middle of the room, staring at the tops of her boots, covered in hay dust.

"You're safe here for now. I must report to the kitchen. There is water for bathing," Sema said before closing the door behind her.

Troy turned her head. A large barrel tub sat against the wall on her left, full of steaming water.

Salvation.

Troy could not move fast enough, struggling out of her tunic and breeches. Hay rained on the stone floor and cascaded from her boots when her feet came out of them. She stepped around the mess and into the tub, leaving her hair wrapped in the scarf for the time being. The water smelled of citrus, and caressed her with blessed softness. She drew the moist steam into her lungs, cupping water to her face and scrubbing at aged mud. Dirt and blood smeared into the water, staining it black. After she had rubbed herself clean and could see her own skin again, Troy leaned back in the tub, observing the room.

There was not much to see. A cot with a thin blanket stood along the far wall, and took up most of the modest space. A rough-woven maroon dress was laid out on the bed. Aside from the tub, there was no other furniture. A small fire crackled in a hollow in the wall, a strange sort of fireplace. The room had no window.

When she had washed her hair and dried herself before the fire, she reluctantly pulled the dress over her head. The skirt fell to her ankles, and when gathered about her waist beneath a wide belt of matching color, it pleated together in generous, impractical folds. She had to sit down and tuck the skirt beneath her to pull on her boots. It snagged on her heels when she tried to walk. It wound about her ankles, threatening to trip her at some inopportune moment. Thankfully, it had no sleeves.

Her own belt and dagger waited on the floor on top of her discarded clothing. The knife had been confiscated when she was taken in Kcen, but Maon slipped it to her through the side of the wagon after pushing her beneath the hay. She was not sure about his motives for helping her, not that he did so entirely from charity.

"What is it you're so desperate to trade me for?" she had asked.

"My daughter is very sick. She needs medicine, and I have no money."

Troy listened as he explained the symptoms, and then said, "That is easily cured. I can get you what she needs."

"How would you get it?"

"The remedy is simple, and the ingredients are easy to find if one knows what to look for. I'll steal them if I have to."

"Dangerous business, to steal from the Inatru."

"I have little to lose."

And so she had spent nearly two days buried in a purgatory of hay. Now that she was out, she was ready to forgive the curly-haired warrior for cursing her with the help she had asked for. Escaping certain discovery was well worth the torture.

She cinched her belt around her hips, below the cloth belt owned by the dress. The dagger hung from its usual place on her belt. It looked ridiculous on top of a flowing skirt, but her itch-filled breeches were no longer an option. She drew the dagger from its sheath and turned it over in her hands. Many times, early on, the dagger had saved her life.

If only it could have saved the lives of Terra's family. Troy closed her eyes briefly. He was there, vivid, before her mind's eye. Gazing at her across the table in his family's home. Grinning at her behind his upraised practice sword. Striding happily beside her through the snow. Leaning toward her, eyes earnest—

Mytch, falling against her. Mytch lifeless in the grass.

The door opened, admitting Sema. "It is time to go." Her voice was hushed.

Troy's eyes sprang open. She touched the rough writing on the hilt of the dagger and returned it to its sheath. "I am ready."

Sema led her down the empty corridor and around a sharp corner. A tall young man with straw-colored hair and big hands waited beside a thick tapestry. A vertical scar marred the left side of his face, disappearing beneath the hair at his temple.

"This is Teyeda. He will show you how to get out." Sema cast a quick look over her shoulder. "You must go quickly."

Troy touched Sema's elbow. "Thank you."

"We will meet again." Sema smiled graciously, nodded at Teyeda, and then hurried back the way she had come.

Teyeda watched Troy from under his haystack fringe. Too many people were taking too much interest in her features of late. She was suddenly glad in her decision at the last moment to wear the filthy headscarf. It did not make her one of the accepted, but it was one less thing to make her memorable to them. "Teyeda. May we go?"

He blinked at her prompt before leading her down the next corridor.

"Where did you receive your scar?" His strides carried him quickly over the stone floor. Troy matched his pace, kicking yards of cloth that dragged against her shins with each step.

Stupid dress.

"I don't know. Perhaps your king could tell me."

"He is not my king." His fists clenched at his sides.

Troy resisted the impulse to step away and widen the space between them. "We have that in common."

"The Inatru have been raiding since long before the Seawolves began—were forced to begin, I should say. But I can give little of those details here." He fell silent, and they reached the end of the corridor before he spoke again. "Scarring is an Inatru tradition. It began as a sign of mercy toward the defeated, before Cathylon was brought to order by the Inatru. There were no chieftains and no order, only the wanderers from other islands, the skopi. The Inatru battled for and won control of Cathylon, but instead of killing the surviving skopi, they made them servants. That was how peace began, and the tradition continues. Now, though, it means possession more than peace."

"What of the Seawolves? The warriors who brought us here were not scarred."

"Theirs is a different mark," he answered. "I was brought here from Telracs in the northern mountains when I was a child, to serve the Inatru when Machaun was chieftain here."

"I know of Telracs."

He glanced at her with renewed interest. "Have you been to the mountains?"

"Once. I stayed briefly in the foothills."

"And beyond that?"

Troy shook her head.

His glance this time lingered. He seemed about to ask another question, so she spoke first.

"What is it you do here?"

"A number of things." He looked forward, respecting her attempt to redirect the conversation. "When I'm not required at the smith I am training the new servants. Several of us share that duty, me because I've been here so long."

"Do you train the Seawolves?"

"I have in the past. There are not many who would suffer it though, even if it were a choice between servitude and death."

"But those who do, how are they treated?"

His glance this time was mildly skeptical. "Are you hoping to return as a servant?"

"I need access to resources. For a little girl. She is sick."

"What kind of resources?"

"Medicine. Or simply the ingredients. I may be able to make it, depending on what ails her."

"Where is this girl?"

"Here in the city. She is a Seawolf."

Teyeda did not seem troubled by this. "What you seek will put you in a dangerous place. You will have to maintain direct contact with the king. His seal is required to buy at the apothecaries."

There was no way around it. She had already given her word to Maon. If she backed out now he would no doubt reveal her to Machaun. She would have to face the king one way or another, but at least it would be on her own terms. Infiltrating as a servant might not be so hard. She already looked the part.

They came to a door, and Teyeda let her in before him. The room was almost identical to Sema's in layout. Teyeda bolted the door, then dragged his cot away from the wall. "Beyond this wall is a tunnel leading outside the Hall."

He pushed, both hands flat against the wall, and it shifted inward silently. A draft of air, stone laden, crept into the small room. "Stay to the right, against the wall. You will come to a cave. A man named D'tanesse waits for you there."

D'tanesse.

The name evoked sudden images: A young boy with a lively round face crowned with a curtain of thick black hair…leaning, laughing wide, out an open window…small hands lifting soggy, spongy plant matter with the end of a deadwood stick like a fishing pole…small bare feet trailing wet footprints across a tiled floor…

"You are not the first captive we have smuggled out," Teyeda assured her. Troy realized she was staring past him into the darkness of the tunnel. The sound of falling water filtered out from its depths.

"I have few options, regardless." She stepped past him, setting a foot inside the sepulcher, then another. "Thank you, Teyeda. Perhaps I can repay your kindness when we meet again."

The stone door closed almost before his answer came. "…already have."

The light from the room behind her shrank to a sliver, and then was gone.

Blackness pressed in around her, and the faint sound of water filled her ears. She took a step forward, into pure nothing. Then another.

The stony ground beneath her feet changed to softer dirt. She kept moving, pressing her right hand against the wall until the rough peaks and bumps rubbed her fingers raw.

The splashing sound grew louder, like buckets spilling down from a great height, sometimes louder, sometimes quieter, with lulls in between. Troy winced, closing her eyes as a shard of pain spiked in her skull.

Not buckets. Waves.

She breathed deeply. The smell of stone and reality comforted her, and she pressed on.

Her steps had become shuffling monotony and the burning pain in her fingers a dull sting when finally she heard a new sound ahead of her. She paused, listening hard. The sound was like footsteps following a slow, measured pace on a known path. Someone was pacing. She moved forward again. Her eyes were suddenly drawn to a pinprick of light ahead. It grew longer and brighter as she approached, until she recognized the curved shape of another tunnel entrance.

The scraping tap cut short suddenly. Troy also stopped, holding her breath, while her eyes adjusted to the new light. There came a soft thud and then slow, shuffling echoes. Troy slid forward on her toes, sliding her dagger from its sheath, and stepped into the light.

On his hands, feet in the air, a young man shambled slowly around a small fire in the center of a small cavern. A quick glance around the space showed there was nothing more than the fire, some wood, a patchwork blanket and a gray-blue uncorked jar as big as her open hand. And the acrobat.

"Are you D'tanesse?" She squinted, coming dangerously close to shutting her eyes. Visions of waves hitting rocks loomed behind her eyelids, and she pried them open again.

The young man hopped—rather, dropped—to his feet, flipping a jet black braid over his shoulder. His clothing was outlandish: a long-sleeved tunic that stopped just below his hips, one half a vertical slash of black and the other half white. His breeches mirrored the tunic, white and black. The resulting spectacle hurt her eyes. The shard of pain in her head twisted deeper, aching.

"You are not Sema," he said.

Replying to the obvious would be a waste of time. "I am looking for the way out."

He approached, gliding on the balls of his feet, to inspect her more closely. He was scant inches shorter than her, forced to raise his eyes to meet hers. Disbelief crossed his round face as he took in the scarf over her still wet hair, the dress, her belt, her scars and finally the knife in her hand. "A captive?"

She narrowed her eyes for an instant and raised her chin, looking down on him.

"Did you get the scars from fights, then?"

"Some of them."

D'tanesse perused her further with curious green eyes, as a child would investigate a rock wall before attempting to climb it. "You look like a Seawolf."

"And I am marked property. Yes, I am aware."

"I was not about to mention that." His eyebrows lifted and he tucked his lower lip between his teeth before saying, "I imagined you…would be wearing jade green. As opposed to maroon."

"You imagined."

"Not in the same way as I do my wife. She smiles."

"You are extremely improper."

"Unintentionally. I meant…you look like someone I once knew. She preferred green."

"Would she cut your throat to gain her freedom?"

His slim shoulders twitched – something of a shrug. "Hard to say. What is your business here, Lady Seawolf?"

"I just told you. Sema sent me. She said you could show me the way out." She returned the shrug. The pain above her ear hammered away, trying to crack through her skull.

As much as D'tanesse's answers were provoking Troy, her answers also seemed to frustrate him. Perhaps he was the sort who needed to make a game out of everything, and everyone must play along. His jaw swiveled back and forth, and his eyelids lowered to half-mast. Troy met his sullen stare with her own. The crash of waves echoed around them.

"If it is passage you need, take it and welcome. I wouldn't dream of stopping you." He waved a hand toward the back of the cavern, keeping his eyes on her. "Unless there is something else you were hoping for."

Troy realized she was rubbing her temple with three fingers through the scarf, and D'tanesse was watching her do it. She lowered her hand. "From you? Unlikely."

"Are you sure?"

"Fairly. Why?"

"You seem the curious type." He was not being coy. He wanted a certain answer, a key to some riddle. Or maybe he wanted her to be someone else, someone who was the curious type.

"I was told you have what I need, and here I am," she said.

"What is that?"

"A way out!" *Was he dense?*

"Is that all?"

The hammering became a throb that sent black specks wafting through her vision. "Yes, that's all!"

"Very well, then!"

Clearly if she wanted an escape, she would have to find it herself. Troy took two steps toward the back of the cave before the world collapsed into darkness.

* * * *

She dreamed.

Rhythmic waves rolled onto a shore scattered with round stones. Black, choking waves. She was lost in them. Silver foam covered her eyes and rushed into her nose and mouth. Bubbles of sound, voices shouting somewhere above her, trickled through the rushing, sucking liquid. She heard her own struggle to rise: lurching, coughing, vomiting water into water and sucking more in again. Her lungs were filled with it—

She didn't remember falling. She didn't remember D'tanesse catching her, saving her from a nasty skull injury and worse headache later. However, she did remember what he said when she opened her eyes and saw his face above her, his arms supporting her.

She would remember those words for the rest of her life.

"My name is Llynx," she corrected, struggling to sit up. She pushed against his shoulder with the heel of her hand, demanding space. He pulled back when he was certain she could support herself and did not say the words again.

"My apologies. Are you alright?" He searched her face, watching her the way Mytch had watched her, protective of a younger sibling. She turned away.

The jar she had noticed upon entering the cave sat within reach, nonchalant on the floor. Troy reached for the cork and set it firmly in the jar's open mouth. The incessant sound of waves diminished, then stopped.

D'tanesse's eyebrows jumped, two peaks of black pushing wrinkles toward his hairline. "You recognize elaa." He pronounced it ay-lah.

"I knew a warrior," Troy lied, moving the jar away using just her fingertips. Still, her skin tingled with the remnant of the elaa's inherent energy. She swallowed and rubbed her fingers against the inside of her palms. They stung, grated skin protesting further exacerbation. "His sword was forged from elaa. I learned from him."

"What else did you learn?"

His eagerness made her uneasy. She'd learned a great deal about elaa in Yettmis, a great deal more than she was willing to admit to a stranger, regardless of his own knowledge about the energetic blue stone. "I learned how to kill quickly."

"Who are you?"

His questions were leading to a dangerous place of no return, begging answers she wouldn't give. "Who are you?"

He shifted and turned his head, suddenly uncomfortable.

"When you tell me your story, I'll tell you mine."

"Tell me how you came here, then. Please," he added softly when her expression stilled, a quiet mask of pain. The fire threw orange light between them. Its natural muted roar and occasional hiss of burning sap were now the only sounds in the cavern.

"My family was slaughtered," she said at last, "in Kcen."

"Mine was lost in Carmul." He offered empathy as an olive branch, and she accepted it for the time being. They might inherently be at odds, but they were kindred where it mattered most.

"Machaun was there," she said. "He and the Seawolves brought us here. Sema and a warrior named Maon helped me escape."

"Machaun goes where he thinks he is needed most, compensating for his lack of proficiency with elaa by sheer force. Where the Seawolves might show mercy, he is incapable." D'tanesse shook his head. "I am sorry."

"I have little remaining to motivate my survival, except this—Machaun and his king cannot succeed. Whatever their goal, I will thwart it. Whatever their desire, I will destroy it. They have made me an animal cornered—they will learn to fear the hunted."

"Llynx." He said her name carefully, averting his gaze toward a distant point on the cavern wall. The firelight cast shadows over his mouth and the hollows of his eyes. They shone out of the dim darkness like green plate glass backlit by quiet sadness. "Don't turn an honorable desire into a dishonorable quest. Let your motivation be for Cathylon and its people. That is worth every breath you take to survive."

"Cathylon has done little for me. Even less for my family."

"Then I will make a start." He stood, brushing dust from his black-and-white breeches, and strode to the back wall of the cavern. He ran a hand along the face of the wall at eye level. His fingers found a hidden mechanism and a crack appeared behind a thin avalanche of dust. It split the wall from ceiling to floor, widening to reveal a crisp night tapestry of sky and stars as two rock slabs swung slowly outward.

Fresh air crept beneath the hem of Troy's skirt and brushed against her bare arms. She inhaled the stench of the desert and remembered dragging footsteps, sand particles blasted against skin, the endless pull of rope on her wrists and shoulders. The rope burns at the base of her hands stung faintly in response.

"Through this door is freedom and, if you wish it, an alliance." All the energy of mirth he possessed now turned into sincere passion. "You are exhausted. Sema would be most upset if I let you wander off to collapse in the streets, after all the trouble she has gone through to help you. There is a refuge, a home where you will be welcome and safe. Our home. I can take you there."

She had not been safe since leaving Kcen the first time, as a young frightened girl. Now she was alone in Camil Askanda, and she must survive.

"Very well." Troy stood, pacing toward him. "Where is this refuge?"

Part Two

The Warrior

Chapter Eleven

Estimal

All was well until the Seawolves came to Carmul.

They arrived in a long boat with one spindle mast, cutting through the waves to our shore, thirteen years before the fall of Carmul. I had just arrived myself, back from negotiations in Camil Askanda. The coastline spread like a long green skirt from the Aigroe pass to Klenit in the distance. A bristle of pine trees along the mountain base edged the green on one side; a moon-colored ribbon of beach laced the other.

Carmul was there, between mountain and beach, where the land smoothed out before the ocean. I viewed it from above, riding west toward the edge of a plateau: lovely round dwellings looking like white stones scattered over the grass.

On my left was a cliff that plunged straight to the beach. Beyond its edge I could see the slim Seawolf vessel easing into the shallows, tacking around the standing rock formations. Those rocks, charcoal against glassy gray water, were the same L'estim and I climbed as children. The boat slipped past, unconcerned.

I turned my mount down the steep path winding across the cliff's broken face and met them as they pushed their boats onto the shore. The glistening hulls left damp scars in the mud, lines dragging away from the reach of curling waves.

The woman herself approached first, wetting her bare feet and the hem of her skirt in the foam-streaked surf. Her oarsmen came behind, observant guards. Deep pits of black their eyes were, in skins drenched with shadow. Straight to me the woman strode, sand clinging to her wet toes. Two silver strips like open petals crested above her bare shoulder, nestling against the tang of a bluish blade. A sword. The woman carried it strapped to her back as if it were a child, some precious cargo. A leather satchel hung over one shoulder, crossing the baldric strap over her chest.

"I have a message for your king," was her greeting and introduction.

"I am the High King's brother and ambassador," I answered, inclining my head with respect she didn't deserve. "Well met, Lady. I will take your message to him."

She ground into me with a look, her chin tipped up in the way of rulers. "Well met. But the message is for your king, not you."

I made her wait with the oarsmen and her boat while I rode to the Hall to fetch the High King, L'estim Glor. Though I had news of my own, I was obliged to withhold it until this woman could be dealt with and sent back from whence she came.

"I am Natug, queen of the Seawolves," she said when I returned with him. I was still in my traveling clothes, coated in travel dust. Not that it mattered to her, or apparently even my brother. Facing each other, the two royal persons tried to overcome the other's presence with their postures and all-knowing stares.

"We know of the Seawolves," L'estim replied evenly. "My brother has done extensive research."

"We do not know him." She was galling in her observation. One did not have to meet people to become acquainted with them. *History tells all stories*, I wanted to say. *I know yours from the exodus, even before.* Perhaps certain pieces were still in need of settling, but the whole picture was easy enough to guess.

She surveyed me with a look, beginning to end, and was satisfied that I knew nothing. "We would be willing to teach you of our people. Having lived as ourselves for so long there are insights to be added, perhaps, to research."

"Be that as it may, we know enough about your violence."

"We do as we must to protect ourselves. I admit many have let self-interest overshadow mercy. But we have discovered a new way of living." She opened the satchel and produced a book wrapped in aged leather. A compass star, or seastar as the Seawolves called it, was stitched with black thread on the front.

My brother cast an appraising glance at the hilt of her sword then down at the book, lingering over her figure on the return trip to her face.

She did not seem to mind. "This is the book of Aenti EirNin, first of the Esobir."

Life began to descend, along with a deep silence, after she spoke those words. I knew what a book was. I had already seen one on visits to Camil Askanda. She had probably never seen a desert, which probably hovered clandestine and arrogant above water eternally. In knowledge, at least, I was vastly ahead.

"Perhaps the High King—" My emphasis on the title was as much to remind her of his position as to remind L'estim. "—will later grant you an audience. As it is, I have just returned from important business which we must discuss, m'lord."

I prompted a dismissal of the woman by turning toward the Hall behind us. L'estim, hesitating, pulled his cloak around him as it tried to escape in the sudden wind. With his arms folded beneath the brown garment, standing straight, he wondered, "The Seawolves have sent their queen to deliver a message?"

Natug's arms were at her sides. One hung casually by her hip and the other cradled the supple spine of the aged book. Her hair hung straight over her shoulders (there being no room on her back due to the exquisite sword) where the wind could play with it. Her hair was constantly being lifted and tangled, looking more ferocious each time the wind set it back down on her crimson bodice.

I tried again. "We will accommodate you as befits your status, and the High King will see you after you've had a meal and bath."

"You speak very quickly for the High King."

"It is my place as his ambassador."

"The queen of the Seawolves speaks for herself." Her gaze latched onto me now, eyes fully open. "Perhaps your research failed to discover this. We will forgive."

I looked to L'estim, who was still studying her face. Finally he smiled. "Indeed, you will have a room. And, after you deliver your message, Estimal will learn from you about your people."

The smile stayed in the corner of his mouth, hidden only somewhat by his beard, as we finally proceeded to the Hall. The queen of the Seawolves left her oarsmen to watch the boat and followed us.

The Hall was decorated by several outbuildings: private chambers, a medicine room, and the armory, all squarish shapes pressing against the long, stately Hall. A circular portico sheltered the front doors, lovely in contrast with its white dome roof, rounded by scalloped pillars.

"She is very smug," I muttered, stalking up the portico steps shoulder to shoulder with L'estim. In the center of the round stone floor a fire burned in a black pit hearth, sending up hot fumes that shimmered before the doors of the Hall.

"Self-assured, yes, but that is no fault for a leader. She is just the person I imagine the Seawolves would choose to follow."

"Don't speak to her without me." Inside, the Hall with its regal dining table was lit with myriad candles against approaching dusk. We stepped through the doors. The woman observed from behind.

"I wouldn't dream of it. Natami may try to keep you though."

"She will understand. Don't smile like that." I left him in the Hall, hurrying to the other end of the room and through a door leading to the private chambers. His smile worried me.

L'estim was the firstborn, son of a pure Inatru lineage, and his birthright was his people. In truth, the kingship could have gone to me—though I came second we shared our day of birth. However, the kingship was his right and I never desired to take it from him. Tradition, and the preservation of such, was my calling. I never looked for more.

Through childhood lessons, an education neither of us took lightly, we progressed to our coming of age and passed it. Our duty to the people and their traditions overshadowed us. We invested our lives in Cathylon, tirelessly working for the good of the villages and the lives of our people. Every choice we made was in Cathylon's best interest, and in making sure the traditions and order set by the book of Inatru survived. Each year we grew closer to complete integration with our ancient heritage.

I chose a wife first, Natami of Redllew who was Inatru, and our son D'tanesse was born the following year, named in the fashion of royal firstborn. I expected L'estim to find a wife just as quickly, but he was reluctant.

"Come with me to Daehexa, there are plenty of women there," I often urged him. "After we negotiate the plans for fortification, the chieftain can introduce you to his daughter."

"I have already met Melaine, and her father Yessac. I do travel out of Carmul from time to time. Yessac and I have had several engaging conversations." L'estim would stare at the sea as he answered, or at his plate, or at the sky, hoping something would materialize to distract the conversation.

"You act as if not a girl in Cathylon will prove worthy."

"Perhaps one will. I have not found her yet."

"The people look to you for an heir," I reminded him. "And D'tanesse needs a playmate."

"I will take him riding by the cliffs."

"But someone his age, as we had."

"When she comes, I promise to marry her forthright and we will give you a playmate and heir and the answer to all your problems," he would grumble, and receive an elbow in the ribs. "Truly." He ended the discussion this way every time. "As king I promise it. You shall have what you ask. But in time."

And so the best of the Inatru's daughters were claimed by others, while I was slowly robbed of patience and L'estim of options. All time ever brought us was this troublesome woman, who no doubt was causing untold damage in the hearthroom in as many minutes as it took me to change clothes.

Natami was waiting for me in our bedchamber, smiling a greeting before I even crossed the threshold.

"Well? You were successful, I take it." Her dress was a muted orange tone, silken like her brown hair which she was braiding neatly, threading the tails of her headscarf into the weave.

The laugh wrinkles fanning out from the corners of her eyes deepened when she spoke, grinning. As usual, grinning. Natami was like a rising sun, laughing and always gaining lightness.

"You always hope for success." I shook lingering irritation away, rolling my shoulders.

"I think you sometimes hope to fail." There was no edge to her words, no guile. Her fingers hurried to finish the braid so she could embrace me. We came together and I forgot for a moment the brown woman intruding on my time with L'estim. A bright scent languished on the air, cinnamon and orange. My wife's body carried it as well, stronger. I breathed deeply. Outside, the gulls squealed as they spun above the water.

"L'estim was distracted, is all," I said at length, sighing deeply. "He has a visitor and did not listen well to my report." Irritation returned, needling its way in. I sounded like a jealous child, which was not the case. Which made the needle of irritation that much sharper.

"A visitor?" Natami poured cold rosehip tea from a pitcher glistening with condensation and handed me a glass. "Never mind, I'll eagerly hear your report."

There was little she could do with the information, but her interest was gratifying and eased the sting.

"Machaun is a good strategist but a poor leader. He welcomes an alliance and will supply our warriors with training. In return I offered the use of our quarry in the mountains to fortify the outer walls of Camil Askanda. I hope—" I swallowed the tea and took the clean tunic she held out "—to one day have the desert city as a refuge, a fallback should the worst happen here."

"But the chieftains are peaceful now." Natami sat on the edge of a chair and crossed one knee over the other, with her slippered toes pressed against the floor. Her skirt swept to one side, rippling playfully in a slight breeze that puffed through the open windows.

I dressed quickly. "The chieftains are peaceful and, moreover, content with what they have. Yet people change."

Natami nodded, watching me. Change was a matter of course and had never bothered her. I preferred to guide the change rather than be surprised by it. Though she was aware of this also, at the time I was not sure she understood.

Now I know she did not.

"L'estim will have to be told again."

"Where is he now?"

"Preparing to eat."

"And the visitor?"

"I hope she is bathing."

Natug had not bathed and her hair was still uncouth, a tangled veil hanging to her waist. For some reason L'estim chose to give her audience on the portico instead of at the table in the Hall. She sat on the stone bench that circled the hearth pit, already seated beside him. They were turned toward each other on the bench with a large platter of food between them.

"Natami could have served," I reminded him, descending the short flight of steps leading down to the hearth pit. "I'm sure the queen of the Seawolves wouldn't begrudge a few minutes' wait for the sake of propriety."

"I am honored to serve this once, as our initial welcome was not so cordial." L'estim picked an orange from the tray. He was playing chameleon, taking on the traits of the woman near him so as to understand her. I stayed standing.

"In the past my people exhibited aggression. My presence here is meant as a show of good will." She lifted a hand to accept the offered fruit. It scraped across her callouses when she turned it over to peel it. "If I wished to conquer you, my warriors would have gone before me." The rind, pierced by her fingernails, released yellow condensation as it split open.

L'estim was satisfied. "Your presence here is welcome. And peace, always welcome."

I was not satisfied. We did not know if she told the truth. We did not know her at all. "Peace is always hoped for, less often expected and rarely delivered."

"Let this be the rare occasion, then."

"And what peace have you come to offer?"

L'estim ignored me, leaning toward her as he sliced the bread.

Drops of moisture seeped from the ripe fruit and ran over the pale scars dotting Natug's knuckles. "I come with a warning. The book of Esobir has described your destruction."

"You should know," I countered, "that there is more than one book."

"Do you have the book of Korah?" She straightened as if to rise, eyes lit with anticipation. Juice ran down her wrists. I was about to fetch a cloth for her, but she licked the juice away and rubbed her hand dry on her skirt.

L'estim looked on in amused silence.

From then on, I looked only at her eyes while she finished devouring the orange. "The Inatru possess the writings of Anithe."

"His words cannot be trusted." She remained upright on the edge of the bench.

"I would say the same of your book, Esobir."

"He was Dnae and a traitor. In his time the Dnae nearly destroyed the entire mortal race."

"So you say."

"You must know of elaa then?"

"I have some proficiency."

Unexpectedly, she drew back. A hesitation quick as shadow crossed her face. "Have you spoken to the Mind? I would guess not."

The Mind was not mentioned, even suggested, in anything so far translated from the Inatru's book. I groped for an answer.

L'estim waited, bread and knife forgotten in his hands.

"The stone, elaa, is not only stone," explained Natug. "It is part of Elaa, the Mind. That is where its power comes from."

The fire at my back was suddenly too warm. "What of this warning? Is the Mind angry that we've ignored it?"

"Yes. And no." She stood, went up the stairs and turned toward the ocean. Sunset slanted across the water and cast a bronze sheen onto the portico. When the warm light touched her clothes, she seemed transformed, a being of the heat and air. The sword on her back took on a grainy texture, blurred as if by a haze. Only her hair remained tangible in color, the same dense tangle slanting over her head and shoulders. A shadow rose between her and the light. My throat dried instantly. I tried to swallow and nearly choked.

Afterward I would remember the shadow appearing shortly after she began singing, but I was not at first aware of her voice, so shaken was I by that shadow.

Then there was the feeling of flying.

My feet remained on the ground—I stamped twice to be sure—but my body wanted to be weightless, floating. The sky suddenly felt vastly close, the ceiling of the hall paper thin. My stomach twisted, sinking and expanding.

Her song came to life in the trembling air.

"In the Place Between, agreement made
Fast flies the word, far until spoken changes
Through doorways into stone living

Become stone, become ruler living
Elaa, elaa, warrior's hand receiving."

I felt L'estim hit the ground and turned my head to look. He was on his knees, face lifted to the pressing sky that was by now a presence weighting the atmosphere of the Hall. I clenched my fists and set my feet, tense in every muscle.

Natug raised her right hand and the shadow mimicked her. She was reaching toward the presence, reaching into it—

The song was over.

The sky's weight receded and we were left in the void, silent. A small hand pressed against my hip, hot and startling. It was D'tanesse, just six years old at the time. He had wandered onto the portico at some point during the demonstration and now slipped beneath my arm, clinging to my waist.

"Father? What happened to uncle?"

L'estim was still on his knees, staring upward. His face was the color of paste but his eyes were vivid as if he still heard the song.

"He is overwhelmed."

"Overwhelmed by what?"

"Power."

Chapter Twelve

"Imra is back." Core's shadow stretched across Sienna's grave, darkening the lupines covering the earthen mound.

Terra remained crouched beside it. The plants had taken over quickly after the fire. The copse was filled with them. He put his hand into their mass, slipping his fingers through stalks of purple blooms until he found the ground beneath. "Did she speak to you?"

"She seemed close to it."

Two years had passed since Kcen was razed by the Seawolves and its people slaughtered. Two years since Troy gave herself up to save him.

Terra reached to the mound on his right. Now one hand rested on his sister's grave, the other on his mother's. "She's never close to it."

After the night of the attack, in the light of a dismal sun, Terra, Core, Cail and Imra emerged from the copse to find themselves the only remaining residents of Kcen. Little was salvageable from the burnt houses, though the fires died in heavy snowfall. Regardless, most of Kcen's resources were lost. Those final weeks of Derrh had been the hardest of their lives.

"You might try to speak to her."

"She doesn't know me anymore."

"Neither does mother, but you speak to her." Core relented at his brother's narrow glance. Cail had fallen sick and died a few weeks after the attack. They had buried her in the copse, visiting once a year on the day of her death. "I'm sorry."

Terra rubbed his thumb and forefinger over the scant stubble on his jaw, watching Core's shadow, the rise and fall of his shoulders. A blackbird whistled a melancholy tune above them. He had spoken to Imra many times. His sister had always been gentle and reticent. After witnessing so much carnage she had withdrawn completely.

"We should be taking care of her." Core's voice, already a man's, deepened further with conviction.

"We would if we could find her." Terra finally stood. "She's happy wandering and sleeping outside, and I think she eats better than we do."

"She sleeps in trees. She could die—the forest is dangerous."

"Imra wants nothing to do with us!"

The blackbird cut its melody short, listening to Terra's gruff shout travel through leaf and branch.

They had argued this many times from both sides. Both of them had alternated reaching out to Imra, then resolving to leave her alone. The truth of loss was bitter in both their mouths. Worse, it was undeniable in their hearts.

"Come on. The sun is setting." Core retreated, shoulders heavy, from the copse. A small quiver of arrows strapped to his thigh rattled quietly with each stride.

Terra turned away from the mounds with a sigh. The haven from his childhood was now a graveyard. His father's grave was beside his mother's, and Mytch's beyond that.

Remember me, its presence said. *Troy is waiting for you. You may be her only hope.*

Her only hope. He dwelt on the thought, drawing reason for existence from it. Every waking hour was devoted to learning the skills he would need to survive in Troy's world. Lack of those skills had cost Mytch his life, and Troy her freedom. He would not let that happen again.

Their home was a rude log cabin a mile or two south of ruined Kcen, amidst the trees. The boys had constructed it over a period of months with salvaged tools from Kcen. They also raised a shanty barn for the horses, Laic and Makala, who found their way home after the massacre.

Outside the house was a small potato garden and a log target, chipped and cratered across its pale round face. Terra's hand brushed the weathered wood, then felt for the bow slung over his right shoulder.

Core passed him, stepping over a chilly stream that cut between their cabin and the log target. "See what you can find in the root cellar for stew," he said over his shoulder.

Terra dropped his hand from the target, brushing his palm across his breeches. Tiny flakes of wood rained to the ground. "We need to make more arrows."

"We need to eat, Terra, sometime before tomorrow."

After their meal they sat before the dirt hearth stripping twigs and bark from thin branches for arrows. The house was close and comfortable, warmed from the heat of the fire and the lingering scent of vegetable stew. Their beds along the wall near the hearth were piles of heather covered with deer skins. Scant household items littered three of the four rough-hewn shelves along the opposite wall. The door occupied the wall furthest from the hearth where they sat.

"We need to find feathers." Core tossed a handful of bark chips on the hearth fire. It consumed them, exhaling sparks.

Terra nodded absently. Troy's bow languished on the top shelf beside her sword and baldric. He could recall the moment she was taken as easily as yesterday, and feel her pushing the weapons into his hands.

He had to find her. He had to give them back to her and show her what these weapons had taught him. His own bow hung from a wooden peg by the door where he placed it upon entering. He had studied her bow to make it. The wood was so thin he resorted to pounding a long, curved branch with a stone to take off tiny chips instead of using his knife, which peeled off too much. The string was deer sinew. He had spent a long time seasoning the branch with rabbit fat before he could bend it to fit the string, with the correct tension, without snapping the branch.

"And a new target," Core continued, his eyes on his work. "That log is starting to splinter." He pushed his blade down the branch in his hands, chipping bark away in long curls.

Wood scent mingled the air, quickening Terra's memory to long days spent shooting arrows at the log, until his fingers bled so he could not pull the string back, and his palm was raw from the snap of it. His stubborn persistence—and Core's—was rewarded as his aim became sharper, his draw quicker.

"It is time," he muttered. He could get no better with his arrows or be more prepared if he practiced every day for the rest of his life.

"What? For what?"

Terra broke his stare from Troy's sword, turning to Core. "It is time to leave."

"You have never been farther than Tarrom's Hall. Where do you hope to go?"

Terra shrugged and shuffled closer to the fire's heat as the coldness of night pressed into their hut. "I know the Seawolves traveled southwest. They followed the merchant road, and the road leads to the river. Camil Askanda is the only city on the other side of the Aganus River. What else is there to know?"

"There are snakes," said Core. "Wolves, bears, bandits, bottomless pits. Also, a desert."

"Those things are here as well as anywhere else in the world," Terra pointed out.

"Except for deserts and bandits," grumbled Core.

"We can get past those. We have been living almost like travelers for two years. Surely the real thing cannot be much different."

"Except we will have no stream, no root cellar, and no beds. There are one hundred details you have not considered. What if your horse dies?"

"I will walk."

"What if you lose your way?"

"I will find it again."

"And how long will finding it take you? You will run out of food before you are halfway there."

"Food can be found along the way. We have survived in a forest for two years by ourselves. I think traveling for one or two weeks will not be as difficult as you believe."

"But what if—?"

"Core. Remember that Troy lost all to save you and me when we would have died in the battle against the Seawolves. She protected us and gave up her freedom for ours. Now she is a captive, while we are alive and well here."

"We are hardly alive and well."

"We could be worse off."

"I remember being much better off, don't you?"

Terra scowled. "I promised her if she left again I would find her and I would protect her. I will keep that promise, if not for the sake of the promise itself, then because she saved my life three times. If I turn away now, and let what she has done die with her in captivity, then the life she saved was saved in vain, and I may as well have died."

Core stared into the fire, sullen. "Well…hang it. I may as well go with you. Imra doesn't need me as much as you surely will."

Terra grinned. "Good. We leave in the morning, then?"

"In the morning? Terra, use your senses! We need to gather provisions, blankets, tools—"

"Core. Your blanket and mine. Our bows and arrows and Troy's weapons. Snares for rabbits and small mammals. Our clothes – two cloaks, two tunics and two pairs of breeches each. Is that not all we own?"

Core grumbled an unintelligible reply.

* * * *

Neither of the boys looked back as they rode away from their desecrated home. They took the horses, Terra riding Laic and Core riding Makala, following the merchant road south and west to the river. Troy's weapons were strapped to Laic's saddle in a bundle with Terra's clothes and blanket. He wore his bow on his back, and his quiver was on his thigh as usual. They rode past streams, moss clinging to dark boulders in brushy patches, huge gnarled oaks and slender aspens. They trotted through lupines and layers of fallen leaves from countless years before. They leaped over fallen logs and caught the scent of earth kicked up from the horses' hooves.

They rode past familiar landmarks: the green boulder hollowed out at the base, forming a natural cave, the honey tree swarming with bees and the dry riverbed, among others.

Finally they reached the end of the woods, their lifelong home, and stopped. Thin shafts of long coarse grasses waved before them and they heard the heavy rush of water ahead.

"The river Aganus," Terra breathed.

"Yes," rejoined Core. "Shall we be on, or should I build a platform so you can gawk at your leisure?"

Terra pursed his lips and urged Laic into a trot.

Chapter Thirteen

A boy swathed in cream linen walked on the dry street past the open door of the king's bake room. Two full buckets of water hung from a wooden yoke across his shoulders, making his faint shadow wider than it should have been. He was one of the many children who came to the well each dawn. It was the size of a large pond, reflecting the shapes of their small, robed bodies as they leaned over the gently bubbling water and filled their buckets.

The strong ones pushed ahead to fill theirs first so they might return to their home duties that much quicker. Those shoved aside hurled sharp insults which were ignored or answered with another shove. The Seawolves, outcasts, waited to one side until they could have the well to themselves. The few minutes of cool shade were too precious to waste with unnecessary fighting. The sun was already baking the top of the city, sliding gold heat down the walls. Soon they would all be drenched in it.

Troy sat with her knees together in the frame of the doorway, watching the boy trudge past. Behind her, the cook murmured instructions while her subordinates thumped dough onto flat stones, splashed mint tea into tall pitchers and scraped nut paste into serving dishes. Nuts were a delicacy in Camil Askanda. They could satisfy hunger much longer than bread, Troy mused. If she could get her hands on it, she could give it to the Seawolves.

The boy trudging past her was Inatru, strong and stocky in the shoulders. They were all strong. They ate well, that was part of it. The Seawolf children with their long, thin bodies were like young trees in comparison. Given the right nutrition and training, they would be more than a match for the bullish Inatru.

Patience. It was only a matter of time, as long as she could keep them alive. The Inatru had strength and dominance; the Seawolves had depth and tenacity. She had recognized that common thread quickly, beginning with Maon. It ran through them all, a center cord stronger than blood, colder than fear.

"Hurry with the pastries. No, fold them over just once, then pinch the seams flat. You are not folding laundry."

"Don't spill the spread! That is all we have."

She paid limited attention to the kitchen chatter, waiting for her name to be mentioned. One of the Seawolves, a girl standing at the far side of the well, was watching her. She came for water every morning along with the rest. Dark hair draped over her forehead in a tangled curve (the Seawolves did not wear headscarves), partly covering one eye but not hiding the steady confidence shining there, a trust that had grown with each brief encounter over months and years. Troy inclined her head, acknowledging her, and then her eyes moved to meet those of a boy standing behind the girl. He was also Seawolf, and his look was one of hope.

"Where is Llynx? She should be here already."

Troy grasped her crimson skirts at her sides when she stood to keep from getting tripped up ascending the steps. The girl and the boy watched her. His eyes were like living polished stones. They bored into her, alight with approval. She should know his name, to know his talents and where he might fit. By the look of his straightened shoulders and his hands clenched around the bucket handle, he knew her name already. Llynx, the Seawolf who lived in Camil Askanda by choice, to undermine the king. Llynx, the warrior. Llynx, who watched over her people, provided for them and—on occasion—led them.

The woman with a lie for everyone.

Those capable of good are equally capable of evil, she had said once to Mytch. She was a warrior, maybe, but she'd left her weapon behind, with no intention of returning to it. *What would they say if they knew that?* she thought. *How long would their hope last?*

The boy was still watching when she turned her back and stepped into the shadows of the kitchen.

"Llynx!"

"There she is."

Her eyes adjusted slowly to the room. Feet thumped toward her, and the cook's voice followed. "Ready for duty, I trust."

The other women put in their opinions from various places around the bake room. "Llynx is always ready for duty."

"As a widow should be. And grateful for the opportunity."

"Look at her," said another woman, slicing hot bread at a board nearby. "She is. Every Seawolf should be so eager to serve and redeem themselves."

Here in the king's Hall she was Llynx, the widow who desired nothing more than a way to survive. Llynx the widow was not interested in conquest or politics. She wanted only to earn her next meal.

Most of the cook's underlings were Inatru, and were paid for their services. They were not scarred, as those brought from other villages would be, or marked as the king's possessions. They were Inatru, privileged and compensated. Troy was not paid but she was fed, and allowed access to all the kitchens. Llynx the widow was grateful.

The woman continued slicing the bread. The knife slipped through the crust and into the bread's brown flesh with a brittle crack. Troy kept her arms close at her sides, palms inward. Her own knife was hidden beneath her skirts, strapped to the inside of her thigh, only to be used in dire emergency. She avoided handling knives in the kitchen or anywhere else in the Hall. She could pretend a great many things, but her hands could not lie about their experience.

The cook's outline came into focus. Her fat shoulders bulged on either side of her neck, spilling two thick arms down her sides. Her headscarf made a red circle around her flushed, round face. She pushed a stone tray at Troy using the round protrusion of her stomach beneath her white apron as well as her own hands.

"Go on, then. The king is waiting for his breakfast. He'll be in the scriptorium." Her round face glistened with fervor. She took her duties very seriously and demanded the same from everyone beneath her. All cooks seemed to possess those qualities. Troy had never encountered an apathetic cook, or a thin one.

Except for D'tanesse—but he didn't count for much of a cook. His recipes were better known for their combustion than their taste.

Troy left the bake room and its voices behind, following the narrow stone-lined passages to a long corridor lined with gray plank doors. There were no windows here. Darkness clustered around candles trapped in hanging lanterns along the walls. In this corridor were the cells—the Inatru called them rooms—that housed the king's servants. There were faster routes to the scriptorium, lighted and warmed by the hot sun, but Troy chose this one to remind herself what she was. She reached the far end of the corridor, where it turned a corner and shot like an arrow into distant shadow. Teyeda's cell, and the reassuring presence of the tunnel, lay behind the door on her right just past the dehydrated wood. It was the same tunnel she'd escaped through and where she'd found D'tanesse that first and last night of her captivity in the king's Hall. Now, here, she was something more.

"I'm not inside, if you were wondering." Teyeda came out of the corridor on her left, surrounded by a small circle of luminescence. An oil flame burned above the fluted mouth of a lamp in his hand, filling the space between them with its singed perfume. His other hand gripped a wrought poker. Its triangle head hovered beside his knee.

Troy turned on instinct at the first sound of his approach, shifting the tray of food onto the palm of one hand to free the other for use. Defense, even though it proved unnecessary. "I wasn't bringing your breakfast, if you were hoping."

"Is he in the scriptorium today?" Teyeda did not seem amused by the quip. He was not easily distracted.

"He usually is."

"I'll be trimming the lamps."

"I appreciate the light." Troy inclined her head and began to move past him toward the stairs at the other end of the hallway.

Teyeda set the poker down and rechecked one of the lit lanterns. "Machaun has returned with an Esobir. He's been questioning him."

Troy slowed and pulled in a deliberate breath. Machaun kept busy uprooting the Esobir who seemed to sprout underfoot in recent months within Camil Askanda, searching for the source of the uprising with no promising results so far. Those he tracked and caught were taken to the Hall, where they defended the name of their leader and her location with their silence at the cost of their lives. But that was Sema's realm. She led the Esobir. Troy's business was the freedom of the Seawolves and the identity that helped her gain it. Each knew the risks of their choices before they made them, and each respected the other's decisions.

The walls seemed to converge as she walked, turning the corridor into a crevice that dipped into the roots of the Hall. Troy followed it down, passing from each island of light to the one beneath until the stone steps bent into the vaulted entry of the scriptorium.

Her mouth began watering. It had nothing to do with the steaming brown loaves beneath the linen cover. She tasted salt, the nearer she came to the banded door of the scriptorium. The same taste was in the scriptorium at Yettmis, though much fainter. The door opened silently when she pulled its latch. Languid yellow light barely made an impression on the stone wall beside her, but its stale presence declared the king was still inside. Troy swallowed and stepped over the threshold.

Needles of awareness dug into her skin and her lungs opened. The boxlike room should have felt cramped. The facing wall, which was shortest, was faintly blue outside the reach of the candlelight. A mock arch of the same dull color bent across it, calling attention to the wall's blankness and an exit that did not exist. Shelves stacked with scrolls crowded the side walls, closing in on the center of the room and the long silver table taking up the floor.

She drew a breath, air rushing in as if it were blowing down from the mountains to meet her. The wall flickered with sudden color that spread like drops of dye in water. A golden field of grain appeared within the rectangle frame of the wall, the knobbly heads bowed beneath their ripe weight. The colors blurred, bled together, then resolved into a different picture. This time it was a lake. Then a white bird gliding in a steel blue sky.

Troy pretended not to see anything but a blank wall. Elaa stone was saturated in energy, and responded in different ways to each individual, but its effect on the user was universal. Those who used it most—for any reason—were the ones Machaun tracked down. Like the knives, Troy avoided using elaa at all. She couldn't avoid its presence, especially in the scriptorium where the king studied it, but she could pretend that it didn't exist. She could pretend sand was water if that would bring her nearer to her goal.

"I've brought your food, m'lord."

"I'll take it in a moment." The High King, Estimal Glor, stood over the silver table with his back to the shelving. He bristled like a maned dog—wide in the chest, thick in the limbs—as he studied a map spread across the tabletop. A bright red cloak, the most colorful thing in the room, covered the hill of his back and stopped short of his knees.

Troy nudged the door shut with her hip and waited.

The king's thick fingers roamed over a large map, tracing the circle outline of Cathylon as if that were all it took to know the island. A medallion of bronze, silver and gold in descending circles with a large bead of blue glass in the center and a bronze candlestick held the curled edges at bay on either corner of the map. His other hand suppressed a third corner. The candlestick was just a candlestick. The medallion was actually a Looking Glass, replicated from one described in the book of Inatru. She had never seen the book itself. The king kept it secret, where no one could take it from him. He'd told her as much when she'd first met him, a new maidservant trained and recommended by Teyeda.

"I find it a marvel." The king frowned at the map. "That the Ancient ones wrote so much using so little space. Our language is a shameful waste compared to theirs. I should very much like to know how the Esobir handle so much information, and where they hoard it."

Troy fixed her eyes on the tray balanced on her hand. Every scrap of parchment could so easily burn, at a word, but those copies could be replaced. The original must burn as well. It would if she ever found it, and then she would be free to act.

The king's eyes were bright, set above dark circles in his wide sockets. "A page of knowledge unfolds from a single line from the book of Inatru."

He mentioned the Inatru often when she was serving him.

"Did you know—of course you don't—the Ancients could cross entire continents in mere minutes? There is an account here by the one who wrote the book, Anithe of the Dnae."

He mentioned that name as often as he did the Inatru. Sometimes they became interchangeable: Anithe of the Dnae. Anithe, Dnae, Inatru. Anithe, Inatru. Soon he would have the Inatru writing the book of Anithe, instead of the other way around.

"He reached through a window to the other side of the world! I copied the entire story right here over the course of the night. And the original text covered less than a page of the book."

Troy followed the sweep of his hand over a stack of parchments beside the map. She parted her lips as if she wanted to speak, but said nothing. The king did not like many questions about his book or his parchments. Troy could not risk making him suspicious, but if she kept silent he talked on his own. So far the information he bequeathed hadn't taken her to the book's physical location, but as his trust in her grew, so did his exposition.

"I think the Esobir would be surprised to know how much I've learned. If they knew what I could teach them, would they learn from me? But why would they, as long as they possess their book." The map curled into itself when he suddenly lifted the weights at its corners. "I will eat now, Llynx."

"Yes, m'lord," Troy answered to the name out of habit, but it sounded foreign, especially in the benign way the king used it. Enemies were supposed to scream one another's names on the battlefield, spitting them into the dirt as filth. He spoke to her as a servant—as he knew her.

If she could just kill the king and Machaun, none of this subterfuge would be necessary. D'tanesse argued adamantly against that, because killing a man wouldn't bring the truth to light. He insisted if they could win the people over with the truth, more death would not be necessary. Sema had agreed, and besides, they were already making headway. Their efforts kept the king and Machaun focused on their city in recent months, leaving the rest of Cathylon alone for the most part. Troy had to be satisfied that more villages weren't being raided, and focused on undermining the king's control over the Seawolves in Camil Askanda. She left the spreading of truth to Sema and the Esobir, whose numbers climbed, then dwindled, as the new converts became proficient with elaa, and Machaun found and silenced them.

"Clear those parchments away while I eat."

"Yes, m'lord." Troy left the tray in front of the king and stepped to the other side of the table where she lifted the first parchment from the top of the stack. Black script was scratched across the yellowed surface of the parchment. She was careful not to let her eyes linger on the words. As far as the king knew, she could not read and had no interest in learning.

"You need only ask, and I myself will teach you," he reminded her, tearing one of the brown loaves of bread in half. Troy knew he never would, even if she did ask. He ruled through ignorance, only speaking thus to point out his superiority, his control over her education, and her people by association.

"I am content with what I know," Troy replied quietly, eyes downcast. The parchment smelled like a garden of fresh dirt, smudged with dried plant matter from the king's fingers. "I am good at what I know. Too much knowledge might ruin me."

"Impossible. You can never know enough. Knowledge is the means to change and nothing satisfies more than knowing you're changed by what you've discovered and making sure everyone else knows they ought to change as well. There is nothing better."

"Yes, m'lord."

"You do not believe me."

"I don't presume to contradict you, m'lord." Troy cast a modest glance at the king before turning back to her chore. At times she didn't know what to make of his speeches. Often he would go on as he just did, almost mockingly, then become suddenly serious. It felt as if he were conversing with two different people, though there was only her. "Tell me why you fear knowledge." His hands were pressed flat on either side of the breakfast tray, supporting his weight as he leaned over the table.

"I don't fear knowledge, m'lord. Some knowledge requires understanding. The deep knowledge."

"The deep knowledge?"

"Knowledge that comes with a price, m'lord. Knowledge that is a door to evil." Troy finished rolling the top parchment and tied it with a pale thread plucked from the pile between the map and the parchments, then carried it silently to its niche. Standing so close to the picture wall, she could feel its sound, a spark thrown against her bare arms. There was no good way to describe the sensation, except perhaps pain. Pain with a taste. The taste was slightly bitter, the after-swallow tang of salt water. She wondered if everyone tasted it when they came close to elaa stone, or if it were just her. Mytch apparently had not, or their mentor Yessac, though Yessac might not have thought it worth mentioning.

The lifelike pictures changed one into another across the surface of the wall beneath the blue arch. Now there was a grass-covered hill, warmed by sunlight. The individual blades seemed to stand out like real grass ruffled by a cold sea wind. She was often tempted to touch the pictures, to see if they really did stand out, or if perhaps her fingertips would actually brush real grass. She never reached out a hand to try, not even once. It was only a wall.

"Knowledge is never evil. You must understand that, or you will never understand anything. You can never get enough of it, and any price you pay is worth acquiring it."

"Yes, m'lord."

He was still watching her when she returned to roll another scroll. His lit, black eyes were on her face instead of her busy hands.

"Was it today?"

Troy's breath caught, squeezed by an uncomfortable knot in her chest. Her fingers continued to curl the parchment slowly over into itself. The dry scrape of it surrounded her.

"Your husband, he died two years ago if I remember."

"Yes. It was today."

He died at the hands of your own warriors. And he was not my husband.

Being a widow, a Seawolf desperate enough to serve the king who had ruined her people, was the guise that gained her entry here and so she used it. The king didn't know Mytch died in the raid on Kcen, or that she had never been married. Or, most importantly, that she was the one who had escaped with the Otnas and the book in the first place, when they were brought through the mountains by the Klenit Esobir. He only knew what he saw and what she told him, and he trusted it because he wanted to. Perhaps in a remote sense they were connected in their grief. Perhaps his grief was a storm beneath the calm surface, like hers.

Troy did not want to care about his reasons. Mytch had died because the king commanded it. Machaun had carried out the command. They were responsible as much as she was for Mytch's death. For Terra's family. For Kcen.

"My wife's death still grieves me, though it was many years ago. You would have been very young when she died."

"I hoped the pain might fade with years." She knew it never would. A swordbrother was not a husband, but death made no distinction. His words were just words. It was not comfort. It was not a common line between them.

"A life sacrificed leaves wounds that never heal, I'm afraid. But Mytch would consider the price worth paying, I think."

Troy's throat burned, throbbing. She regretted ever mentioning Mytch's name to the king. She had done it to show vulnerability and desperation, but it was too close to the truth. From the beginning it had been a trapdoor to her emotions, and when he spoke the name they swirled into chaos.

"Do you think your wife would consider your life above her own?"

He pressed his mouth closed, and his eyes cooled. Troy's hands stilled, silencing the rustle of parchment. They stood like animals tensed in a cage until he spoke again. “Yes. I think she would.” He pushed away from the table and dismissed her with a grumble. “I will finish with the parchments. I want to read them again.”

She released one still in her hands, and it relaxed on top of the pile where she left it. “Yes, m’lord.” Troy smoothed the anger from her voice. “Thank you.”

The door opened as she reached it, and Troy found herself in a new standoff with the king’s second in command.

“That tray is not empty.” Machaun tended to snarl whenever he spoke to her. Troy stepped aside to make way for him, bowing her head. It was true. The nut spread was still untouched in its dish on the marble tray. Estimal Glor had lost interest in the bread and ignored the pitcher of mint tea altogether.

“Have you not eaten?” Machaun spoke past Troy’s shoulder to the king, but did not step inside.

“I am not hungry now.”

“You should eat to feed your mind, regardless.”

Troy listened to their voices before and behind her while her eyes lingered on the sword hanging above Machaun’s right hip. The hilt reached past his ribcage and was tilted toward her. If the worst happened and he attacked her, she would try to draw his sword before he could. Easier than trying to reach her dagger, hidden securely behind a curtain of skirt.

“I welcome your good advice, but I know my own strength.”

“Then I will whet your appetite for news.” Machaun’s hand was like the desert, hot and abrasive. He pushed against Troy’s shoulder, restraining her while he helped himself to a portion of bread. “I have been questioning one of the last Esobir. An old man.”

Troy stiffened. At the edge of her vision, Machaun’s snarl changed to a sneer.

“Has he told you what he knows?”

Machaun scraped a chunk of bread through the dish of nut paste and pushed it into his mouth. “He says he is the very last, but I can still see lights walking throughout the city. He did know something about their book. It was moved from Klenit, and no one has heard news of it for two years. He was adamant that we were responsible for the loss. I told him there would be no loss if they had not been skulking about, hiding instead of using it.” He licked flavor from his fingers and released Troy’s shoulder. “He also says the Deliverer is going to…deliver them.”

“They always do.” The king felt for the circle medallion resting on his night’s work of writing. His palm covered it, soaking up some reassurance.

Troy disciplined her lungs to breathe normally. The Esobir were careful, but they were also passionate, devoted and adamant about Cathylon's deliverance. Passion—or perhaps desperation—overtook common sense in some of them.

"The Esobir are dwindling in number. In time—I think a very short time—they will be no more."

"That is not good enough. The Esobir who run from you are of no concern. The one who does not should concern you greatly."

"They have no real power besides the Otnas, and if they did I doubt they would use it. You said yourself, they shy away from the source of power—"

"Pride, man!" The king snatched the medallion up into his fist, and parchments scattered. "See to your pride before it ruins us! Change comes by one, and is changed again by one."

"Carmul's power is long broken. The Seawolves are cowed and even happy to serve." Machaun's fingers grasped Troy's jaw in a pinching grip, forcing her to expose her face to him. Her breath jumped from her mouth and she quickly lowered her eyes. "What can my sword do?"

"It can end my life." The bronze hilt hovered at the base of her vision. Her left hand was nearest to it. Troy shifted the tray, resting the weight on the palm of her right.

"Do you want to live, Seawolf?"

"Yes, m'lord."

"What will you do to live? Anything?"

"Yes, m'lord." She had never feared a weapon. A sword had no power on its own. Power lay in the arm lifting it. Even the Otnas responded according to the will of the one holding it.

Will is the most dangerous thing of all.

"Would you fight me to win your freedom?"

"No, m'lord."

"Why not? Tell the truth!" His fingers bored into her jaw until the bone began to hurt. He was pushed close against her. His tunic was damp with sweat.

The tray overcame her efforts to balance, and two loaves of bread fell to the floor when it tipped. Troy caught the pitcher of tea before it followed suit, quickly righting the tray without looking at it. "Freedom means little to the dead."

"Some would not think so." The king turned his hand over, pensive, examining the medallion for some hidden memory.

"I am not one of them." Her voice was strained. No one, not D'tanesse, not Sema, knew what she knew about the Otnas. Mytch had known and they'd argued about it from the first.

"I don't blame the Klenit Esobir for trying to get rid of it," she had said when they found out its function. "Something so powerful draws enemies. I would not want to own such responsibility, were I them."

"Are you afraid of your potential for evil—"

"I am wary. As you should be."

"—or your potential to do good? Of being so good that the weight of it crushes you, the weight of responsibility for those less capable?"

"I don't know what you're talking about."

"I think you do. Or will. Perhaps I'm ahead of my time."

Mytch may have acted differently here, in her place, but the dead had no say in her actions. She lived and the man gripping her face lived, and that was consuming enough.

Machaun's lips drew back, baring white teeth like a dog cornered. "The Seawolves and the Esobir could have destroyed the Inatru if they'd realized their strength. If you will survive, you must have strength greater than your enemy. Otherwise you will serve him. And you do!"

Troy rocked backward when he pushed her away and the wall thumped against her shoulder blades. "Yes, m'lord."

The picture wall observed them from the back of the room, constantly offering its possibilities. Troy shut her eyes against it.

"Let her go. She is frightened enough."

That emotion was strongly present in all three of them. Troy kept her head turned toward the door while she gathered the spilled loaves and hurried from the room.

Chapter Fourteen

The sky bled orange and red fire as the sun set behind the harsh silhouette of Camil Askanda's Great Hall. Cicadas droned into the dusty haze, lulling the city into a grateful stupor. A black shadow cast by the grim stone walls stretched over parched streets and sun-baked adobe dwellings. It shaded the wealthy who took their supper on flat rooftops. It chased beggars back to their deadwood shacks. It crept over dirt yards in the Seawolf quarter and down empty cracked lanes that perspired shimmering, musty heat waves into the atmosphere. And it followed a young woman who hurried alone through those lanes.

She clutched the frayed edges of her brown cloak close around her, concealing her servant livery as well as she could. By memory she traversed the route to her home, tucked deep in the folds of the decrepit city quarter. Darkness had descended completely by the time she reached the battered shell of a windowless house, mottled with a shameless patchwork of new boards over old. It sat at the back of a narrow lane that threaded through a gauntlet of ramshackle buildings. Light flickered faintly through thin gaps in the brittle planks. She paused and listened a moment, turning her head to make sure the lane was empty, then grasped the handle and opened the door.

She surveyed the cramped space with ironic satisfaction before turning toward the other door in the room. A strand of light brown hair fell over her eye when she slipped her hood off. She smoothed it back absently. Even a farmer would have been embarrassed to entertain guests here. A proper Lady would have been mortified. A chieftain would refuse to consider it.

The room was sadly bare save for a thrashed chair sitting next to an even more abused wooden table. Upon the gnarled surface sat the only source of light in the room, a small iron lantern. The young woman lifted this and took it with her through the second door, then down a short flight of stairs which groaned under her feet. The steps ended abruptly in front of another thicker door, with a sliver of light glowing along its base. A dry, musty essence reminiscent of parched sand and death seeped from the wood. She held her breath against the urge to cough. Her comrades would be preparing supper on the other side of the door. They were waiting for her arrival and her news. Their voices were muted, absorbed by the thickness of the door and the sandstone walls of the large room on the other side.

"...sure you haven't seen it?" That was D'tanesse, his usual lithe tenor now low and serious.

"I know nothing of your stupid book. For the hundredth time." Llynx. Impatience sharpened her normally smooth alto.

"Perhaps he moves it often."

"I'm his serving girl, not his accountant."

"Perhaps he keeps it in his bedchamber."

"I'm not his mistress, either."

"That might improve your chances of success."

Silence. One could imagine the frostbitten stare Llynx was focusing on D'tanesse, chilling the air between them.

"However." D'tanesse backpedaled toward a warmer climate. "I doubt you meet the requirements of womanly companionship. That is—"

"The soup is burning, D'tanesse."

"Oh, thank y—"

There was a crash, then the shuddering impact of bodies hitting the floor, and fists pummeling flesh. She yanked the door open and stepped through, observing the room with a sweeping glance: three chairs toppled on the floor, a black soup tureen hanging from an iron hook above the hearth fire and D'tanesse and Llynx sprawled before it. All movement stopped. The aroma of salty broth and vegetables filled her sinuses, chasing away the arid scent of deadwood. She breathed deeply.

"Sema!" Llynx brushed coarse black hair from her eyes with one hand. The other cupped D'tanesse's narrow chin, directing his head backward to the ground. Her voice was surprised. Her shadowed eyes beneath her brows and the tilt of her head as she raised it were wolfish, expectant. She knelt with one knee across his stomach.

"Get off me!" D'tanesse arched and twisted, grappling with her locked arm. She gave him a stoic look before releasing his head, standing up deliberately.

"He was about to burn the soup."

"She attacked me when my back was turned!" At times it was hard to tell D'tanesse was a grown man of twenty years and abundantly educated. Sema maintained her silence and paced toward the fireplace, an alcove chiseled in the pale wall. A tower of crates housing stacks of folded laundry stood to one side of it. She placed the lantern on the top crate. The candle inside threw warm light through star-shaped holes punched in its six sides, magnifying the sandy prickles on the surface of the sandstone behind it.

"I suggest not showing any body part you wish to keep to a woman you've just insulted." Llynx stooped, facing him, and picked up a black cloak from the floor, shaking it out before draping it over her shoulders.

D'tanesse sat up, flipped a dark braid over his shoulder and brushed himself off. His shirt was a strange orchestration of tight-woven linen, black on the right, white on the left. His pants were that in reverse. He stabbed a finger at her. "You are not a woman! You are a…a…" Words failed him.

Llynx tilted her head a fraction to the side. Her eyes flickered amusement above the bitter twist of her lips. "Am I a Maanx, D'tanesse?" she said softly.

"You—what?"

Sema glanced between them, as shocked as D'tanesse to hear the Ancient language coming from Llynx's mouth. Translated, Maanx meant a female outcast, on the same level with a murderer. Few people recognized the words when spoken, and even fewer understood them.

D'tanesse stood rigid, dark eyes wide. His fists clenched at his sides. "Who are you, Llynx?"

"Who are you, D'tanesse?"

He stiffened further. This running stalemate had plagued Llynx and D'tanesse since their first meeting. It was the one question that penetrated his coltish armor, pricking him where he was most tender. His identity was a sore secret, one he would not reveal until he was sure of Llynx's. She was not forthcoming, and so the question had remained unanswered for both of them.

Llynx raised a black eyebrow. A scar ran down her face from temple to cheek, elongating the corner of her left eye and tugging her expression from maudlin to devious.

"Is the soup ready?" Sema's light touch on D'tanesse's arm pried his eyes from their deadlock with Llynx. He turned to her. Silence stretched for the space of several heartbeats as they searched each other's faces. Her soft smile reasoned with him, while her fingers reassured with lingering pressure on his forearm. His shoulders lost their defiant hunch. The energy in his slim body calmed to a warm simmer, and he reached for her. Sema caught his hand and squeezed it gently before turning to the hearth.

"We were waiting for you." His eyes followed her.

"What did you learn, Sema?" Llynx was also watching, arms folded, impassive.

Sema lifted a warped wooden spoon resting on a folded towel on the edge of the hearth and dipped it into the soup tureen.

Four years she had spent in Camil Askanda, posing as a servant in the king's kitchens. When captives were brought in from the Seawolf raids, she smuggled them out to Yettmis with the help of D'tanesse, Llynx and the servant Teyeda, who lived and worked in the Great Hall of Camil Askanda. Teyeda had come as a captive himself, years before Sema arrived, when he was a child. D'tanesse came from Yettmis with Sema, and Llynx had been among captives taken from Kcen in a raid two years ago.

Recently the inflow of captives had ceased, leaving Sema and her comrades with no way to leave the city themselves, undiscovered. At first they had considered simply walking out—the city was not closed to traffic—but Troy and Teyeda both had vertical facial scars marking them as the king's personal servants, his human property. They, as well as the Seawolves, were not allowed to leave the city without signed permission from the king himself, which they could not get. The only hope, then, of leaving the city without the king's permission was to be smuggled out with a raiding party, but those had stopped months ago, without warning.

Sema sighed, lifting the spoon out of the pot. Diced goat meat and onion comprised the bulk of the soup. Only a few small shreds of greens could be seen in its bubbling brown depths. She missed greens, served fresh with churned butter and warm flatbread. "First, let us eat."

D'tanesse moved behind her, laying his hand over hers to take the spoon. She allowed him to serve her a bowl, and smiled approval when he served one to Llynx as well. They retrieved the scattered chairs and pulled them to the hearth fire, sitting close together as they ate. Sema felt their eyes on her as she stirred the brackish liquid and lifted spoonfuls to her mouth. She had promised to find a way out of the city and back to Yettmis, but her options had just been severely limited. She knew no way to soften the truth. "Teyeda says there will be no more raids," she said at last.

Llynx's lips came together, and she lowered her spoon, staring at the floor.

"Excellent news for the rest of Cathylon," D'tanesse offered with a sigh. "We can at least assume he found what he's looking for."

Sema wrapped her hands around the clay bowl in her lap and felt the heat seep into her fingers. "I am sorry."

"I'm surprised the king kept up the raids as long as this." D'tanesse leaned forward, elbows perched on his knees, balancing his bowl on the palm of one hand. "We will find another way out."

"I will speak to Maon. He may know something Teyeda doesn't." Llynx maintained a profitable relationship with certain Seawolves, mostly children and widows of the warriors in forced service to the king. It had begun with a Seawolf warrior named Maon: Llynx had presented him with medicine for his sick daughter, gaining his instant trust and loyalty. After that, she took to walking the streets of the Seawolf quarter with him, learning landmarks and faces. Three times a day her presence was required at the Hall to serve the king his meals, an arrangement Teyeda helped her procure—and one that worried Sema and D'tanesse. When not working for the king in the open, she conspired against him in secret.

She discovered gems of persons, hidden deep in the filth of poverty and misery. "That one is intelligent." She would nod at a young man—a Seawolf—as she walked through the market with Sema. "He would benefit from your knowledge. Start with economics."

She gleaned information from every quarter, making use of pickpockets, weavers, blacksmiths and keepers of wayhouses. "That one oversees the Crock and Leather, a favorite wayhouse of the Inatru. Send D'tanesse to perform there and you'll learn more than you ever wanted to know about them."

With Maon's help, she hand-picked and oversaw combat training for promising young men and a few young women. They worked in secret, meeting every night at a different location. Though she refused to even touch a sword or spear in the open, she often came home practice-weary, with small cuts across her knuckles and bruises on her forearms. She caked her hands in flour to hide the cuts and wore long sleeves whenever she served in the Hall.

She arranged a watch for their home and center of command. She pilfered food from the king's kitchen and gave it to the Seawolves as payment. Sometimes she gave it to them for no reason at all.

She was a saving miracle, a godsend.

D'tanesse believed it, regardless of her tendency to antagonize him, but his opinion was strongly weighted by his hope that Llynx was who he wanted her to be. Sema was less biased, coming to her own conclusion by listening and watching. Truth was found in action, she knew all too well, and not in words.

Llynx returned Sema's unintentional stare, awaiting an answer.

"That is a very good idea, Llynx." She gave herself a mental shake, dropping her gaze to the bowl in her hands. "One I hadn't thought of."

"Thank you." Llynx's tone implied her doubt there was anything Sema did *not* consider, even if she chose not to mention it. Sema did not argue the point. If Llynx thought her smarter than she was, all the better. She smiled innocently, and received a flicker of a smile in return.

"Your soup is not so bad, D'tanesse." Llynx scraped the last spoonful from the bottom of the bowl and lifted it to her mouth, swallowing thoughtfully. "I must be developing a taste for blackened onion."

"Must you goad me?" He scowled.

"Really, 'Tan, I almost like it." Llynx carried her bowl to a bucket of hot water beside the fireplace.

For some reason Sema had yet to discern, Llynx enjoyed their verbal sparring. Perhaps her capacity for friendship was more extensive than she conveyed, like her ability to lead.

"Are you leaving?" Sema asked, before D'tanesse let himself be pulled into another bickering match. "I'll wash that."

Llynx let the bowl slip into the steaming water, pulling her fingers back at the last moment to avoid the splash. "There was a surplus of bread made today. Teyeda is waiting for me, to help him distribute it."

"Fare well."

"And you." Faint yeast essence, reminiscent of flour-covered tables and sweltering ovens in the king's kitchens, lingered with the swell of air stirred by Llynx's cloak as she stepped past them toward the door. She let herself out, pulling it shut behind her. Her steps thudded up the short flight of stairs, then creaked overhead as she walked through the upstairs entry. The muffled thump of another door closing shuddered down to them, and then silence.

* * * *

Surviving the fifteen-day journey to Camil Askanda proved a small victory compared to surviving inside of it.

"Eggs, I need eggs!"

"This beast is crushing my foot!"

"Then watch where you're stepping!"

"Fresh rolls! Fresh rolls! Feed them to your little ones!"

Even if Terra could have imagined roads crowded with three times the population of his village—which he couldn't—his mind's eye would never have captured the scene before him as he passed alone through the yawning gates.

"Flowers, young man! Buy flowers for your lady!"

Terra started to shake his head, startled to be singled out by a short bald man standing behind a ramshackle table. "Um, I don't—"

The bald man thrust a fistful of yellow blossoms beneath Terra's nose with a soiled hand. "Come, young sir! A special offer for you. Three cantie and they're yours!"

Terra stammered. He had no idea what a 'cantie' was. Everyone in Kcen had bartered for goods, and the merchant who came for collection never mentioned cantie. Core might know, but he was waiting outside the city at an oasis with the horses. Neither expected the city to be such a storm of activity. Terra was saved by a rough shove from behind as a man leading several horses bumped past. The horses gleamed gold, silver and bronze, as if their coats were woven of precious threads instead of coarse hair. Their legs were thin and their polished hooves cut thin crescents into the road. Even Tarrom's horse, though the same breed, had not been so well cared for.

"Out of the way, boy!"

Terra gladly obliged. He spun and hurried to the other side of the road, only to be hailed by three other men all standing beneath bright colored canopies with wares spread out before them on patterned rugs or low tables. Terra quickly learned to keep his eyes forward and his stride quick.

As he went deeper into the city he began venturing down the side lanes. Some were just as crowded as the main road but others were deserted, much easier to navigate.

There were signs hanging over the doors of certain buildings announcing what services were offered inside. There were common occupations like smithy, leather-making—they called it 'tanning'—and alchemists. There were others Terra had never heard of.

In Camil Askanda there was not one wayfaring house. There were many. Here, a wayhouse was something different. Their large double doors were flung open all hours of the day. Merchants did not collect contributions in the wide common rooms. Instead of dusty boxes there were long tables, blazing hearths, kitchens stuffed with food and drink, and constant comings and goings. The wayhouses were for the rich and important. They were places of feasting and entertainment for weavers, warriors, blacksmiths and cantie counters. Entertainment was another new concept. In Kcen they rarely sang and never danced, and there was no need in the village for a musician. Terra knew without going in that a meal in a wayhouse would cost plenty of those 'cantie' things, of which he had none.

He walked for hours, and the scenery underwent a gradual but steady change. The houses went from shapely stone to deadwood huts with sagging walls. There were no yards, no stables around these houses, no simple comforts of home. Women stood in the doorways clutching their ragged dresses, staring through tangled black fringes as he passed. Dirty, dark-eyed children played in the dust outside their doors. Even the dogs roaming the gutters were disarrayed and had thorns woven in their mud-crusted fur. They too stared at Terra, sunken eyes glazed with hunger. There were no fathers and no youths that Terra could see. Just women and very young children.

The sun set before he knew it, casting long shadows down the streets. Women emerged from their homes, walking on the road in small bunches toward him. Terra shifted nervously, now aware of his vulnerable state, a foreigner alone on the streets. Did they watch him with malice—how does one look when they're about to rob a stranger, he wondered—or starved desperation? Desperation, he decided, when the knots of women and children parted around him. He shuffled to the side of the road as the knots became bunches, then small crowds converging at one destination. Terra flattened himself against a wall to let a particularly large group pass, craning his head to see where they were going.

"Waiting won't help you, boy."

Terra jumped as a hand touched his elbow.

"If you want your bread, get in line now," said a scarecrow of a woman, barely held together beneath the bundle of rags over her shoulders.

"How many…uh…cantie?"

"Free, lad, from the king himself. His servant brings it every night."

"Whose servant?"

The crone's dark eyes widened beneath the folds of skin on her brow. "The king's, lad! Do you have sand for brains? Come get some before it's gone!" She pressed ahead into the crowd and Terra followed.

It was amazing. Even the children grabbed desperately from the brown wicker baskets on the ground. A wagon stood nearby filled with more baskets. The king's servants, two cloaked figures blending with the deepening shadows, were in attendance. As soon as one basket was picked clean, they replaced it with another. Terra dipped into a basket, taking a small loaf before they were all gone. The old lady filled her apron and tottered off into the crowd. Terra turned to thank her, but the words stuck in his mouth as he laid eyes on her retreating form. Starkly tattooed on the white skin of her bare neck was a four-pointed compass star, the sign of the Seawolves. Unlike Troy's tattoo, there was no thin circle connecting the points through their center, but the mark itself was enough indication.

Staring, he backed toward the servants who were heaping empty baskets onto the wagon.

"There's a…" He glanced around, not wanting to cause a panic.

"Yes?" The servant who answered was a woman. Her companion, a hulking man with blond hair showing at the edges of his cowl, paused to listen.

"There's a Seawolf over there."

The servants exchange glances, but the dying gold light of evening obscured their expressions. "Yes," the woman said again. The man tossed another empty basket into the wagon.

"Shouldn't we warn someone? They might—"

"Are you mad?" She pushed her face close to his, lowering her voice. Her eyes were dark fires in their sockets. "They're all Seawolves. I should warn them about you."

Terra's mouth dropped open, and his voice fled. It was her.

"Look at them. Look!" She grabbed his chin and turned his face toward the women and children digging for the last crusts of bread in remaining baskets.

"If you—" She forced his head back to look at her, and her breath caught. They stared at each other. Her face filled his vision. Blazing dark eyes. A shred of coarse black hair twining against her high cheekbone. The jagged scar, tugging the corner of her left eye…

Terra lurched, grabbing her shoulders. "Tr—"

She clamped a hand over his mouth and he tasted earthy yeast. He struggled, shocked. Troy glanced at something behind him. A shadow crossed her face, blotting it out so she was a mere shape against the alley wall—

The blow against the back of his skull shocked the world into white fragments of pain, which flooded together and then dimmed into nothing.

Chapter Fifteen

Sema collected Llynx's empty bowl, taking it and her own to a pail of hot water waiting beside the hearth.

"Sema." D'tanesse's chair scraped the floor as he stood and moved to her side. His hand caressed her hair and she leaned against him. "Come lie down. You must rest. I'll clean up."

"I hate to sit and do nothing. Bring me yours, please."

His brow darkened, but he complied. While she dipped the bowls in the water, using the towel to wipe them clean, he pulled a clean nightshirt from one of the crates.

"Llynx hasn't found the book yet," Sema ventured. D'tanesse walked to a patched sheet suspended by a thin rope across one corner of the room and draped the nightshirt over it before removing his white-and-black tunic. A red, silk headscarf spilled from inside his black sleeve and flowed to the floor. He bent to pick it up. "So she says."

"She has no reason to lie."

"Then why not tell the truth?"

"Perhaps she is." She caught a glimpse of his bare torso, tight and wiry, as he pulled the nightshirt over his head. His skin was painted dark amber in the flickering light. He had draped the headscarf around his neck.

"She knows the language of the Ancients."

"One word is not all." Sema stacked the clean bowls in the bottom crate as she finished wiping them. D'tanesse returned, stole the towel from her hands, draped it over the edge of the pail and then picked her up.

"D'tanesse—"

"Your father would behead me if I let you work yourself to death."

"And yours will behead us both if I do not think of a way out of his city."

"It's not his city. The Inatru still control it, like they do everything. Do you think Teyeda is teaching her?"

"Not unless you taught the word to him." She slipped an arm around his neck as he carried her around the partition sheet. A pallet covered by a pretty patchwork quilt of various blues occupied most of the space behind the sheet.

He laid her down carefully. "We've studied botany, infusions for medicinal purposes—the simple things. He hasn't much use for the language and no discernible proficiency with elaa stone."

"Not yet." She tugged at his hand, lying on her side on top of the quilt. He sat beside her with his back propped against the rough wall.

"No, not yet."

"When we get to Yettmis, Yessac can show him the other scrolls. Teyeda will make a splendid Esobir, proficiency or no."

"Yes, if—" He closed his mouth, but the words were as good as spoken.

If the Inatru do not kill him.

Sema pressed her fingers around his, warm and hopeful. "He will survive. You have, well enough."

D'tanesse rubbed his thumb lightly over her knuckles, then leaned down to kiss the top of her head. "I must." His words were soft, breathed into her hair. "Or there will be no one to make you sleep."

Her smile was hidden in the shadow cast by his body as he leaned over her. "And there will be no one to wear my scarf for me."

"How else will I remember who I married?"

One gray eye appeared between her slitted eyelids. "If you forget that, the Inatru are the least of your worries."

D'tanesse plucked at the headscarf peeking up from beneath the collar of his nightshirt, tugging it free. "I believe it." He draped it lovingly over her caramel hair. "You are fearsome terrible when angered."

She smiled. Her eye drifted closed again, and her breathing grew long and steady. At length, D'tanesse eased away from her and stood. She heard him moving on the other side of the partition and the familiar sounds of his nightly activity: the musical chink of pottery as he took jars from miniature alcoves carved along the wall beside the door, the faint hiss and patter of dried leaves and herbs poured from containers. Then came the click and grind of mortar and pestle, his weapons of choice.

He hummed as he worked, bending pleasant notes to his vocal will. Delicate floral scents seeped past the sheet, filling Sema's mind with images of their bedroom in Yettmis, of laughter-filled debates on the lighted balcony, whispered secrets over blue silk pillows in the cool dark while music from the Hall murmured faintly through the open windows, carried on humid currents through blue embroidered curtains…

"There's trouble." Llynx's voice woke her.

Instantly, Sema was on her feet, stumbling to the partition and sweeping it aside. D'tanesse sat cross-legged before the fire, ceasing motion with the mortar and pestle, staring at Llynx. She stood before the open door, face hidden in the recesses of her dark hood. Teyeda's shadowed outline loomed behind her on the stairs, cradling something in both arms.

"I need your help."

* * * *

Terra. You idiot...

Troy didn't know if the idiot was Terra for coming to Camil Askanda or herself for taking him straight to Sema. She should have pretended not to know him. She should have walked away. Instead she let Teyeda think he was accosting her and knock him out. Sema and D'tanesse deduced he was probably sent by Machaun, and D'tanesse promptly put him to sleep with an infusion. Troy left as quickly as possible, claiming a need to inform Maon about the incident. Maon took it as proof of coming attack and sent Seawolves to keep vigil over Sema's hideout. The night, spinning out of Troy's control, was over almost as quickly as it had come.

Troy had never been so glad to return to the king's bake room the next morning. Yet, now the day was almost over. She dreaded the night, when she must return to face the real consequences of Terra's appearance.

Flour hung in clouds above the two long tables lined by girls kneading dough for the next day's baking. Troy hunched over her own lump of dough at the table closest to the open pantry. The dough twisted, doubled and mounded beneath her moving hands. Bits of it clung to her fingers, absorbing more flour, drying into little dough callouses.

All around the square room maidservants bustled about in their red livery, headscarves tied around their heads and knotted at their necks to keep flour out of their hair and the cloth from clinging to perspiring skin. They moved deftly around each other, measuring flour from clay jars, wrestling with spongy dough, struggling to stir acrid starters and perspiring before the gaping maw of the brick oven.

Troy liked the bake room because it did not smell as bad as the meat room, and she could coat her hands with flour to hide telltale cuts from sparring. Machaun was present while she served the king, often as not, watching her every movement.

Sema brushed past her, making contact, on her way to the pantry. Troy shaped the dough into a half dome and covered it with a nearby towel before following her. The bustle of bodies and slap of turning dough diminished somewhat inside the smaller room. They would not be overheard.

"No way out yet. Still waiting," Sema said, pretending to inspect a shelf of covered pies. She had donned a headscarf, folded in a thin band and tied beneath the bright braid hanging down the center of her back. Her neck and shoulders flowed into the scoop of her collar. In servant livery she looked like a gold and crimson flower.

"Did you decide what to do with him?" Troy lifted cheesecloths arbitrarily, not looking at what lay beneath them.

"Maon will question him after dark." Sema's sideways glance pierced her, as if she knew the boy was not sent by Machaun or anyone else. "He seems an innocent young man."

"Machaun is employing better tactics," was Troy's ready reply. The one thing she knew better than Sema was combat, a high ground to which she quickly retreated. Indeed, it was the only expertise she could boast in the face of Sema's apparent omniscience. Sema was considerate enough to downplay her gift of perception, but Troy was no less aware of it. "If he suspects there are rats in the kitchen, easier to send one in coated with poison than to send the cats after them. Cleaner, too."

Sema ran her fingers along the dustless shelf. Troy collected a slow breath, pretending to adjust the leather cuff around her throat, tugging at the short laces where the ends met at her trachea. If Sema did not believe her, she would start to question what it was about the innocent young man that set Troy so on edge; clearly they must have a history. Then it would only be a matter of following the trail leading back to Kcen and a sword, two missing Esobir and a book that was lost forever because of Troy's failure to avoid Terra in the first place.

"If you are sure," Sema said finally, turning her hand to inspect the pads on her fingertips.

The cook's bellow saved Troy from further lies. "Llynx!" The king's supper was ready.

Troy's eyes met Sema's on her way out of the pantry, and they nodded farewell. Terra must leave Camil Askanda. He must stay alive. Of that she was very, very sure.

* * * *

"So you come again, young servant."

Troy caught the uncertain emphasis on the last word. "I have no greater purpose than to serve." She raised her voice, resonant, to carry across the long dining room. The king sat at the far end of the marble dining table, with his second in command looming behind. From where she stood, Machaun appeared a wavering silhouette backlit by the small fire glowing in the oversized fireplace.

"I am neither your kinsman nor countryman." The king's answer was half laugh, half growl, and made no sense. He exuded hostility, like a trap set to spring. “Why should that be your desire?”

Troy shuffled forward, mindful of the delicacies balanced on the marbled tray in her hands. “M’lord, you of all people know my position. We speak of it every time I enter your presence.”

She could see him beyond the quivering jelly moulds and the gleaming mound of black olives, seated in a grand chair garnished with splashes of green and gold silk that made his black hair seem even darker. His barrel chest was covered by a bright red, long-sleeved tunic. Thick hands rested flat on the board. Thicker legs were hidden beneath.

Machaun, the iron fist, stepped up beside his chair. Both hung heavy gazes on Troy as she slid the tray onto the table.

“I find it fascinating that your story never changes, for all the retelling. I am determined to find the flaw, though.” The king rested his forearms on the table, leaning forward to examine the array of dishes.

“The story never changes because it is true.” Her shoulders retained their humble slouch. “I suggest the sugared junipers, m’lord.”

“Coated with poisonous crystals, no doubt.” The king’s hand hesitated over the tray, fingers curled slightly, talon-like. “Why don’t you try one first.”

Alarm prickled over Troy’s skin. Her throat tightened, and her pulse fluttered against the leather cuff. Their conversations had always carried the undercurrent of a duel – thrust, parry, counter – verbally circling and feinting to gain the upper hand. All conversation held this facet in some measure, but this one had the hallmark of a death match. Something had provoked him.

Troy focused on keeping her arms still at her sides, not fidgeting, and her eyes on the mound of black olives. Machaun would be watching her, if she chanced a look at him. Perhaps studying her hands, searching for signs of skills beyond serving. Strong hands could hold a sword as well as a spatula.

The king plucked one of the olives, the one she was watching, and popped it between his thin lips. His drooping mustache writhed on either side of his mouth as he chewed. “Tell me, exactly what happened to bring you here?”

The words nicked her memory, and images bled out: frozen faces of young women. Waxy skin. Blue lips. Porcelain dolls, discolored by death. More than two years had passed since then. The memories should have waned. Instead, they throbbed. Troy stared at pinpoints of light smeared across the oily olive skins and said nothing.

“I knew a Seawolf, in Carmul.” Estimal Glor selected a small pastry and bit into it. His lips pulled back to reveal his teeth as they pierced the flaky crust. Chew. Swallow. "You remind me of her very much. She was married to my brother, the High King. Who died in Carmul." He raised his thumb to the corner of his mouth, smearing away a bit of red currant filling. "She took advantage of him, of all Cathylon. She was Esobir. And I cut her throat."

There it was: baited words, the veiled threat. The trap was already set. The question was, whether to keep her head down, her steps light and pray to avoid decapitation when the jaws snapped shut, or spring the trap and hope she could jump out of the way in time.

"What have I done to displease you, m'lord?"

"Your face has always seemed familiar. Machaun shares the sentiment, though I think for different reasons. He thinks he saw you once near the mountains."

Troy tensed as Machaun stepped behind her. He reached over her shoulder, and she in turn leaned forward so he could not feel through her clothes the tense cords of muscle lining her back. Muscles a maidservant should not have.

"Pursuing you was such a fine chase. Through the villages, into the dark. Did you not think of the victims you left behind?" His words puffed through the contemptuous slit of his mouth, warm against her neck and jaw. A bitter green smell rode his breath.

"Did you?" Troy turned her head slowly until she could see part of his pudgy cheekbone and porous, ruddy skin. Some hopeless piece of her mind insisted pretending weakness could still convince Machaun she could not be the warrior he was looking for. So she did not fight, she did not struggle. Her pulse thrummed, pulsating in her chest and nudging against the cuff at her neck.

"I thought only of the book and the Otnas."

"You should know I wouldn't keep such power."

Machaun stopped breathing for a moment. Then he slapped a medallion, the same one from the scriptorium, in front of her on the board. Troy swallowed. A faint, bitter taste rode her tongue.

"Do you know what this is, woman?"

The medallion had a name in the book of Esobir, which could not be translated into the common language of Cathylon. Hence, they called it as it was: a Looking Glass. A window to see other places without being physically present in that place. She had never seen one put to use before now.

Estimal picked up the medallion by the edges with his thick fingertips. The back of it was perfectly flat, circumscribed with the thin lines of gold and bronze circles. The center was translucent, faintly blue. When he held it up Troy could see his face, compressed within it to the size of an acorn. He breathed on it, then lay it flat-side down on the map of the city. Beneath the blue bulge in the center of the Looking Glass, the map was magnified several times its actual size. A grainy circle as big as Troy's hand materialized in the air above the blue center, a perfect copy of the ink directly beneath the Glass.

"This Glass is a window which will show me anything I wish to see. Right now it shows me an Esobir, pretending to be a servant in my very own Hall." The grains inside the circle shifted, and as she watched them, she realized the grains were people. There were walls, carts—real people moving around on a street in Camil Askanda. A street in the Seawolf quarter. A street she had walked down many times.

Troy's mouth was suddenly dry. Sema came into view from the edge of the circle, hurrying from a dark side street. She was returning home to D'tanesse, who would be waiting, guarding Terra. Two warriors followed her at a distance.

"She did not think we would miss the stolen food." Machaun's arm moved around Troy's waist, his hand coming to rest on her hip. "So we set a simple trap. Surplus bread. Watch where it is taken. You led us to her, as we hoped. Imagine our surprise when we saw a face so familiar."

Adrenaline sliced through Troy's chest. A rat coated in poison. How right she'd been, and realized it too late. The room seemed to rotate when she raised her head and broke off her stare from the Looking Glass—pillars directly across from her edging to the right, the floor twisting left.

"I know what you are, Esobir," Estimal declared. He was standing now with both hands pressed against the table. "I knew your face the moment you came pretending to serve me."

"I am not Esobir—"

"You are a Seawolf—you are from her—and that is enough. I thought your mind would change with time. I hoped perhaps you would be useful as a servant. I kept you close to me to watch you."

"What do you want of me?" Troy refused to look down at the Glass again.

"Your name, to begin."

"I am called Llynx."

"But that is not your name," Estimal countered.

Machaun released her waist and grasped the back of her neck forcing her forward and down. His boot hit the back of her knees, and her upper body slammed forward onto the board. Her pelvis hit the stone edge and bruised on impact, instantly throbbing. The air left her lungs. Olives and jelly smeared, smashed between her dress and the board.

The king's fingers worked the laces of her collar free, and it dropped quietly onto the table. Machaun leaned on her shoulders, with his leg across the back of her knees beneath the edge of the table.

"Now, L'abri." Fingernails lightly traced the back of her neck, round and round the tattoo now exposed. "Tell us again. What will you do to live?"

"My name is Llynx." Her words were slurred behind her teeth. Adrenaline pooled behind her eyes, flashing red, and she thought she might vomit.

"Liar!" Estimal bent over her. His fingers scraped her scalp, grabbing a fistful of her hair. He yelled, close above her face, "Tell me your name! Own it!"

She yelled back. "My name is Llynx!"

Machaun pushed his elbow into her back, forcing her to breathe short.

"You were born in Carmul!" Estimal's lips were almost touching her ear. His voice vibrated inside her skull. "Your mother was queen of the Seawolves!"

"I am nothing! I came from Kcen, they found me—!" She shut her mouth, snapping her teeth together.

Estimal flinched back, blinking. "They found you…in Kcen? They found…?" His quiet wonder was worse than yelling, worse than the hot weight of Machaun's body pinning her to the table. Estimal released her hair. "All the time we knew of you, we expected you to attempt an uprising, or some retribution for her sake. All who knew her were bewitched enough to do it, but you…" He leaned in again, examining her face with disbelief. "Don't you know who you are?"

Chapter Sixteen

Terra woke lying face down on a hard surface. Wood, he found, upon opening his eyes. He rolled onto his back—a wood floor in a dim room. Dusty wood essence filled his nostrils and he sneezed.

"The spy awakens." The voice, female, came from a wavering figure standing too far away for Terra's fuzzy vision to define. He blinked a few times, but didn't answer.

"This is the spy sent by Machaun himself? I could do a better job." This second voice was lilting, male.

Terra squinted. "Where am I?"

"Far from safety," intoned the male, "or the king's Hall. Don't struggle, it will just make a mess and Sema likes to keep a clean house. You're our plaything until you tell us what you know."

"I know nothing. Where is Troy?" Terra struggled to sit up. His hands were bound behind his back.

There was a short silence before one of his captors stepped forward. "Why are you looking for Llynx?"

"I don't know who that is." Terra could now make out some details of the nearer speaker: a girl whose hair was pulled cleanly away from her face. It shone golden in the paltry flickering light, haloed by a folded red headscarf. He could see no candles on the wall behind her.

"You will only make it harder for yourself by pretending ignorance. Our business will be far less painful if you loosen your tongue," she said.

"I don't know what to say!" Terra winced at his own voice. "I'm not in service to the king. I'm Terra of Kcen and I'm looking for my friend Troy."

"You must take us for raving idiots—" the man began, but the girl cut him off.

"You are from Kcen?"

"My brother is outside the city waiting for me. I'm not after this Llynx or whoever you're worried about."

The man's outline finally came into focus. His hair was black, encasing a round, glaring face. His eyes were green, clearer than glass.

The girl knelt in front of Terra, filling his vision. She was a woman, he realized, with mature gray eyes set wide apart in a young face. Her cheeks were soft curves above a demure mouth. She watched him with compassion. "Tell me what happened to Kcen."

Terra's face scrunched in an uncomfortable way as he answered. He couldn't help it. "It's…gone. Destroyed by Seawolves. They killed our chieftain's brother and when we went to challenge them, they were waiting for us. Warriors against…against farmers and weavers. We had no chance of victory, didn't even know it."

She moved suddenly, and Terra cringed. Her hands were gentle, though, as she loosened the knot binding him and pulled the length of rope free.

"Sema, he could be saying anything—"

Terra faced the girl, Sema. "They killed them all," he said, lowering his voice. Aside from Core, who didn't need anything explained to him, Terra had not spoken of that night out loud, or tried to describe it to anyone. Now he was telling a stranger in a foreign city, and it felt like being gutted. "My sister Sienna was dead when we found her." They didn't care about names, but he did. "My father died fighting them. Troy and Mytch hid my mother and Imra, me and Core in some trees. They burned the village. Everyone—" He was talking into heavy silence. "She hid us, and then she was taken by them. The Seawolves took her."

Sema's eyes flickered, back and forth across Terra's face. "I was there that night, D'tanesse. He is telling the truth."

D'tanesse remained silent, looking from her to Terra and back again.

"I was one of the servants who attended that raiding party. D'tanesse and I help the captives escape to freedom after they are brought here." Her hand rested lightly on his shoulder. "I am sorry for this. We live in dangerous times. I am sorry for your loss."

Gratitude welled in Terra's eyes and distorted his vision for a moment. To collapse weeping on the young woman's shoulder would have been improper and embarrassing in retrospect, so he just shook his head, as if it were all past now and did not still gnaw at his insides. She released his shoulder.

"I am only here to find my friend," Terra said thickly. "I saw her when she brought food to some Seawolves—"

"That was not your friend." D'tanesse spoke up again, cutting the heavy emotion in the room with nonchalance. "That was Llynx. Our friend." The last was said with a slight sneer. Terra returned it.

D'tanesse arched his eyebrows. "Perhaps if you had described your friend, we could have helped you find her. It would have saved time. Teyeda wouldn't have hit you to protect Llynx, she wouldn't have brought you here to be questioned, Maon will stop skulking about our front door, and everyone could get a decent night's sleep once a week."

"Troy is tall, dark skinned, with a scar down her left cheek."

Sema stood quickly and faced D'tanesse. They stood close together, whispering urgently. Terra moved his shoulders, trying to loosen aching clusters of muscle.

The conversation ended with Sema abruptly leaving through the only door in the room. She gave Terra a quick, reassuring smile before closing the door behind her. Light steps could be heard, and then creaking wood overhead.

"She is going to fetch Llynx, who should be finished with her duties by now anyway," D'tanesse explained, settling into a tired wooden chair and folding one leg beneath him. "In the meantime, we should get better acquainted. Llynx is my close friend."

"Alright."

Silence.

"So…are you a warrior?" D'tanesse formed the word skeptically, eying Terra's slim frame.

"No."

"An ambassador, then? You must have seen much of Cathylon."

Terra's slanted look was answer enough.

"My word. Are you good for anything?"

Terra was weary of mincing words in a losing battle. "I could shoot out your left eye from the city wall."

"Oh, terrific." D'tanesse grinned. He had a wide, triangular mockery of a smile. Terra wasn't sure if he liked it or not. "You may prove quite handy, then."

Terra raised both eyebrows, hoping his expression didn't let on he couldn't tell if D'tanesse was serious or not. "I would leap at the chance," he said, trying to be equally mysterious by not indicating if he would jump at the chance to prove handy, or shoot D'tanesse in the eye.

The door slammed open overhead, startling them both. Sema had only left moments ago. Steps pounded overhead, wood creaked outside the near door, and then, sure enough, Sema's voice preceded her return to the room.

"Llynx is being arrested!"

D'tanesse was on his feet, meeting Sema at the door as it came open. He caught her hands in both of his, examining her face anxiously. Terra also stood, slightly unsteadily.

Sema convinced D'tanesse she was alright with a look and a brief tensing of her fingers. "I was followed from the Hall as well but Maon stopped them."

A tall, tanned man strode through the door behind Sema, wiping a bloodied blade on his charcoal tunic. He was laden with weapons: quiver, belt knives, bow and even a sword. In one hand he carried a thick staff, while the other inserted the knife back in its sheath. “Teyeda is the vigilant one. He sent word to Siegra, must have been as it was happening. She ran all the way here.” His black, heavy-lidded eyes absorbed the room and Terra, roving beneath a curly fringe of dark hair across his brow. Terra felt small even standing up. Maon was a Seawolf, he knew, even before the warrior turned his back, exposing the stark tattoo on the back of his neck.

“We must leave.” Sema swept forward into the room, already knowing what to do next. “Take what you need. We will not be returning here.”

“When did it happen?” D’tanesse retrieved a sleeved cloak from its hook beside the door, plunging his arms into the multicolored sleeves. It was tighter than a robe, and fastened up the front with small wood toggles, coating his figure completely in patchwork. Sema pulled small jars from their wall nooks, uncorking them and pouring leaves and powders into the patchwork squares on the coat. Every one of those muted blues, greens and tans were pockets. D’tanesse would be an essential spice rack when they finished.

“What of Teyeda?”

“Freeing Llynx at any cost, if I know the man.”

“What about Troy?” Terra frowned. He had just found her, almost, and now she was arrested? Would she die? Did she face torture? He recalled the bread she gave to the Seawolves. Stolen bread, most likely. What was the punishment for thieves in this city?

“Who is this?” Maon’s frown was heavy. “And who is Troy?”

D’tanesse hardly glanced at them. “We think he means Llynx.”

The warrior did not seem pleased. “Her name is not Troy.” As if such a name for such a woman was ridiculous.

Terra folded his arms. He thought the name was very fitting.

“Can he go with you, Maon?” Sema slipped a cloth satchel over her shoulder, while D’tanesse tucked shining leaf-shaped knives into the tops of his boots.

Maon turned his disapproval toward Terra.

“He can shoot your left eye out from the city wall,” D’tanesse piped, bouncing on one foot while fidgeting with the opposite boot.

Terra nodded at Maon’s raised eyebrow and unspoken question. Now was not to the time to be left behind, and these people could help him find Troy—not to mention rescue her.

“Have you a bow?” Maon could see he didn’t.

“I left it…with my brother. Outside the city.” Terra cringed inwardly. What kind of bowman left his weapons behind when he might need them? It was a stupid thing to do. He vowed never to do it again, if he lived through the night.

"We will give you one."

"'Tan and I will distract them at the gatehouse." Sema's cheeks were flushed. She did not seem so concerned with Terra's lack of weapons. She did not appear to carry them herself. Then again, with Troy and this Maon watching over her, she would hardly need to. "Signal us when you see her." That she may not come at all was not even mentioned.

"Time to go, children." D'tanesse doused the fire with water from a small bucket, and the room darkened completely.

By the time Terra stumbled up some rickety stairs, through an upper room more barren than the lower, and outside onto a narrow street, his eyes were already adjusted to night. A presence beside him made him flinch and shy to the side, bumping into D'tanesse. Something hard inside one of the sleeve pockets jabbed Terra in the shoulder.

"Careful. Don't want to explode something," D'tanesse muttered, eyes forward as he stepped past the threshold.

Terra looked to his right and saw a tall warrior standing against the wall directly beside the door. Terra's eyes moved up to the warrior's shoulder, and then further up to his face. His eyes were small and close together, gleaming in the shadows cast by the curve of his brows and long nose. He loomed over Terra, staring down at him, absorbing him as Maon had moments ago.

Terra stepped back, turning to find Sema, and saw two more warriors standing against the opposite wall. They were shorter than the first, faces obscured by gray cloths wrapped around their foreheads and mouths.

Maon rested a heavy hand on Terra's shoulder. "He comes with us, Mikal."

A murmur came from the tall one, Mikal, and Maon lifted his hand. Two more warriors glided in from either end of the alley, and all five closed in around Maon and Terra: coal eyes glinting, black hair pulled back from narrow foreheads, true warriors of dark Seawolf blood. Each brandished a bow, and crow fletching bristled from the tops of their hip quivers. Their arms and necks were wrapped in a haze of gray cloths.

Maon looked into each of their faces. "This is Terra, a friend of Llynx. Sema vouches for his loyalty. Siegra, he needs a bow."

One of the unhooded warriors—a woman, Terra realized—responded immediately, removing her bow and quiver. Terra took them, fumbling a little in the dark with the quiver straps, but grateful he at least knew what to do with them.

Sema edged in beside him. "They are the Watch," she said quietly. "Llynx helped train them. They are deadly marksmen, and loyal to us."

If she meant to reassure him of his relative safety, she had misread his nervousness. Beside these warriors, he felt pale and delicate. His fingers were too spindly and fragile, his callouses paltry in comparison to theirs. His shoulders were not wide enough, and he could not stand tall enough to be counted among them. They were sure and collected, scanning their surroundings with experience. Terra was beginning to tremble with adrenaline, and his brown eyes jumped from one point to another haphazardly.

"Siegra will follow you," Maon said to D'tanesse, who had both hands tucked into green cobble pockets near the coat's waist. "Mikal, Norem, Ivel and Emori will go to the Hall and aid Llynx."

"Take the roofways," Siegra put in to the four who were named, while Maon continued.

"Terra and I will clear the way to the gate."

"Yes, yes, that's lovely." D'tanesse spun toward the far alley entrance, flaring the bottom of the green-blue-maize garment. "We'll have a welcome ready at the gatehouse."

Sema and Siegra followed him. Siegra held a small ax in each hand. Sema touched Terra's arm as she passed him. "Fare well." She said it as if she hoped, rather than knew, he would. He wondered if every parting held the same uncertainty for them.

Into a city covered by desert night, cooled by sunless sky, and with warm earth beneath his feet Terra strode, surrounded by his former enemy. He shone like a pale flame in their center, clutching his borrowed bow, baggy sleeveless tunic rippling in the turgid air. Maon turned his head and the Watch dispersed, fanning out to either side of the road, joining with the nothing that surrounded colorless adobe dwellings, reappearing briefly on the rooftops and then were gone again like passing shadows. Terra continued with Maon, who deviated onto a smaller street as well, but kept sure bearing toward their destination.

When they reached the gatehouse, D'tanesse had already set it on fire.

Chapter Seventeen

Faint chinking of metal in the corridor announced the arrival of warriors. Inatru.

Ki...

Sema was in danger because of her. And Terra. Ki, Terra—! All of this was happening because she needed a fight, because she needed...what did she need? It made no sense. Troy struggled to raise her body and gain a full breath. Machaun's hand pressed her head against the board, grinding olive pulp into her cheek.

Warriors filed into the dining room. Her hands were bound. She was hauled upright, dripping olive pulp and currant jelly. Machaun moved to stand beside the king. His face was more flushed than usual. Troy's throat burned, coated in bile.

"I had hoped we'd be allies, but you've proven even more meddling than your mother." Estimal raised his chin, looking at Troy through slitted eyes. "At least now I can be rid of several nuisances at once. Sema will be dealt with. She's turned out worse than you, considering what she came from. I hoped...well it doesn't matter now. We will do what we must for the good of Cathylon."

The next moments passed in flash-step, vivid. Fleeting.

Narrow, overcast halls. Her hands, bound. Skin chafing. Four warriors, two walking ahead, two behind her. Passing pools of shallow candlelight. Statues. Black windows. Teyeda, walking toward them, blacksmith hammer in fist.

Four against two.

He waited until the rear guards had passed him, then spun. His hammer thudded into the back left warrior's skull. Three to two. Troy kicked twice: back of the knee, then back of the neck as the rear right warrior turned—and fell. Two against two. No—two against one, as the front right guard met his unfortunate end on the spike of Teyeda's hammer. The last warrior lunged at Troy, arms spread to capture her in his grip. Teyeda wound back. Troy collapsed to the stone floor, twisting to land on her shoulder instead of her face. Hammer caught forehead and the warrior dropped on top of her. Stars pricked her vision.

Teyeda hauled the corpse off her, untied her hands and jerked her to her feet. They ran down the corridor to the servants' quarters and finally the tunnel entrance in his room.

"Maon is with Sema," he said when Troy began to talk. "We must leave the city."

It was not how she would have preferred to leave, but at least the trap was sprung and she had escaped with her head. New clothes, especially breeches, must be found as soon as possible. Her pleated dress and wide cloth belt would only get in her way once fighting began. It already made running difficult. She pulled on a leather vest, stowed just behind the tunnel door for such an emergency, and felt a tiny relief. At least she had some protection.

She emerged from the tunnel behind Teyeda, sprinting away from the Hall into the city. The hem of her dress was folded into her cloth belt. The surplus material stopped above her knees in front and fanned out on either side of her hips, a proper train for the lady she wasn't. At least now she could move unhindered. She would go naked if it meant escaping with her life.

"We need horses!" she yelled at Teyeda's back.

He turned his head. "No time!" Sweat was beading on his temple and streaming down his neck.

A shrill blast of the warning horn behind them. Warriors would be pouring into the yard and through the wide doors leading to the city.

"Where is Maon?" she bellowed, pulling even with him.

"At the gate!"

The Hall stood in the city's center. The tunnel came out on the east side of the Hall. They would be forced to veer perpendicular, crossing the path of the warriors leaving the Hall's front gate to reach the gate in the south wall. It was too far on foot. Especially if—

Hammering thumps of hooves on dirt echoed over the narrow street, chasing after them.

—pursuit was mounted.

"Get back to the main road!" Cobblestones were slick and treacherous for running horses. Troy shoved at Teyeda. His momentum absorbed it.

"This way is faster!"

"Not against them!" They burst into an alley, Troy leading, crashing over crates and rags and refuse. She sprinted, bearing down on the rectangle of open space ahead, and burst out into the wide main street.

Horsemen. Cantering forward on her right. Much too close.

Four-bladed spears swinging down to pierce her body.

Do not stop.

Troy pivoted to her left, grinding loose pebbles beneath the balls of her feet. Springing, flying down the road, trying to stay close to walls. Their backs were vulnerable. Firelight, smoke rising above rooftops, black lines of windows and doors all slid past. Not fast enough.

She began to slow. She could turn and face the line of horses gaining on them, give Teyeda a chance at freedom. “Teyeda! Go without—”

His hand clamped down on her arm in a shackle grip. “You run!”

“Teyeda!”

“Run!” He jerked her forward as he bellowed, red-faced.

An archer stepped out as they passed a gap between houses, bow bent to arrow. He turned toward the pursuing Inatru. Released the string. A singing whistle, barely a noise itself, nicked the air. A warrior cried out behind them. Troy did not look back.

All along the street the Watch ran in the shelter of shadows. They moved with her in the shadows of the walls and along the rooftops. Arrows zipped across the road in crisscross patterns, a gauntlet of stinging needles that sang as they flew to their marks. Horses squealed, high-pitched like wild children, hopping over fallen bodies. Their hooves lost traction on smooth stones. They fell, rolling and sliding. Some clambered to their feet, forelegs churning, and continued to run riderless. A few broke through the gauntlet and dodged past the fugitives, tails flagging high above their surging hindquarters. Troy glanced back, back again, crouched and sprang up as one began to pass her. Hands caught mane, pommel, and she swung up onto its narrow back. Teyeda caught another and they coaxed the animals onto a safer side lane.

Mayhem reigned when they reached the gatehouse with the Watch on their heels. Searing flames poured from every orifice in the structure, devouring wood and blackening stone. Beyond the open gates, Sema and D’tanesse waited, mounted, holding four more horses ready for escape. Maon stood beside one of the open gates, arrows springing from his bowstring. Teyeda leaned over, galloping through the archway. Maon caught his open hand and was pulled up, riding behind him.

By the other gate stood Terra, feet set, loosing arrows calmly into the fray. His face was livid in the firelight, fearless. Troy stretched toward him, offering her hand. His fingers caught hers, skin stinging skin, and he swung up, settling behind her. His arm snaked around her waist. The Watch came behind them, some already riding, some launching from the ground when they reached Sema and D’tanesse to mount as well. They thundered over the sand following Teyeda and Maon, leaving flames, gates and city behind.

* * * *

“Llynx, are you deranged?” D’tanesse shouldered his mount alongside

Troy's. The city was now behind them, a dim mass of sand ahead. They had cantered and galloped at first, putting quick distance between themselves and the city. Then to save the horses, the group jogged and walked them in turns. Real pursuit would be slow in coming, at least several hours, while supplies were gathered, warriors summoned, and order restored at the city gates.

Several members of the Watch had managed to snag horses the same way Troy and Teyeda had done, catching those whose former riders had fallen. Still, they were short two horses. When it was deemed prudent, the group took turns walking or jogging alongside those riding.

Terra's arm was a constant pressure against Troy's ribs. They had both been silent after regrouping outside the city, where Core had been waiting for them.

Core too. Ki misin!

They were all here. Sema, Teyeda, 'Tan, Terra and Core, and the entire Watch—Maon, Siegra, Mikal, Norem, Emori and Ivel! Might as well call themselves a caravan.

However, Troy couldn't complain much about the Watch's timely appearance which had saved at least her and Teyeda. After such a spectacle, and killing a few Inatru warriors, they could hardly stay behind if they wanted to live. Besides, there were only five of them. Six, including Maon.

Core was riding Laic—Laic, Terra's horse, which was hers once upon a time. Now Terra, Core and Laic were trudging in the middle of her nightmare. Her bow and quiver were visible, strapped to Laic's saddle. She prayed the rolled-up blanket didn't have the Otnas hidden inside. It was certainly the right length for it. How could this be happening?

"Arrested! How could you be so reckless?!" D'tanesse raged on. "Do you realize you might have died? You are so…so impetuous! Your antics exasperate the most patient of mortals!"

"Surely you do not imply yourself." Troy's hands trembled, resting on her horse's pommel. Terra was there, behind her, breathing on her hair—

She inhaled deeply, trying to focus on the irregular swish of hooves in the sand. Calm, dark desert. The wind picking up. Throwing sand in her face.

"Mark my words, Llynx! If you ever try such a trick again—"

"D'tanesse! I am not your possession, and you have no right—"

D'tanesse raised his voice as she raised hers. "—I'll grab you with my own hands and—"

"—to tell me what is dangerous—"

Terra's arm tensed around her stomach. Troy jerked on the reins, sidestepping toward 'Tan. The horses flattened their long, prim ears.

"—drag you down and sit on you—"

"—and I'll do as I wish—" Her horse began to dance, springing stiff-legged over the sand. Terra's other arm slipped around her, hanging on either for balance or in an attempt to calm her.

"—until you get enough sense to be reasonable—"

"—because I can! And if you dislike that, you can—"

Sema urged her horse to the other side of Troy. She leaned far over, snagging the braided hackamore bridle. The horse jerked his head, blowing irritation through distended nostrils as it stopped short.

"Llynx, stop this." She did not need to say 'be ashamed.' "D'tanesse, come with me and allow Llynx a moment to speak to her friend."

D'tanesse grumbled something Troy couldn't hear, ambling forward after his wife. The others had moved on. Maon walked beside Siegra, talking quietly as if nothing were going on behind them. Most likely they were strategizing. Siegra loved to strategize. Mikal rode behind them, slouching as best he could between Emori and Ivel, but he still towered above them. Norem rode on the other side of Siegra, happy because something was happening and he was part of it. His cowl, rarely used for its intended function—to hide his features—was pulled down over his shoulders like a miniature gray cape. Teyeda rode beside Core, their conversation stilled for the moment. They all seemed preoccupied, but Troy was aware of the discreet distance they maintained from her and Terra after Sema moved on.

Terra's hands were knotted against her stomach, a foreign presence generating low levels of adrenaline to maintain the tremble in her fingers. The desert whispered quietly to itself, waiting for her to talk.

"Troy?"

"Hm."

"Did they hurt you?"

Troy turned, twisting to catch a glimpse of his face. It was closer than she expected. His eyelashes hovered thick and dark above the gentle curve of his cheekbones. A shadow of stubble peppered his jawline and chin. His mouth was set, worried, and a little brooding because of his underbite.

"No." She faced front.

He rested gently against her back, rocking in time to the horse's steps. It was a pale, smoky color, even its mane. Slivers of light danced over the coat, gleaming as if on oil rather than hair. But it was hair. Troy wound a strand of the tough mane around her fingers and tried to breathe.

"Don't worry. We're with you now."

Exactly the reason she was worried. "Terra. You should go home."

"You are my home."

He couldn't know what he was saying.

The sky curved above them, a giant overturned bowl. Her skin prickled. Estimal Glor might be watching her now, gazing down at her through the Looking Glass. The prickle changed, and her whole skin shifted, shuddering.

Terra felt that. He moved his chin to rest on her shoulder, speaking quietly beside her ear. “I’m sorry I didn’t come sooner.”

She shook her head. “Please.”

He leaned back, dropping his hand. The other stayed around her waist, but looser, uncertain.

“Please…” she began again, but suddenly couldn’t finish. Instead she reached over her shoulder for his hand, and he took it in his solid grip. His fingers absorbed the trembles in hers and warmed them, reassuring.

Chapter Eighteen

They rode in silence again, listening to the desert languish beneath the window of night, until Maon called a halt. "We must stop here. The horses cannot go farther without rest."

Troy quickly slipped to the ground, leaving Terra to clamber down on his own. His legs shook with fatigue, unsteady in the deep sand. Troy turned her back on him, loosening the girth of her mount's saddle. Resigned, Terra turned away to look for Core. His brother was lying on his back in the sand, succumbed to exhaustion, several yards ahead. Terra settled down beside him in the surprisingly comfortable bed of grit.

I've become something more than a warrior, Terra.

He closed his eyes. The weight of her words, years ago in Kcen, had imprinted upon his memory the moment they were spoken. He saw her in his waking dreams. With his memory he touched her clenched, calloused hands. He traced the laces of her scars with care, following the short hard ridges up her forearms to her shoulders. He tucked errant, coarse hairs behind her delicate ears. He smoothed the worry from her forehead and her stubborn eyebrows. He covered the scar marring the almond shape of her left eye. He kissed her strong mouth.

Terra opened his eyes and saw Troy, who was now leaning against her horse, folded arms propped up against the saddle. He understood now. Fear had already cut her, already hardened beneath scar tissue, spreading its slow poison to her soul. She couldn't ask for help. She couldn't remember how.

Hunger woke him. Hunger, and the quiet roar of water. Terra sat up, immediately looking to the horizon, anticipating a line of horsemen along the rim of the night sky. Nothing.

Core lay beside him, arms folded over his chest, breathing evenly. The others were obscure human-shaped lumps near the standing horses. D'tanesse was on Terra's other side, lying on his stomach, narrow chin resting on the cushion of his arms. A small blue jar was cradled in the sand before him. Sema was visible on his other side, curled up on his cobble-colored jacket. Terra wasn't sure how anyone could manage to sleep on such a lump-riddled surface.

"Do you hear water?"

Terra squinted. Perhaps he was still dreaming.

The whites of D'tanesse's eyes shone, outlining circle pupils. He winked.

Troy's steps swished through loose sand, trudging between them. Her headscarf was gone, her hair braided and tied with a scrap of gray cloth. "Close it, 'Tan." She sounded in pain. "The sound will lead them to us."

D'tanesse languidly plucked a cork from the sand and stopped up the jar. The sound of water ceased.

"What is that?" Terra asked.

D'tanesse chuckled, watching Troy pretend to ignore him while she checked her mount's hooves for embedded rocks. "An ocean jar. It holds the ocean."

"It does?"

"No." He grinned. "It holds the sound of the ocean."

"How?" The jar seemed so ordinary—a deep shade of blue, barely big enough to hold a draught of liquid.

"Salt water, inside the jar. The jar is made with elaa," he said casually, as if that should explain it.

"Get up, 'Tan. We're moving on." Troy threw D'tanesse an irritated glare before trudging away to rouse the others.

"Elaa?" Terra forced himself to his feet, groaning inwardly.

"Yes, well. I'm not supposed to talk about it." He rocked to his knees, resting on his elbows and pushing his rump in the air before sitting upright on his heels.

"Then why did you open it?"

"To annoy Llynx."

They traveled in the gray dawn until the sun colored the atmosphere with pink and gold. Soon they were perspiring under a brittle blue sky. Core rode beside Terra, saying little. He did not like this development, traveling with Seawolves, one little bit. Troy obviously was not included in that sentiment because, well, she was Troy. Core knew Troy, or had known her once. Oh, he had gone willingly enough when they left the oasis—Core was not one for altercations unless he was very mad or knew he could win. He was not at all interested in a scuffle with armed Seawolves, and he feared what lay behind them more than he feared their present company, so he had gone along without a word.

Words were there, however. Terra could tell from the forward set of Core's jaw and the intense stare he maintained on the horizon ahead. It would only be a matter of time until the stew boiled over, so to speak.

They sipped stale water from dusty flasks and ate shreds of jerky while they rode, supplied from the stock in D'tanesse's pockets. The man had brought on his person more leaves, herbs, dried meats and even infusions than Terra knew existed. Each time they stopped to rest, which was every six hours or so, he would produce a new concoction of leaves or roots, to 'fill the stomach and raise the spirits', he claimed. Even though their stomachs were never actually full, they did eat very well compared to Terra and Core's fare on their first journey through the desert.

"What is elaa?" Terra, on foot, reached up to accept his meat ration from D'tanesse. He had to concentrate on chewing slowly to savor the food, instead of giving in to his ravenous hunger and scoffing it whole. D'tanesse leaned far over to drop the jerky into Terra's hands without dismounting.

"Elaa is forbidden by the Inatru. To use it without their sanction is cause for death without trial. Or so I am told," D'tanesse answered with a mocking sideways tilt of his head.

"Yes, but what is it?" Death without trial was no real threat—they faced that and worse already, he was sure.

"Elaa is…well, it's complicated. Put simply, it is a type of rock found in the mountains. It acts as a catalyst, a doorway connecting one element to a separate element to produce a certain reaction. It makes the impossible a possibility," he added when Terra frowned, uncomprehending.

"Such as…the sound of water where there is none."

"Such as, yes. Llynx knows how it works." He raised his voice, directing it toward Troy, who rode on Terra's other side. She stared straight ahead, guiding her gray gelding by its reins with one hand.

"The Inatru claim it is the source of power, a talisman. But we know better."

"We?"

"The Esobir, man."

"The Esobir know less than the Inatru," Troy broke in, then frowned deeply as if she'd spoken without meaning to.

"Not true. We just know different."

Instead of countering, Troy dismounted and handed the reins to Terra. "Go ahead. I'm going to walk with Maon."

Terra climbed up, not too reluctantly, and Troy dropped behind to walk with Maon, who was also on foot.

General endurance was flagging by the time the sun receded below the shimmering edge of scalloped landscape on the second day. Terra found himself slouching further and further over the saddle, until he was leaning on the ridge of the gray's bobbing neck.

In his mind, Terra named the horses according to color. His, the smoky gray, was Gray, the gray with slate blue mottling its coat was Blue. The white was Ivory. Laic was, of course, Laic. He was a different shape, thicker, and his black fetlocks feathered out over his wide hooves.

Siegra, one of the Watch, came alongside him on Red, a rust-colored roan. She actually smiled, almost, when he returned her bow and quiver the night before, at their first rest stop. It had shocked him greatly. Now she waved a hand at his own bow, which rested across his back and over one shoulder. She had unwrapped her arms and tucked the charcoal cloths into her boots, and her skin was already a few shades darker from the relentless sun.

"I have never seen a forest bow."

"Core and I have the only ones." He shrugged, embarrassed. "I simply copied Troy's...Lynx's bow."

Siegra inspected it, then showed it to the one called Ivel who was riding beside her. He reluctantly pushed his cowl back and wiped sweat from his forehead with one hand, then squinted at the bow. Four scars curved around his neck, like trails left from long claws.

"Resourceful." Was all he said—almost grunted—and passed it back to Siegra, who handed it down to Norem. Besides Siegra, who was the only female in the Watch, Norem was easiest for Terra to recognize. A dark, short beard covered his lower face and he was constantly flashing toothy grins at his companions, usually Siegra and Mikal. His hair was a mess of tangled ropes, twisted together and clasped with a bronze band. The gnarled ends stood out from the back of his skull, an uneven sheaf.

He took Terra's bow and the grin appeared, a white crescent splitting his lower face. He seemed more amused than any Seawolf should be. Norem jogged ahead to the other warrior who still wore his cowl over his head despite the heat. Norem called him Emori. When he pulled the damp cloth back from his forehead, Terra glimpsed pocked skin and a flat, wide nose, nothing more. For the most part, he recognized Emori's hood better than his face.

Ivel moved to ride alongside Emori, and they seemed identical in build and height. Emori bent over in his saddle, examining the bow in Norem's hand without touching it. He said a soft, terse phrase, and Norem clapped him on the knee before jogging ahead to Mikal, who was taking his turn on foot with Norem. Emori and Ivel nudged their mounts closer together, conversing. Together they were like a double vision, if their mounts had been the same color.

When Terra looked back at Mikal, he had the bow in both hands, drawn. His elbow was folded back beside his ear, his long fingers hooking the string. Norem kept up a trickle of commentary while he drew and then eased the string.

They were all—except Maon—Seawolves without families, or whose families had died in one way or another, Siegra told him, which was why they agreed so readily to join the small resistance.

"Llynx discovered us. Pulled us in from the four winds, it seemed. She and Maon. I was the first one on watch." Siegra snipped sentences between her teeth like a weaver biting through threads. Her squint pulled freckles into the wrinkles around her eyes, and bits of escaped hair clung to her high forehead. Her skin was bronzed in the setting sun.

Terra's bow was passed from hand to hand, until all of the Watch had examined it. Over time, all of them spoke to him about weaponry, about how they came to know Llynx, and asked, how did he know her? Where had he come from?

He told them how he'd found Troy and about his family caring for her. He realized they were kindred souls, not only because they shared a skill in archery. Each of the Seawolves were fiercely loyal to Troy, especially Siegra and Maon.

"Maon's family was smuggled out. Wife and daughter. Llynx sent them to Yettmis." Siegra cracked a smile, imparting the tidbit with mild pride.

"Did she get your family out as well?" Terra asked.

She closed her lips again and shrugged, all the answer he would get for the time being.

Core rode apart from the Seawolves, staying beside Teyeda or Sema when Terra was speaking to any of the Watch. He had no interest in them, loyal or otherwise. "Sema has been telling me some disturbing things," he imparted, sitting down beside Terra when the group stopped for a reluctant rest. The horizon remained empty, but now and again a wisp of cloud nosed the line of the sky, there and gone, enough to make them all go a little faster for a while.

A covered well stood lone sentry, poking its head above the deviant sand, and they gathered around it. Core and Terra sat at its base, keeping their backs from touching the sun-baked sandstone.

"Everything they do is against law," Core said, keeping his voice down. Teyeda and Ivel were drawing water, while the others busied themselves arbitrarily. "They live underground. We are going to a city of lawbreakers."

"What are you so afraid of? We've already lost everything worth losing."

"Not everything," mumbled Core.

"The Inatru made the Seawolves go raiding." That got Core's attention, and held it. "Ask Sema. She was there when they came to Kcen."

"She was there?"

"Do you really think we're better off doing as the Inatru say? Sema kept Troy safe in Camil Askanda, she helped save all our lives. The Inatru would have killed her."

"Why would the Inatru come to Kcen? Why kill them all for nothing?"

"They were following Troy. They're after her still."

"But why, Terra?"

Terra shook his head. "I will find out."

They rested for two hours, all asleep, or appearing to sleep in dug-out hollows where the sand was cooler. All except for Terra, who couldn't sleep ten minutes without waking to check the horizon, and Maon who was taking his turn on guard.

"Drink water," Maon said as Terra approached, handing him one of the flasks. Each Seawolf carried one at all times. D'tanesse and Sema had brought their own along as well. "This is the only well until we reach Yettmis."

Terra stood alongside the tall warrior and stared back the way they had come. "Have you been to Yettmis?"

"Not inside, but the raids passed it on their way to the Aganus river. This is the last well between here and the river so it's the last one until Yettmis. Drink."

Terra drank, trying to fix the sensation of cooling in his mind as he swallowed and knowing he would forget it tomorrow, once wrapped in the sun's heat.

"You need a new bow. Something that will endure use," Maon said abruptly. "Yours was not seasoned long enough."

"You know how to make bows?" Terra was impressed.

"I was Seawolf long before I was slave." Maon's eyes narrowed, either from hard memory or because he saw something in the distance. Terra followed his gaze, suddenly anxious, but saw nothing. Maon was proud of his race, regardless of their reputation. He made no apologies about who he was or what he'd become a part of, perhaps because an apology would do no good. It wouldn't change the past and it couldn't bring the dead to life. An apology from the Seawolves might have set Core more at ease and avoided some trouble, but there was nothing Terra could do to instigate that.

By midday on the seventh afternoon they had eaten the last of the jerky, the peppered goat and even the strident marl root. Terra already felt he was in the throes of starvation—D'tanesse's root concoctions notwithstanding—and now it seemed the journey, and his torture, were endless. After resting, they pressed on through the night and into another pale dawn. Dawn quickly gave birth to a circle of blood-red sunlight leaking waves of heat and melted pools of sky along the horizon. Translucent outlines of hills swam there, a cluster growing slowly clearer.

"Ki, D'tanesse! Someone silence him!"

D'tanesse had taken to singing quiet rhyming ditties about sand turning to food, clouds raining candied nuts and, of course, about his friend the ocean. Troy had had enough. "Shut your mouth or I will stuff it with sand."

"I'll hold him down," Ivel volunteered.

"I'm not the only one whose mouth needs attention." D'tanesse raised an eyebrow at Troy. "Where did you ever learn such language?"

"He's diverting himself from this misery," Core spoke out, surprisingly. "Allow him the small mercy."

"We leave his tongue in his mouth. That is a mercy." Siegra slapped the end of her reins against the hatchet sheath strapped to her upper thigh.

Conversation split, following separate courses. Terra listened to the storm of argument brewing while he stared at Teyeda's broad back in front of him. Of all of them, Teyeda seemed most content, happy to be outside and a free man. Freedom seemed to be all he needed to act amiable.

Not so the others.

Troy rolled her eyes at D'tanesse. "Where does anyone learn such words? I know of no one who does not use them on occasion." Laic bobbed his dark head, as if he agreed.

"I don't," D'tanesse scoffed.

"Perhaps the true injustice he bears is riding with the lot of you." Core threw a heated look at Siegra. Her face darkened.

"You are Esobir." The word left Troy's mouth like an arrow of venom. "Of course you don't."

"The words mean something, Esobir or not," D'tanesse pointed out.

"The 'lot of us' saved your sorry life," Siegra growled at Core, who shot back:

"I will tell that to the dead. I'm sure they will be comforted."

"Isn't it dangerous for you to admit your alignment with the Esobir? I could sell your head and buy something quieter. A cat, perhaps." Troy minced the insult through bared teeth.

D'tanesse snorted, throwing Troy's sneer back at her. "Your head is worth just as much as mine, Llynx. What is your real name?"

"Our dead outnumber all of yours." Siegra turned on Core. "If you knew anyth—"

"An entire village?" Core's neck was bright red. Terra winced.

"An entire race!" Siegra raised her voicc.

"You seem well enough!"

Siegra reached for her hatchet. Core's eyes flared open. Both of them jumped down from their horses with violent intent. Terra dismounted and dashed to intercept Core.

Troy finally noticed them and kicked Laic forward, between Siegra and Core. "What is this? Stop—"

Siegra ducked beneath Laic's neck, and was knocked over by Norem on the other side. Terra hadn't even noticed him moving. Siegra barely had time to turn her head before she landed hard on her back, arms pinned, the hatchet harmless by her left hand. Terra grabbed Core from behind and held him.

Siegra bucked against Norem, but found he was more than her equal in weight and strength. He rocked back, and she was hauled to her feet, shouting. "We lost every village! Along the coast, every one to the Inatru. No fault of ours! We gave Cathylon our queen, and Cathylon let her die!"

Core strained against Terra's grip, but Siegra's hoarse bellow cut his anger. Terra stared, aghast at her words. She continued to struggle, adding force to truth with her body weight. Norem's fingers blanched, holding her arms in a shackle grip.

"My family, killed! My sisters barely able to draw bowstrings! What reason after that to resist? None! Cathylon abandoned us!" Her shout cracked like a whip, vehement. Adamant.

For so long, Cathylon had feared the Seawolves, accepting their villainy without question, without looking for the reasons why. The Seawolves were not animals. They were not savages. They were flesh and blood, their hearts cut beating from their chests, their spirit stolen away. Oh, but they were not without hope. Troy had become a light of relief in the darkness for these few, and they followed that light without wavering. They would die before giving up pursuit.

Core deflated against Terra, and Terra released him. The boiling point was past. Now the group stared at each other in heavy silence. The other members of the Watch had dismounted and gathered around Siegra, with Troy behind them still mounted: eight Seawolves facing the brothers, with D'tanesse and Sema lingering beside Core. Sema's face was unreadable, but D'tanesse looked faintly sick, as if Siegra's tirade had been directed at him. Teyeda stayed back from all of them, his eyes following Troy.

"Enough of this." Terra was surprised at his own voice, tightly controlled in spite of the pounding in his chest making him feel lightheaded. He strode forward and picked up Siegra's hatchet. Sandy grit clung to the wrapped handle and sprinkled to the ground when he handed it to her. "Cathylon is not your enemy. *She* is not your enemy." He turned to look at Core, then back at Siegra.

He had felt small, meeting the Watch the first night. Now he faced an armed woman consumed with bitter fury. She had been a giant then in comparison. Breath charged from her chest, flaring from her nostrils and mouth. Veins throbbed just beneath the skin of her forehead and temples. She glared down at him through inky, distended pupils. In a moment, she was going to sink the hatchet he'd just handed to her deep in his chest and let him lament his stupidity. Even the horses took on her aggression, lashing their tails and jerking at the reins, showing the whites of their eyes.

Terra forced his words through dry lips. "Our enemy rides behind us. The king and Machaun. This is exactly what they wanted from the start. They began your pain, yes, but don't continue it for them."

Troy was looking down at him, her expression something between pride and disbelief. That faded quickly as she glanced at the sky. Terra stepped backward to put space between himself and Siegra's hatchet. Norem released her arms, resting his hands on her shoulders. Core was remounting Blue in stricken silence. Terra had not heard him shout in years, and he hadn't physically fought since the rout of Kcen.

D'tanesse clapped Terra on the back. "Well done, ambassador."

Terra swallowed, hoping it would rid him of the queasy feeling swimming in his throat. "…I hope never to do it again."

"We'll have time for arguing in Yettmis," Maon said, checking the desert behind them out of habit. "It is only a few hours more to reach it."

"Not even hours." Sema's smile was hopeful of absolution. "Yettmis is that center hill."

She must have meant beyond it, Terra thought as he followed the line of her pointing arm to a bulge wavering in the distance. They stood less than a mile from the curve of an incline dipping between several beehive-shaped hills clustered around the center one Sema indicated.

"Start riding, then." Maon's voice was grim. "The Inatru are here."

Chapter Nineteen

It was worse than Inatru. It was sand.

The horses sensed it first, shuffling away from the oncoming cloud, lifting their hooves as if on springs, preparing to bolt. The wind suddenly jumped at them, flapping against their clothes, tossing sand in their faces.

Troy snapped her attention down from the sky. It was blanched with dust. “Get the horses!”

Terra and Core stared disbelieving as the sandstorm rose behind them, a seething gray-brown wall of sand, riled by sudden vicious wind. It pushed fat fingers through the shaking ground, speeding toward the group. Everyone else was scattering to mount the squealing, kicking horses. Troy leaned over and smacked Core’s mount, Blue, hard across the hindquarters. Blue squealed and sprang away at a gallop. Laic was right beside her, ears laid flat against his skull. D’tanesse pulled Sema up behind him on Gray. Ivel caught Terra’s arm, wrenching him into the saddle before urging Ivory to a dead run with the rest of them.

The sun was doused, hidden behind a haze of sand. Sema, sitting behind D’tanesse in the lead, screamed something back at them, but Terra couldn’t hear it above the hungry moan of the gyrating sandstorm behind them. Ivory clamped his tail down and bounded on the very tips of his hooves, slamming Terra about. It was like riding a boulder bouncing downhill. They barreled down the incline and through the cluster of hills. The center hill came into view, and it was not just a hill. It was a curving rock face, the pale surface smoothed like glass. It rose from the base of another incline, and a path funneled straight to the blank rock. It was too wide to ride around—they didn’t have time. Terra’s back and neck were burning from the sting of wind-lashed particles. The storm howled behind them like an animal, like a wolf on the hunt.

Teyeda had dropped the reins, gripping fistfuls of streaming mane to stay upright. Siegra crouched over Red’s back, standing in the stirrups to lift herself out of the saddle. Maon was slapping Makala’s flanks with the ends of his reins. Troy was dropping behind. Foam streamed from Laic’s mouth and chin. Core was being thrashed about as violently as Terra. He looked about to topple.

“Core!” The wind bit at Terra’s lips, swallowing his voice. Before them, a wall of rock; behind, a grinding mountain of sand and wind. Terra looked down at the heaving earth, which tossed itself into the wind like evil smoke. It was upon them. It was enveloping Troy. It was surging around Laic's thrashing hind legs, coating them in gray. It was licking at Troy's back. Terra screamed her name.

Troy twisted to face the storm. The reins flapped against Laic's surging, sweating neck. Her sword was in her hand. The rag wrappings flagged away in straight lines, fighting their bindings to escape the onslaught. She swung futilely, horizontal. Cloth disintegrated from the sword point. A fault line of shadow shot across the roiling monster as it began to swallow her, and it buckled. Top and bottom folded inward and the storm staggered, collapsing into its severed heart. She shot out of its clutches. The storm howled, then choked.

"Terra!" Core's scream reached him above the dying wind. Terra whipped Ivory around and ground to a halt. Ivel sprang down, pulling Terra with him. They had reached the wall.

An opening that wasn't there before now gaped wide, revealing the space behind. Sema sprinted toward it, her skirts hiked above her knees. Teyeda was on her heels, pulling Blue along. Siegra and the Watch went next. D'tanesse stopped, facing the onrushing sand, squinting and gaping to see Troy. Core's fingers pinched Terra's forearm, dragging his younger brother headlong to what safety lay beyond the opening. Terra swiveled back, searching for Troy in the vacuum of gray dust. She barreled toward them, leaping from Laic as he slowed, hitting the ground and rolling. Grabbing her sword. Gaining her feet. Running.

Terra gasped. "Ki—!"

It disintegrated even as it stretched overhead to grab Troy's body with giant fingers: a hand.

Core jerked him into the crevice, and they were doused in darkness. A blast of debris and dust chased them through, followed by silence.

* * * *

Troy stumbled past the closing stone doors into cool darkness, choking and coughing. Her hair and skin were smoke gray with debris, her vest and savaged dress caked with it. She stood, panting and choking in the shrinking shaft of cloudy light. Her mouth hung open. Wet trails glistened on her cheeks.

More debris cascaded from her upper arms as Terra gripped them, catching her when she sank to the ground. There was movement around them, the Watch hurrying to her side as well, but Terra reached her first.

"I thought you were dead." He pressed his lips to her hair and came away caked in chalky dust.

"We were all dead." Her voice cracked, more confession than comment. They were safe now, safe beneath a blanket of darkness, inside a circle guard of Seawolves. Time and fear stepped away to let them be. Terra spoke to her quietly with short, calming words. Not conversation, but proof of his presence. His voice resonated through his throat and chest as he cradled an arm around her back and brushed filth from her hair. Water oozed from her eyes and smeared dirt around her eye sockets, leaving dark lines on her cheeks. Someone handed Terra a flask, and Troy held her breath while he poured cool relief over her face.

"This dust smells worse when it's wet," Terra observed, brushing grime from her cheeks and eyebrows with his thumbs.

Troy blinked hard. Dusty faces became visible above her. Maon, rubbing his now filthy beard. Emori, with his dusty hood for once hanging loose about his shoulders. Mikal craning his head toward her, concerned. Voices began to register. The others were moving around in the shadows beyond.

"Troy…" Terra hesitated, conflicted briefly. "There was something in that storm."

Between Maon and Emori, she could see D'tanesse standing a few feet away. Holding her sword. He ran his palms over the flat of the blade which felt like stone but looked like metal: sword, yet not sword. The Otnas.

"I saw a hand reaching for you."

Troy forced her head back to Terra. He still cradled her with gentle arms, but the firm set of his mouth demanded truth, and she was not ready to give it. Not yet.

She looked back at D'tanesse. There was no escape from either of them, their searching eyes, their questions. D'tanesse stared back at her, and suddenly she was transported in mind to years previous.

Mytch, alive. The book still with the Klenit Esobir. The Otnas simply an idea, myth. Her future, brightening. Their last adventure. A mission from Yessac, friend and teacher. *Klenit, on the coast beyond the mountains, has kept the book of Esobir until now…* The crunch of sand on the hard path beneath their feet—the same one she knelt on now. A grinding bellow as the great stone doors of Yettmis had opened, letting them enter bright daylight.

Klenit sent word that a perilous time is coming, and they believe the book would be safer in Yettmis, underground… All living in Yettmis, their allies. Mytch at her side, fearless.

The doors were closed now, and how dark it was.

"Sema. We must go to your brother." D'tanesse was still looking at

Troy, still with the shock of revelation stiffening his features. "We've only escaped one danger out of many yet."

Maon and the others parted to let him through, and Troy took the sword when he held it out to her, flat across his palms, bequeathing it respectfully to its owner. For once he didn't goad her, or mock with smiles. She swallowed, resisting the urge to gag on the sharp taste rising in her mouth when she took it from him.

"The light is fading," muttered Mikal. He still stood with Maon and Emori, crowded close behind her.

"And it is not torchlight…" Emori pretended to study the ceiling, as if he did not notice Troy still huddled against Terra, a miserable little girl harboring miserable little secrets.

"Circles of sunstone, set in the ceiling." D'tanesse stepped past them, suddenly ignoring Troy completely. The others raised their heads to peer at the glowing shafts stabbing down to the bottom of the cavern, proof of the sunstones' presence. "The stone mimics daylight, brightening with dawn, dimming at sunset. See, the city is already lighting the night torches."

"There are thousands on the center mountain alone." Emori was fascinated, or at least interested. Much of his interest was to know his surroundings. He was one of the Watch, after all.

"Those are windows," corrected D'tanesse. "You are looking at Yettmis."

* * * *

Before them rose a towering conical stalagmite, covered with lighted, diamond-shaped windows almost to the top, to the Hall of Yettmis. It was chiseled out of the rock, adorned with white pillars and hanging greenery that glowed faintly golden in the light of myriad torches. A rock bridge spanned the shadowy distance between the group and the chieftain's Hall carved into the top of the stalagmite.

"Be careful." Sema stood several yards away, holding the horses they'd managed to recover. Laic was among them. Makala was not. "The bottom is hundreds of feet below us."

Core was beside Terra, pulling on his arm. Finally noticing this, Troy stood. Terra followed her lead.

"We're not alone," Core said quietly.

"I would assume not." Terra shrugged free of Core's grip, an irritated gesture. "Someone had to open the doors for us."

That someone was approaching, walking beside Sema: a stocky warrior carrying a double-bladed ax. Siegra and Norem trailed after them, heads bent close together, speaking in murmurs. Using a full ax as a weapon was of course possible, but unheard of in Cathylon. The Inatru did not train with them, and only a few warriors had learned ax combat in Yettmis. Troy and Mytch had both preferred the lighter weight of bow or staff to an ax.

Dread found a reservoir in Troy's middle, growing rapidly as she walked with the others to meet the warrior from Yettmis.

"Fortunately I was diligent on my watch or you would all be dead," said the warrior to D'tanesse as they came closer. His flat, serious mouth quirked at one corner. His small eyes flickered over the group, taking them all in at once. A bronze armband shone above his right bicep.

"Fortunate indeed, Alan of Yettmis." D'tanesse's answer was subdued.

"And it would be just like you," said Alan, crossing thick forearms over his chest as he stopped before D'tanesse "—to leave our chieftain without anyone to punish for the loss of his sister."

"D'tanesse and Llynx have kept me out of danger." Sema stepped up to D'tanesse and slipped her arm through his. "Where is my brother?"

"Inspecting the crops. He may have returned to the Hall by now."

"We must see him immediately." D'tanesse's brusqueness was unnerving. His face was a solemn mask. Sema didn't seem to notice, though she folded a firm hand over his. They looked like ghostly pillars of sand in the artificial light, with only their eyes and the dark slashes of their mouths as proof of life. Siegra and Norem looked much the same.

"Allow us to escort you, then." Alan turned and began leading them over the wide rock bridge to the Hall of Yettmis.

It was a long walk. The bridge was nearly half a mile long. They led the horses on foot, following Alan toward the lighted top of the stalagmite city. The sunstones cast faded yellow light on the floor of the cavern, illuminating squares of greenery—fields—growing as crops would under the sun. Questions began, slowly at first, as they walked. For each answer Sema and Alan gave, another question arose. The fields below were Yettmis's main source of food, mostly greens: lettuce, tubers, and a plant called yusa that they said tasted like lemon. Yes, they lived on what they grew, even the animals: chickens, ducks, some cattle, even a few horses. The dark segmented patch of dirt that made a giant half circle around the center stalagmite was the training yard. The warriors slept in tent barracks at the stalagmite's base.

"Look Terra—that's a river." Core gripped Terra's shoulder for the tenth time.

"Where does it come from?"

"We think it runs beneath the desert past Camil Askanda, all the way to the ocean, and is fed by the Aganus in the north." Sema looked down at the snake of water bending around the outside of the limestone columns, smiling faintly as if reunited with an old friend.

Terra touched Troy's elbow. "Am I…and Core…the only ones who have never been here?"

"The Seawolves have not." Troy looked back at Maon, who confirmed with a shake of his head. None of the Seawolves had. Emori and Ivel walked on either side of him, making a wall with their bodies behind her. Mikal and Norem strode just in front of her, soaking in their surroundings. Each rested a hand near their quivers—nowhere was entirely safe. Siegra roamed ahead, sometimes walking with Teyeda and sometimes close at Sema and D'tanesse's heels. Her own hands strayed often to her hatchets. She was probably pleased at her choice of weapons, which had set her apart in Camil Askanda. Pleased to be on the same level, in a way, as this warrior from Yettmis.

This was a rare experience for them, welcomed with acceptance rather than hostility. The warriors of Yettmis would see them as equals—or at least, not enemies—accepting these Seawolves because they had already accepted Troy herself. She, a Seawolf, had lived among them and had even been respected.

Moisture slicked Troy's fingers. She tightened them around the leather-wrapped handle of the Otnas, as if to crush the very tang. The sword had a heart of elaa stone, forged together with metal ore—it could not be destroyed. Elaa was forever. Yessac had been right.

If there were any way to undo what I've done, I would.

Mytch's words, in the forest after her exile from Kcen. Troy felt she could eat her own fingers to escape the conversation she knew was coming. Shame seared her to the bone at the thought. Such cowardice.

Alan's shout made her jump. "She has returned! The Lady of Yettmis has come home!"

Ki.

It might as well have been the entire city running to meet them. It was at least half. Over one hundred people came cheering, shouting, practically tripping over one another in their eagerness to greet Sema, the Lady of Yettmis, their chieftain's sister. Young ladies in red headscarves giggled coyly at Terra, Core and Teyeda, then stared wide-eyed at the Watch. Little boys tried to climb up D'tanesse's back and clung to his legs. Everyone tried their best to block their path and shower them with praise. Terra and Core watched the fast-forming ambush with wide eyes and slack mouths. Emori and Ivel pulled their cowls further down over their foreheads and waded through the rush, impervious. Mikal soon pulled his cowl up as well, though his eyes shone large from its shadow as he stared about, searching for danger and finding none. Norem grinned and waved at a cluster of young girls, who immediately succumbed to nervous squeals and giggles, hiding their faces behind their hands.

"This is no time to make friends, Norem," Siegra growled without deviating her straightforward gaze.

"I think I've made more than friends just now." He grinned wider.

"You'll make a quicker enemy of me for acting idiotic!" Siegra retorted. Her voice echoed in the sudden silence.

Troy pressed the Otnas against her leg, moving it in tandem with her stride, but it was too late. The whispering hush expanded over the small crowd as it parted to let them through to the steps of the Hall. Their eyes were not on Sema anymore.

"Troy…it is Troy…"

"Troy has returned…"

"Mytch is not with her…"

Tiny ribbons of whispers flurried around her. Troy fixed her eyes on the path at her feet. Stepping forward took an eternity. Her body felt light, while the sword in her hand was a sudden immense weight, difficult to grasp in her damp palm. She pulled air into her lungs. Glanced up. Saw pale grimy legs and tunic-wrapped torsos lining the Hall steps. Raising her eyes further, she saw hands clasping together, felt their eyes drinking in the sight of her. Old men laid their hands on their sons' shoulders, and young wives clutched at their husband's arms. She might as well have been walking down the road naked, exposed completely with nothing to cover, not even a shadow.

Before, it had always been Mytch who caught their gazes. Mytch who smiled at them. Mytch who argued her case, and any case of injustice presenting itself. Mytch, who gave them hope. Now it was left to her to tell them. Now she must face Yessac. He was old and wise, the oldest living Esobir, and still sharp as any blade. He had loved Mytch as a father would. He'd demand to know everything and she would have to tell him. Mytch, dead. The book destroyed. Hope, gone.

Sema hurried forward to embrace the chieftain, Raelcun, who stood at the top of the steps. A fond smile split his long face above his thin, red-gold beard.

"We might have known she is a chieftain's sister," Norem said to Mikal, who leaned down to listen. "She certainly acts as one."

"He dresses as plainly as his surroundings. All green and shadow,"

Mikal observed with a nod.

Norem grinned and shrugged. “Just came in from the fields, too busy to sit on a chieftain’s throne, I suppose.”

“So that is where Llynx learned it…”

Troy turned to scowl at Maon. He stared past her as if he had not said anything out of the ordinary.

She faced forward again, then stopped with one foot resting on the bottom stair. An old man shuffled past Sema and Raelcun. He stopped at the edge of the stairs, searching the faces before him with quick eyes. A stiff, white beard jutted from his chin, hiding his thin neck. A deep blue robe edged with a wide silver band hung from his bony shoulders. He saw Troy immediately and nodded. It was a silent request to approach that she dreaded to answer and dared not ignore. Better to lay her shame bare in private than here with the entire city and Terra looking on.

“Maon,” she said without taking her eyes from Yessac. “Go with Sema and the chieftain. Terra and Core, you as well. I must speak with someone.”

Chapter Twenty

"He fell in Kcen. He was protecting me. The Seawolves found us. A man—Machaun, Inatru—he was there. He killed their chieftain, and the entire village was burned when they tried to fight back." Troy spoke before Yessac had closed the door to his private study. Before he could voice sympathy. Sympathy was the last thing she needed. Emotion was the last thing she wanted. "I was taken to Camil Askanda, and saved by Sema. She brought me here."

Yessac was silent, shuffling to the fireplace, where he disturbed the coals with a wrought poker. Almost everything was stone here, softened with cloths and pillows, rugs and tapestries. Even the beds were woven pallets laid on the stone floor. A clever maze of holes bored through the stone siphoned smoke from the fires to be dispersed in the river, where no sign of life would betray the underground city's presence. The room was faintly familiar, like a distant dream. She'd stood in this spot, beside the low writing table, many times. Mytch would stand by the diamond-shaped window opposite the door while they talked, looking out every so often at the illuminated fields below by day, or the vast darkness pricked by torches at night.

"We were right about the sword," Yessac said at last. "They did have it."

"The sword is yours now. I do not want it."

"It was never a matter of desire, Troy. The Otnas was given to you because you will need it." He turned his head, openly examining it for the first time. Troy wished she could sheath it out of sight, out of memory. It was not hers. It had been handed over with the book. So much, shoved onto her without permission or apology.

"I saw him. The king."

"The man who calls himself king."

"He said my mother was a Seawolf. He said he killed her."

Yessac set the poker down noiselessly on the hearth. A trickle of smoke wafted from the blackened tip, adding its scent to the room.

He had stood just there, stirring the fire, when he'd given her and Mytch the assignment in the first place. *In time long past, I would have gone myself to get what I needed from the book,* he told them. *My wife, stubborn woman, made the journey with me many times. Now I am too slow, and the roads are too dangerous for an old man. The Klenit Esobir sent word about the perilous time approaching. They believe the book would be safer in*

Yettmis, and I agree...

The book had not been safe with her. They could not have known. Yessac never would have sent her if he'd known. Then again, he had seen the warnings. He had copied them down himself, kept them with his other scrolls. Even if he did not know what the Esobir from Klenit had found at the end, might he have acted on suspicion alone?

Troy searched the tabletop for a place to set the sword. The surface was carpeted with parchments, quills and translucent white shavings. She considered brushing them aside to clear a space. "Do you know something, Yessac? You are from Carmul. It was close to Klenit."

Yessac watched her, daring her to disturb his sanctuary. "My life has been devoted to three things – Elaa, my wife when she was alive, and the Esobir. I left Carmul as a young man." His lips flattened, pushing wrinkles of skin toward his narrow cheekbones. "I have not seen Carmul or Klenit for many, many years."

"He said my mother was their queen."

"Do you believe it?"

"He lies about everything."

"Partial truth can be very effective. Not whole truth, but the idea of it. Enough to cover the lie." Yessac slipped into the lilt he used when teaching, shuffling through the mess of parchments on his table. Their layout was a mystery to Troy, but he knew them like old friends, handling them with care.

"Why did you send me to get the book? Did you suspect—?"

"Did I suspect what?"

The room was suddenly too warm. She took a breath. Then another. Yessac remained bent over the table, hands still, waiting for her answer.

Troy stepped toward the stone shelves stretching along one wall. The carved recesses—pentagon-shaped slots—made a honeycomb pattern pleasing to the eye. She fingered the edge of a scroll, one of many from Yessac's translations. Nearly every slot, fifty or so, was occupied by scrolls of varying thicknesses. Handwritten copies from the book of Esobir. They represented barely a quarter of the original text.

"You would tell me if you knew something. If you knew…about my past." The last words stuck in her throat, but she pushed them out.

"My suspicions, and I dare say yours, do not make fact."

"And emotion does not make truth."

"Emotion has its uses. Someone here may know you."

Heat condensed into a hard ball above her sternum. "The book is gone."

Yessac selected another parchment and examined its script. "Did the

Inatru take it?" He sounded less eager to hear the answer than she was to speak it.

"No. We left it hidden in Kcen when the Seawolves came. To fight for our friends." The hardness convulsed and something gave way in her chest. *Sienna. Mytch. Terra's parents. Imra.* Troy filled the dead space with air, pulling it into her lungs, but not before Yessac noticed. His eyebrows sank low over his eyes, and he turned toward her.

"The book was destroyed. It burned with the house." As soon as the words left her mouth, she was weightless. The confession stretched between them, stealing sound and heat and motion from the room, leaving just their still bodies, facing each other. She looked into Yessac's dark eyes and saw nothing. His thoughts had turned inward, the horrible news churning through his mind.

She couldn't apologize. Not enough. The hope of the Esobir was gone. That she alone survived was punishment enough. Yessac seemed to decide this much as well. He demanded no further explanation. Instead, he tucked his long hands into the looped cuffs of his sleeves and inspected the scrolls in their honeycomb nooks, still searching for a certain one. "He was better than family to you. An unforgettable young man."

"I know."

"You may have other family. Blood family." Yessac eased toward her, scanning the scrolls as if they were the focal point of the moment.

Troy stepped back. The sword dipped toward the floor, suddenly heavy. She steadied her grip to keep the point from grinding against stone. "I should return to my friends."

"If you decide you want to know, talk to D'tanesse. He knows the truth of many things."

D'tanesse. She might have known.

Her past was not just a weight. It was a black shadow stretching forever in all directions. She could search all her life and never find the end of it. "I wasted two years in a fight none of us could win. Years before that learning to make explosive powders and...concoctions from elaa. I thought I could make a life of it. I should have been running. I should have run as far as I could."

"Why do you think running would make you any safer? That by hiding you would remain obscure?"

"Nowhere is entirely safe." Troy stared at the tiny crack between the door and doorway, thinking of the hallway beyond it and the cloak of darkness beyond that, outside. "But this war will be fought without me."

"And the Esobir? They have put their hope in the Deliverer."

"They will have to hope without me."

"They have no hope without you."

Troy turned back to him in spite of herself. "They have Elaa. He will have to be enough."

Yessac chose a small scroll finally, caressing it between his leathery palms. "Elaa has given them you. Do not run from this."

"You're wrong. It was because I faced the king that he finds me a threat. Becoming a warrior and Esobir brought the Inatru down on me and destroyed Terra's village. I have destroyed lives already, and I myself have lost everything. If I had remained obscure the king and the Inatru would have no reason to chase me. Mytch would be alive. Right now."

"Where are you going?"

Troy was already lifting the door latch. "The Inatru were following us. It is only a matter of time until they figure out where we've gone. How we escaped the storm. Someone must lead them away."

"A lie fears the truth, Troy. Fears it so much, because truth is its death. That is why they hunt you." Yessac stepped toward her, holding the scroll against his chest with one hand, like a promise. Hope of life.

"And that is why I run." Troy swallowed the bitter taste rising in her throat and opened the door.

D'tanesse was standing on the other side.

Chapter Twenty-One

D'tanesse

Her hands hold my soul captive. Hands that stay young, though the years age me. Her ghost follows me, dancing on the edge of awareness. A jade green dress swirls around her bare legs. The hem is muddy from playing on a wet beach, crouching above tide pools hidden in volcanic rock. Tiny fingers poke into the water. Coarse hair escapes the sloppy ribbon tying it back, drapes about her cheeks in black waves, shielding her face from sight.

Sand clings to her bare feet, spraying from her heels when she runs to me. Her outline is stark, green and black against a gray fog sky.

Oh, L'abri…

She brings me treasures for safekeeping, gifts for her mother. White, grooved shells. Bright fingers of coral. Chips of rainbow abalone.

She swoops over a hard, smooth beach, arms spread to imitate the seagulls, pursued by the reflection running upside-down beneath her. She shrieks when I chase her and lurches into the salty waves.

She trails puddle footprints over the black and white tile floor of the Great Hall…and is promptly scolded. She sits beside me at feasts, racing to finish her pile of crab legs before I do. Stealing from my plate. Trying to wrestle me to the ground. Failing. Trying again.

She grows a little older but still leans against me, knees hugged to her chest, on the clifftop among long tufts of yellow grass. They hiss as the wind coming up from the sea and over the cliffside rubs against them. Her bony ribcage expands against mine when she presses close, shivering a little in her damp summer dress. I feel a hundred feet tall with my arm around her shoulders, warming her with my body heat. We watch the stars appear and travel along the horizon, marking the passing hours. Fog rises up from the sea.

"…Are you afraid of the water, D'tanesse?"

She confides to me many secrets. Desires. Fears. Woe to the man who pursues her: I will see that he proves himself worthy many times over.

L'abri, my sweet cousin. She holds my soul still.

I see her face in my dreams. When they are pleasant, she is laughing. Leaning over the sill of her open window, windblown. She is embracing salt spray as it crashes into the rocks and peppers her with foam. She is grinning up at me, flashing a mouthful of little white teeth.

I remember that smile when nightmares wake me. Truly, nightmares are nothing worrisome. Dreams can be forgotten in a day. Memories live and breathe. Memories, traitors within, tearing at my walls of reason and self-control.

I was not dead when the fires began. Oh, I did look it. I was too afraid to move for fear my father would return and end my life with his own hands. My mother's body was as stiff as the table she'd collapsed on, one arm curved above her head, sleeplike, except it was resting in a plate of steaming scallops. She was one of many, nearly a hundred, who died while they feasted in celebration of L'abri's twelfth birthday, while poisoned pine cordial worked away at their insides. Pine can cover nearly any taste with its pungent flavor.

My father knew this. He'd learned it from me.

The High King, L'estim Glor, was the last to die. For a short moment we shared more than a blood relation, staring into each other's eyes. Our breaths were shallow in the silent Hall. I held him up, my arm around his twitching shoulders and a hand against his head. His circlet crown was skewed; braided gold, bronze and silver strands sloped across his damp forehead at a sharp angle.

L'estim Glor, so regal and strong, full of life, who could not be felled by combat, and so his own brother resorted to cowardly poison. Let it always be said our High King was a True Man among men! Even I did not fully know, then, the care he took for his people.

He pushed two words through blue lips ringed by stiff brown facial hair and bubbles of saliva. "L'abri…Natug…"

I blubbered a response. L'abri had complained of feeling lightheaded. Natug, all splendor in her crimson robe and divided silver skirts, had carried her from the Hall. Natug, queen of the Seawolves, queen of Cathylon. Light resided in her olive skin, and veins of sun pulsed just beneath the dark freckles at her temples. L'abri was a bright splash of jade silk against Natug's robe, her hair swept back by twin braids like her mother's, flowing over her shoulders on a river of black tresses. Minutes after they'd gone people began to die, choking on the food still in their mouths.

My father had watched it all, arms folded impassive across his barrel chest, then left—no doubt to find the queen and her daughter.

I cried harder, trying to make out the High King's last words on earth, pressing my ear close to his lips. "Take them…Klenit…find Yettmis…"

A crash behind me, tinkling glass. Flaming pitch-covered arrows shot through the tall windows. Some plunged into corpses, burning through clothes, skin, flesh. I was soon choking on the sweet metallic stench. I abandoned the High King's body and fled outside through the kitchens, retching into the crook of my elbow. Fire was everywhere, loosed into houses and shops by black silhouettes of men, cantering through the narrow streets.

I stumbled into the embrace of deep flickering shadows, staying silent and hidden. Where were L'abri and Natug? In her room? The medicine room? Had they escaped the fires? Succumbed to poison like the rest?

At last I reached a decision and sped on my toes to the medicine room, the closest building from where I was hiding. It was just beginning to burn, from the inside. Through one of the low, open windows I could see a table overturned. Rolls of burning cloths and shattered jars littered the tile floor. Flames licked around the queen's body, consuming the remains of her crimson robe. A pool of blood congealed beneath her in the crackling heat.

L'abri was not there.

* * * *

Sema leaned back against the rim of the limestone tub, gratefully breathing in the citrus-scented steam that curled around her face. Her clothes lay in a dusty pile by the bedroom door. A blue robe and long, white tunic waited for her on the pallet bed, on top of the various blue-shaded squares of her mother's quilt. A quiet reminder of time gone by.

It was almost too quiet now. No screaming sandstorm. No flurry of bodies, chaotic in welcome. No struggle to survive heat and cold, day and night. She could hear the splash of running water coming through the embroidered curtains. The river: a constant murmur in the dark, her companion through countless lonely nights. Lonely, until D'tanesse appeared.

He had come to Yettmis in Grano, one quiet night seven years ago. It was a month after Yessac's wife, Sema's grandmother, had passed away, and only two since Sema was sent to Yettmis to live with her brother Raelcun. She was honored to be a part of the secret establishment, but aside from Yessac and Raelcun, she had no close friends.

Sema was reluctant to sleep alone the night D'tanesse came, and was sitting with Raelcun in the dining hall.

"It is begun." Kilar's rasping voice preceded him into the dining hall. He never tried to swagger, but he was so broad in shoulder and long legged he couldn't help it. Dust rose with each ripple of his green travel cloak, hurriedly thrown back from his shoulders. D'tanesse, staggering at his side, was escorted to a stool beside the warm hearth. "Where is Raelcun? He should hear this man's story."

"Here, Kilar. It's late to be dragging in half-dead recruits, even for you. Did you make him run before you all the way from Daehexa?"

"Late for you to be up mending tools, on the table no less." Kilar tipped his head back, squinting disapproval at Raelcun. He was a close friend of their family, and most trusted of her father's warriors in Daehexa. Yessac even said her father made Kilar his successor, since Raelcun was now chieftain of Yettmis. "And keeping your sister up from sleep as well to help you. The shame of it."

"I wouldn't sleep knowing he's working." Sema quickly poured a cup of water—all they had at the moment—and nudged it between D'tanesse's limp fingers. He lifted his head after peering at the cup's contents, and her breath caught.

Oh, those eyes.

Even bloodshot from sorrow and heavy-lidded with fatigue, they were striking. Brilliant and clear green, they snared her gaze. She continued holding her breath until he raised the cup, releasing her to pour one for Kilar.

"He found me in Daehexa," Kilar said, nodding thanks. "Sent all the way from Klenit. He asked me to take him to Yettmis. Once I heard his news I could not decline."

Sema retreated with the jug to stand by the fire. The flames in her cheeks rivaled the embers for heat.

"Tell us what has begun." Raelcun remained sitting, but his shoulders were rigid. He had always been wiry, but tough muscle corded his arms and back. Raelcun could hold sway over a king's court from the middle of a field. Even his silence influenced.

"This used to be D'tanesse of Carmul." Kilar swept a thick hand toward him.

"Used to be?" Sema swallowed, venturing a glancc.

Raelcun waited, passing the weight of response to D'tanesse, who sat hunched and miserable on the stool. Sema, knowing the agony of withstanding her brother's silences, refilled his cup, giving him something to do besides sweat out an explanation. She was careful this time not to catch his eye.

"Carmul is no more." He spoke at last, echoing Kilar's words. "The people died without much struggle. Poison. L'estim—the High King—told me to find Yettmis."

"The High King is dead," Kilar put in.

"The Inatru came. They set fire to the city. They killed…" D'tanesse swallowed.

Oh, he was wretched. Sema felt sick to watch him, bent beneath his burden of memory, while they leaned forward, desperate to hear more. "L'abri was gone, and the queen was dead when I found her. My father had some connection to the Inatru, but had done nothing blatantly treacherous until that night."

"The Inatru simply wandered across the island and happened upon Carmul after the people were slaughtered." Kilar's mouth tightened in contempt. His brown beard nettled. "They were blessed with impeccable timing."

"It was bound to happen. The Inatru want possession of Cathylon, but this is brutal." Raelcun shook his head gravely. "Even they would not slaughter a city in such a fashion."

But they had.

"My father helped them. He made it possible. Then the Seawolves—"

"What have the Seawolves done but lose their queen to a coward's treachery?"

Sema frowned deeply at Raelcun, but D'tanesse didn't seem to notice the slur.

"When I left Carmul for Klenit, their ships were pulling into the harbors. The Inatru were waiting for them on the beach."

"Cathylon is without a king," Raelcun mused. His eyes were bright and hard above his steepled fingers. "The Inatru control the coast and the desert now. The land in between is weak, the will of the people watered down. Now not even the Seawolves on their island are safe."

"Yettmis is safe," Sema said quietly, speaking at last. They turned toward her, three sets of eyes burning with fury and vengeance and guilt. Her fingers tightened around the handle of the clay jug. "And we know the truth about Carmul. That is reason to hope. We must not forget hope."

She felt small in the large room, facing three men—two of them her elders—but what she said rang true. It needed to be spoken. She did not lower her eyes.

Raelcun nodded, harboring a slight smile at the corner of his mouth. It was there and vanished again, but not before she saw it. "We should tell Yessac what has happened."

"Not that he will act," Kilar muttered, crossing his arms.

"Yessac is wise, and we need wisdom as much as action. Much as it pains me to sit still."

"I have seen you do nothing but sit since I came through those doors."

"I did not want to make you look bad." Raelcun remained sitting. If ever two men were like brothers, it was Kilar and Raelcun: always at odds, yet fiercely loyal.

Yessac was awakened and brought from his apartment. The story was told again over warm cups of lemony yusa cider and leftover brown bread. Sema sat beside Raelcun at the table as was proper, but kept a watchful eye on D'tanesse's cup, refilling it as soon as it was empty. He drank nothing but water, refusing her offers of cider and wine with a small shake of his head.

"Natug thought my father was interested in Elaa, maybe to become Esobir. But he wanted the power of the stone, not the life of Esobir. He grew suspicious of everyone, even my mother. He would always say, 'everyone is against me!' even though no one was.

"Natug, I think, realized what he was about, but too late. He killed her. And I couldn't find L'abri."

"What do you know of Elaa?" Yessac asked.

"I was studying the book of Esobir with Natug before she sent it, with her sword, somewhere else. When my father couldn't find the book, he grew sullen and suspicious. He stopped experimenting with me. We would try new recipes to see what elaa could do. I knew he was communicating with Machaun but I didn't think… I didn't say anything. Even at the celebration, I watched everyone drink the wine, wondering if it really was…"

"The book is in Klenit," Yessac said, drawing bony fingers down his chin and stiff beard. "But I have some of the writings here with me. Copies. You may study them as long as you are here."

D'tanesse's mouth went slack. "But I am his son…"

"You know our enemy better than any of us," Raelcun told him, "and he will not be watching for you. Take refuge in Yettmis."

Of course, D'tanesse accepted. He had nowhere else to go.

He continued his training with Yessac, and Sema learned alongside him. They studied lists of ingredients from the scrolls and learned how to use the elaa stone as a catalyst, as the Ancients had in the beginning. Gradually, he began to tell of his life in Carmul before it was ravaged. Sema told him about her childhood in Daehexa before being sent to Yettmis earlier that year. She told of Raelcun's appointment to chieftain of Yettmis under their grandfather Yessac, while his son Remus, their father, worked in Daehexa to support the spread of Esobir knowledge.

Not many weeks after D'tanesse brought his news, Sema's own parents were killed in a raid on Daehexa. Both Inatru and Seawolves were reported as present in early communications, only Seawolves in the later. Kilar became chieftain of Daehexa, as her father had directed while still alive, but the Inatru watched him closely and communications between Yettmis and Daehexa by necessity grew scarce.

Sema and D'tanesse found solace in each other's company, and soon they were inseparable. She learned how to see past his personality to his character, and liked what she saw. She began to recognize when he was nervous, snipping humor through tight lips with his eyes fixed somewhere distant. She searched for ways to make him smile. She learned about his tendency toward mischief. He began to wear laughter like a second skin, with all his dangerous fears and raw emotion tucked away beneath. That skin rarely broke after the first few days, but she learned to recognize the slant of his eyebrows and the certain tension around his eyes when, remembering, he was close to tears.

Months passed. News reached them from the world above ground: the Seawolves accused of treachery, of killing the High King—nothing mentioned of their queen—and war arising between them and the Inatru. Raids continued across Cathylon: Seawolves attacking and burning villages. Vicious lies of the Seawolves were spread by the Inatru, which Cathylon was content to believe. However, one truth did find its way through: a Seawolf, a young girl without a name, was encountered in one of the lesser villages. The story was a scandal—some reports saying she'd killed men, women and children before disappearing. Others said she cast plague wherever she went, leaving a trail of dead behind. D'tanesse only heard that a young girl, a Seawolf, had been found somewhere, alive. Hope sparked within him.

They continued their studies, memorizing entire scrolls of carefully selected texts. They tested one another, playing memory games, until they could recite the words verbatim.

A light began to grow in D'tanesse's eyes, gradually, when he looked at her. His questions became more pointed, discovering her mind and venturing bravely into her emotions. When he touched her hand, she wanted to laugh with joy. When he kissed her, he owned her heart.

They spent their first night in this very room, not long before they left for Camil Askanda. Raelcun, who gave his consent to their union readily enough, had not been happy about her decision to go there, but she insisted and promised they would stay out of danger.

He would have things to say once he learned how quickly she'd broken that promise. For four years she had put herself in danger purposely, mingling with the king's servants and accompanying both Inatru and Seawolves on their raids, and then helping the captives they brought back to escape. And now this: fleeing to Yettmis before the king's army and a sandstorm, barely escaping to safety. Oh, yes—a tongue lashing was surely imminent. He was waiting for her in the dining hall while she bathed and put on clean clothes.

Sema finished her bath, squeezed the water from her hair and stepped, dripping, onto the black and silver rug. She missed the sound of birds and the whisper of air over endless sand. The realization surprised her. She'd found the outside so unnatural after living underground, but had grown accustomed to the sounds of the desert over the years in Camil Askanda. Yet there was that distant splash of water from the river and the echoes of activity coming from the rest of the city. Later there might be gentle music or driving renditions from stringed instruments in the dining hall. Yettmis was a warm place, warm and safe.

She had just finished dressing when D'tanesse entered. He stood in the doorway, mouth slack as it had been the first night they met. His eyes stared around the room, seeing nothing.

"It is her. I'm certain. She came to Yettmis soon after we left." His hands clenched at his sides, blotchy white beneath a brown coating of dirt. His chest jerked irregular beneath the cobble jacket. Fine streams of dust sifted from the pocket seams and hung in the air close to his body. "She studied, became Esobir. She lived just down this hall. Yessac told me. He knew her, but he didn't know…for sure who she was. Until now."

Tension broke across his face, and Sema went to him. His fingers gripped her shoulders and he shook against her. "She was so…good. She loved green, she came to me when she had nightmares—" His voice was muffled, face pressed against Sema's shoulder. "She doesn't remember any of it."

For years it had weighed on him, tension building up and up since their first meeting in the tunnels of Camil Askanda. Llynx was familiar yet she was not, his cousin in his memory only. Gone was the little girl who had followed him everywhere, who snuck out of her bedroom to sleep in his when she was scared, who climbed rocks and played in the ocean with him. Llynx was distant and wanted no one. At least, she tried to make it seem so.

"Now she carries the Otnas," he said when he'd regained his composure. "The Otnas, Sema. Cathylon's Deliverer, the queen of the Seawolves, ruined before she even started."

"She is not ruined yet." Sema placed her hands on his shoulders and looked into his eyes. "Llynx is distant but also fragile. Her need for people, for us, is so great she feels she must ignore it or be overwhelmed. Yet, she is not entirely wrong to distance herself. The Deliverer, or I dare say any female warrior, must be able to fend for herself, because her friends will not always be able to."

"It is so much worse than that. She wants nothing to do with us. The Esobir. Yettmis. She told Yessac she is going to leave."

"Then we will leave with her."

"She doesn't want us!"

"Then it is good we are not her servants." Sema forced herself to smile: courage to create courage. "Some of us stand on the front lines, some sit on the thrones. A favored few are able to guard those warriors' backs and stand at the right hand of rulers. That is us, D'tanesse. She may not remember what your father did or who she is, but you know her—and her enemy—better than anyone. She needs you now more than ever."

Chapter Twenty-Two

Troy's room—her former room—was on the outside curve of the mountain, above the warriors' barracks. She walked quickly. The corridor was wide and warmly lit by pillar candles sitting on limestone outcroppings. Floral carpets of blue and brown silenced her footsteps. She practically leaped over the gaps between, chasing the shadow just visible beyond the turn of the walls. Mytch's voice came from somewhere in her memories, speaking up uninvited.

He's right, you know. Cathylon needs a deliverer and Elaa sent you.

I don't have to admit it.

But there you just did.

Mytch had great respect for Yessac when he was living. The old man had taught them all things Esobir, from the basic concepts of economy to the intricacies of the supernatural, and everything in between. His teaching—the truth of it, the concepts, the knowledge—had made so much sense to Troy. It had given her a place to exist outside of the rigid social structure set up by the Inatru. An Esobir was Esobir regardless of race or status.

If only she could have remained simply an Esobir. Or skipped becoming one altogether. Becoming a warrior had been hard and dangerous enough.

Now I am done being either.

Mytch would have disapproved. He disapproved from his grave her argument with Yessac, and her decision to abandon the Esobir. He especially disapproved of that. Very well, she would let him. The dead had no say in her decisions.

If that were true, you wouldn't have argued with Yessac in the first place.

Troy kept walking.

Rectangle rugs, candles and walls slipped by, turning with the shape of the mountain. She came to her door, listened for a moment with her fingers on the handle, then opened it. Candles in two corner sconces lit the empty room. It was the same shape as Yessac's scriptorium, but smaller. There was no table, no honeycomb nooks. A single straw pallet languished beneath the curtained window. A change of clothes, folded breeches and tunic, was stacked on the pallet. A leather cuff sat on top of the tunic, a thoughtful gesture. Even though the Esobir in Yettmis knew the truth about the Seawolves, she preferred to hide her mark. She took the cuff automatically and put it around her neck, sighing softly as she tied the laces. This familiarity, at least, was a comfort.

The air tasted like dust. Chaff rose, disturbed by Troy's boot when she nudged the pallet. She touched the thin curtain hanging across the window, then turned back and pinched out all the candles.

Now she could breathe, hidden even from herself.

"I am nothing," she whispered. "I know nothing."

The sword was still in her hand. Troy set it on the floor, leaning but not crouching to do so. A little light glowed through the curtain, shaded green. Its natural golden color showed around the edges of the cloth. Noise came in through the window as well, and a little through the plank door, but the walls closed out most of it. The river hissed in its bed, far off. Troy was glad her room was above the barracks and not the water. She sank down, stretched out on her back beside the sword and stared at the ceiling. She did not want to think anymore, but she couldn't help herself. Sleep was not forthcoming.

Many nights, she had come to this very room and dropped onto her back on this floor. Sometimes, Mytch would come with food if she missed the evening meal. He would talk while she ate, or if she had already eaten, until she fell asleep. She closed her eyes and saw the Looking Glass. At any moment, the king might use the Glass, might turn the river into a maelstrom or simply reach though bare sand and rock to crush her. But, if he could do this, by now it would be done. There was no reason for him to wait. She was only his prey now. So why was she not dead?

Troy opened her eyes. There must be a contingent. Either he knew where she was and needed her alive, or he could not pinpoint her. Or—a third idea crowded after the second—perhaps desire and location were not enough to use the Looking Glass. In the eye of the Looking Glass, she'd seen Sema—had known it was Sema, but not just by her face and dress though they were both visible.

A faint color like the gold light edging the curtain over there, had shown up around her, almost totally eclipsed by Sema's body. Or escaping from it. Something had marked her.

Troy groaned and thumped herself on the forehead with the soft side of her fist.

Machaun himself had said it! I can still see lights walking throughout the city…

She saw it now: the strangeness of their conversations when he was there, the king berating Machaun for his confidence, the security she derived from their apparent confusion about the Esobir—all contrived. Her escape had been so easy. He knew she would run if fed just enough truth to ignite her fear—if it were true—and once she ran, he could give chase and destroy all of them. Follow the rat back to the nest, as it were, and stamp out the infestation for good. Sema was not his target. Even Troy herself was not. All of the Esobir were.

And Terra had followed her! Terra, Sema, Maon…all of them…right here. With the book of Esobir destroyed, all the knowledge they had was in the minds of the Esobir, and a few handwritten scrolls here in Yessac's scriptorium.

I am such a fool.

A hand at the door, knocking briefly then tugging the latch, propelled Troy to her feet.

"Yes?"

"I have your meal." D'tanesse offered from the other side.

Her shoulders bumped against the wall before she knew she was backing up. She wanted to refuse, tell him to go, but she needed to eat and this saved her a trip down open corridors to the dining hall which would be full of people and questions she didn't trust herself to answer. Conversation with Yessac was hard enough, but Raelcun would be unbearable. He was immune to diversion.

Coward.

"Come in."

He opened the door, then stood in the doorway backlit by a haze of light from the rounding passage. "Do you need candles?"

"No."

His head turned, taking in the dim space. Some light touched his neck and one round cheek. His eyes were just dark hollows with vague outlines of the whites of his eyes. "So this is where you lived. Warrior, Esobir. Breaking law underground was not enough—you knew you must do it in the king's city, to his face, or never be at peace."

She expected him to start in with questions. *Why did you not tell us you knew Yessac?* or *How long have you known about the Otnas?* He must have heard some, if not most, of her discussion with Yessac. The D'tanesse she knew would be bursting with enthusiastic antagonism, picking at the new gaps in her armor. "I did not know the king until I was brought to Camil Askanda. I came from Kcen."

"So Terra told me." He waited for her to respond, and when she didn't, he set the tray on the floor beside the sword and pulled the door closed behind him. In the ensuing gloom she heard him stepping toward her. "When did you come here?"

She felt his presence and saw the outline of his shoulder in the feeble glow cast from the window behind her. "Four years ago. We left on an errand for Yessac, my brother and I."

His steps stopped. "Your brother?"

"His name was Mytch. He adopted me. We traveled to the northern mountains to meet the Esobir from Klenit and carry the book back to Yessac. Mytch lost his horse in a skirmish with Seawolves on the plains, and we were forced to stop in Kcen."

"But you are not from Kcen."

"I don't know where I'm from."

"And the Otnas?"

"Given to me by the Esobir from Klenit. I was going to give it to Yessac as well, but Machaun found us. He was following us."

D'tanesse sat down, hard, on the pallet. The wall was cold against Troy's back, a welcome discomfort.

"Four years…" His voice was distant. "Sema and I had just left for Camil Askanda." His head slumped forward. "Four years…"

"I am not Esobir anymore."

He scoffed, a harsh sound in his throat. "This was your secret? Hiding all this time, yourself, but so much more."

She turned her back to him and pushed the curtain aside. "I am nothing."

"It was not nothing I saw on the faces of the people here when we arrived."

"Then I pity them. And you."

"Do you know who you are, Llynx?"

Her muscles grew rigid. *Please don't say it.*

"Do you have a suspicion to voice?" Her words came out louder than expected, brittle with emotion that the dark could not mask.

Silence pressed between them. Troy realized she was looking, not down at the barracks, but at the far walls of the great cave. A dead end. For once, she knew exactly what blankness filled the mind of a cornered animal. She did not know what to say next or how to escape. Her next instinctive move would be to turn and attack him with her fingernails. The realization was horrible.

You are not an animal. You are not an animal! Don't act as one.

Her stomach clenched, shrinking in her middle. Acid pushed up into her throat—how familiar this sensation was becoming—and settled there to burn.

"The king has a Looking Glass."

"Estimal Glor is my father."

Their revelations came simultaneously and collapsed into each other.

Troy turned toward him. He was obscured in the dark, a human shape sitting on the edge of her old bed. If this were another time, another day, that shape could have been Mytch. This could have been another bantering conversation over a small evening meal. But it wasn't.

"That was why you argued so strongly against killing him," Troy said at last.

"I should hate him by now. I hate what he's done. I'm ashamed of him. But he is my father and I can do nothing about that."

"He is going to find us if I stay here. The Looking Glass marks users of elaa. I saw him use it to find Sema. Your jar probably betrayed our location in the desert, and the Otnas—" She looked automatically toward the sword on the floor where she'd left it "—probably has again."

"Yes, I realized," he snapped.

"What should I tell you then? What could I have said that would have made any difference?"

He thrust an arm toward the sword. "This? This is no difference?"

"I did not know what he would do, or what it can do!"

"This is the Otnas, Llynx!" As if she needed reminding. "What can it not?"

They were yelling now.

"It can't give me what I want! It can't save anyone, D'tanesse! If it remains here, it will do the opposite! Your father will come and he will kill them! He will kill Sema!"

"Then what do you want? The truth? I think you're afraid of it!"

"I never asked for it!"

"If you did I would tell you!"

"I don't want to know!" Any louder and she would be screaming. "I want to find a safe place and make my home there! I want Terra to be safe with me, I—" She couldn't say that. "I want Core to be safe with his family, and I want to never see a village burn again, ever!"

"And it's never occurred to you the only safe place possible is the one you make when you face that question you're so afraid of?" D'tanesse asked, suddenly quiet, overcoming his temper.

Mytch's words came again to mind. *The life you want will not be handed to you, little sister. You must fight for it. You can fight for it.* From a conversation once held in this room. She'd said much the same thing to him about what she wanted, and what she did not want. *You are who you are*, he told her frankly. *Do not be afraid of it.* She'd forgotten the discussion until now.

"I'm not staying here, D'tanesse."

"I'm not suggesting you do."

She blinked. "Good."

"Fear comes first. You're never safe from fear, but you can be safe despite it. More important—" He stood and made his way to the door "—is the moment you realize what is stronger than fear, and reach for that."

She watched him pause in the slim rectangle of light that appeared when he opened the door.

"You will never be safe, but you can be something better."

When he was gone, she stood in the dark, hearing his words over again in her mind.

You will never be safe, but you can be something better. Fear comes first. You will never be safe, but...

The conversation with Mytch butted in. *Fight for Terra. Fight for the Esobir. Fight for Cathylon. Fight so you can continue to fight with me...*

She shook her head, closing her eyes as if the dark room were not dark enough.

You will never be safe, but you can be something better...

I will always fight with you, and beside you, Troy. You'll not be alone...

She stood, forgetting the food growing cold on the floor, while D'tanesse's words followed Mytch's words over and over in her mind, until the new words overcame the old and Mytch's voice was lost.

She cried.

Chapter Twenty-Three

In a room much the same as Troy's, Core and Terra struggled against one another in front of the filled tub.

"You cannot follow her every second!"

"I just want to know where she is. Let me go!"

When Troy had walked away with the old man, Yessac, Terra started automatically to follow her. Core grabbed his arm and practically forced Terra along when Raelcun, the chieftain, led them to the dining hall. There they were given water while a few of the women who had followed them in were sent to prepare rooms. Others began clearing dirty dishes from two long stone tables, and scavenged clean cups and water for the travelers.

D'tanesse took a few sips and then excused himself, saying he needed to talk to Yessac as soon as possible. Sema seemed torn between going with him and staying with her brother. The others sat down around the table nearest the hearth while the other table was being cleared. Terra sat also, forcibly encouraged by his brother. They talked little save for short enquiries such as, "I wonder how long we have until…?" and "How are you doing?" and "Did you see the…?"

"I saw a hand in the storm," Terra declared at last, and they began to rehash the whole event from the beginning. Raelcun stood back, with his head tipped down above his crossed arms, listening. After a few minutes of discussion, Sema suggested everyone go to their rooms to bathe, and by then a meal would be ready for them. They could talk more, and think better, then.

So Terra was dragged by his brother down a slanting, curved corridor to their borrowed room, and was fighting to leave it not two seconds later.

With strength he didn't know he still had, Terra shoved against Core.

Core gave way just slightly and came back at him. "At least take a bath first! She's probably hiding from your stench!"

"I don't smell!"

"You smell like a cart of manure!"

"I'll bathe later, I don't have time! Troy i—" His teeth clicked together when Core punched him.

Terra reeled away, more from surprise than pain. His shins thudded against something hard. Too late, he remembered the bath tub. Core caught him with an arm across the chest before he pitched headfirst over the stone rim into the water.

"Listen to yourself." Core pulled Terra tight against him, talking over his shoulder, hooking his other arm around Terra's throat. "You're acting like a child now, even after that speech in the desert had us all convinced you're a man."

"I am a man!" The blood in Terra's body seemed to rush into his head and neck, squeezing behind Core's arm.

"Then act like one, and don't cling to her every second!" Core pushed him away, and Terra threw his hands out just in time, catching either side of the tub as he fell toward it. His reflection rippled gently, inches away. His eyes blinked up at him. A film of gray dust quickly formed, falling from his clothes and hair, obscuring the surface of the water.

Alright, so he was dirty. Filthy, even. He was certain he didn't smell as bad as Core claimed.

He rubbed his chin where Core had hit him, feeling for split skin beneath the scattered, short bristles of his new beard. Core hadn't hit him very hard, just enough to bruise his temper. Yet the rebuke stung. Terra rolled his shoulders, turning to scowl at Core until he realized he was pouting rather than threatening. The scowl receded after a brief inward struggle and Terra sat down, relenting. There were no chairs so he sank to the floor and rested against the tub. His feet were braced apart, flat on the stone floor, scraping over tiny particles. A black and blue rectangle rug, laid out to soften the room, barely reached Terra's toes.

Core pulled his tunic over his head, walking toward the pallet. Dust fanned out on either side of him and drifted down in his wake. His hair clung to his neck, a mix of lax curls and knotted tangles. It was still darker than Terra's, auburn like their father's. "Why do you still try?"

"Try what?"

"She is not the girl we once knew. You must know that."

"We are not the same boys," Terra returned. "She knows it and we know it."

"You hope she knows it." Core looked down at his bare torso, as if to ensure it was still intact, every rib accounted for, no surprise gashes.

"She does, when she's frail." Terra closed his eyes and tangible memories crowded toward him: in the desert, when she reached for him the first time with trembling fingers. Those quick moments when he would turn to find her also turning toward him. She always looked away quickly, and usually searched the sky for some invisible observer. But again, eventually, her eyes sought Terra's. At the entrance to Yettmis, when he caught her, she stayed pressed against him, in the refuge of his arms, unable to stand. It was the same way she sought him as a young girl, terrified of her nightmares. Core might not know how she was frail but Terra knew. And when she was, she came to him. That meant something. Or perhaps he was making more of those moments than he should. Perhaps they meant nothing to anyone but him.

Core thwacked his tunic down on the bed and dropped down on top of it. "She will be the death of you."

That would not be so bad, Terra thought, opening his eyes, but he said, "She saved us, remember?"

"She's not the same girl we knew."

"I don't care."

Core shook his head, pillowed in his folded arms. "Get in the bath."

"Troy has the arrowhead Imra gave her," Terra said after he undressed and stepped into the tub. "I saw it when I was holding her."

"I'm surprised." Core closed his eyes.

"Me too, a little."

"Wake me when you're done."

* * * *

Terra returned to the dining hall clean but dressed in his old clothes, wearing his bow and quiver. Just in case he didn't have time to return to his room, he reasoned. He needed to be ready for anything. He retraced his path from before and came to the double doors of the hall. They were slightly open, emitting faint orange light and the voices of Sema and Raelcun.

"You don't fool me, sister. Half a plan and overmuch confidence in hope will not win battles! You are my only family—"

"There is Yessac—"

"How can you so selfishly put yourself at risk?"

"Where are the plates?" she interjected, changing and lowering her tone.

"On the shelf there, beside the oven."

Terra stepped silently into the room. Only a few of the torches lining the walls were lit now, probably to save fuel. The hearth, set in the stone wall like the hearths in Camil Askanda, was filled with red-gold light from a bed of coals. The dry heat was welcome in the damp and perpetual chill of the air.

Raelcun, dressed as before in plain brown breeches and a green tunic, was crouched beside the hearth skewering long tubers to roast over the coals. D'tanesse stood at the head of the table nearest the hearth, frowning deeply at a block of white cheese, which he placed on a warped wooden tray waiting on the tabletop. Sema was at the far end of the oval room, with her back to them, pulling plates from a stack on a tired wood shelf.

Terra sat down on the stone bench at the end of the table, near D'tanesse and facing the hearth. Upon closer scrutiny of the uneven tray, he saw a mess of leaves, some circles of flat bread and a thick mug of steaming liquid that smelled of lemons and yeast. The thick scent stuck in the back of Terra's throat when he leaned over the mug and breathed in. D'tanesse briefly noted his presence, frowned again, then went in search of utensils.

Sema spoke again to Raelcun. "Should I wait in my room while the Inatru kill my brother like they did my father? He was only supportive of the Esobir. You are teaching from the book of Esobir. Leading them! You speak of my selfish tendency, when yours is a governing habit!" The plates rattled when she set them on the table. Tears threatened, clouding her voice, and she swallowed them away.

Raelcun finished skewering the tubers and thrust them alongside a row of eight more already roasting on a rack suspended above the coals. His face was a tight mask of skin, drawn over the hard lines of his chin and the slit of his mouth. Red, hot light shone into his eyes, reflecting anger and frustration back into the coals. It was not an expression that belonged on the man's usually stoic face, but then again Sema was his sister.

Terra lowered his head. His bow was stiff against his spine, but he didn't want to call attention to his intrusion by wrestling it off now. D'tanesse came back to the table with a knife and a scrap of yellow linen. He thrust the knife into the block of cheese, spread the linen over the tray, then carried the tray out of the room without speaking. Terra glanced up at Sema. She was watching D'tanesse. For a moment her countenance changed completely and the rims of her gray eyes glistened. She was struggling within herself, perhaps wanting to follow him, but she did not. Terra blinked and looked away from her face, almost ashamed at seeing her so vulnerable. It was an emotion she did not mean to share with him or even her brother—only with D'tanesse. Perhaps that was how it worked with women—certain emotions were only revealed at a certain depth to a man who had earned the right to see them. That made him think of Troy, and the way she'd remained in his arms at the entrance to Yettmis. Perhaps he was not just speculating after all. Perhaps there was something between them—just between them.

"Where did you find her?" Raelcun stood and examined the dustless mantle.

"Kcen." Sema sounded in control of herself, though her eyes might have betrayed her if Terra looked. "Machaun was following her and caught her there. Apparently she left the Otnas with her friends Terra and Core before she was taken. I recognized her servant scar; Teyeda has the same one. She lived with us in Camil, but she never said…Raelcun, she is a miracle." She began setting the plates out, speaking in a rush. "She can fight, she is intelligent, cunning…She trained those Seawolves on her own, she knows about elaa, and now the Otnas—"

"I know she can fight," Raelcun cut in dryly. "Her tenure in Yettmis proved that to all of us." A story lay in those words, some history of experience Terra would not hear now, or possibly never. No doubt Troy had earned quite a reputation among the Esobir of Yettmis, as she had in Camil Askanda with the Seawolves, the warriors in Daehexa and in the other villages she'd visited with Mytch. Terra couldn't help a small smile. She was indeed a miracle, a legend, and he'd held her in his own arms. He remembered how she felt, leaning against him, and heat seeped into his face.

They'd stopped talking. Why had they stopped talking?

Terra raised his eyes and saw they were both looking at him, the intruder. Well, if he must intrude, then he must. He needed to know what they knew, what danger Troy was running from. Terra drew a breath in the silence, pushing his back straight against his bow and trying to make his eyes hard as they studied one another. He felt if he spoke first, some ground would be lost.

"Why are the Inatru chasing Troy?" He couldn't help himself. Terra was willing to lose ground, blood, sleep—anything to solve the mysteries surrounding his friend. Anything to be with her.

"Which one are you?"

"Terra."

"Terra, I am Raelcun, and not your enemy. You may stop murdering me with your eyes."

"I am sorry, but I do need to know. I need to protect her, and I can't if I don't know what to protect her from."

Raelcun seemed pleased, somehow. A knowing smile curved across Sema's face.

"What do you know about the Inatru?" Raelcun asked.

"I lived among them, recently."

"But what do you know?"

Terra hesitated. Not nearly enough, and the truth was not all truth, if Siegra's story counted for anything. "I know they force the Seawolves to fight for them. They burned my village to the ground. They are chasing Troy, and I think she is part of something bigger. Something she can't say."

Raelcun's eyebrows were suspended high on his forehead, but there was no betrayal of emotion as there had been a moment earlier with Sema. Neither seemed inclined to speak, so Terra pressed on.

“She had brought the Otnas to Kcen but because she’s a warrior I didn’t know what that meant. She can use elaa as an Esobir can, and her sword controls the sand, and the king wants to harm her, I think.” If not for the ‘I think’ he added (without thinking), it was overall a convincing statement. For a moment, he was on solid, even footing with them.

Then Raelcun said, “Troy knows elaa is of Elaa, and power is only an agreement. I know because I taught her that very fact. I know she came to Yettmis with a friend seeking refuge from the Inatru. I know she left as an Esobir and returned as the Deliverer. She carries an agreement between what is flesh and what is of Elaa, and that agreement could be the saving of Cathylon from worse than the Inatru. The cups are over there, Sema.”

“That is the last place I would have chosen to put cups,” Sema noted, opening the sideboard Raelcun indicated.

“You were not here when the dining hall was expanded.” Raelcun bent and poked at the thin skewers, rolling tubers over to expose their browned bellies. “Otherwise I would have gladly asked your opinion.”

“I assumed you would have the common sense to put them near the jug.”

“Apparently that singular trait does not run strong in the family,” he quipped without looking up.

“Elaa is of Elaa?” Terra was trying to digest Raelcun’s banquet of information, delivered in a form far too rich for immediate understanding.

“Yes, elaa,” Raelcun enunciated slowly, turning toward him, “is of Elaa. The Esobir refer to the physical source as elaa stone.”

“Are there two kinds of elaa?”

“No. There is elaa and there is Elaa.” This time Terra caught the slight emphasis on the second word: a proper name. “The stone and the Mind.”

Chapter Twenty-Four

"We should fetch the others, so they can eat before we must leave again," Sema broke in quietly.

"I am here," Core said, stepping into the room. He too was dressed in his old clothes, but his hair was damp from a good washing. "The others are on their way. I think they were waiting for Troy."

Terra sat down slowly. Stone that could do the impossible was one thing, but this? He was not on even footing at all. He was standing in a quagmire and fast sinking. "Is the stone a person?"

"No, the stone was made by a person."

"What are we talking about?" Core sat on Terra's left on the end of the bench and folded his hands on the tabletop.

Terra was hardly sure, himself. "And you call them both elaa."

"This is not how we usually teach about it," Sema apologized, setting plates down in front of them.

"But you insisted, and we are short on time, so try to pay attention." Raelcun rested the poker against the hearth stones at his feet, balancing it on end with his downturned palm. "There is a book, written by the Ancients—"

"Actually, three that we know of. The Inatru have another."

"—which was in the middle of being translated, before it was sent to Klenit for safekeeping. It was a tedious process in any case, and much of it could not be translated."

Sema brought Raelcun a platter, and he piled steaming gray tubers on it while he talked. "Through the book, we learned the ways of the Esobir, and how to use elaa stone as a catalyst—"

"A doorway connecting elements to produce a reaction." This time Terra interrupted.

"Who told you that?"

"D'tanesse."

"He did a poor job of explaining it."

"I don't think he was trying very hard."

"We could hardly educate him while fleeing for our lives, Raelcun." Sema set the platter down before Terra and Core. It scraped quietly over the stone surface, a pleasant but cold sound.

"He said the Esobir know different than the Inatru." Terra tried to keep the conversation on track, before he lost it completely.

"The Inatru claim the elaa stone is power. There is no mind or reason behind it. It simply exists as an element. Yet it is much more than that. The use of elaa is an agreement between the user and the source of its power."

"May I have some of this?" Core pointed to the platter of tubers. Terra swallowed, suddenly realizing how hungry he was.

"Please, eat." Sema filled a thick clay cup from a brown jug and set it before Core, then did the same for Terra. She flowed into the function of hostess effortlessly, perhaps from her years spent as a servant.

Terra sipped some of the golden liquid. It was the same thing D'tanesse had on his tray. It tasted strongly of lemons, with the yeasty bite characteristic of ale. It stung his throat when he swallowed.

"How long have you been living underground? Why are you hiding instead of helping?"

Terra elbowed Core. Core elbowed him back, watching Sema for her answer.

"I myself have lived here for six years," she replied. "Construction of Yettmis was begun when L'estim Glor had a warning from the Mind itself, that a great destruction was coming, a refuge needed. Yettmis is that refuge."

"Did you build it?"

"We are still building it," Raelcun said, settling in his chair by the fire. "Not all the stalagmites are inhabitable yet. My grandfather and a few others are overseeing the work."

"Yettmis has been a closely kept secret since we were children," said Sema. "Only our parents, Yessac and a few Esobir from Klenit on the coast, know of it. The L'estim Glor and his queen of course knew of it, but Estimal Glor was never told."

The doors opened again and Siegra strode in, followed closely by Maon and Norem on her left and right. Mikal ducked through after them, bending his uncowled head to avoid the lintel. Emori and Ivel in tandem slipped in after him, stepping to either side of the group like silent guards. They stopped together, hesitating, as Raelcun set the poker down and turned toward them.

"Welcome, friends." He did not wait for them to speak first. He approached with easy steps to greet them, inclining his head to Siegra, who was foremost, and then to Maon. "Welcome to Yettmis. Sema told me how you saved and protected her in Camil Askanda. I am honored to meet and thank you all."

"For taking my wife and daughter into your protection, I thank you," Maon returned, meeting and holding Raelcun's gaze when the chieftain raised his head. He reached out and gripped Raelcun's forearm, their wrists touching in a kinsman's greeting. His voice thickened. "I thank you."

Raelcun accepted the gesture which usually came from one Inatru to another, and rested his hand on Maon's shoulder. "They are safe here, as safe as anyone can be in such a time, for as long as you want them to stay."

Maon's hand tightened on his arm.

Sema stepped forward and directed them to seats at the table. To Terra's surprise, they sat close around him—Siegra on his right with Norem beside her, Mikal, Emori and Ivel across from him. Maon sat on Norem's right near the far end of the table. They were all famished and tucked into the plain meal as if it was a king's banquet. Emori and Ivel pushed back their hoods, and Terra was almost surprised to see they were not identical. Ivel's face was narrower, his nose long and thin like Mikal's, and the four scars, slashes, curved along one side of his neck. Emori's face was wider and pale in comparison to the others, who were darkly tanned from riding through the desert. His nose was wide and flat, his mouth wide and thin.

Teyeda joined them a few minutes later, entering alone. He moved silently, eyes down, to sit at the end of the table on Maon's right. Maon pushed a platter of tubers at him and he nodded thanks, heaping them on the plate Sema set before him.

"Where is Troy?" Core asked, while Terra had his mouth full of ale and tubers.

"And D'tanesse," Norem added. "He did not look well."

"D'tanesse is resting in his room, and I believe Llynx—or Troy—is with Yessac. He is my grandfather, and Raelcun's," said Sema, setting another platter of tubers on the table between Ivel and Emori. She then sat down in an empty seat beside Ivel, across from Norem. "He and our grandmother raised me when our parents sent me to Yettmis to live and learn to be Esobir."

"Yessac is here," came an aged voice, as the man shambled through the doors. He held a scroll in one fist. Raelcun gave up his chair by the fire, and went to sit beside Sema at the table. No one was at the table's head, but as soon as Raelcun sat the general focus oriented toward him, so he might as well have been.

The doors opened again almost immediately and D'tanesse entered, minus the tray of food he had carried out earlier. His forehead was creased, his mouth tight. The blue-green-gray cobble jacket hung loose on his shoulders, flaring open with each step. Sema went to him at once, and they shared a whispered conversation standing close together.

"There is a mystery surrounding Yettmis," Core spoke up after a moment, "and I would like to know it."

Raelcun remained silent, passing the answer to Yessac, who was staring into the fireplace. The old man's face was painted red by the glowing embers. “Then you shall know it,” he said at last, turning and tipping his head back so his pale beard jutted toward them.

Core felt the need to clarify. “I don’t ask out of curiosity. It is necessity. My brother and I need to know what trouble we’ve become a part of.”

“We are all in trouble most dire, I’m afraid. All of Cathylon is threatened by the Inatru, and the man who calls himself king.”

“But you began building Yettmis years ago, before the king, or whoever he is, was any threat.”

“The High King knew what was likely to come, but he was loath to make an enemy of his own brother, to affix on any person such a doom and fear. Instead he waited and watched. Meanwhile, we prepared Yettmis in secret.” The old man watched D’tanesse take a seat at the empty table, further from the hearth, sitting near the doors but still within earshot.

“How did the High King know what was coming?” Core asked.

“From the book of Esobir, and words from the Mind itself.” Yessac nodded, ready with the answer. “As for those words, L’estim never spoke them to me. As for the book – ‘In the heart of the Betrayer grows the weed of darkness. He will banish all light from Cathylon, and the land will live in his shadow.’”

“The book of Esobir was written by a woman named Aenti EirNin, whose race was dying of a horrible disease,” Sema explained, also returning to them. Her face was unreadable, her voice composed. “Elaa gave them the cure in nine Dreams and their people were saved. The book records one of those Dreams and the life of the writer. While the other Esobir, as they were called—the other eight who were given Dreams—stopped having them, Aenti EirNin continued to Dream, and one of them was of Cathylon. A warning.”

“Where is she now?” Core looked as if he already knew the answer and didn’t want to believe it.

“Long dead. The book was written hundreds of years ago, and was brought to Cathylon by ship. By the Seawolves.”

Yessac recited into the ensuing silence. “‘In the heart of the Betrayer grows the weed of darkness. He will banish all light from Cathylon, and the land will live in his shadow. When the Light of Life emerges in his midst, the Bearer of Darkness will give chase to destroy it, and he will become the Hunter. In the Age of Darkness the Deliverer will come as the dawn overcomes the night – the root of the tree, the lifeblood of the people. Life will be born through death. What was once rejected will be received with gladness, what was unheard of will be spoken, and the traitor will be pardoned. As the rock withstands the blazing fire, so the Deliverer will escape the Betrayer's inferno. The Betrayer will reign for six years, and a warrior will be fashioned, as hard as stone, cold as the snow which falls on the mountains, who will wield the Otnas and stand in the Place Between.'"

Core set down his cup and dropped his hands to his lap. Terra stopped chewing. A bit of tuber sat forgotten on his tongue. The Watch kept on eating, but they were all listening.

"'In the time of Eulba, season of the Sun, past, present and future will be joined. Mighty and terrific evil will awaken with the return of the Deliverer to the foundation of the past, where light was born in the midst of darkness. Great will be the destruction left in the Hunter's wake, from the plains to the very shore of the sea. The cry of the orphan and the widow will rend the heavens, and there will be no escape from the grasp of the Hunter when the cities are tainted by his evil. Yet flee, flee while it is still light, and refuge will be found in the depths of the earth. There will flock the homeless, the orphan and widow, to take refuge until the final outcome. As the river seeks to become the ocean, so the Hunter seeks to become greater than he is able. The Deliverer will come when death is reversed and fear has been put to rest. So ends the Dream and warning. Let him who hears take it to heart and remember it well.'"

Terra stared at Yessac. The words repeated in his mind: *a warrior will be fashioned, hard as stone, who will wield the Otnas and stand in the Place Between...*

Troy.

The Inatru wanted power, would stop at nothing to get power, and they would be most afraid of the one person who could take it all from them. They would do anything to get at her.

But why not in Camil Askanda, when she'd been in their grasp—for years, at that? She could be their undoing, why let her go?

"They don't know who the Deliverer is." Terra spoke even as he realized it. All eyes flicked toward him. "That is why she is still alive."

"We can assume they know now," Maon said. "And we should decide how to proceed before they come for her."

"Yettmis is hidden in more ways than one," said Yessac. "Not even a Looking Glass could penetrate here."

"To them it would seem we disappeared with no trace. Once they determine the place where we disappeared," Maon observed, "they will make short work of discovering Yettmis."

"We can go to Kcen," Terra said quickly. "No one travels through it anymore. The village is gone. We could hide there."

Core gave him a dark look, but Maon was considering it.

"There would be no casualties if we were found, outside of ourselves, of course."

"I think we would all rather not be casualties if we can help it," Core pointed out.

When the door opened again, Terra almost didn't expect it to be her. There was a moment of stillness after she stepped into the room and set her bundled belongings on the floor beside her. The rolled-up cloak sitting on top rested against her leg below the knee. She was wearing clean breeches and a tunic that seemed to have been designed for her. The tunic cut away from her shoulders and hugged her neck like a second, dark brown skin. A new leather cuff was around her neck, overlapping the collar of the tunic. The pale scar tracing the oval curve of her face, and the thinner white scars tunneling her arms like long thorns, added a sort of violence to her appearance.

"Raelcun." She bent her head, bowing to the chieftain. Her hair was gathered loosely at the back of her neck by a strip of gray cloth. The thick strands seemed to grow sharper and darker as they absorbed shreds of light from the candles and fireplace.

"Troy." Raelcun returned the gesture, rising to stand with his hands close to his sides.

Now Terra understood why the people of Yettmis had stared and quieted when she passed them on the road. There was a controlled wildness about her, in the straightness of her back and shoulders and in the wide, solid stance of her booted feet. She was like a thing of the earth, a rock underneath the thorns.

Terra was on his feet before he knew he was moving. The others rose an instant later, and soon they were all standing, facing her, except for D'tanesse.

He was facing her, but he wasn't standing. Troy strode toward him and laid her hand on his shoulder. His eyebrows sank down, and he looked like he might cry, except for the relief creeping from his thin lips to his eyes. Her hand remained on his shoulder while she looked to the rest of them still standing at the other table in front of the hearth. Her eyes were red around black irises, but her gaze was steady. Her expression was so identical to D'tanesse's that they could have been siblings, except his hair was not as dark as hers.

"Talkative as ever, I see," she said to Raelcun.

"When I need to be."

"I thank you for your kindness in sheltering us, but I'm afraid we can't stay very long."

"When will you be leaving?"

If she expected him to be surprised, she didn't show it. "Right now, after we discuss a few things."

"By 'we', I gather you mean these good people."

"I do."

"By all means, then."

Troy was not frail now. She gathered that into herself, so far hidden it was hard to believe she ever had been. "Please sit down."

Terra had forgotten he was still standing. They sat, but nobody resumed eating while she talked.

"We are not safe here," she began, taking her hand off D'tanesse's shoulder. "Moreover, Yettmis is not safe if we stay."

She said *we*, but Terra guessed she meant herself. Herself and the sword.

"We know that," put in Norem, turning on the bench beside Siegra, but staying close to her. "We were discussing what to do."

"In Camil Askanda, the king and Machaun found so many Esobir for a reason. That reason is a thing called a Looking Glass, an instrument made with elaa. It can detect and locate those who have used elaa recently."

"That would be most of us here," said D'tanesse.

"I haven't," Core protested.

"Nor I," echoed Maon.

"Neither have I, since we left Camil Askanda." Sema stared at the table top. Her hands were hidden beneath it, folded tense in her lap. "We should warn Daehexa and the Esobir in Klenit about this."

"Kilar will need to know," Troy agreed. "The only reason the king has not razed Daehexa or Klenit that I can see is because his attention has been elsewhere until now."

There were nods in response. They all knew what, or more precisely who, she meant.

"Yettmis is protected," Yessac said from his seat by the fire. "Estimal Glor would have invaded it by now if he knew where it was. Remember that he wants the book of Esobir as much as he wants the Otnas and its keeper. He wants control over everything that is powerful."

"Why can't he find Yettmis?" Terra turned to Yessac. If Yettmis had a way to be shielded from the eye behind the Glass, perhaps they could use it to shield Troy. He saw again the hand, extending from the sandstorm, and quelled a shiver. The Looking Glass seemed to him less like a window, more like an open door.

"Have you ever seen Estimal Glor use the Looking Glass without a map?" Yessac asked Troy.

She shook her head, thoughtful. "No."

"It is very likely—almost certain—that the Glass requires a map to function properly. If it can only show that which corresponds to locations marked on a map, it cannot show him Yettmis. One might look through a window at the grass, but they cannot see beneath the grass. If he could have looked through walls into houses, none of you would have remained hidden from him as long as you did."

So much for any hope of a shield. Unless they intended to tunnel their way out of the desert, the threat of discovery remained. Troy could not hide. Terra let out his breath slowly, turning his mug with his fingertips. The rim moved in a slow circle above the trapped liquid rocking gently in the bottom of the mug.

"But Yettmis is only hidden as long as the king does not know where to look." Maon brought up his point from earlier. "With the Looking Glass, he will soon know Llynx is not in the desert beyond, and he will return to the point where she disappeared, which is at the entrance to Yettmis."

"That is why we must leave." Troy had obviously reached the same conclusion. "But I have something to ask of you, Maon, and of Sema. Daehexa must be warned about the Looking Glass. The Esobir living there may need a place of refuge." She paused, realizing her choice of words—words from the Dream—closed her eyes for a heartbeat, then continued. "Sema is the best choice to tell them, since Yessac cannot travel and Raelcun must stay to lead the Esobir and warriors here. Maon, I would ask that you and the Watch escort her. It is time the rest of Cathylon learned the truth about the Seawolves."

The stillness that settled over the table was tighter than before, like a bow drawn out, not quite full but close. Terra, between Core and Siegra, kept his eyes on his cup. He could still see their hands moving on the table on either side of him, fingers folding and unclenching. If the silence stretched, tension might break over all of them and the backlash of the argument in the desert sting them again.

Troy spoke before that could happen. "D'tanesse and I will lead the king the other way."

D'tanesse shifted on his seat. "And when they find us?" Terra could imagine him turning to look up at her.

"Then we will do what we must. They will not have what they want. Not while I live."

Terra swallowed. Premature protests were already fighting to leave his mouth. *D'tanesse and I,* she'd said. Not *we*, not anyone else. She hadn't looked at Terra since entering the room with a plan already in mind. She was going to leave him behind.

"Maon, what say you?" she asked.

"I am your man, now more than ever. Whoever will come is welcome, but I will go where you send me, even if I go alone."

Now Troy was silent. When Terra ventured to look at her she was staring at Maon, trying to come up with a suitable reply to his declaration. "Yes or no would do."

"Then yes, I will go."

"Thank you. Everyone should gather their things, and we will meet at the entrance to Yettmis. Please hurry."

"Troy, we would speak with you alone," Raelcun said as the Watch and Teyeda rose to leave. Sema went to D'tanesse, and sat close beside him. Neither seemed surprised at Troy's request, which would both separate and endanger them. D'tanesse's posture was resigned, but his eyes were narrowed. They were not surprised, but neither were they much pleased—understandably so.

Terra and Core stayed where they were, still processing what was happening. Conversation sprang up around them: Sema talking earnestly to D'tanesse, Maon planning with Siegra and Norem, Emori and Mikal passing observations back and forth with Ivel…

Terra saw only Troy, passing by their table. Troy outlined by the light of red embers, standing between Yessac and Raelcun. Troy still refusing to look at him.

Teyeda laid a hand on Terra's shoulder, covering it with his long, large fingers. "Terra, Core. We should get the horses."

Terra could not stand. He did not think he could talk, but he surprised himself by muttering, "She is leaving without us."

Teyeda's hand tightened. "She can try." He sounded almost amused. "She is not going as alone as she thinks if we have anything to say about it. Deliverer or not."

Chapter Twenty-Five

Torches glowed on either side of walls, marking the opening to the passage between the city and the stone gates. Troy's shadow stretched behind her, reaching toward him. Terra ran faster, pulling even with her as she neared the passage. The Seawolves, D'tanesse, Sema, Core and Teyeda were behind him, leading their horses. It had taken longer than Terra wanted to retrieve the horses from the stables at the bottom of the cave, then saddle them and lead them back up to the bridge. They were new horses but the same desert colors, and except for one their names in Terra's mind were the same: Gray, Blue, Red, Ivory. The only one with a real name (besides Laic) had a splash of white across its face and was called Pie. By the time they reached the bridge Troy was leading Laic—who had already been saddled and ready—across.

"No, Terra." She did not turn her head. Laic paced dutifully beside her.

"You cannot go alone."

"Yes, I can."

"Well, you won't."

Troy maintained her stride, moving with the frightening beauty of a stalking wolf. "Terra, you are not coming."

"And you are being childish."

Troy halted at the entrance to the narrow passage and turned on him. "I do not have time to watch after you."

"I do not want you to. Nor do I need it."

"You don't know what you need." She glared at Terra. He glared back.

Norem edged past them, and his mount slashed its tail against its flanks as it stepped into the passage. Ivel, Emori and Mikal moved by silently, but each of them glanced in approval at Terra.

"Perhaps you'd be better off giving yourself to the Inatru, to do as they please with you," he snapped before Troy could speak again. "They will find you eventually, and how will you fight them alone?"

She leaned toward him, her hand fisted around Laic's reins. "And where would you take me that is so safe? Where will they never find me?"

"You will go to Kcen."

Teyeda came up behind them, tugging on his mount's reins.

"The Inatru will track us if we go there. Are you so eager to repeat that slaughter?" Troy was hardly diverted.

The others were clustered behind Teyeda, who stood in the center of the path with his loaned horse, the one called Pie. He moved on reluctantly. Core followed him, then Sema and D'tanesse in close conversation. They stopped not far away, within earshot, waiting to see what would happen.

Terra ignored them. "Then what is your plan, Troy? I know you won't face them."

"Terra, you are not coming!" Her shout, vehement, cut into the darkness around the bridge, echoing toward the city.

"Then kill me!" He pulled his bow over his shoulder and shoved it into her hands. "I swore to stay with you and face your enemies! If I am of no use to you, then I can make no use of life!"

Troy started to push the bow back at him, but he grabbed her arms and held them. She stiffened, finally meeting and holding his gaze. Terra blinked and faltered. Her eyes were wide and red-rimmed, glistening with tears. He lowered his voice. "Don't make me break my promise. Please."

"If you keep pushing him away, one might think it's because you care what happens to him," D'tanesse observed, still watching with the others.

Troy's lips parted. Terra drew breath to speak again, to reassure her, but she gathered herself quickly and jerked away, shouldering his bow. She spun and disappeared through the passage, pulling Laic after her.

Siegra stepped forward and laid a hand on Terra's shoulder. "We will do what we choose to do, and she will learn not to waste her time fighting us who are not her enemy." She slipped a sidelong glance at him, along with a faint quirk of her lips.

Terra clenched his empty hands at his sides. "Where is Maon?"

"Speaking to Raelcun about Daehexa. It seems that is where he and Sema were born. Maon wants to know what we can expect from them."

"I am surprised you would do this. Pleasantly surprised," he added quickly.

"I think Llynx is wise to send a warning to the Esobir in Daehexa. Even if Llynx did not ask us to go, Sema sacrificed much in Camil Askanda, and we know her cause is true." She turned toward him. "Maon knew Llynx from the beginning. He was the first to see her mark. Some of us who would not have fought for her before may have a reason now. In truth, many would—and do—follow her regardless. They believe she has a plan for us. I myself have never seen the mark, but I have been with her, and I have seen her heart. Even if I did not see that, all she's done for us is enough."

Terra finally tore his eyes from Troy's fading outline as Siegra's meaning became clear. He felt he should speak, but Siegra shook her head and continued.

"I would stay at her side always, but you will have to do it now. Here."

She handed Terra her bow. "You must watch over her now, Terra of Kcen. Watch over our queen."

* * * *

The night was silent, observing the five horses and their riders cantering up the narrow incline. The sandstorm was long dead. The dust was back in its bed, but the stench of scorched particles remained. Sand churned beneath five sets of scooping hooves. It was turned into a fine gray mist hanging behind the horses as their feet found purchase in the coarser sand at the top of the hidden road, and the riders shot away from Yettmis beneath the watching stars.

For a few moments the horses ran together in a close bunch, a surreal burst of movement within the container of the suspended world. They soon separated, stretching their strides. The desert stopped moaning and listened to the horses blowing long, hollow breaths through their nostrils. Over the flat ground they ran, flat out as if the warhost was just behind them, skimming toward one of the dunes.

Troy went up first, at one with Laic and his clawing strides. Then D'tanesse on Blue, his coat lurching with each leaping gait. Terra's fingers tightened on the reins, then loosened to give Gray her head. He lifted himself out of the creaking saddle by pressing his thighs against her ribs. Up they went: Gray bending her neck, nearly touching her nose on the sand, pawing with front legs, jumping with hind feet, up the deep slope until they lurched, panting, over the crest. Core and Teyeda were clambering up on either side of him in a spray of white particles. The landscape was blank in all directions.

Laic came to a stop and Troy turned in her saddle to look back the way they'd come.

"We're on top of the southernmost mountain of Yettmis," said D'tanesse, reining in beside her. "From here we go south and east."

On top of Yettmis. Terra imagined he could feel slight heat seeping out of the sand, from all the fires and candles and bodies warming the air in the cavern beneath him.

Laic stamped a foot, impatient to run again. Troy frowned down at the middle hill, the central dwelling of Yettmis.

Terra followed her gaze; seven more riders emerged, rising out of the ground on the hidden causeway. Their shadows floated over the pocked sand, pushed by the moonlight into long sharp strings of black, the stretched shapes of legs and ribcages. At that distance they seemed to float, restless, like a flight of birds, curving slowly toward the southwest. Then one rider jumped forward, breaking into a run, and the others followed. Six dark gray figures, hardly more than wisps of flagging mane and tail under vague human outlines, swept over the sand. In their center was a figure in lighter gray, a dot of light in the heart of the dark riders.

"You didn't need to send all of them..." Core sounded apprehensive watching them go.

"Yes, Core." Troy's expression had not changed when Terra looked back at her. "I did." She turned Laic, cutting across D'tanesse's line of sight and making him frown deeper. His eyes snapped up and they exchanged a silent, tense dialogue. She dared him to run after Sema and be with her. He shifted unhappily in his saddle and Blue responded, shifting as well. Finally he shook his head. They both knew Sema was safer the farther she was from them.

Troy's eyes narrowed. *So is Terra,* her look implied.

D'tanesse was unmoved. Not the same.

A weight settled over both of them, and Terra knew what it was. The same weight hung from his shoulders, hunkered in his chest.

D'tanesse ended the conversation not happening by nudging Blue into a trot then a gallop away from Yettmis, the Watch and Sema. Terra sat for a moment, until he remembered D'tanesse probably did not know the way to Kcen. He kicked Gray forward and caught up to him.

"I know the way," he said.

D'tanesse's jaw was clenched. Eventually he rolled his eyes toward Terra, his expression a tangle of relief, sorrow, amusement and derision. "You know the way from Yettmis, a place you've never been before?"

"Well..."

"Great burning pots, man, what are you good for?" His pained grin dulled the cutting edge of the insult.

Terra stared forward, but continued to match his pace.

The weight of care, Gray's rolling canter and the dry air pushed into Terra's airways consumed the next hour. Though the stars still told direction, and the sun promised with its eventual dawn to rise as usual, the world had changed. The night deepened with each passing hour but it did not cover them. Barren ground did not promise to hide them with a blind of expanse. The hollow dents in the deeper sand seemed like dark staring eye pits. Terra saw a hand—*that* hand—everywhere. He saw it in the shapes of vagrant clouds, against the dunes, and even in his own shadow. It was a hand reaching out of nothing, seeking Troy.

He clenched his own hand, pricking skin with his fingernails, and made himself look at something else. Teyeda had pulled just ahead of him on Pie. His shoulders were wider than the rest of his body, almost wider than Pie's curving ribs. Teyeda was always calm about things. Terra wondered how he managed it. D'tanesse tugged on the reins. Troy loped past them as Blue slowed.

"Llynx. Llynx!" D'tanesse called again, louder. "We have gone far enough for now."

She did not respond.

"The horses need a rest!"

Still no answer from Troy, but Laic broke his stride and eventually came to a halt.

Terra was briefly grateful to dismount. He groaned a moment later, when he tried to take a step. His thighs felt like taut strings. It hurt to stand. It hurt worse to sit. He'd been aware of a dull pain in Yettmis, but now that pain was doubled. His backside throbbed beneath him. He stood up again.

"We'll set up a watch," Troy finally spoke as she dismounted. "Two hours' rest and then we move on."

"I'll go first." Terra didn't exactly mean to speak so quickly.

Troy breathed sharp, turning to him with a glance just as sharp. He held his ground, looking back at her.

"I'll watch after you," Teyeda said. He was already lying down beside Pie. His thick arms were folded behind his head. He looked up at the stars and then closed his eyes. "We must all sleep if possible."

Terra did not want to sleep, but he said nothing.

Troy relented. "D'tanesse, show him how to count the hours."

D'tanesse was loosening Blue's girth. He paused and squinted at the horizon. "Dawn comes in an hour or two. A little less than." He swiveled the same painful grin toward Terra. "Think you can tell what dawn is, or shall I draw a picture?"

Terra grinned back, more with his teeth than his humor. D'tanesse chuckled, a soundless burst. He finished the girth then went to Terra and turned him east with both hands on his shoulders.

"Look on the horizon, there. That red star will be invisible when the sun rises, but it is a lateral star. That means it moves across the horizon instead of toward or away from it. You can count the night hours by it. It's all very technical. It is the fourth hour currently, that is all you need to know. Dawn will come just before the sixth."

"I know about the time stars." Terra did not know about that particular one, for the time stars were hard to see in the forest, but he wasn't going to admit that to D'tanesse. Besides, he knew about it now.

"He knows about the time stars," D'tanesse echoed, calling over his shoulder to Troy.

"Be quiet, 'Tan."

"What should I do if something happens?" Terra asked low, close to his ear.

D'tanesse knew what 'something' meant. The grin faded. "If something happens," he said, staring at the wells of sand near their feet. "You wake us up, of course. And pray she uses that sword."

Something did not happen before dawn. Terra paced a square around his prone companions, watching the edge of the sky and the friendly red star, until it was swallowed in green-yellow light. Siegra's bow remained in his constant grip. Occasionally he switched hands, rubbing away moisture from his palms. Troy had his bow still. It rested across her torso, held in place by her fingers across the grip. A smile tugged at Terra's mouth.

Teyeda sat up during the false dawn, rubbing his face, and stood to take his turn on watch. When Terra began to protest, Teyeda laid a hand on his shoulder and pulled him closer.

"Things will get harder," he confided. "This may be the last rest we have before it's over."

Terra couldn't argue Teyeda's logic. He would not be able to put off sleep forever. If he wanted to protect Troy he must be able in body. It was comforting, too, that Teyeda was very strong, regardless that his strength would help little against another sandstorm or other attack of the elements.

Still, he lingered. "Why did you come, Teyeda? You could have stayed in Yettmis."

It was hard to tell in the pre-dawn, but Teyeda's blink seemed surprised. "I will tell you, sometime."

Sometime, meaning not now.

Terra wondered, as he lay down beside Troy, if the thought of staying behind had entered Teyeda's mind in earnest. That was a comforting thought. It meant the man was trustworthy, whatever his reasons.

Troy was awake. Her head was turned so the scar near her left eye was hidden against her rolled-up cloak. There was no obvious emotion on her face as far as Terra could tell. She didn't seem angry, and he decided that was good enough. They both were still beneath the mutual weight neither would voice. She did not reach for him except with her eyes, a line between them. He might have imagined it, but he was grateful nonetheless.

His eyes closed on their own. When he opened them again, she was on her feet in the full daylight, tightening Laic's girth. Terra struggled to stand and went, stumbling, to mount Gray.

Chapter Twenty-Six

The day passed as quickly as a week. Troy took the lead, loping and then trotting southeast. Terra tried to ride beside her, but Laic's longer legs easily outpaced Gray's and Terra soon fell a full length behind. It was just as well, he decided. His duty was to watch and protect, and he could do it better from behind anyway. If anything came up behind them, he would meet it first, and whatever threat she did not notice, he would notice for her.

They rested. They rode. They ate scraps brought from Yettmis, relieving hunger for a few short hours. They rode then rested again. Nothing happened in the afternoon or in the evening.

Night. The sky sank down close to the earth and woke him. Terra felt the sensation against his skin, a new physical weight added to the one constantly in his chest. The air felt like it was being compressed from above, but it did not resist him when he sat up and grabbed Siegra's bow. D'tanesse was on watch, standing just to Terra's left. He was singing very softly. Terra looked at the sky. The stars were as small as they were usually, but they felt too close.

"D'tanesse." Terra tried to speak. His voice struggled to stay in his throat, from thirst or panic.

"Elaa, elaa, warri—" D'tanesse turned around and the song stopped. "Yes?"

Beyond the warning meant to alert D'tanesse of the obvious—the sky is sinking—Terra didn't know what to say. He sat with his arms propped in the sand, blinking.

"Try not to wake everyone." D'tanesse turned back around.

The compressed sensation abated slightly, enough so Terra could stand without fear of bumping his head on the sky, or whatever it was hanging over them.

"Did you feel that?" His voice still resisted him. Thirst, this time.

D'tanesse slid his hands into two pockets near his waist, one green and one blue, and searched the distance. He rolled his shoulders once, scowled, then widened his eyes at Terra. "Did you feel it?"

"Something is wrong with the air." Terra ground the words through his teeth. Was he dense?

"Nothing is wrong. Not yet."

"Does the sky always collapse when you sing?"

"It wasn't him if that's what you're worried about." Now he looked amused.

"It's not funny."

"It is, a little."

"What did you do?"

"You're becoming hard to resist, do you know that?"

Terra closed his mouth and tipped his head to the side, waiting for the answer he wanted. Raelcun would have approved.

"Alright, I was singing. Calling really, to Elaa. So there, nothing to worry about."

"Will you shut your mouths!"

They both turned toward Troy, who burst into a sitting position as she spoke, grinding fistfuls of sand at her sides.

"Now look," D'tanesse complained, "you woke her."

"You were the one who was singing," Terra snapped.

"Was I?" D'tanesse sounded aghast, but he may as well have been laughing. Neither did he flinch when confronted by Troy's stare that threatened to chew through him.

She reached over without quitting the threat and shook Core's shoulder. "Get up. We're moving."

Again she took the lead, still heading southeast. Terra brought Gray beside D'tanesse. "Tell me what you were doing. I would like to know why as well."

"I told you. I was singing."

"What does it mean?"

D'tanesse fiddled with the reins. "It's the essence of an agreement." He took a breath, saw Terra do the same to speak again and hurried on before he could. "But it's more than that. In the book of Esobir, there are many songs and sayings exploring Elaa. The Presence is a mystery, was a mystery even in the time of Aenti EirNin. They did not even have a name for the Presence in the beginning."

"Didn't they have elaa? The stone?"

"They knew of it, but it was extremely rare. Almost no one was proficient with it and few knew of its properties. No, they found out about Elaa through the Dreams."

"Like the one about Cathylon?"

"Aenti EirNin was very perceptive, but on her own she could never have predicted what would come of the people who lived after her. Look at it this way." D'tanesse switched the reins to his left hand and twisted to face Terra, resting his right hand on Blue's hip behind the saddle. "You had no idea I existed and lived for all these years, until we met in Camil Askanda. If

I knew about you and decided to meet you, I would have to make myself known to you. I would send you a message by some means or another, or send someone to tell you about me, or go meet you in person."

"But I might run into you by accident or hear about you from travelers, without your knowledge."

"Yes, indeed you might, because we live on the same piece of land. But if I were someone altogether different, someone you could not sense or see on your own power, who even lived somewhere you could not get to unless I took you there, or hear about unless I told you, then it would be up to me to make that happen. If I wanted you to be able to find me, I must look for you first."

Core, riding just ahead of them and listening to the conversation, turned around then. His mouth was a little open, his expression incredulous. Terra was sure he himself looked about the same. He closed his mouth and swallowed. His tongue scratched the back of his throat.

"And that is what has happened with Elaa," D'tanesse progressed. "The Presence wished to make itself known to Aenti EirNin and did so by the Dreams. Aenti in turn wrote it all down, and the book came to us. Then we realized we had a Dream of our own, a message from Elaa: the stone, which we call elaa because there is no better way to describe it."

"The Mind and the stone…" Terra was glad Gray still walked on her own while he sat reeling with impossible thoughts. Except, these thoughts were not so impossible. Terra's mind moved back over what D'tanesse had told him, looking for somewhere to latch on.

"You said the song is an agreement. What is the agreement?"

D'tanesse did not answer right away. Core turned back around eventually. Terra blinked, coming to himself—he was forgetting to keep watch. A search of the area around them revealed nothing unusual, but he made sure to pay attention to his surroundings better. The only sound for a few moments was the steady mush of hooves pushing through sand. When D'tanesse finally spoke, it was with complete reverence.

"'In the Place Between, agreement made fast flies the word, far until spoken changes through doorways into stone living become stone, become ruler living. Elaa, elaa, warrior's hand receiving.'"

After a pause, Terra asked, "What does it mean?"

"It means a lot of things." D'tanesse shifted back around and studied the tangle his fingers had made in the reins. Blue bobbed his head to the rhythm of walking, ignoring the fiddlings going on that tickled his mouthpiece. Muddy foam obscured the corners of his wide mouth and dripped occasionally from them.

"Llynx, we should water the horses." D'tanesse directed his voice over Blue's head, between his speckled ears.

"I'm out of water," was her reply over her shoulder.

D'tanesse looked at Terra, who shook his head, despairing to be reminded.

"I have some." Teyeda patted the flask tied to the back of his saddle. "We will need more soon though."

"It's another day at least to the river," D'tanesse muttered, and began to dig through his pockets.

"No, D'tanesse." Troy hardly had to look back to guess what he was doing.

"One flask is not enough for five horses," he defended. "Unless you'd like to walk the rest of the way after they are dead."

"Using elaa now will bring the king straight to us."

"He is going to come to us in any case."

"There is no well in sight," Terra pointed out, looking from Troy ahead of him to D'tanesse beside him. Then for good measure he scanned in all directions.

"That's alright." D'tanesse dismounted and squatted in the sand where Blue stopped. "We don't need one this time."

Core slid from his saddle as well and lay down, closing his eyes. Terra, reluctant to lose at least the impression of traveling, guided Gray around to see what D'tanesse was doing, and to finish their conversation. "Will it protect us? Is that the agreement?"

He was scooping a hollow in the sand. "That depends on what you mean. If you mean at certain times a certain person is shown the means to use elaa as a defense, then yes."

Troy made an irritated noise. She also remained mounted.

"So, Elaa will protect us with the stone. It is on our side," Terra reasoned.

D'tanesse stopped digging and peered up at him. "Do not misunderstand. The stone is not our friend. Elaa is not your mother, at least not as far as I can tell. The Mind does not take any special consideration for us except as much as it has already shown—which is substantial if you think about it. Following certain laws produces certain results. I can't tell you how most of it works and I can't tell you why. I didn't invent the Mind, I'm just telling you what we've found out so far."

"We won't be finding anything more either, now that the book is gone."

D'tanesse turned, directing his squint toward Troy. "Don't sound so satisfied."

He might have slapped her, for the way she flinched. "I'm not."

"I'm sure." He turned back to the hole in front of him. He had made a shallow well the width of a bucket. Now he tugged from a small pocket over his breast, a tear-shaped stone as long as his thumb and twice as wide. Troy moved away. Teyeda followed.

"Why do you provoke her?" Terra watched them go.

"You ask a lot of questions." D'tanesse extended the hollow lengthwise, making a trough about six inches deep. Into the center of this he dropped the tear-shaped ornament, draping the attached leather string over the side. Over the stone he splashed some water from Teyeda's flask. Little shimmers, blue, pink and silver pearl, slicked the stone's surface.

"That's what one does to find out what they don't know."

"You may not enjoy the answers."

"When enjoying myself becomes more important than living and protecting Troy, I'll keep quiet."

D'tanesse looked up at him again, and again he was chuckling in mockery, a sound Terra was growing used to. "You can protect her alright, except can you protect her from herself?"

"I don't see how that m—"

"It matters very much. You might follow behind her, keeping all danger from reaching her, and you'd probably do very well." He flicked the leather string back and forth across one side of the trough. The stone resting on the bottom was now surrounded by a patch of sand several shades darker than the rest where the water had seeped into the ground. "But unless she comes to terms with certain fears and decisions, she will destroy herself from the inside."

"How do you know that?"

"How can you not?" He tugged at the string again, like a boy bored with his fishing line. "It is something we all do. My father, my mother. Me. My father and I spent hours perfecting little potions and concoctions made with elaa. I thought he did it to spend time with me as much as to learn. Even when he extended into the destructive properties, poisons, things that twisted the potential of the stone for the worse, I thought little of it. I simply wanted to be with him.

"My mother tried so hard to please my father—she tried too hard. When he needed to be challenged, she acquiesced, until he grew intolerant to command or change. It was her only flaw, but it was key to their ruin. There you are, old fellow. Drink up."

Blue pushed his lips into the puddle forming around the tear-shaped stone. The dark stain had grown while they talked.

"That makes water?" Terra pointed at the stone.

"No, it attracts water. Also, as it does, the water seems to pull on itself, attracting more water at a faster rate." He lifted the string, and as the stone began to come out of the puddle, the puddle stretched up from its center to follow the stone.

"And the water comes from…"

"Underground. It is there in minuscule pockets of trapped moisture. This will be enough for the horses until we can reach the river." He dropped the stone back down, and the water mushroomed over itself without splashing. The trough was half full within a minute, and filling fast. Terra climbed down from Gray and freed his empty flask from the saddle bindings while she drank.

"We've crossed the hottest part of the desert," D'tanesse said, watching him. "I thought by now they would have caught us."

"I'm glad they haven't."

"I'm not sure if I am glad or worried."

Terra remembered Sema and lowered his eyes. He dipped his flask into the trough. D'tanesse observed with lowered eyelids, as if he were watching something else happen and didn't like it at all. Before Terra could think of something to say, D'tanesse rose, stepped over the trough and walked after Troy who was crouched with Teyeda near a small formation of rock. Terra finished filling his flask, drank from it and filled it again. The water was very cold, and it had a peculiar taste that made Terra's mouth tingle. His stomach stretched reluctantly around what was not food, but his throat and mouth were relieved.

Even with the horses sucking great gulps of water, and Terra filling five flasks, it filled and then overflowed the trough. He found the leather string and lifted it out of the water. The stone came up dangling on the end of the string, pulling a cone of liquid with it. Terra raised his arm higher. The water rose, stretched, thinned, and finally dropped back into the trough. This time, without the stone, it splashed.

D'tanesse returned with Troy and Teyeda. Terra shook Core awake, gave him some water, and then they rode on.

"What is it made of?" Terra handed D'tanesse the tear-shaped stone on its leather string.

"Elaa stone, ground to powder. One abalone shell also ground, and liquid jasper from Seya Wul, the island of the Seawolves." D'tanesse wiped the stone with the hem of his sleeve, blew on it, and wiped it again. "Then it's pressed and fired like a piece of pottery." He wrapped the string around the stone and tucked it into the pocket from which it came. “Also there is a pinch of mint.”

“Mint? That is a little odd.”

D’tanesse shrugged. “I did not invent this recipe. I merely used it. They work out for the most part.”

“You mean not all the time?”

“Elaa stone responds to different people in slightly different ways. Very strongly to one person, not as much to the next. If Llynx had used it, we might have an ocean. Or at least a flood.”

“I am not stupid enough to draw that much attention to our location,” put in Troy, who was listening but of course not looking at them while she rode just ahead.

“I hardly touched it,” D’tanesse informed her, “and besides, we don’t want the king to forget about us.”

“We don’t want him to catch us in the open desert either, if possible.”

“He will not catch us in the open,” D’tanesse insisted. “We are barely a day away from the river, and the forest is just beyond that.”

Troy did not answer.

At dawn, they stopped again to rest. Terra took his turn on watch, walking a rough square around the others in his self-trained method. Counting his steps. Counting the stars that slowly vanished in the growing light. Watching the wisp of dust or cloud that occupied a point on the horizon from the direction they’d come. Ignoring his hunger and roaring thirst. Ignoring fatigue by distracting himself with movement. Counting his steps again.

Troy was up after him to take watch. He saw her sit up, dragging her upper body out of its comfortable hollow in the sand, and went to offer her his hand. To his surprise she took it and stood.

There was nothing to say, and he didn’t want to wake the others, so Terra decided to smile and release her hand. He turned and walked back to his point of lookout roughly two yards away at the edge of a sand embankment. From there, he could see the round brushes of treetops along the far line of the world. They were nearly transparent at this distance, but he knew them. The ground stretched away below the embankment, marked here and there with hesitant bushes like twisted sentries at the edge of the wilderness.

“Here.” Troy pressed Terra’s bow against his hand.

Terra shook his head. “I have another. You will need that one.”

“I already have your knife.”

“It is your knife.” He rubbed his hand across his eyes.

She lowered the bow. Terra squinted, trying to count the trees.

"Aren't you going to sleep?"

"Yes." Terra stepped over the sloped edge of the hill and sat down, sinking into the sand a little as it made way for him. "I was going to sleep right here."

"Why not stay with your companions?"

"You don't." Terra made a pillow of his hands and smiled up at her. "And I can't see the sun as well from where they are."

"Why do you need to see the sun?"

"Because I like it. I like knowing we've lived to see it rise again." He tried to resist, but the yawn came up anyway and made his eyes water.

She sat down beside him. "How are you always so pleasant? You're exactly the same as when we first met."

"I don't know. How can you be so unpleasant?" Fatigue made his body feel numb. It also made him a little careless. "You were not always so."

Troy looked at him, perhaps trying to decide what to say. She seemed to give up, instead resting a hand on his shoulder. "Go to sleep."

Terra felt a light chuckle forming in his chest. Troy looked away. Her face in the dawn was stoic, but there was a clear brightness beneath her skin and the scar.

While he slept, he was aware of her hand still resting on his shoulder. It stayed there through his dreams, real and warm, while the world grew brighter against his eyelids.

* * * *

"Where did you find those?" D'tanesse's voice ripped through his sleep.

"Ki, 'Tan, will you shut your mouth!"

"Where did you find those?" he asked again, quieter.

"They grow under rocks, out of the sun."

"Why didn't I guess so?" His voice held a tinge of sarcasm. "I know where they grow."

"Ki…" She growled. "Teyeda and I found them under a rock last night while you were playing with the stone."

Terra opened his eyes. Troy was sitting cross-legged beside him on her cloak, shredding some pale green plants with her dagger. They were no longer than her forearm, with round leaves resembling hearts. The sun had rushed up the sky, and now the small bushes had stark shadows stretching out from their bases.

Troy stopped crushing leaves and looked at the sky. "Your name means Head of Knowledge. You might at least live up to that."

D'tanesse was lying on his stomach, looking down over the edge of the incline. His arms supported his round chin. "I promise you, my head is full of knowledge. But knowledge does no good if there is no one to listen."

She twisted the knife, severing stalk from leaf with a wet snap.

Terra sat up, rubbing his eyes. They began to burn, and he quickly stopped. "Are we moving?"

"Soon." Troy stacked the stems in a pile before her and held up her hand. D'tanesse handed her a small, square stone, and she struck the knife blade on it, sending sparks flying. The roots smoldered then blossomed into a flame at a gentle breath from her lips. The stalks were consumed in a moment, sending up an earthy scent and making Terra's mouth water. He had not eaten a full meal since leaving Yettmis. Troy made sure the stalks were incinerated to powder ash and then scooped up a handful of sand. She mixed the sand and the ashes, scattering them around her, leaving no trace of her activity. She gathered up the leaves and said finally, "We should wake the others."

Terra took a deep breath for strength and stood up. His muscles protested, pinching his bones, but he stood up anyway. He blinked heavy eyelids and watched Troy roll the harvested leaves between her palms. "What are those?"

"Strength." She handed him one. "Eat it."

He put the offered leaf tentatively into his mouth. It had what he thought was a 'green' taste, like the forest after a spring rain. Fresh, with a hint of washed earth. After rolling it around in his mouth for a moment, he decided he rather liked it. Troy handed a leaf to each of the others, and they chewed on them while they climbed back onto their saddles.

His hunger faded away as they rode down the dune and jogged the horses ahead through the scattered twisted bushes. The green taste of the leaf was still on his tongue. As Gray broke into a gentle lope (she did not like to fall far behind the others), he realized his muscles no longer tightened in pain with each rocking stride. His eyelids felt lighter, and he felt refreshed and warm all over. The others seemed to feel better as well. Even their voices seemed brighter when they talked.

Terra pulled even with Troy. "What were those?"

"Khoni. The Ancients ate them for strength on long journeys. The leaves take away the effects of cold, hunger, fatigue and pain for a time. They are rare, especially in the desert. This will be enough to last us through the day, at least."

"I wish we had enough to eat every day. Imagine what it would have been like to forget hunger altogether on this journey."

Troy shook her head. "It would not be good," she said. "The relief is deceiving. If one never knows fatigue, he will never sleep. If he never knows hunger or thirst, he will never eat or drink. He would soon die for lack of nourishment. The leaves are good for a short time, but to take them every day would be fatal."

Chapter Twenty-Seven

The sun arched from horizon to horizon. Clouds tumbled over and over themselves in front of it. The ground stretched beneath Troy like a taut hide marked with liver spots of rock and brush. They had seen only hints of pursuit since leaving Yettmis three days ago. She hoped it was because of the war-host's size, keeping it to a lumbering speed.

The steady mush of hooves pelting sand became rocky thuds then pleasant thumps and swishing over brown dirt, ferns and foliage. The Otnas bumped her left shoulder blade every time Laic's lead leg reached forward and caught ground. She wore it not for protection but as a beacon, begging pursuit. She left it wrapped, indulging in the unreal hope of never using it as more than a beacon. If they reached the forest in time the hope might become a reality.

Terra and even Core were more practical: their bows were ready in hand, lengthwise in front of them. Sometimes when they walked the horses Core hung his over a shoulder to free his fingers, but Terra was ready at any moment to lift and shoot. However, their bows were only made of wood and sinew. She had the Otnas, a beast among weapons. She also had Terra's bow and her two hands if the need for fighting mere men arose. In truth, flesh and blood hardly worried her anymore.

She looked at the sky again. The clouds were like foam surging over blue water. She felt dizzy as if she were sinking headfirst into its mass. The wind fought with itself, hot and cold, trying to make up its mind.

"There it is." Terra smiled down at the leafy shrubs congregating along a snake of water. They had reached the river Aganus. It was wider than Troy remembered. It looked nearly half a mile to the far bank and the trees. She tried not to stare at the water.

They crossed on one of the merchant rafts. Teyeda worked the towrope, pulling them across the water toward the trees. Terra and Core watched them grow closer with eager eyes, but their smiles were pained. D'tanesse rested his forearms across Blue's damp shoulders. "Does anyone live in the forest anymore? Maybe we should warn them who come behind us."

Troy stood facing Laic with her feet braced apart. Her fingers tied and retied leather saddle bindings. Her lips pressed against each other until she could feel the blanched ring of white forming around them.

"No one has lived in Kcen since it was—" Terra turned on the edge of her vision toward Core.

"Burned." Core made the word an audible grimace.

In heavy silence they reached the far bank, remounted and rode into the shadow of the trees.

Terra and Core led them past many landmarks: a dry stream bed, a tree swarming with bees in the warm, damp air, a blue-black rock formation with a hollow at its base. They rode past streams with moss-fringed boulders. They rode past shingled hickories and spindle aspens. A perfume of wet, vivid earth rose around them when they hopped over branches fallen across the shrunken dirt road.

Evening was losing its luster when they came over a small hill and looked down on the ruins of Kcen. Troy climbed the rise crouched forward in the saddle, then sat back hard. Laic halted, stiff-legged. A curl of dark brown dust lifted in a final shaft of sunlight left by the evening. Terra stopped beside her.

The road had once cut through the middle of the village all the way to the chieftain's hall. Now it was obscured by overgrowth, and only one wall was still standing to mark the grand structure. Even less remained of the houses that once lined the road.

Troy dismounted, landing softly on the balls of her feet in a thick carpet of purple lupines. Black dirt smudged against the toes of her boots as she began walking.

This is Kcen, the forest village… Terra's young voice spoke from Troy's memories. Green aspen shoots poked above the flowers, tugging at the hem of her cloak as she moved. Charred sticks and debris cracked underfoot.

"We shouldn't stay here tonight." Their voices were muted behind her.

"It's going to be dark soon."

"Is the well open?" D'tanesse had caught up with them.

The well. There it was, standing vigil between the ruined Hall and wayfaring house, claimed by the forest. Troy toed the plants encircling its base as she passed it and glimpsed blackened stones.

Ki, you have a spine. What's your name…? Mytch's voice surfaced, from their first meeting. She turned her head and swallowed automatically.

"It's only overnight, Terra. We can't travel any farther…" They were still talking, arguing.

She turned and left them behind, wading through the flowers and between crumbling skeletons of log houses. Her palm brushed the remains of a wall and came away black.

To her left was the copse. New, young aspen trunks were growing thicker than before, covering the blackened remains of their predecessors.

"I hereby bestow on you the name Troy. Rise Warrior, and live a life worthy of the name..."

In her mind Mytch still lay in front of the copse, lifeless eyes staring at the sky. She kept walking straight ahead. Eventually, as she left the burn radius, her steps crunched dead leaves, then swished through overgrown potato plants. Ahead of her was a thick, gnarled tree. Its branches spread out from the trunk in an upward spiral. She stood at its base where two roots bulged up, forming a small hollow. She nudged the heel of her boot into it, resting her shoulder on the tough brown bark. Here, Terra had crouched beside her while she dug her toes into the soft soil...

Are you lost, Llyna...?

I don't know...

With both hands she reached over her shoulder and lifted the Otnas out of the baldric.

Are you lost, Llyna? Are you lost?

Troy knelt down and lay the Otnas beside her.

The soil was just dirt now, buried in a layer of decaying leaves. Troy set the sword beside her and pawed the mess aside with both hands. Filaments clung to her skin in clotted strings, smearing brown over the black stain on her palms. She dug into the dirt with her fingernails and tips, scraping a long hole in the earth.

A tinge of smoke cut the air and she froze for a moment before realizing where it came from. The others were building a fire. That meant meat. Good. They were all past malnourishment, not to mention exhaustion.

The wind came down through the trees, nudging loose debris about on the ground. It ruffled the aspens and they sighed, a chorus of dry rattles. She dug harder, scraping in time to surfacing memories.

She was walking into the copse with Mytch, seeing Terra for the first time in four years. She was in the warm hearth-room. She was talking with Sienna. Crying with Imra. Being hugged by Cail. Gazing up at Harok.

A shadow fell across the trunk in front of her. Troy looked, then jumped to her feet. Her knife was instantly in her hand.

A girl stood in front of her. A threadbare dress of dingy gray clung to her slight frame. One sleeve was shorter than the other, stopping in a frayed line at her sun-browned shoulder.

"What do you want?" Troy was angry at herself for not hearing the girl approach, even though she did not appear to be a threat.

The girl's wide gray eyes played over Troy's face before she turned her head, watching a deer rustle through the potato plants to their right.

"What do you want?" Troy tried again, putting her knife away in its sheath. The initial shock of seeing her began to wear off, and Troy wondered just how the girl had managed to surprise her. Perhaps she had been in the tree. The girl moved a few noiseless steps toward the deer and crouched, holding out her palm. The deer gazed at her with shimmering black eyes then advanced and shoved its nose into her outstretched hand. She turned toward Troy. Ash-blond hair drifted across her cheek like thistledown. One side of her mouth lifted in a smile.

Troy stepped forward. "Imra?"

The girl's smile faded, and she stood suddenly. The deer shied back and bounded away.

"Imra…it is Troy. I have missed you…"

Imra maintained her queer smile, but did not reply.

"Are you hurt? Ill?" Troy tried in vain to make her speak. "Do you have food? Do you need anything?"

Imra blinked at her.

Troy remembered the arrowhead she still wore. She searched for the string under her tunic and pulled it from her neck. It spun at the end of its thread, suspended from her fingers. "See this? Do you know it?" Troy held it up before Imra's face. "You gave it to me."

No answer. Not even an acknowledging look.

"Please tell me you remember…"

Imra smiled again, but it seemed only a polite smile now. Her eyes moved past Troy as footsteps crunched, coming nearer. Imra withdrew to the far end of the potato field. Troy watched her wade through the leafy tops that reached her thighs and sighed. The arrowhead fell to the dirt at her feet.

Terra stopped beside her a moment later. "What are you doing?"

"Your sister, Imra, lives."

He lowered his head, pressing the toe of his boot on the dirt mounded around Troy's digging. "In body, yes."

"Does she speak to you?"

He shook his head.

"That plant she discovered…"

"I remember it." He bent to pick up the arrowhead.

"Mytch was going to take it to Yettmis and show Yessac. He thought she could do well as an Esobir, being naturally gifted."

Terra looped the string around his fingers, making a crimson line between his second and third knuckles. "Are you burying your sword?"

Troy pressed her mouth closed so she couldn't bite her lower lip. The urge had been recurring in the desert, ever since their reunion. "I thought when I was given it that it was just a sword. They told me it was made of elaa but—"

"Who told you?"

"The Esobir who live in the village of Klenit, beyond the mountains." She had mentioned this to him, but briefly, on her last visit here. It was no surprise he didn't remember, though she could never forget. She would never forget telling him either. They had been on that hill in the clearing just beyond the grandfather tree, as Terra called it. The hill where she finally told him the truth. The hill where he'd kissed her.

No, she would never forget.

"The Otnas is what they called it, a weapon but also a counterpoint—light met with dark. One element can null another element, or can undo it altogether."

Terra shifted, but was listening. His eye was a dab of clear brown above his cheekbone. His mouth was closed and his head tipped to the side, attentive as she spoke.

"I used it for the first time, not long after it was in my possession. I told you Machaun and his warband found me."

Terra nodded. She had said 'us' when she related this the first time. He didn't seem to notice, or if he did, was not inclined to remark.

"Do you remember the first time you shot your bow and hit a target in the center?"

He nodded again.

"Do you remember the elation, knowing you could do something you couldn't before? Knowing you would feel it again, stronger each time your skill increased, and as you hit new targets?"

"I know that is how I kept going. If I could not progress at bow and arrow, I would have to start over with something else."

Troy looked at him and briefly lost control of her thought. His face was unchanged, but he seemed older and wiser than she remembered, even from yesterday. Suddenly she was glad she chose to confide in him. She found her words again. "That is how it feels to use elaa. Some describe it as awakening. A certain thing slowly becomes clearer and you realize how to command. The Otnas is elaa. It was made by the Ancients with methods we have not been able to duplicate. It functions as no other thing made of elaa. It is far more powerful than any of them."

"How did you find this out?" He rested his weight on his heel, turning to face her straight on. His head was still lowered and tipped to the side, eyes concerned beneath the soft ridge of his eyebrows.

"I used it on a man." She hadn't spoken about it out loud to anyone since it happened. "He dissolved when it cut him."

The wind pressed between them, rippling Terra's tunic and Troy's breeches while he stared at her. The arrowhead was hidden in his fist, and the crimson line tightened on his fingers.

"It responded to my will. I wanted him destroyed and he was destroyed. I have killed men in combat when it was required, to stay alive. But no man should die as that one did. We were not meant to be undone. Sometimes I wonder if we were meant to die at all. We do, I know, but not like that. Not by my hand." Her voice faded as her soul shrank away from the memory, refusing to engage.

Terra stood and put his hand on her shoulder, drawing her a little closer. "It's good you understand the danger of that power. It makes our situation a little safer, if only a little, knowing we can trust your discernment."

"I don't know what to do with it."

He smiled, lowering his voice as well. "Neither do I."

That was not exactly helpful, but for a moment the iron trap around her heart eased its pressure.

"What can we do for Imra?" She cast a look in Imra's direction. The girl was crouched, pulling potatoes from a plant she'd unearthed.

"Nothing that I know of." Terra sighed. "Core and I tried to care for her, but she prefers the forest to a family now. I think her mind has withdrawn."

"I wish I could give her something. Even a dress, if I had one."

Terra muttered something she could not hear and studied the dirt, withdrawing somewhat himself. Imra selected a potato from her small pile. She held it up, brushing lumps of dirt from dusty brown peel, and then bit into it.

"May I take that?" Troy held out her hand for the arrowhead.

He lowered it by its thread into her palm, then pressed his hand over it, flat against hers. His skin was cold, mottled white from clenching his fist.

For the instant she held her breath, his eyes seemed to grow softer, ardent, saying the things his hand could not. She breathed in against the sensation of drowning and tasted a remnant of smoke doused in the turgid salt-tinged air.

"I want—" She breathed in again. Pulled her hand away. "To leave it for her. Maybe it will help."

She wrapped the string around a branch close to the trunk and tied it. When she turned around, he was struggling to smile. His gaze quickly dropped to the ground. Little leaves skipped and rolled over the dirt, getting trapped in the rut between their feet.

Behind him, D'tanesse was approaching. Both hands were in pockets at his waist to hold his coat closed. The bottom belled out around his legs, a windborne half-circle.

The iron trap began to close again in her chest, pinching so hard she thought something would snap. "I can see why Core is so protective of you."

Terra's scoff was faint. "Core does not want me involved in anything unusual."

D'tanesse was close enough now that Troy could see him open his mouth, about to call to them.

"You're a treasure." The words instantly stung her ears, and she shut her mouth against anything more.

"So are you," Terra breathed without looking up.

"Teyeda snared a rabbit—" D'tanesse began, then saw the Otnas on the ground beside the rut. "What are you doing?"

Troy turned her back to him and stared down at the product of her digging, deciding how to answer. Her strong resolve had waned since she began digging. Yet by keeping the thing she endangered them all, and for what? They could not hide with the Otnas, and they were already exhausted. Things could not continue this way forever.

D'tanesse pinched her shoulder between his thumb and fingers and pulled her around to face him. His coat flapped open on one side. "Tell me what you are doing."

"I'm doing what I came here to do." She raised her chin. "Let go of me."

The wind pulled thin wisps of black hair onto his tight forehead. His eyebrows slashed down toward the bridge of his nose. "I cannot believe this."

"Let go of me."

He pushed her away and thrust his hand at the ground. "This? This is your plan? Do you think—do you honestly think you can run forever?"

"He is chasing us because of this."

"He is chasing you! Because you have this!" D'tanesse drew each word out as if she were deaf.

"Then let him find me in a normal way. With his eyes."

"And when he catches you, how will you defend yourself? With sticks?"

"It is a big island."

"The people living on this island need what you have. I need you. Sema needs you! If you care for nothing else think of her!"

"What do you want me to do, D'tanesse? Run back into the desert?

Fight to the death in glorious battle?"

Terra grunted, half turning away before turning back to scowl at them both. He began to speak, perhaps to mediate, but it was too late.

"Better than this nonsense! You have the means to help us all, and you would bury it in the ground?" D'tanesse's cry strained high and broke.

The giant hickory groaned above them, twisted by a sudden wind flurry. Heat rose in her chest and neck while she forced her expression blank, one lifted eyebrow daring him to continue.

He dared.

"She gave up her life in Yettmis to help me look for you! She has put all of her hope in you to deliver Cathylon. She risks her life at your request and for her sake, as well as yours, I will not let you play the coward!" He was poised on his toes, ready to jump at her. He probably would have, but he was not done yelling. "If it kills me, I will not lie down and let him have this victory! I will not sit back while the one I love dies because of your stubborn, thick ignorance! Now pick up the sword!"

He was beyond angry, she realized, well on the way to hysterics. Small wonder since they were all exhausted and worn thin, waiting for something to happen. "I don't want her to die. I wish no one had to die. I know where she has put herself, and I did not ask her to go to Daehexa for frivolous reasons. But the Otnas is too dangerous to keep. If I am killed and the king or Machaun takes it—"

"If you keep running we will all be killed, one by one as we drop on the road!"

"You don't understand what the Otnas is capable of!" She finally raised her voice. He would now raise his, but she couldn't help herself.

"I know what he is capable of! I only hope the sword is able to end what he started."

"I said I would do what I must. I did not say I would use the Otnas."

"You have a responsibility—"

"And I am doing what I must!"

"I cannot believe what I am hearing!"

"I am not the Deliverer! Why can't you understand?"

He shouted, his face shaded red. "Yes, you are!"

Unbelievable. Anger chewed the last shreds of her self-control. "Why? Because I have a weapon? You don't know how much power this agreement holds!"

"But you know! You have known it from the moment you first held it."

She shook her head, eyes clenching shut on their own. "Stop it."

His words kept coming. Terra had given up trying to interject and just stood watching. Imra ignored them all, dining placidly beside the swaying potato plants.

"You knew before you went to Kcen, before Camil Askanda. All that time helping the Seawolves, pretending to be ignorant, and you knew what you were!"

"I did not—"

He stepped forward as she drew back. "What are you waiting for, the world to end? The Otnas was passed to you because it was meant for you!"

The hot flush pounding through her died and cooled into a layer of bedrock. "You don't know what you're talking about."

"Do you want me to prove it to you? I was there the day it was brought to Cathylon by your mother! By the queen of the Seawolves!"

"Stop it! I don't know what you're talking about. Don't you dare say that!"

"It is passed to every ruler of the Seawolves since time out of mind, and they found out—your mother found out—"

She hit him. One second he was leaning forward, pressing the verbal attack, and the next second the back of her open hand flashed across his face. The snap reverberated, cutting through even the rustling gusts in the trees.

No one spoke.

D'tanesse clutched his face, twisted away by the shock of her hand. Then he recoiled. Sprang at her, hands reaching.

"You cannot turn awa—"

She raised her forearms, knocking his hands wide, and punched her palms against his chest. He crumpled. Landed on his back. Sprang up again. This time Terra caught him from behind and pulled him back.

"That's enough. Enough!"

"Don't you see Estimal wants you to give up?" D'tanesse struggled to wrench free. "He wants you to abandon your sword, so you cannot stand against him!"

"I don't mean to stand against him. That was a foolish thought I had, years ago." Troy shut her eyes briefly. She was tired of this. Tired of fighting him; of fighting everyone.

"You wanted revenge, years ago! You wanted to make him suffer because you had suffered. You cannot fight him with something so small!"

A line of blood slid from his grimacing mouth toward his chin. Troy stepped up to him and touched her thumb to the corner of his mouth, gently wiping the blood away.

He finally quieted, though his narrow chest heaved and he leaned against Terra's restraining grip. "If you hide, if you try to be someone you are not, it will destroy you and your companions. You were set apart for this. When you became Esobir, when you took the sword, you were marked. You cannot reject that so simply. Easier to take your heart, beating from your chest and replace it with a pebble to keep you alive."

Terra watched her over D'tanesse's shoulder, still holding onto him. Troy stepped back. The wind pressed up behind her, resisting. She took another step back, then turned her back on them. The clearing with the hill was visible from here, and she escaped to it with quick strides.

Chapter Twenty-Eight

In the clearing, the wind was stronger and colder. It scraped low, white clouds over the points of the trees. Troy turned her face away from them as she climbed the hill. She sat on the other side with the crest rising between her and the overgrown potato field. The grass hissed around her and the sky darkened. She looked up. It wasn't darkened by the coming of night only. Something had changed.

The pale clouds, streaming smoothly overhead, became a curtain between one space and another. At the same time they were the other space. They were impossible.

The hazy veil—what used to be sky and clouds ringed by tops of trees—cracked like glass in its center. The cracks shot in all directions outward, meeting green jagged points around the rim. It was a window. An overturned bowl. A long-legged spider straddling the trees over her.

Strings of black dripped from the crooked legs straight down to where she lay gasping on her back. Her skin was coated, drenched. Black, wet threads hit her face and slid down her cheeks, her temples, into her ears, mixing with the salt drops coming from her eyes.

The round body above her dilated, widened, and through it came a fingertip. Her mind, stretched to snapping for some comparison to reality, coiled tight around this horrible new image.

Through the hole came the finger, then four more fingers as the hole crackled open: a hand.

As her mind determined this was a true reality, her soul came alive to resist it. She knew the hand. She knew how it found her. Now she knew why D'tanesse hoped—could only hope, he said—the sword could counter the king.

It kept coming. First fingertips, then knuckles, then palm and wrist all translucent gray, thick as storm clouds, wearing the sky like a glove. Troy could not move. She was not even sure of the ground, or of her own limbs. She might try to stand only to find herself falling, drowning in the wet, black deluge. All of creation came to a crux at this point above her, outside of her, turned and pointed like a live blade at her center. Like an arrow in the hand of a hunter drawn full in the bow. She wanted to die, but to die would be an end. The world continued and she continued with it.

Get control of yourself, Troy! Get control! Get...

Her eyes closed on their own.

Breathe.

The black rain still soaked her. She heard it splatting the ground, crashing on swaths of grass. The grass was sharp beneath her arms and neck. Rubbing against her breeches, her thighs, her face.

Breathe. Breathe. Breathe.

She opened her mouth wide and drew a deep shuddering gasp. And another. Wet drops splashed onto her tongue and teeth.

Nothing has changed.

Resolve formed in her soul.

The grass stopped rubbing against her and was silent. Energy shivered through the air, not quite tangible, like the weight of a charged storm.

Nothing has changed. Open your eyes.

Her mind rejected the thought.

"L'abri…did you think you could hide here?"

Those words were not in her mind. They resonated like stones grinding underground, like thunder. Her hand found her dagger still in its sheath on her belt. Much good it would do against this.

"Are you…tired?" The last word died into a quaking thrum like laughter.

"Who are you?" She knew the answer, but she needed to speak. To hear herself; a real voice.

"You don't know?" The last word was drawn out in disgust.

Open your eyes. The thought came again. *You must move.*

She knew she could not. She could not fight now, alone against…this.

Nothing has changed. Our agreement stands.

It was shock, more than anything. Just as she knew who was profaning the sky and the very air she couldn't help pulling into her lungs, she knew where the whisper in her core came from. That shock set something at ease in her mind and she opened her eyes.

Two hands. Thick legs. His body was wrapped in filmy gray swaths of clouds like animal skins. Long stripes of black vapors stretched from the body to the cracks behind it. Two slashes of milky light were set in a face covered in streaming wisps like black hair. Like a doll on strings, moving on its own power, the body moved its head and then its lipless maw opened and the thunder came again.

"I…end this."

An arm lifted, dripping black strings of rain. The strings clung together and slid through his tightening fingers.

Move.

Her body was heavy. Troy's arms strained, pushing her shoulders and waist out of the fast-forming mud.

Now his hand held the strings in a bunch. They melted together into a single glistening rope. Their ends dragged in the grass, up the hill, a fishing line at the end of a rod. They snapped free, tiny curling tendrils whipping, arching up to follow the lead of the hand. They reached their pinnacle far above the trees, hanging in the salt-ridden air, and then snapped back down.

"Ki!" Troy gathered her feet and launched to the side. Displaced grass and mud shot into the air, stinging her cheeks and eyes. Troy leaped up and dashed down the hill. She couldn't tell which direction to take through the uneven circle of trees. Her mind registered only trees, nothing more. The Otnas, her key to lock away this nightmare, lay waiting somewhere beyond them.

The cloud hunter flicked his black whip into the trees ahead of her. The tendrils sliced into silver trunks, leaving charred black slits as they passed through. The trees toppled into one another like matchsticks, forming an impenetrable tangle. Troy struggled to stop in the slick mud. Her feet flew out from under her. A thick branch dropped across her leg, pinning her down. She twisted around to see the sky. The hunter heaved the whip back again. She grabbed her calf with both hands, working her leg free with hard jerks. The whip came down.

* * * *

"It's going to rain," Teyeda said as Terra and D'tanesse trudged up to their little camp by the well. A small fire glowed beneath a lashed spit. Teyeda slowly turned a skewered rabbit over the flames. "And the meat is close to done."

D'tanesse dropped the Otnas beside Troy's saddle and collapsed beside it in the dirt, stretching out on his stomach. His head found refuge in his folded arms.

Core looked a question at Terra.

"Troy is taking a walk." Terra did not say D'tanesse provoked her, but the assumption was general. He put his hand toward the fire, then worried a bit of meat from the steaming carcass. He could taste it even before it was on his tongue, burning hot. Food.

"She is very temperamental about the sword." D'tanesse's voice was subdued in the circle of his arms.

Terra sat down beside him, making himself chew the succulent tidbit longer than necessary before swallowing. "You might have approached the subject with some tact. She didn't know what she was going to do with it."

"She knows what is at stake. I see no point in wasting time."

"She won't come to your side if you goad her."

"I know that!"

"Then why do you do it?"

"Because I have secrets of my own and I don't know how to share them."

"You might as well be siblings. You're similar enough."

"I am her cousin."

Teyeda shook his head and nudged the fire with a blackened stick. A glowing log crumbled into a heap of orange embers.

D'tanesse lifted his head, finally speaking directly to them. "My father was the High King's brother. The High King, L'estim Glor, married Natug, queen of the Seawolves. L'abri was their daughter."

"Troy…"

"Or Llynx, or whatever she calls herself lately." D'tanesse sat up and brushed dirt from the front of his jacket, then pulled it closed to shield against the sudden chill wind.

Terra moved closer to the fire. Faint thunder grumbled in the distance. "Do you know why she calls herself Llynx?"

D'tanesse didn't answer for a moment, staring at some point beyond them, head tilted as if listening to a whisper.

"D'tanesse?"

"I have a fair enough guess." He blinked, coming back to the conversation, but his voice was distracted. "The word for Outcast in the Ancient language is Maanx. Llyna is the proper address for a young woman. She must have taken the two meanings and merged them, coming up with Llynx."

"That is just how she might feel. Neither true lady, nor true outcast."

D'tanesse's answer was drowned out by a second growl of thunder that could be felt as well as heard. His eyes snapped wide open, and he was on his feet. In the next instant, they were pelted with a sheet of rain. Water dripped from Terra's hair, over his nose and into his open mouth. The fire sizzled, hissed then died in a cloud of smoke and steam.

"Get up!" D'tanesse ran stumbling the way they had just come. "Llynx is in trouble!"

The wind carried a remnant of a scream to their ears. Terra's skin crawled as if to escape his body. He still had his bow over his shoulder, and his quiver now held a good amount of water as well as arrows. He pulled a shaft free as he sprinted after D'tanesse.

The air was hazed with falling water. They passed shapes of crumbling walls, ruined foundations slick in the deluge. The potato field was barely visible on their right.

D'tanesse suddenly doubled back, dodging Terra who was right behind him, shouting, "Keep on! I must get the sword!"

Terra recognized a human shape coming toward him. He started to cry out Troy's name, but it was Imra's dress and pale hair that became visible.

"Imra!" He caught her in his arms and held her. She twisted, tossing her head to look over her shoulder. A thick rope of hair struck his open mouth, and a sour earthy taste nearly gagged him before it was rinsed away. Imra moaned, a constant sound of wordless terror. Terra struggled to hold onto her, peering ahead into the murk. The trees just ahead stood in dark shadow, shimmering like a night-lit waterfall.

Before he heard the sound he felt it: the thud and crack of some huge thing hammering the earth. Imra convulsed, screaming into her hands. Terra clutched his sister against him and screamed also. "Troyyy!"

It was too late. Troy was surely crushed by what lay ahead. Defenseless without her sword. Killed because he hadn't sided with D'tanesse and made her take it.

"Imra, stay here. Core!" He screamed for his brother. Imra went limp, folding over on herself as she sank to the ground. "Core!"

Core was running toward them, but Terra didn't wait. He lowered Imra onto the leaves before stepping over her and running into the looming shadow that once was a hill in a clearing. Further into the shadow he could still see, but the view was weak and grainy. The hill was just a gray-green curve blocking his view of the trees beyond it. The grass was obliterated by the pelting rain.

Two shafts of light flashed over the clearing and he saw Troy hobbling away from a fallen tree. Patches of mud mottled her breeches, clinging to her hips and legs. Her skin looked like reflective wet glass beneath smears of more mud, as if she had been dipped in one then the other. The tree was snapped in two places, broken like a brittle twig beneath a cartwheel. Terra ran forward, shouting her name.

Troy looked up and saw him. Her eyes flew wide open, seeing not a friend but a new nightmare. Black mud streaked her forehead and dripped from her cheeks. "Go back! Back!"

Terra did not slow. Troy's hands were empty—even her knife was gone. He reached her side, ready with bow and arrow; ready to protect her with his life.

Troy dove into him and he went over onto his back. His chest and spine crunched together, squeezing his lungs. A thin black line snapped overhead, slamming into the ground beyond them. Grass and mud concussed, covering their bodies. Terra lay on his back beneath Troy. Choking. Spitting mud. Staring at the storm above them and…a man?

A human shape was suspended from the clouds. A human shape holding a solid black, curling…thing. As he lifted it, Terra saw the mass was long and tapered to the curling end. A whip. A whip of black water.

Ki, ki, ki!!

Now he knew what made that hammering thump, what had snapped the trees like dead pine needles. His chest released his lungs and he shouted, struggling from under Troy's weight. She rolled off him, limp on the ground.

"Troy!"

Her eyelids were partly closed. Blood ran from her temple in a pulsing rivulet. Terra looked up again as the specter's eyes narrowed and the whip whined as it snapped up again.

His bow was of no use. Terra scooped his arms beneath Troy's armpits and began to drag her backward toward the trees. At least they might have cover there. His heel slipped on a pocket of mud and he staggered, almost buckling. With a groan, a shout, he pulled Troy up and ran, lifting her body as high as he could. Her boots left two lines in the mud.

D'tanesse charged into the clearing, dropping the empty baldric to grip the Otnas in both hands.

Crushing pain stabbed Terra's ribs with each hoarse, desperate breath. He must reach the trees—he would reach the trees! His heels caught on something he couldn't see, and he crashed down. Troy landed face down beside him.

The specter dropped his hand.

D'tanesse hurtled the remaining yards toward them.

The whip twisted in the air, then cracked as it hurtled down. Terra threw his body over Troy and shut his eyes.

D'tanesse, screaming, slid to his knees. He swung the sword mightily over them. "Elaaaaahhh!"

A jarring impact shuddered above Terra's head. Energy shivered over him. He felt it like a puff of air tousling his hair, skin—and then it was gone again.

Terra raised his head and saw D'tanesse, gaping at his own hands clutching the sword hilt.

"It worked…" His eyes and mouth made three perfect circles in his head. Rain dripped from his nose.

Terra gaped back at him, trying to breathe. The sword flickered, bright white and then its usual blue.

D'tanesse didn't notice. He shook himself and got to his feet. "Go!" he yelled. "Take her!"

Terra picked up Troy again and this time made it to the trees. Teyeda met him, arms stretched to take her. Core knelt with his arms wrapped around Imra's shoulders. Only her hair and back were visible, and the bottoms of her feet as she was kneeling. Her face was pressed against his chest. Her shoulders heaved and shuddered. She might have been screaming or crying, or even laughing, but Terra was listening only for another thud and crack, the whine of the specter's whip coming for them again.

Troy's eyes fluttered open. "Terra—"

Terra and Teyeda lowered her to the ground. Teyeda knelt behind her, supporting her upper body. Terra clutched her hands.

"You are safe now, Troy." Of course, she wasn't. None of them were, but he said it anyway.

Troy twisted around, searching above her and seeing only trees. Her gaze dropped down and she saw D'tanesse standing alone in the clearing, a muddled figure in a long sodden coat. His profile was obscured by the gloom and haze of water. They could only see that his face was turned up to the man in the clouds.

Thunder, just thunder without the recoil of impact, rolled overhead.

"Because it is wrong!" D'tanesse shouted. His voice was keening, thin. "Because I cannot let you continue!"

"He is speaking to it!" Terra realized. "Ki! Why is h—"

The thunder responded: a longer roll, sharper.

"Because it is speaking to him." Troy sat up, gathering her legs beneath her. She flinched faintly, and Terra remembered her limping run.

"No, you cannot stand against this!" D'tanesse thrust the sword in the air lengthwise above his head. "Stop this now, and everythi—"

The trees convulsed. D'tanesse swung the Otnas in a wide arc. As before, there was the shuddering impact but this time Terra also saw it clearly. The end of the whip slammed—no, was pulled—into the sword. It lingered, a wringing wet line, and then from the edges inward it frayed. Undid itself. Gray shimmers of water peeled off and rained onto the ground around D'tanesse.

Troy pushed to her feet, leaning heavily on Teyeda's shoulder and Terra's upraised hand. For a moment, there was no sound or motion except the slap of water and wind against every surface.

Then a new lash came down. This time it went astray, smashing into the grandfather tree. The trunk splintered, severed. Massive branches spun through the air as it fell toward D'tanesse. He dove to the side, out of the way. A branch snapped from the body of the oak and flew end over end, smacking him in the back of the head as he jumped to his feet. He fell heavily to his knees, then collapsed. The Otnas fell from his limp hand, bouncing harmlessly away.

Chapter Twenty-Nine

"No! Estimal!" Troy launched forward before it had stopped rolling. "I am the one you want! Let him live!"

"Troy, don't—!" Terra bounded after her.

Troy's airway burned, charred from screaming and heaving for breath. Her temple pounded spikes of pain inside her skull, but she held onto one thought as she ran up the hill.

I can stop him.

"I…will end this…Esobir. It is over."

She heaved again, one more lungful of air to reply, and lifted the Otnas, looking to the sky. And then breathed in deeper, sharper. Sharp enough that she felt air like sandpaper grate the walls of her lungs.

Look.

She did look. She *was* looking. Straight through the cloud specter. Through the crack in the sky still oozing black thick rain. She could see—not with her physical eyes but with a vision deep inside her mind—the sodden edge of that hole above her. A jagged edge. A frayed edge that she now realized was the source of the black rain. All along that edge were tiny fiber-like threads that drooped, stretched, broke at the tips, grew and then drooped again. Then the image changed and the threads were shards of glass, filaments of light spurting patterns into the air. Then they were threads again. Glass and then thread, again and again and again.

She was seeing a thing that could not be explained because it did not exist in the physical. Therefore it could not be understood. Since it could not understand, her mind made up its own comparisons, pretending to understand. This revelation saved her sanity, and she was able to focus.

With the inner vision she was able to push past the edge of the crack to what was beyond the crack. There was the man, the real man: Estimal Glor. His hair was real hair. His eyes were human eyes. His face shone with sweat. His upper lip, beneath the stiff hairs of his mustache, was beaded with it. A cloth wall, red and gold swirled embroidery, was behind him.

"I see what you are doing, man." The word described all that was filth, all she did not have time to say. She was not meant to linger here, split by two spaces of mind and body. An agony bloomed, trying to come forward, but she shut it down. "You found me once, and again as I knew you would. Now I will find you. I am coming."

Terra was running up the hill toward her. She opened her mouth to tell him what she saw through the crack, but the words that came were not for him. The solid, muted voice—the one telling her to look, the one instructing from the epicenter of her being and at the same time from far outside of it like a beam of hot light shooting through her—began to consume. It was a voice and a heat. It had weight and texture like sand, flowing in the thin line between her mind and her body, rising to the sky and the king's face beyond it. She lifted the sword.

In the Place Between...

Black threads began shooting toward the Otnas, striking the flat of the blade. Terra slowed as he came nearer.

Agreement made...

Troy swung the sword up, flat out as if throwing a heavy weight from the point.

The rain reversed course. It shot back up to the sky. It needled through the specter's body, reducing it into a mess of slate-colored filaments. The black water continued to leave the ground, every last drop returning to its origin: the hole in the sky. The drops rejoined with the ends of the severed threads at its edge.

On the other side of the opening, in his traveling tent, the king blinked. Winced. Then laughed. "You still run from me. You can only r—"

A single black drop shot through the threads meshing and weaving together across the opening. There was a snap. A shatter of glass.

Clear bluish light from the full moon washed over the clearing as the crack faded like a vapor.

Troy closed her eyes. She could still see it. She pushed toward it with every bit of strength she had left inside. There was no time to explain to Terra, even if she could have spoken.

She felt her body but she felt it from the outside as well. She was here and she was there, in the world but no longer of it. She stood on the hill with the Otnas lifted above her head like a banner...and she stood at the edge of another place, peering through the rent. This was the way she had to go. It was like being in a waking dream, but she would wake in the king's tent, and there she would end the nightmare. Certainty filled her mind at the same time as power whipped through her body, uncontrollable.

You have found it too, haven't you? The wind and rain and all the elements obeyed you. They answered to you. The mountains might have shifted in their beds for you. You are a wave rising over deep waters—you know nothing of their weight.

The Otnas filled her hand, and her hand grew with it.

He was a wave, but she was the ocean.

Troy stepped forward.

* * * *

If it were daylight, if there was any light at all save for the brief flickers emanating through the slits in the cloud specter's head, Terra would have thought it radiated down onto Troy. Her upturned face shone. Her eyes were round pieces of black glass above curved glistening cheekbones.

If there were a light shining on her…but there was not.

There was no way she could cast a shadow in all this darkness, but there it was just the same. This shadow enveloped her like smoke. It stretched above her head, brushing the clouds. Or else the clouds were suddenly very close. Terra crooked his head backward, staring up, disbelieving it still, until he lost his balance and sat down hard. Mud splattered his arms and saturated his breeches. A knife of pain bored from his tailbone into his spine.

Troy's hand was still lifted, fingers curled around the handle of the Otnas, but the Otnas was gone. Or it had changed. Instead of the curving silver handguards and the thick blade, there was only a bright white cord winding over her knuckles, down her arm and straight through her chest. She didn't seem to feel it or know it was there. Her feet remained strong, set apart. Her hands were lifted; one empty, open, and the other clenching the glowing white cord. Her mouth was open, but not in pain or agony. She was speaking into the force of the storm, the same cadence of words D'tanesse had used in the desert.

"…Fast flies the word until spoken changes through doorways into Stone Living…"

The shadow—her shadow—moved on its own. It reached one arm long, into the center of the storm, where a calm circle floated in the middle of rolling clouds.

"…Become stone, become Ruler Living…"

He did not notice the rain stopping or the moon coming out. He only knew his stark relief when the specter began to fade.

"…Elaa, elaa, warrior's hand receiving."

The white cord erupted at the point where it penetrated the cloud specter's abdomen. It was like watching, all in one instant, the unfurling of a flower's leaves. Except this wasn't a flower. It was a cord made of white light and, instead of delicate tendrils, this thing grew jagged streaks, intricate white shoots. They spread quicker than a blink across the sky, until the clouds looked like a circle of pottery crushed beneath a flat weight. There was a loud crack. Terra fell back. He would have screamed, but his lungs were occupied trying to gulp air as fast as was possible. The thousand jagged lines burned a pattern into Terra's vision that moved as his eyes moved. As it slowly faded, he saw the clouds were gone. The storm was gone. Troy's shadow—and—cord still towered into the sky with her upraised arm holding the other end of the cord thrust through a shrinking black hole—

For the first time, Terra heard the words of the ancient language in tandem with their translation. A young woman's voice came down from the heavens. Troy's voice rose to meet it and the sounds mingled, resonated—

As Terra lost consciousness, mercifully put to sleep by his self-preserving mind, he looked at Troy once more.

She was not as he had just seen her, standing on the hill plastered with grainy mud. Her arms were clean. She bore no marks, not so much as a scratch or a bruise. Her body, a graceful deadly form, was wrapped in filigree white lace. The wind pulled at her long hair, making it brush along her high cheekbones like tapered fingers. Her shoulders were bare. Her feet were bare. One was cradled in fine gray sand, the other disappeared beneath a surge of white sea foam. He could see the lines of her ankles and the curve of her calf muscles below the hem of that gleaming white garment. She had whole, healthy skin. In one hand she still clutched the Otnas—not the sword, but the bright white cord. It wound around her arm, along her shoulder blades and through her back. It curved up her chest and neck over her hair and snaked around the crown of her head.

She was looking down at her feet, at the line between land and water. Choosing one or the other. Then she lifted her eyes and seemed to look right at him. An emotion, something like apology or perhaps affection, filled her expression. She knew him—

She was gone.

* * * *

Only a fool jumps into the fire because he enjoys the heat.

However, Troy had not stepped into a fire. She had stepped into a wall of writhing threads. They closed around her, sticking to her skin through her clothes. Little wet sensations streaked across her back, wriggled along her ribs and slid over her abdomen. Simultaneously, the wet was a stinging, shocking burn burrowing into her flesh. It covered her like a new skin; her toes felt seared off. Her knees and inner thighs contracted beneath the new pain. She felt the tingling shock inside her head, even her eyes. Her eardrums swelled. In a second, she would burst into a spray of red droplets. Troy thrashed. She arched her back—the threads sucked up all space as she moved, adhering to the shape of her body, and then in a frantic, desperate push she threw herself forward. She pulled the Otnas with her. It was still there, solid in the center of her fist, but she saw nothing. She slashed with it as if through thick foliage. It moved, but did not sever the threads. Instead it passed through them like a stick through water, barely disturbing the surface except with the vibrations of its own movement.

Elaaaaa! She tried to scream. Maybe she did scream, but her ears were useless.

"Only a fool jumps into the fire…" a voice said, and then, before it became a booming roar, "And where did you think you would go?"

Chapter Thirty

Troy

In that moment, and for that moment only, I remember everything. It all comes in a thick rush, every memory I lost happening at once. A few memories stand out large against the rest.

I ran, a little girl, into the bedroom where my father and mother were sitting close together. My mother had black hair, wild and thick, falling like a horse's mane to her tanned shoulders. My father held her hand. They smiled and called my name. A special name…

In the evening, sunset peeked through the bedroom windows. A breeze stirred the curtains. I was cradled on my father's lap. Between slow blinks I watched his bearded chin moving as he spoke to my mother.

"I hope it will come to nothing." My father, the peacemaker. That is what mother called him. Even when his jaw was set in resolve and his mouth little more than a straight slit below his nose and eyes, though he was a rock of a man, steady and unyielding, he was always struggling to understand the opposition. "I hope I am wrong. But if I cannot reach him soon he may turn against us. We must be prepared, if only in our minds."

"I have not forgotten what you told me in the beginning," replied my mother, "after the Mind spoke to you. You also could have turned away from the warning but you did not."

"Still, I hope I have misunderstood it." Father dropped a kiss on the crown of my head. His lips were warm and full of care. I nuzzled closer against his chest, his voice fading as I fell asleep. "If I have not…"

They led me one day to the edge of the water and held before me a sword with silver, curving handguards.

"This is your mother's. It is not a sword, though it looks like a sword. The Otnas is a sacred thing passed from one to another. Look."

My mother explained while he drew a line in the wet sand with a stick: "The body and spirit are one—body Here only—" she pointed to one side of the line, then the other as she continued, "—and spirit both Here and There. In the center where both sides touch we can hear the Mind speak. In a place that is both Here and There, and neither. That is where the agreement is made."

In the sand, my father wrote:

In the Place Between,

agreement made

"When the Otnas is passed, one to another, that agreement ends for one and begins with another," my mother said. "My mother passed the Otnas to me, with the command to pass the Otnas to my child, to protect with the Otnas and to serve the Mind through the ways of Esobir."

Fast flies the word until spoken changes

"Elaa stone, you know, is a catalyst or a vessel, or a passage where the Mind gives a little of Itself to us, and we become something more than what we are."

Through Doorways into
Stone Living
become stone
become Ruler Living

"*A*nd the flow from the Mind to the Place Between the Mind and spirit, to the stone we can touch and command, appears like this…"

My father finished writing:

Elaa,
elaa.
Warrior's hand
receiving.

"It is time for me to pass the Otnas to you, my daughter," my mother said, turning to me. "My little lioness. It is yours now, if you would have it."

I loved my mother. In every way I wanted to be like her, to walk tall on the sands, unanxious and unintimidated. I wanted to rule carefully, like my father. As my young hand closed around the hilt of the sword, my mother pulled hers away.

And I was asked a question.

Why do you live?

I knew why I wanted to be alive—I did not want to be dead. But what kept my life Alive, purposeful, vibrant?

D'tanesse.

My heart panged when I thought of him. I thought of feasts, sitting on his lap when I was tiny, picking at his plate and drumming my tiny heels on his shins…

Estimal, even when he disapproved of my romps through the halls, and my proficiency with projectiles. We argued our way through history lessons and economics, but he was thorough in his efforts. He brought me a string of blue pearls for my fifth year, when I'd memorized all twelve of the primary recipes from his secret book. I knew my numbers because of his persistence and unyielding nature, well fitted to my childish stubbornness.

I thought of nights spent beside the circle hearth, listening to Natami's stories while munching roast sweet grain. I thought of the beautiful people who worked so hard on our coastal town. I thought of the children who played with me and raced their horses up and down on the beach. I thought of their smiles, their bright eyes, their warm breath on my skin as we played and wrestled. My heart swelled, aching to burst—

Now I am falling. Consumed by a black, endless howl that is wind, but not wind, breath, but not breath. My hair whips back from my face, streaming behind me. My stomach squeezes hard as a rock. My lungs collapse, leaving me to consider the starved blood exploding into my legs and toes. My heart still works very well, a repeating explosion in my chest and neck and even my ears. Bursts of phantom light crowd my vision, red and silver lines that live behind my eyes.

Outside all this, I can feel a shadow covering me like a set of clothes. The shadow is alive. She thinks, she loves. She is me, but she is better than me. She remembers everything. She understands.

With our eyes we see only in part, because we do not know. We are left with comparisons, hypothesis, because a sword looks and feels like what we know is a sword. We see only as much as we know. The Otnas is not a sword. I do not know what its true form is. When I look at it, I see a blade: hilt, handguards, pommel; but here Outside, where I know again what I do not know Inside, I know it is not a sword. It is Otnas.

I wake, lying on my back beneath aspen trees.

It is light—day. It is cool—morning. The sky is fresh and blue. The storm is gone.

So is everyone else.

Part Three

The Lioness

Chapter Thirty-One

Estimal

"Start over, from the beginning."

Sheets of narrow light split the gap between Natug's boots as she shifted her feet. Her divided leather skirts were coated in dust kicked up by the scuffle. Kilar of Daehexa backed away from her and dug in his heels. Natug waited. He raised his blade, advancing. She slid her foot forward, deflecting with an upward sweep. The wooden blades thunked, echoed, thunked again.

They were alone in the practice yard, making use of spare time before the evening meal. It was the turn of the year and the long sweeps of grass covering the ground were turning yellow. Horses passing on the dirt path to the stables reached for clumps of it. Their riders snapped the leather reins, and the beasts moved on.

Dust rose to meet smoke and both pressed toward me. I closed my mouth and squinted—again—at the low sun. Negotiations about the new warrior training system proposed by Natug had ended before midday, strongly in her favor. The chieftain Remus and his wife Melaine had long been taken in by Natug and her book of Esobir. I should have known how the day would end. The chieftain sent one of his warriors, Kilar, with Natug, to work at once on drills, deciding what to teach the warriors of Cathylon once the old system I'd developed from the book of Inatru was replaced. Everyone, Inatru and skopi alike, would have the opportunity to learn each warrior level. Power would be given to all, and any weapon available to those who could learn to use them, bow or spear or sword.

L'estim, of course, would not protest. I lost my brother to this Seawolf by marriage twelve years ago. I shouldn't be surprised that Cathylon went next.

Machaun also expected as much. His exact words in correspondence to me were "ripping out the seams of our history, reforming Cathylon into something unusual." He and the Inatru in Camil Askanda were disturbed to the point of violence since this woman had come to stay. By marriage she was considered Inatru, but it was an affront to tradition. It was the Inatru, not the skopi outsiders whose ancestry was lost to history, not the Esobir, not the Seawolves—and certainly not this woman—who controlled Cathylon and the power of elaa stone. If Cathylon converted to the ways of the Esobir, then power would belong to anyone who wanted it.

If everyone is in power, as Machaun wrote, no one is. The words were scrawled in dark ink, furiously penned. He ended with a request to meet in Camil Askanda to discuss resolutions for the problem "even if I must commit the most heinous acts for the sake of the Inatru and our traditions. I know you share my convictions. If we do not act, our way of life will be lost."

Machaun's passion was encouraging, if not convincing. His heritage ran back to the very first Inatru who came to Cathylon and forged order from the chaos of the rampant outsiders. All were once refugees, skopi from other islands—even the Inatru. But only the Inatru possessed strength to endure and establish themselves through decades of fighting amongst the forming villages and clans. They had forged our way of life at great cost and maintained it through generations, tradition unbroken from that time to this. I had no doubt Machaun would stay to his convictions, every bit and thought, to the point of death. Better death than to be remembered as the one who broke the line of command and let the island revert to chaos.

"She is not what I expected."

I turned, scowling at the intrusion on my thoughts. An elderly man stood beside me. He observed Natug with a low-lidded squint, tipping his head back and thrusting his chin forward as if he were reading a parchment.

I folded my arms and allowed my gaze to follow his. My scowl stayed. "Indeed. It is disconcerting."

"Who would have thought a woman could be capable of so much influence. I have known her for years now and I am still amazed at her tenacity." He arched his eyebrows, amused.

"I hope it remains a novelty. Women are both headstrong and weak-minded in such a way…" I couldn't conjure a meaningful comparison and fell silent.

"I think you mean guided by an inner character we cannot understand? I have told my wife as much on many occasions."

"My wife is a joy to know, much less have." Natami lately seemed more attentive to my well-being than ever. At least there was one person still on my side.

"My wife as well." He smiled and tucked wrinkled hands into the wide cuffs of his sleeves. His features were familiar, somewhat resembling those of Daehexa's chieftain.

"You were present at the negotiations. Remus called you his historian."

"I keep track of what records I can," he allowed. "He also calls me father, on occasion, but titles have a way of obscuring even blood ties."

"What did you think of the outcome, historian?"

"Please call me Yessac."

"Yessac, then."

"I think, after some study of the queen's book, I may have my own proposal to make."

"It is not her book, or the Seawolves'. They do not have House blood."

"Are you so sure?" Yessac's glance was a roll of the eyes. He was amused.

"The Inatru, however, do have House blood. It is undeniable," I said. "We have the final, most accurate authority of our heritage in the book of Inatru. That is what sets us apart from the skopi."

"That may be, or it may not." Yessac could not argue outright with what had already been written, though he seemed bent on trying. "Neither book has been translated entirely, though I think the writings of Aenti—" Here he gave credit to the book's author "—could be very soon. Then there is the matter of the prophecy."

My jaw tightened. They were calling it prophecy now. Even L'estim called it that. It was nothing more than a few paragraphs on a loose page tucked into the book of Esobir. They thought it was the truth, undeniable, unchangeable. Most of it made no sense. It was so cryptic that practically any meaning could be drawn from it. The woman took advantage, telling us exactly what to think.

"If the Prophecy truly is that which will come, it should be more specific in terms."

"I think it is very specific," Yessac began. Then he considered my words and closed his mouth. His white brows sank toward his eyes.

"How do we know what this prophecy means, or if it means anything at all? There are other kingdoms. Their futures are none of our concern, and our future is none of theirs."

A young woman walking across the yard toward the hall stopped between us and the practice ring, where Natug and Kilar were beginning yet another drill. The young woman's back was turned to us. She was mesmerized by their display of violence.

"And what are we teaching our children by allowing tradition to be so openly challenged? That women are not treasures to be protected? They are made to give life, not take it."

"We are all made to give life," countered Yessac. "Some of us are able to protect it with strength. Some stand on the front lines, some sit on thrones. A favored few protect those who lead and stand at the right hand of rulers. That is you," he added, to remind me as well as compliment, I think.

But he was wrong. It had been me. Now L'estim went to her as often as not for advice. He went to her for everything he needed, and only allowed me what was left of himself after she had her share.

"I hope Remus will at least teach his children to follow good tradition."

"Remus is a good chieftain, and his wife an excellent woman." Yessac did not try to conceal his pride. "Daehexa prospers under their leadership."

"Their children are no doubt happy to be raised in such a pleasant situation. Melaine's ambition was to raise her children well, she told me once."

"She is rare among her people, that is the truth."

As we spoke, the young woman, Melaine's daughter, turned her head, possibly hearing her mother's name. I had once harbored hope of L'estim taking Melaine as his wife, and making her the queen of Cathylon. Melaine's daughter would then have been D'tanesse's cousin.

I had imagined it all before: she would have L'estim's light skin and his kind brown eyes. She would be slight like Melaine, neat and soft of voice. She would sit beside D'tanesse for tutoring sessions. His eyes (green like Natami's) and hers (brown like L'estim's) would be trained on me while I taught from the book of Inatru, all our traditions. They would learn from me what was most important.

Ours would have been the happiest of families, had not the Seawolf come to Cathylon.

"I will begin teaching them the ways of Esobir very soon," Yessac said, with a deliberate glance at my face. "Raelcun is more than ready for some improvement of mind, and Sema is surprisingly observant."

My turning to look at him was delayed, as my eyes stayed forward wanting to study Sema. She was close enough to hear us, perhaps. I could have called to her and formally introduced myself, but the circumstance was all wrong. She would not have L'estim's eyes. Besides, she was too absorbed with the clash before her. Natug and Kilar beat their weapons together, louder as the drill picked up momentum. Sema braved their dust as if it were not there.

"In fact," Yessac pressed on, regardless that I was ready to be done talking. "In fact, I hope the High King will hear a proposal on that subject. I've been thinking once we have translated the book of Esobir completely, Daehexa might become the training grounds for Esobir as well as warriors. Natug has started the reformation, but we must continue it. She will not live forever."

"No, she will not."

"Remus and Melaine are willing to take on the responsibility."

"You have spoken to them about it already, then."

"They are willing, as I said. We believe it is time for a change of mind."

"For the good of Cathylon."

"Exactly."

"I will speak to L'estim."

A young man—Sema's older brother, most likely—came from the Hall and stood beside her. They stood side by side for a moment, and then he took her hand and led her away toward the Hall and their supper.

Natug and Kilar came to the end of their drill.

"Shall we start over?" One of them asked.

"From the beginning."

I left that night and rode alone to Camil Askanda. I traveled there many times in the next months, through Derrh's snow and Grano's growing warmth. It became more my home than Carmul, Machaun more my brother than L'estim. It became the place of a new beginning for me, and for Cathylon.

* * * *

"Brother, where have you been?" L'estim caught my arm as I stepped through the door into the Hall. Inside was awash with candlelight and laughter. This Eulba marked L'abri's coming of age, and the whole city had gathered to celebrate. Nine months had passed since the negotiations in Daehexa. I had just returned from Camil Askanda and all was ready. Messages had found their way to the island of the Seawolves, warning them that their queen was in danger. They would come, believing to her aid, tonight, but too late to save her. This night would be Carmul's last.

"Did you fit all of Carmul under one roof for this celebration?" I asked, turning my head as if searching the room.

"Of course not." L'estim laughed. "Many of the children have already been taken to bed, and a few foot races are still going on along the beach."

"Ah."

"Your presence has been sorely missed." L'estim walked beside me toward the tables set up on the other side of the dining hall.

"I was called to Camil Askanda for negotiations. Natami was supposed to tell you."

"Yes, but it was sudden. Natami has waited anxiously for your return. We hoped you would arrive in time for this."

I shook my head, diverting the conversation. "Your daughter has been pilfering knives from the armory."

"Natug taught her how to throw. She is excited, that is all."

"It is dangerous. She could injure someone by being careless, or kill them."

"L'abri is coming of age, and Natug is seeing to her training. I assure you, neither take it lightly."

"I am assured." My gaze jumped from his face to the crowd of diners, the feast, the smiles. They were happy that Cathylon was decaying. These favored ones who chattered and chewed and shut their eyes to the darkness about to close in. Joy was painted on every face. It was loud in the rattling of utensils, in the scuffle of boots beneath the tables. Here they gathered: the lifeblood of Carmul. The reward of our labors. To a man, I hated them.

"Estimal." L'estim laid a hand on my shoulder, pulling me to a stop.

I stiffened.

"This is a great night for us. I have a beautiful wife and a beautiful daughter. You have your heir, and D'tanesse loves his cousin. They are the best of friends." He was smiling, but his eyes were desperate. "See? I have kept my word."

I have seen that glance many times in the years since Natug came. Since the first night she sang, and the sky pressed in. Something changed him on that evening thirteen years ago, and he struggled ever since with an inner pain I could not discover. He would not speak of it.

I turned away from his smile and his hand, and found Natami seated at the king's table beside Natug. She was laughing. Our son had grown to develop her humor, and her laugh. He laughed the most with L'abri.

Natami's laughter stopped when she saw me, but her smile grew. She held my gaze steadily. Her eyes seemed to glow, clear like green sea stones. She leaned toward Natug and whispered, conspiratorial, close to her ear.

Natug took Natami's hand in a brief squeeze. Natami forgot me and turned back to the table, adding her laugh to the noise filling the hall until it was only noise.

"Brother." If my tone was cold, the coldness was absorbed by the noise and the heat of the bodies around us. "Your celebration is well deserved. I have a gift from Machaun: pine cordial put to barrel when we ourselves came of age. We shall drink to your health and the health of your daughter."

L'estim put his hand on my shoulder again. "When we are finished this night, we must talk. I have something to share with you."

"Indeed. After the meal."

Chapter Thirty-Two

Troy woke slowly, keeping her eyelids closed as she became increasingly alert. An easy wind brushed through the trees, nothing compared to the previous gale. Birds warmed their voices to greet the morning. A dull brightness against her eyelids told her the sun was up or almost up, lifting the blackness of night to a translucent blue-gray. She forced her eyes open and stared into an empty sky, trying to remember the night. Everything was so muddled and inconceivable, like a nightmare. Perhaps it was. They had ridden to Kcen, made camp, slept, and she had dreamed of a storm. That was to be expected; the threat of danger consumed her thoughts and her days since leaving Camil Askanda.

Troy moved her left leg, and her muscles cramped down it like iron shackles. She winced.

No, not a dream.

She touched her head, remembering something had struck it. The storm specter's rain-whip. Her fingertips brushed the raw wound, crusted in a layer of blood.

She had faced and fought Estimal Glor. She had used the Otnas—there it was, by her hand. She had seen through something…to something else.

That was all she knew.

Troy sat up stiffly and looked around, blinking. She was lying at the bottom of the hill in the clearing. A swath was sheared from the forest where trees had been mowed down. The grass was ravaged with scars of black mud. The air smelled dank, like a bag of overturned dirt.

She was supposed to have stepped through the window made by the Looking Glass. She was supposed to have come out on the other side with Estimal. Instead here she was on her back in the same place she'd started, with her hand still around the leather-wrapped handle of the Otnas.

He had not followed them after all. He had not needed to since he had the Looking Glass in the first place. At least she had taken care of that. The Looking Glass was destroyed, of this she was sure. She had felt it shatter before the window closed on its own.

Now to find the others.

First things first. Could she stand? Yes. Walk?

She took a step forward, holding the Otnas at her side. Her right ankle pinched and buckled, and she fell over. Well, she could limp then. The extra time it would take her to reach their camp at the well would hopefully be enough for her to think of an explanation for where she'd gone–if she had gone anywhere. That seemed unlikely. She found her baldric in the mud, near a mess of fallen trunks. She wiped it, slipped the Otnas in the sheath and strapped the baldric to her back before moving on past the fallen grandfather tree.

Laic stood grazing in the potato field beyond, his long face hidden by a cascade of black mane. Troy called to him and he came at once with his broad ears up. She rubbed his nose in silent apology for forgetting him last night. He wore his bridle still, but not his saddle. Teyeda must have taken it off. She would have to apologize to him too. In truth, she should to all of them. She'd done a foolish thing in the throes of delirious power. She would have to apologize quickly, in the ten seconds before D'tanesse began remarks, or she would probably change her mind. He had the same playful antagonistic quality as Mytch, but Mytch was usually able to laugh at himself as well. It had made Mytch tolerable, but D'tanesse was simply antagonistic. What made it worse was she couldn't help rising to the occasions D'tanesse created by being so like himself.

She limped past wrecked foundations toward what had been the center road. Laic walked behind her, browsing through the crushed lupines for the rest of his breakfast.

Troy slowed, almost stopped, when she saw the well.

Empty blankets lay rumpled on the ground. Near those, a spit stood over a ring of ashes and charred wood. Some half-burnt branches were scattered about, and a pack of travel equipment was overturned, emptied. Her own things were in a loose pile beside one of the blankets.

"Terra?" Caution muted her voice. She listened for a long moment, turning on her good foot to search the surrounding forest. Birds still chirped, unconcerned about the camp below them deserted in apparent haste. Lupines rustled behind her as Laic pulled and snipped them with his teeth.

She looked down and finally saw the footprints of men and horses covering the ground around the well. Too many prints for her friends to make on their own, unless they had raced back and forth for hours. Dread knotted her stomach. She took hold of Laic's reins, drawing him near so she could lean on his shoulder, and they slowly walked along the trampled ground. If she kept following them south she would find their origin at the river Aganus.

"What have I done?" she whispered. "Al ki, me Elaa, what have I done?"

She stared at the trail of prints another moment, then rode back to the well. She repacked her travel gear, saddled Laic and then retrieved her black cloak, shaking the dirt out of it before settling it over her shoulders.

As she began to tie it, she glanced at the ground again. A vertical brown-black streak which she hadn't noticed before ran down the side of the well over the stones and leaves. Dried blood. Looking to the north, toward the ruins of the chieftain's hall, she could see irregular pools of congealed liquid forming a zigzag trail over the trampled foliage. Someone had been badly injured. But had her friends been taken by the warhost, or had they hidden themselves elsewhere, waiting for her to return? Or were they dead?

Troy finished fastening her cloak and shuffled forward slowly, following the trail of blood along the ground until something caught her eye to the right. It was a scrap of bloodied cloth. She bent and picked it up, revealing a dagger hidden beneath. The tip of the shining blade pointed north. Troy's blood froze, and her hand darted to her left side for her dagger, but her hand grasped only the empty sheath.

She examined the handle of the weapon, nudging it with her fingertips. There was the name, etched in the wood: Terra. Her hand closed around the hilt until her knuckles turned white, and her eyes lifted to the trail beyond.

A whisper escaped her lips, but her entire body trembled with a scream.

Terra...

The scream continued in her mind as she struggled onto Laic's back and spurred him down the trail. The scream followed her through the trees, past bushes and boulders, over fallen limbs and small streams, and as she splashed through larger ones. Trees flashed past, blurring with the green of leaves and blue of the sky. She crouched over Laic's neck as they surged beneath low branches. They followed the trail until the full moon was high above them. The ground became washed with a silver glow that made the pale colors lighter and the dark colors even darker.

Laic was trotting steadily, and they were both scrutinizing the trail ahead of them, when Troy caught sight of a shape lying across it. It was too small to be a log or boulder, too big to be a root. Laic stumbled to a halt beside it. Troy slid out of the saddle and approached the prone figure with caution. She knelt beside it and reached a trembling hand to roll it over. It was warm: a body.

Her fingers touched knobby bulges beneath fabric, and then long hair. D'tanesse. His eyes were open, the whites glinting, but he was unresponsive. She shifted onto her sprained ankle and hissed in pain, pitching sideways. Her hand landed in a puddle of liquid. Blood.

"So it was you." She stripped back his jacket and felt along his body for the wound. She found it on his ribs beneath his left arm. The blood coming from it was warm and gooey, seeping slowly but not spurting or pulsing. He was with the living yet, though for how long Troy couldn't say with the amount of blood he had already lost. Her hand worked down his left side, measuring the length of the gash. One, almost two spans long. It began near his armpit and reached to the middle of his ribs.

Troy tugged his arms out of their coat sleeves and spread the garment open on either side of him. It would serve as a blanket, at least, keeping too much body heat from seeping into the ground while she worked over him. His tunic would have to be sacrificed. She sliced it carefully to his armpit and pushed the sopping edges away from his open flesh. Then quickly stabbing, ripping through the thick hem, she cut two long strips from her cloak. She folded one and pressed it against the wound. Working with her other hand and her teeth, she tied the second strip twice around his chest, cinching it tight. The knot sat on his sternum, rising and falling discreetly with his breathing. His pale skin was covered in what looked like shadows, but under scrutiny was actually blood.

She pulled the edges of his jacket back over him, then began going through the many pockets until she finally found a small oilcloth bag no larger than her hand. It was filled with a grain-like substance, which Troy poured out onto another piece cut from her cloak.

She stood, briefly unsteady on one foot, and looked for Laic. The horse had wandered a few yards from the road to a stream trickling through a shallow crevice in the ground. He sucked at the water, laying his ears back and gulping the chill liquid.

Survival was much easier in the forest compared to the desert, she thought as she filled the bag. Then she considered the past twenty hours, her lost friends and the one dying on the road behind her, and changed her mind.

She carried the dripping bag back to D'tanesse and dribbled water into his mouth. His throat worked up and down, swallowing weakly. Troy spread her cloak over him and trickled a little more water over his lips. Laic came and stood near them. His head drooped toward the ground, nipping small shoots at his feet. There was nothing else to do until the sun rose. Troy lay down beside D'tanesse and pulled her cloak over their bodies.

* * * *

Several times during the night, Troy woke, removed 'Tan's bandage, rinsed it in the stream and replaced it. She woke the last time as the sun was shooting early rays into the silver-gray sky.

I do not want to get up.

She had traveled hard over the last two days with little sleep or food.

She knew she was dehydrated and exhausted. If she did not eat soon, she would drop from sheer lack of strength. She rolled over and felt the muscles in her back and legs stiffen into a thousand knots.

I cannot go on. I will never catch up to the others in time. Elaa help me, I cannot go on!

"Follow…"

Troy jerked around. 'Tan's eyes were open, and though they were flat and blank, he licked his lips and struggled to form the word again. It came out a harsh whisper. "Follow her…"

"D'tanesse, speak up." Troy leaned toward him. "Follow who?"

"Follow her to—to—"

She touched his forehead. It was cool. No fever, no delirium.

"To Carrrmm–"

"What?"

"Follow…" His eyelids feathered closed once more.

Troy placed her hand on his neck. A pulse was still beating, and she decided he was asleep. She shook her head, struggled to her feet and limped off in search of something edible. When she returned, somewhat satiated by some wild blackberries, D'tanesse was lying face down in the leaves several yards from where she'd left him. Drag marks in the dirt showed where he had pulled himself down the trail.

"'Tan, what are you doing over here?" She rolled him over. His eyes were open, fixed on her face.

"Follow…follow them…" D'tanesse struggled to raise his left arm. His right hand clutched at the material of his jacket, gathering it inside his fist and squeezing it, releasing it, squeezing it again. Troy had a thought and pried his fingers open. The pocket he had been crushing was slashed with a red-brown stain across the original yellow weave. Inside was a starchy powder she didn't recognize. She put her face close to the puckered opening—it was barely wider than her mouth—and winced back, gagging. A gamy, eggy stench stung the inside of her nose all the way to her throat. Her eyes began to water. Whatever the powder had once been, it was ruined by his dried blood, and now its memory lived in her sinuses. Troy rubbed the underside of her nose, as if that would help the inside of it. She could imagine what he might say if he were able to observe her just now.

No, not that pocket. Try another. Keep trying, keep trying...I don't carry all that stuff around to amuse myself, do I?

"One day, my friend," she muttered, prying her fingers into the pocket and scooping the stinking powder onto the ground, "You will learn to laugh at yourself, not only at others. Then you might even become tolerable."

Troy proceeded to search his other pockets, looking for a leaf or powder she might recognize that would speed his recovery and ultimately their travel. She found it finally on the inside right panel near his hip. A longish blue pocket with a short flap across the opening held several mold-colored wafers. The Esobir in Yettmis called them spirits. She didn't know the recipe by heart but she remembered they were made with extract of khoni, mint, dried fish and ground marl root, and they tasted terrible. Without ceremony she pulled his jaw open and tucked one under his tongue.

"That should help," she told him, wiping her finger dry on her breeches, "with your pain, anyway." Nothing could be done about the taste he would wake up to, like a day-old fish supper buried in roughage. Troy guessed that made things even. Her nose was still burning, oozing mucus down the back of her throat.

She used his jacket as a makeshift litter, pulling both corners by his feet to drag him back to the side of the road. "At least you will feel better for it. And stop complaining, or I won't give you another."

She lowered the edges of his jacket back down and knelt at his side to check his bandage.

"Terra… Go…" He struggled to raise his head.

She stopped with both hands resting on his ribs and looked intently at his eyes. "Where are they, 'Tan?"

He was losing strength by the second, but he took a deep breath and said, "Machaun follows you to Carmul."

Troy stared at him. "Machaun? Ki."

His eyes rolled into his head and he fell back, unconscious once more.

She considered this as she redressed his wound. "You are a wonder, 'Tan. I do not know what goes on in your shell of a brain, but it must be something big to you. Following me to Carmul. Why would I go there?"

Her hands fell to her sides as a thought dropped into her mind. "Or did you tell him I am at Carmul? Did you tell him I would trade my life for Terra's—for all of you—and if he follows me there I would likely give myself up?"

Machaun had dumped D'tanesse on the road when he thought he was dead. The others must still hold value as long as they were alive.

But why Carmul?

Troy stood and whistled once, high and sharp. Laic came at a swift trot. She caught his reins where they drooped under his chin and coaxed the horse to kneel by tapping his forelegs with her boot. Laic was not fond of this trick, but he obediently went down and stayed there while she lifted and pushed D'tanesse onto the saddle. Laic rose again, shaking his head side to side.

Troy rubbed his neck and fed him some leftover blackberries before climbing into the saddle herself. She carefully situated herself behind D'tanesse, holding onto his waist with one arm, and took the reins in her free hand.

Once again they traveled, following the tracks left by Machaun and his warriors to the edge of the forest, where the plains met the trees. She glanced constantly about her, watching for signs of anyone else lying beside the road. If she did find someone else, even one more, she would have to stop and rethink her strategy. It was hard enough riding at a slow jog with one arm around D'tanesse, one hand on the reins. She might make a litter to drag behind Laic, but even more time would be lost. The quickest way to Carmul, that being a straight line across the plains past Daehexa, then through the foothills nestled against the base of the mountains, then forging a trail over those, would still take several days—

She sat back hard, and Laic stopped with his head up, nose extended forward. His energy beneath her felt undecided, rooted and about to spring forward at the same time. The reins slipped through Troy's fingers and she fumbled to catch them, vague in her effort while her gaze, along with Laic's, remained fixed on the horizon.

Up to that moment Troy harbored a notion—stubbornly harbored, D'tanesse would say if he could—that rescuing her friends would put an end to it. She could still run after that, she could disappear into the mountains or even go back to the desert and survive alone. Perhaps she could even take Terra with her. They could go to Klenit on the coast past the mountains, which was so small no one bothered with it. The Esobir would be relatively safe since the Looking Glass was destroyed. All that could reach them now was made of flesh and malice, and anyone could overcome that.

The same foolishness she'd felt after stepping into a place she was not meant to go to, a place where even the Otnas was powerless (and where did you think you would go?) spread over her like a shadow. The king's plan to contain her had failed. His attempt to trap her had failed. His Looking Glass and means of keeping control of Cathylon was irreparably broken. The quickest way to end the uprising would be to purge Cathylon, to start over.

"The line has been drawn, and the line has been crossed." She sat still on Laic, hugging D'tanesse with an arm so tense it felt brittle. They stood at the edge of the forest where the trees became sparse, scattered over a flat landscape of pale green grass. Smoke rose in a billowing pillar, a black mark in the sky above Daehexa. Estimal Glor meant to do more than find her. He meant to destroy Cathylon in the process.

Chapter Thirty-Three

They traveled by day, resting by night and letting D'tanesse heal, which he did with surprising speed. Each day he became more aware of his surroundings, and each night Troy woke less to the sound of his tortured moans when the effect of the wafer spirits wore off.

His first words to her after she found him had been his only words so far. He stared ahead at the spreading black stain, the gravestone marking Daehexa's remains. The trail they followed would pass several miles to the west, between the river and the rising pillar clouds. Troy also said nothing. She didn't know if he were coherent enough to grieve, or seethe, and if he vocalized either she didn't know what *she* would do. They had all known the risk, she reminded herself needlessly. Besides, Sema might not be dead. She might have left Daehexa in time.

It was her home once, some part of Troy—a childish part—moaned. Her home. That is bad enough.

No. Life is what counts now. Homes can be rebuilt and livings restored. That came from a stern place inside her, somewhere cold and deep. They had yet to begin fighting properly.

But we will, Troy promised the smoking city as it slipped past, riding the eastern horizon. *We will.*

D'tanesse gave a muted yelp, clutching at her arm encircling his ribs. Troy realized she was holding him too tight and relented. D'tanesse's fingers continued to dig into her forearm, his dirty nails pricking ridged scar tissue. His head was turned toward the burning city. Toward red and orange flickers, deep crimson glows beneath crumbled walls and foundations. His green eyes blinked wide awake, reflecting pinpoints of blood-colored light across his irises. His mouth opened, pulled at the corners tightly toward his chin. Skin crimped together in the space between, trembling as he pulled another sharp breath.

She expected him to say Sema's name, in fact almost heard it, but he closed his hand over Troy's on the reins and kicked with both heels. He sat so far forward on Laic that he only nudged the horse's shoulders.

Troy sat back and tugged the reins to counter the hasty command.

"Go."

"No, D'tanesse."

"Go!" He thrust Troy's hand with the reins forward and kicked again with his heels. "Go!"

Laic laid his ears back. Troy's counter-order held more authority, so Laic ignored further requests from D'tanesse.

"Go!" D'tanesse was shouting now. "Go! Go get her! Sema!"

"'Tan, listen to m—"

He started thrashing, twisting side to side, ignoring the gash in his side when it cracked and oozed fresh blood into the bandage. Troy dropped the reins and thrust her arm around D'tanesse's neck, careful not to choke him, and pulled him tight against herself with her arm still about his waist. She leaned in by his ear while embracing him thus and spoke low as he sobbed and struggled.

"Let me down! Sema!"

"She is not there—"

"Sema!"

"Listen to me. No, listen. She is not dead."

"You don't know!"

"He needs her to draw us. Stop thrashing, you'll bleed to death if that gash opens further."

"I want to see! Let me go see her!"

"She may have gotten away before Estimal came here. She may be back in Yettmis by now, with the Watch looking after her. If Estimal does have her, he dares not kill her. She is the only way he can draw us now."

He sobbed and sucked air through his teeth, racked alternately by pain and panicked grief, but subsided against her. Troy moved her hand to rest on his forehead, brushing his dark hair back, the sides of their heads touching. She nudged Laic to walk and held D'tanesse as they passed the desiccated city, murmuring into his ear like a mother consoling a child. 'Tan's body shook against her, and his hands clenched at her forearms, her fingers, even reached back to touch her face and hook her neck in awkward needful embrace. They continued this way until finally Daehexa had passed from sight behind them.

* * * *

The days wore on. Troy and D'tanesse traveled in silence, unable to drag themselves from the lethargy which enveloped them like the foul smoke defiling the sky with its sick, brown haze. The heat became unbearable. No wind stirred the dead air. Every morning the sun rose on their right, swollen and orange behind the sickened sky, its light unable to penetrate the haze as more villages in the surrounding countryside burned, adding to the thickening vapors. Every night the sun set on their left, casting a tired, false twilight over the land for hours on end.

They followed the ceaseless trail of savaged grasses that sometimes made thick lines and sometimes the usual track of many hooves. When the trail was obscured through layered ash or packed dirt, Troy just kept heading north. North to the mountains, and Carmul beyond.

Five days from the forest, they passed another smoldering city. Troy thought it might be Engar, or used to be. A thread of people meandered from it to the shores of a lake not half a mile away. The trail left by Machaun and his warriors crossed perpendicular through the line. Either he had ridden straight on, regardless of the refugees, or he had passed the village before it was razed.

D'tanesse sniffed, trying to clear his nose and breathe a little better. Both of them hardly wanted to speak, as much from fatigue as pain whenever they tried. Their throats were raw, ooze-coated shafts useless for anything except breathing. Troy patted his upper arm and his return nod was just perceptible, a lift and drop nearly hidden by his shoulders. He was more than ready to rest.

They spread Troy's cloak onto the ash-coated grasses where Laic had come to a stop and D'tanesse sprawled immediately upon it. Troy lingered a moment, watching the refugees wrapped in their belongings or carrying them in loose bundles. Ash floated on the air, swirling in the spaces between trudging bodies like limpid, dirty snowflakes. Most of the refugees were women and young children. Here and there were old men clutching blackened clothes to their bodies, or a bent grandmother hobbling past with the help of a stick or a family member. Others simply sat on the lake shore, watching a greasy gray film accumulate on the water. A few of these turned to look at Troy and D'tanesse, but most ignored them.

Yes, this was Engar. She'd seen it twice before: once passing through with Mytch on their way to the mountains to meet the Klenit Esobir for the book, and again on the way back with Machaun in pursuit. Their second visit was especially short, not that Troy had much desire to linger in the first place. There was nothing a simple people who made their living from the fish in the lake could do for her—a Seawolf, outcast and Esobir.

Troy sat down on the cloak beside D'tanesse. She rested one arm on her upright knee and watched the nearest woman sitting with her son. He was a slight child. His red hair was powdered with soot. He stared around at the line of walkers, at the smoke, the lake and finally at Troy. She stared back. Burns and scratches adorned his thin cheeks. His clothing, his arms, his feet were all blackened by smoke. He left his mother and crept up to the edge of her spread cloak. One sooty foot came to rest on the last bit of uncut hem. He studied Troy with wide brown eyes.

"Are you going away too?" His voice was low and clotted in his throat. His hands stayed at his sides, unusually still as if he did not have the strength to use them and talk at once. He was maybe seven Eulbas, too young to grasp what had happened, too old to miss that something was going wrong.

"We are trying to find our friends," she said eventually.

"Why?" His eyelids were swollen from the constant sting of smoke, but he did not lift his hands to rub them.

"He took some of my friends. I am going to get them back."

The boy's red eyebrows pushed toward his eyes, more of a nudge beneath the black grime smeared across his forehead. "He took my friends too. And my father." His chin wrinkled with a remnant sob. Troy half expected him to crumble toward her, seeking comfort even in the arms of a stranger, but he just stood still, trembling with emotion.

D'tanesse stirred beside Troy, lifting his head from the pillow he'd made with his arms. "Whu—" The word pinched out before he could finish.

"Why did he take them?" Troy translated (and embellished).

"He made them join his warband. Everyone who wasn't Esobir. Those ones are…" His little throat convulsed in a swallow and he turned to point at the city instead of finishing with his words. His arm was slow to lift, prolonging the movement as if on its own power and will.

Troy's shoulders rose compulsively to shake off the ash coating them. Apparently it was not only the falling remains of wood. D'tanesse wheezed an exclamation into her cloak, dropping his head back down in fatigue or disgust. Then, suddenly rousing again, he patted his jacket on his left, unwounded side. Then he tried with his right, arching his back and turning, wincing. "My—No, it's on the other side. That one. The blue one with the flap."

The boy watched, squinting more than blinking, while Troy found the indicated pocket on the inside of his coat near his waist and pulled out a palmful of the spirit wafers she'd been feeding D'tanesse. She frowned, hesitating.

D'tanesse addressed the boy. "These are called spirits. They will numb your pain. There is also a map—" He reached for another pocket, winced, but persevered and drew out a small folded skin. "Follow it to Yettmis, the city beneath the sand. There you will find refuge."

The boy took the spirit wafers and the skin. He turned automatically, taking the gifts to his mother.

Troy watched him go. "You just gave away your medicine."

"I know."

"And our food, if we can't find game further on."

"Do you want me to take it back?" He started to twist around to look up at her face, but grimaced and gave up the notion.

Troy shook her head.

The boy knelt beside his mother, whose similar red hair Troy could just make out by the braid hanging down her back.

"We have an easy enough trail to follow." D'tanesse was also watching the pair. "Either Machaun…and the king…don't expect anyone to follow them, or they're setting a trap for us."

Troy stood. "They are setting a trap. Whether we spring it sooner or later is the variable."

D'tanesse did not ask her where she was going. Instead he watched her walk over to the woman and kneel on one knee beside her.

"Excuse me, Lady." Troy couldn't help noticing the infant sleeping fitfully, red-faced, in the crook of her arm. "Can you tell me which direction the warband has gone?"

She turned to face Troy. Her son rose and stood facing both of them, closing the conversation into a tight, three-person circle. When her eyes met Troy's, the mother blinked and straightened. The infant mewed, disturbed. "They go to Carmul. Every man who can lift a spear or throw a net." Her eyes went from Troy's face, to the scar on her face, to those on her arms, and then to the knife and quiver of arrows at her waist. "Who are you?"

"I am trying to find a friend. Did the king do this, or was it someone else?"

"The king."

"Did anyone else pass through?"

"Pass through?" The mother's distant expression was overtaken by incredulity, the beginning of anger. She straightened further. Her blackened shawl, intricately weaved and at one time probably beautiful, smeared grit on her shoulders as it slipped to the ground. "Everyone is passing through. Engar is ruined."

"What do you mean, everyone?"

"I mean what I say. You are the first to stop since the chieftain came to warn us. Of course there was no reason to worry at the time, or even think such a thing as this could happen. And when it did, like sheep we walked out and let the king have it. Our village, and he left it to burn." She seemed to be speaking to herself as well as to Troy, waking to an injustice she should have known. Her eyes, brown like her son's, were wide open, staring at Troy regardless of ash and smoke. Perhaps she recognized something else about the young woman, this warrior. Perhaps she recognized a Seawolf.

Troy breathed carefully. Her throat resisted speech, making every question more painful than the last. "What was the chieftain's name, who came before the king?"

"He said if we wanted to escape what was coming to send the women and children away and let the men come with him. Of course, we didn't. Kilar was his name."

"Kilar." Troy leaned closer and put her hand on the mother's shoulder. "Are you sure?"

The woman finally blinked, squeezing tears from behind turgid eyelids. "Then came the king, and we lost our men to him anyway. He said a purge needs to happen, to clear evil from Cathylon. He burned—" She remembered her son, crowded close to them and listening with his head down, staring at his sooty feet "—well, he's burned us all now, hasn't he?"

"Was there a young woman with the king? She'd have caramel hair, fine eyes...perhaps dressed in blue or gray."

The mother could not say one way or another.

"And the king went to Carmul?"

"That is what he said." The mother caught Troy's hand as Troy stood and held it. "Don't go after him. I know...he is the king, but this is wrong. Please, do not join him."

Troy shook her head. "I am going to find my friends and bring them back. I could not follow a man who does this to his own people."

"Are you a warrior?" The mother studied Troy with new interest, rising to her knees and shifting the infant to her other arm.

"I am—"

"What is your name, Lady?" This was a new voice. Others were watching them, listening to the exchange. Troy had not expected them to come alive all of a sudden, especially not over this. The owner of the new voice was an old man, draped with a cloak covered in black patches. She looked harder in the fading, grainy light and saw the patches were actually streaks of soot. She opened her mouth to say, *Llynx*, but a sharp cough from D'tanesse cut her short.

"Ah—hack—Troy L'abri Glor." He had not only found his voice, he was on his feet somehow. "This is the true ruler of Cathylon."

Troy's head tilted to one side, her widening eyes scolding him. Must he do this now? Right now?

There was no outcry following D'tanesse's proclamation. More people noticed the deepening quiet and drew closer to see what was happening to cause it.

"I am no one." Troy began to correct D'tanesse. "I—"

Small fingers crept over her hand. It was the boy, pressing the wafers D'tanesse had given him into her palm. She bent toward him, another refusal forming on her lips.

"I want you to have them." His voice trembled, made husky either from the smoke or sincerity. "You'll need them, while you're saving us."

The old man had come closer meanwhile, stumping through the grass and filth on a lamed foot. His hand was all sharp bones and callouses that abraded her arm when he gripped it. He gripped in that peculiar weak but heartfelt way of the aged, pressing against her bicep with tremorous fingers.

"He told us you might come." His lips curved back over his teeth, making his mouth a rounded wobbly line over his jaw. His eyes crinkled in that sad and desperate way Maon's had, years ago when she met first him. "And we did not listen. We suffer because we did not—"

Troy shook her head, but like the boy still clinging to her hand with both of his, the old fisherman would not be refused.

"—and as you apparently have suffered. We are, maybe, in some ways the same. Chieftain Kilar said Troy L'abri Glor would be the saving of us, and there has never been a people more in need of saving."

Troy swallowed, wishing for water to clear her throat. Instead, a soft lump there made her voice stick. "This may be a fight I cannot win." Her glance took them all in before she answered him. This time, she saw their faces. Each one stood out, vivid, fastening itself in her memory. They were women and children, confusion-struck. Most were ignorant of how they had come to be this way, and their silent gazes begged for a way to be better. Whatever else she meant to say dried up on her tongue, and she said nothing.

"We cannot fall much farther than we already have, Lady. But I know how I may rise, if but a little." Now the old man lowered himself, trembling in his joints but determined, to one knee. "Hail, Troy L'abri Glor. Hail…my queen."

All around her the women, children and old ones sank to the ground. If they were sitting already, they shuffled to their knees. The little boy, in a different expression of loyalty, rushed forward and threw both arms around her waist. He hung there with his hot little face pressed against her hip—the most ardent of subjects in his way.

Troy shut her mouth, which by now was gaping. She looked to D'tanesse for help and found him kneeling in the ashes with the rest. He was, for once, not grinning in mockery.

Chapter Thirty-Four

Smoke made four yellow-gray walls around the warband, shutting them and their prisoners into a private cell where moving ground was the only indication of change. After the first day, Terra would not have noticed the passing landscape even if he could see it. He was too busy trying to stay on his feet.

The ground became a peril, another antagonist among the twenty or so riding ahead of him, pulling him along. Bushes with twisted brittle limbs came up to trip him, claw holes in his clothes and skin if they succeeded or if he tried to step over the smaller shrubs. Grasses and thicker flowering stalks, some coated in ash, rubbed through his clothes and cuts. His legs first burned and then throbbed. He didn't know how they were finding their way, just that they were. Machaun was determined to catch Troy, and desperate enough to believe she was where Terra said she was.

Teyeda and Core, on either side of him, persevered as he did. They verified his claim about the book, even though they must have been as skeptical as Machaun was on first hearing it. They grunted with short bursts of breath, stepping over rocks and around shrubs. He learned to listen for the supple crush of leaves and sharp cracks of branches amidst the leathery drumming of riding warriors that signaled another bush.

His arms flew up, jerked by the rope as the horse ahead broke into a quick jog. Branches, grass, rocks rushed toward him. He ran with his arms out in front of him, trying to watch the ground but mostly feeling it through hard bumps and gouges. They were moving quickly toward Carmul. That was good. Even if Troy wasn't in the forest anymore—he was almost certain she wasn't—Imra probably was. She had disappeared, of course, by the time Terra woke to Machaun standing over him. Terra did not want these men, especially Machaun, to find her. Imra might not be sound of mind, but she was still his sister, too precious and gentle to be discovered by Machaun. The man seemed to like weakness. He liked to crush it.

The rope jerked again. Terra's wrists tried to leave his arms. His elbows were next, and then even his shoulders snapped in their sockets at the sudden force. He stumbled once, twice. The rope still pulled hard on his arms. Terra's feet lost contact with the ground and he pitched forward. Now he was skimming forward on his chest. Tiny rocks grated through his clothes, chewing long lines from sternum to navel.

He arched his back, all of his weight on his thighs, and crashed through a low bush full on. He turned his head just in time to save his eyes. A branch snagged his ear and sliced away. Fuzz-covered leaves got into his mouth and stuck in his hair. He glimpsed Core through the tangle—his mind barely registered what he saw past his own pain and panic—also on the ground. He twisted onto his side and caught the worst of the scouring shrub along his ribs and right hip. His breeches tore open below the waistband, ripping all the way to his knee. Then he was back on his stomach. The constant, relentless moving ground grumbled beneath his dragging weight. He leaned back, heaving with his shoulders despite their warning shriek that they would abandon their sockets, found leverage and rose to his knees. Pebbles cracked his kneecaps, bit into his shins. Teyeda called to him, "Stand up, Terra! On your feet! Terra, stand!"

Core was back up and shouting at the warriors. Terra could not understand it through his own voice in his mind echoing Teyeda's.

Stand! One foot, then the other. One foot—Now lean back, use the rope, stand up!

And then he was up, nearly sobbing with breath and adrenaline. Teyeda went down. Then Core again. Terra shouted them both to their feet, between his own lurching leaps and stumbles. He shouted to drown out the laughter of their captors. He shouted in spite of the consequent jerking that threw him face down again and again. He made no apology. He did not beg them to stop. Imra in the forest, far behind them. Troy—

He was slower gaining his feet the third time. The fourth time, slower still. The fifth time, he did not rise at all.

* * * *

Troy and D'tanesse stayed the night on the lake shore and woke before dawn. They left the remnant people of Engar with instructions to go to Yettmis, following the map D'tanesse had given the red-headed boy.

"Until this purge is over, nowhere else is safe," Troy told them. "D'tanesse and I have both been given refuge there at separate times. The chieftain is a fair man whose heart is for the good of Cathylon."

They rode in relative silence, following Machaun's trail. Troy did not say what she thought of the impromptu, crownless coronation and D'tanesse did not ask. Having revived enough to care what was around him, he probably wished he could have remained delirious. His face was painted with soot. His mouth hung open, breathing shallowly to avoid the stench of the burning villages as much as possible. Troy did not know how many were burning at once. The acrid fumes of scorched flesh and wood burned a permanent scar down her windpipe. Eventually, in the places where smoke hung thick over an indent in the plains, they wrapped their faces with the last scraps of D'tanesse's tunic.

Laic sweated in the hanging heat. Ashes stuck to his drenched coat until he no longer looked like a black horse, but a gray and brown one. Troy walked beside him when the smoke was thickest and tied a scrap of cloth around his halter, covering his nostrils. She had to rest him now as frequently as D'tanesse.

"Laic was a gift from Terra's family," she said during one such rest, as she squeezed water into the horse's mouth from the waterskin. It was midday. Yellow-gray smoke drifted around them—another village was being consumed a few miles away.

D'tanesse attempted a nod. Laic coughed.

"We'll come into cleaner air soon." Troy tried again.

"We can't go on like this." D'tanesse's eyelids drooped above the cloth hiding his mouth and nose, the red rims cutting across his green irises coated in moisture.

"Let's move on." She reached for his hands and pulled him to his feet.

D'tanesse gave a low moan in tandem with Laic as Troy helped him settle on the horse's bare back. They had shed the saddle hours ago to ease Laic's burden. D'tanesse was not quite well enough to walk yet. Troy carried the travel pack rolled on her shoulders, and they made slow progress. She stared ahead, counting red streaks visible on the trail. Dried blood, not yet covered by ash.

"Talk with me," D'tanesse rasped. "I cannot live another moment without conversation."

Troy took Laic's reins in her hand. He stepped readily forward, needing out of the poison air. His breath snuffled through the cloth covering his nostrils, making two rippling circles on either side.

"I found the limit of the Otnas." Her voice scratched out of her throat like it was made of sand.

"I didn't think there was one."

"There is."

Laic's and Troy's mingled steps fit into the long pauses between dialogue. She stared at the ground, counting each new streak of blood. Wondering if it was Terra's blood, and if she would find his body next. "I thought I could step out of one place into another. I meant to go where Estimal was."

"To stop him?"

She nodded.

"If you hadn't, Machaun would have you now."

She stared at another blood stripe, wiped long over bent withered grass. "I would have killed him."

Silence again. Troy glanced back. D'tanesse was slouched over Laic's neck, staring at his fingers tangled in black mane. She breathed in slowly, suppressing the urge to cough.

"That little boy was like Terra. He didn't look like him, but he was like him."

D'tanesse latched onto the name and rallied his own voice once more. "Terra told Machaun you went to Carmul. Said he saw you there."

Troy grunted surprise.

"On my honor he said it."

"What did you tell him? Machaun."

A pause, while D'tanesse gathered his breath to answer. "That he and his warriors were a clod of bumbling idiots and—" Another breath "—came to Kcen for nothing."

"I was going to ask next why you were wounded, but never mind."

The smoke was thinner ahead. They were on an incline now and the ash was for once sparser than the grass. Troy pushed on with her feet and D'tanesse with his words. If they lay down now, they might not get up again.

"Machaun had us bound and took us with him, for bargaining when he found you, or when you came to him. In one sentence Terra made himself and Core essential."

They stopped at the top of the incline and pulled the cloths down about their necks. They could breathe easier here. The smoke thinned above this pocket of shallow hills. The hills swelled higher and longer as they got closer to the mountains showing through the haze, orange and red blurs, roughened with a growth of trees.

The trail went on between the bases of two higher hills and disappeared. Troy slipped the waterskin spout between Laic's teeth and squeezed some water over his tongue. He lifted his head, swallowing gratefully.

D'tanesse continued. "He said he took the book of Esobir to Klenit."

At this, Troy turned to face him, holding the waterskin in both hands before her.

"That's what he said. 'We took the book back to Klenit while you chased Troy to Kcen. While you were burning the village, we were halfway to the mountains. And now she has escaped again while you were distracted by us here.'"

"Twice distracted in the same place. Twice without the book…" Troy mused. Laic pushed his nose against her forearm, reminding her he was still thirsty. She obliged him.

"He turned out useful after all." D'tanesse couldn't chuckle, but Troy sensed his desire to just the same.

"At least they will stay alive a little longer."

"Terra had your dagger, fallen where you dropped it on the hill. So he managed to leave it in case you returned to Kcen." D'tanesse squinted ahead, shifting a hand from Laic's mane to his bandaged side.

"Also." He sighed, wheezing the word out to prolong the last vowel, "Alsoooo, I did not try to staunch the wound in my side as I should have, but let the blood flow freely to make a path for you to follow—"

"Ki, D'tanesse, just tell me what happened. You do not need to go into detail." Troy fixed the cloth over Laic's nostrils again and then took a drink from the skin herself after wiping the nozzle.

"I only want you to know how much I value you that I would shed my very lifeblood—"

"So I could find you. Get on with it."

"Hmph. Well, my throat hurts now. I don't think I want to."

She slapped the skin against his leg. "Let's move on."

Revived somewhat by the less sordid air, they set a good pace. By dark they reached the last set of hills before the mountains. Here, those were like feet, ridges tucked into the lower slopes.

Troy left D'tanesse with Laic when they came to these and walked ahead, following the warband's trail around the bends. She could not afford to lose the element of surprise by stumbling into their camp, especially in her exhausted, half-sick condition.

"Mayhaps we should go in search of Kilar," D'tanesse said when she returned from the latest trek. "He may have ten or fifty warriors with him by now."

Troy dropped beside him on the blanket and pulled the waterskin out of the travel roll. "If any have joined him."

"Even with just his own from Daehexa," D'tanesse pursued. "They would follow him, not my father."

Troy had already begun a reply, but stopped and gave him a sharp look. "You've never called him that before, but once."

The once was long ago, or so it felt, in her dark room beneath the sands in Yettmis. D'tanesse shrugged one awkward shoulder. "Sometimes I do. He is."

"I wish you wouldn't. Anyway, here's what I think. Kilar was ready when Sema came with her warning. He took his warriors and hopefully

Esobir, and sent his people to hide on the plains until they could safely reach Yettmis. Daehexa was empty when the king reached it."

"Kilar and Raelcun were plotting some contingency," D'tanesse allowed.

"So, Sema and the Watch are with Kilar, carrying out whatever they have planned."

"Leaving you free to worry about Terra. What a convenient line of thought."

"Do you think it unlikely?"

"No."

"Then we carry on. After we have Terra and Core and Teyeda we can join with Kilar, then face the king and Machaun on our terms."

"Still outnumbered."

"I always have been."

"We."

She nodded, after exchanging level stares with him.

"Alright." He brushed a dot of ash from his folded knee. "How do you plan to pluck your friends from Machaun's fingers?"

Chapter Thirty-Five

"Eat. There you are." Machaun pushed a bit of jerky into Terra's mouth. Terra clenched his hands out of reflex. Even though they were bound to the wagon wheel behind him, he imagined the movement more than felt it. He chewed because he was starving, but he also bored a hateful hole with his stare through Machaun's wide forehead.

"We covered nearly twenty miles today. You've done well." Machaun picked another chunk of stringy, leathery meat out of the drawstring bag held in one hand.

Terra chewed. The left side of his face was a stinging mask of scratches. He was sure there were tiny rocks stuck in every fissure. His breeches were gone, worn clean away below his knees. Every part of his lower legs also burned. Burned and itched. The left side of his tunic was torn wide open, and a long line of his skin also.

"Try not to hit any more rocks with your head and we may go even faster." Machaun pushed the jerky between Terra's teeth. "We will reach the Seawolf that much sooner."

Teyeda, bound to the next wheel, heard this but said nothing. His skin and clothes matched Terra's except for a crusted patch on his chest. They had all fallen or were pushed over more times than they cared to remember. Machaun did give them periods of rest, riding in the supply wagon, but it was for the sake of time and not kindness.

Terra shifted his weight to one side to relieve his throbbing tailbone. That bruise from falling backward during the storm should have been forgotten by now, insignificant among all the other parts of his body singing in painful discord. It reminded him what he'd seen before he woke up to Machaun standing over him. It reminded him of the storm, their mission and, in a strange way, of Troy herself. It reminded him why he was here.

It didn't mean he wanted to sit on that pain, however.

"You just remember what he is to her," Terra rasped. His tongue felt like a piece of wood turning the jerky over in his mouth, clumsily getting pinched between his teeth. "If he is dead when we reach Carmul—"

Machaun slapped Terra's cheek and the raw skin erupted into tear-jerking pain. "I know her better than you do, boy. Keep your feet under you and your mouth closed. See after your own life."

Machaun knew Teyeda as well. He knew the manservant had recommended Troy to serve in the king's hall and had taught her a servant's ways. Machaun knew Teyeda was with her—or was in her vicinity—more often than not, and had seemed more than a little protective of her even when he did not need to be. All this led Machaun to believe they were attached, a thing neither Teyeda nor the brothers denied. He was a former servant who consorted closely with the woman—Machaun simply called Troy 'the woman' or 'Seawolf'—who was an enemy of the Inatru, the Inatru's way of life, Machaun and the king himself. Unless he had a claim that made him more valuable alive, Teyeda would be dead by now.

Machaun thrust jerky pieces into Teyeda's mouth, one after another with jabs of his thick fingers. It was no less torture to be fed by Machaun than dragged behind his horse. Terra's throat closed whenever Machaun knelt before him with the bag, but he made himself open, chew and swallow because his body needed it to keep alive. Though it was Machaun who bent the knee, they were made to submit with open mouths to take food from his fingers like children, with their arms secured behind them and vulnerable fronts exposed. Core, tied to the same wheel as Teyeda, received the paltry meal last, in silence.

"Sleep well, sirs." Machaun stood, letting the bag dangle by its leather string to close the pleated neck. "We'll be in the mountains tomorrow."

Terra waited until Machaun's heavy strides faded into the general sounds of the camp before turning his head toward Teyeda. His face was turned upward, searching for the stars none of them could see through the haze of smoke.

"It's your turn," Terra whispered.

Teyeda did not respond except to draw a deeper breath. His chest expanded, the dark blood stain riding on top of it like an island surrounded by skin and cloth instead of water. His eyes closed. His jaw bulged and deflated as he chewed, swallowed.

"Come on, Teyeda." Terra felt a jab of panic. "It was my turn last night, and it does help."

"I barely remember them."

"But what you do remember," Terra pressed, desperate to make him talk and keep talking.

Core leaned forward to see around Teyeda to Terra, alert but limp with exhaustion. His face was at the same time sapped of color and overcast by an amber shade from the strange, smoky light.

Every night they took turns talking, reminiscing on memories to keep their spirits up. After Machaun fed them they were left mostly to themselves save for the intermittent visits from warriors to make sure they were behaving. Terra and Core talked about their childhood, years before the rout of Kcen. They told of meeting Troy, of naming her, of the fight with Mytch. Teyeda told them of life in Camil Askanda, of meeting Sema and D'tanesse, of studying passages from the book of Esobir in their lower-story home.

"I don't know what else to tell," he said.

"Tell how you met Troy," Terra suggested. "You haven't yet."

Instead of answering Terra, Teyeda looked to the warriors standing around the fire. Twenty Inatru warriors grouped around the small campfire or lay on the grass. Always their weapons, long spears with four-bladed spearheads, were near them. While they ate, they stuck their spears headfirst into the ground beside them. They slept with spear in hand.

Light from the small cooking fire sent shafts of color through the curtain of smoke and men's moving shadows. The faint glow touched Teyeda's face and broad shoulders, but mostly he was inscrutable. Night was falling.

Terra was about to try one more time before starting a story of his own—just to say something—when Teyeda began.

"The Inatru took me from my home when I was a child. It was part of the tribute my village paid in exchange for warrior training, and also for extra favor in the eyes of the Inatru. There was no greater influence before the Seawolves came to Cathylon. So, I did not consider the Inatru an enemy, but benefactors. I never returned to my village."

He reported this flatly, without aggression, but he rarely said anything out of tone. Terra knew Teyeda held no love for the Inatru now, especially Machaun.

Terra shifted his weight again from his right side to his left, and studied Teyeda's profile. On the other side of Teyeda, Core said, "Sometimes it's better not to return."

"Do you think so?" Teyeda tipped his head back to rest it against the wheel, placing it carefully to avoid gouging any tender spots on his skull.

"Look what happened when we did."

Teyeda made a slight negative movement of his head, without lifting it. "That would have happened anyway. We could not have known where or when."

"Do you think she might have?"

Another shake. Then, returning to the former topic, "The Inatru made us wait in the foothills on the other side of these mountains while they razed Carmul. They brought her back with them. Some said was she dead; others, drowned. Estimal apparently intended to kill her, but changed his mind at the last moment. He was hoping she would tell him where the book of Esobir and the Otnas was hidden. She woke after two days, and her mind was blank.

They cut her face, marking her the king's property. She fought, then. The man who marked her—he was Inatru—died with her hands locked around his throat while others used whips to subdue her. The Seawolves knew nothing of it."

Terra's stomach began to churn. "You saw them do this?"

"To my shame," he answered, "I did nothing for her until afterward. I was a stupid creature, doing whatever the Inatru told me. But she…" He faltered, swallowing as his voice thickened. "The harder they tried to claim her the harder she struggled. I treated her lashings, stole a tunic to cover her. At the first opportunity, as we traveled back to the desert, I helped her slip away."

"And then she came to us," Terra finished out loud, just so Teyeda could hear he was still awake. "She was still wearing that tunic."

"When I saw her again in Camil Askanda…" Teyeda's eyes became distant. "She, of course, did not remember me. It was just as well."

Terra's eyes slid closed against his will. His body felt weighted to the ground by the sheer volume of smoke he was inhaling. He could actually feel it flowing over his tongue. "Who might have thought the girl you set free would return to do the same for you?"

Teyeda answered, but Terra's mind was clouded and slow. He wanted to call to Core, to make sure he was alright.

He dreamed, hearing the real voices of the warriors mingled with the voices of his dream. Core sat with him in the copse of their childhood. Their mother was cooking the evening meal and chatting, laughing with a group of men. The sun beat down on Terra through the branches. His skin was scalding red. Core lay on his back, smiling up at the hot sky.

"We did it," he was saying. His hair and face were clean from a recent scrubbing. "I am so proud of you."

They threw knives at the old target log, taking turns. The log was tall and thin. Then it had shoulders. Then it was Troy, with her hands at her sides.

"You can't take his place, Terra," she said. "Mytch doesn't want to be replaced."

The throwing knives hit her but it was alright. They sank into her chest and disappeared, or curved past her body like steel birds.

Core slapped Terra on the back. "Come on." He ran past Troy into the woods. "On your feet!"

"Terra," Troy called him back.

Terra…

Terra opened his eyes. A face hovered inches from his own. The lower part was a drape of black sagging skin. It had no mouth. A hand pressed against Terra's lips—he was being suffocated. He was going to die.

Well, if he was, Terra would not go easily. He thrashed his shoulders, opened his mouth and snapped down with his teeth on the hand trying to smother him.

Chapter Thirty-Six

They found the camp between two ridges that spread like fingers around the trailhead leading into the mountains.

Troy set seven small fires across the short ravine, which acted as a funnel, trapping the new smoke in its lowest point and concealing her approach to the camp.

In the hour between night and early morning she crawled on her stomach beneath the heavy fumes, stopping at last under the wagon where three figures rested. They were tied to the wheels, two together and one alone.

D'tanesse was busy with his own task: the warriors' horses. Four would go to them (Troy was not interested in crossing the mountains on foot) and the rest would be a diversion. The warriors could not chase them and the scattering horses, and horses were vital to chasing their quarry through the mountains. If Troy and D'tanesse were able to keep the element of surprise in their favor, getting out of the camp might be the easiest part of the rescue.

Troy came to the edge of the wagon and slithered underneath it. From here she could barely make out the smoke-blurred outlines of the nearest warriors stretched out on the grass. Now came the hardest part. She turned onto her back and eased her head and shoulders along the ground between the wheels, digging with her heels beneath the wagon until she was far enough out to see Core's face and shoulders above her. His chin rested on his chest, and he breathed shallow.

Slowly she rose to a sitting position facing the wagon. Core's head was now right beside hers. Troy woke him with a hand pressed gently over his mouth. His eyes flew open and he stiffened, locking eyes with her. She lifted her finger to her own lips, and when he nodded removed her hand.

He mouthed, *where have you been?*

Troy just shook her head and leaned close to whisper in his ear through the black cloth covering her mouth and nose. "When I cut you free, do not move yet. D'tanesse is getting horses. When he creates a diversion, follow me."

While Core woke Teyeda, whispering the same instructions, Troy slid back under the wagon and sliced through the ropes around his wrists, then Teyeda's.

Meanwhile, her mind tracked D'tanesse's progress, trying to predict his movements and time hers accordingly. By now he would have reached the horses, approaching from the hillside and keeping them as a shield between himself and the warriors. He would be preparing to spook them into a frenzy with another of his powder mixtures. He had grumbled about being nearly out of tricks, but Troy had her doubts about that.

There was no time to hesitate. Troy scooted around to Teyeda's other side and pushed her head and shoulders out into the open. As before, she sat up and placed her hand over Terra's mouth to wake him.

Instead of sitting quietly and listening, he thrashed against his bonds and bit her hand. She choked back a startled yelp, clenching her jaw. Her eyes watered. He bore down harder, breaking skin.

"Terra. Let go." Her whisper was strained through her teeth. Immediately he obeyed. She pulled the cloth down and raised her fingers to her mouth, tasting salty blood on her tongue.

"Forgi—"

Her other hand flew up, pressing four fingers over his lips while they stared at each other. The left side of his face was a field of scratches obliterating his cheek and part of his eyebrow. Troy's eyes flicked over his body, taking in the missing tunic, the long gouges on his bare chest and arms. A rash of dark streaks ran down his side below his ribs to the top of his hip, disappearing into the shadow hiding his legs.

"Al ki." She swayed toward him, dropping her head. Her hand moved from his mouth to the wagon planks behind his head. "Ki!"

"I'm alive." His rasped whisper was calm. He turned his head, resting his temple against hers. Her cheek brushed against the stiff, tangled hair on his temple. A vein pulsed faintly beneath his skin. "Don't be afraid, Troy." The sharp smell of his blood and the muted scent of dirt filled her mouth and nose. His breath caressed her cheek as he whispered again. "Remember in Kcen, I promised we would face him together."

She nodded.

"I want more than that for us. I want life with you, after."

Troy inhaled sharply. Her fingers scraped against the dry plank, forming a fist. Surely he was incoherent. This was not the time to speak of feelings. This was the time to move, to run. She reached around him to find his bound hands. His fingers were crusted with dried blood from his wrists, where the rope had savaged skin.

"I couldn't let the king know I care for you. The Glass…" She owed him that much, at least.

"I don't care what he knows." The stone in his whispered voice told her what was in his eyes, if she raised her head to look. Gone was the boy from Kcen who had played with her in the copse and grinned at her behind his practice sword. A man owned that voice now, and those eyes. "I care about my promise."

And there it was. That was why he'd followed her so doggedly. That was how he could comfort her regardless of his tied hands and his beaten body. Troy's own hands involuntarily stilled, the knife blade pressed halfway through the rope.

"I don't want to take his place," he breathed against her hair. "I want my own."

"You have it already." She turned and pressed her lips to his cheekbone, below his uninjured eye. "Now hold still. We must go quickly. Stand up." She motioned to Core and Teyeda. They stood with a struggling effort, bracing for whatever was to come. Terra stood last, weaving. Troy put out a hand to steady him. D'tanesse would be instigating the distraction any second. Any second now. Troy counted slowly to ten. Then to ten again.

"We should be moving," Core whispered. "Before someone comes."

Someone was coming already. Terra saw the outline first and stiffened, dizziness twisting him slowly to one side. One of the warriors nearest them rose to his feet and walked toward them. Core's palms found the wagon behind him and he pressed against the slats, making the whole thing creak on its axles.

Still nothing from D'tanesse.

The warrior's outline sharpened. Now Troy could see the stiff edges of his leather tunic around his shoulders. He stopped. He saw the captives standing up. He saw Troy standing with them, knife in hand.

Time held its breath. The warrior sucked in his own breath to shout. Troy rushed at him. Two steps. Four steps. Her eyes fixed on his neck, hand ready to slice his words from his windpipe.

"Intru—"

BOOM!

The warrior jerked toward the sound. His eyes went wide, wider, staring at the source of the noise and what was coming from it. Behind him, more shapes rose in the gloom, shouting. Troy did not deviate. Pushed even faster by adrenaline, she leaped at him, turning the knife, and punched her closed fist into his throat. He fell choking, clutching his neck.

Core was already running when she spun back to the wagon.

"Wait!"

Terra and Teyeda started to follow him in spite of her warning, but they slowed and turned toward the sound of panicked pounding hooves.

Time asphyxiated.

A wave of heat shuddered past them, rifling smoke vapors as it came.

Throaty squeals rose in the churning air. A backdrop of blue-white flashed up behind twenty charging horses, a wall of flesh and bone. Coarse strings of mane and tail flashed about their white-ringed eyes. They came into the camp with necks stretched up, forelegs stretched out, cutting crescents in the ground with black hooves and shoving with coiled hindquarters, skimming forward, unstoppable.

"Teyeda—move!" Troy shoved Core—who had also stopped by now, staring—forward out of the way. To fall under that stampede was death.

"Here, Teyeda! Terra!"

Troy glimpsed D'tanesse perched on Laic's back, skirting the rush, heading for the wagon. Then she too was sprinting toward the camp with Core, away from the stampede. The running horses trampled through the camp, some cutting between the wagon and dead campfire, some running wanton over men, knocking their spears down and throwing pieces of turf, clothing, even flesh up behind. Those who went down died in moments, rolling then flopping as their ribs and skulls crunched like shells under the rush of hooves.

Troy pushed her legs faster, breathing in the spray of her own sweat as it rolled over her lips into her open mouth. She was just another running body among those scattering for safety. Men dodged around her, hardly glancing at her face. Recognition registered on a few, but she was past them and gone before they could react.

Core, about fifteen yards ahead, was nearly to the boulder at the base of the mountains on the other side of the camp. Behind them was the cacophony of D'tanesse's distraction—and footfalls drawing nearer.

Troy glanced over her shoulder and saw a lone man sprinting after them. He was shouting something, trying to alert his companions probably, but she didn't see any more warriors joining pursuit.

The warrior behind her suddenly stopped. The stiff twang and hiss of an arrow separated from the other noises. Troy threw herself to the side too late—the bolt bit into her thigh. She twisted as she fell, reaching for her knife and landing hard on her back. Her lungs seized on impact, cutting off her breath for a moment. She rolled over, dropped her knife and caught the warrior's arm with her both hands as he pounced down on her. One hand grabbed his wrist, one pushed his elbow. Twisting. Pulling weight and momentum to one side. His knife pushed into the ground beside her head.

Troy kept his arm firmly grounded, with one hand on his wrist, and hammered at his elbow with her other fist. He lifted one knee and slammed it down on her thigh, pushing down over the place where the arrow protruded. She screamed, anger and agony.

The weight and heat of the man on top of her vanished as Core bowled into him. Troy rolled to her feet, retching as pain pushed nausea into her throat. She heard whistling gasps from Core and the warrior, and brought her head up again. Core was on top, flailing wildly. He latched onto the man's knife hand, trying to wrestle it away. Troy searched for her knife in the grass, found it. Looked up again. Core was bearing down with furious strength, forcing the warrior back. For a moment it seemed he would win…until the man yanked his arm free and stabbed his knife into Core's side. Core gasped for air and found none. He toppled onto his back.

Troy's knife left her hand, spinning point over pommel. It drove into the center of the warrior's chest, cracking bone as it sank in. Troy grabbed the shaft in her leg with both hands and snapped it off near the bloody flesh. She stood. Made her leg bear her. The warrior's mouth hung open, his eyes lidless and bugged. Troy grabbed a fistful of his brown hair, pulled the knife from his chest and slashed it across his throat. She threw him face down and turned, sobbing for air, to find Core.

Blood leaked from his side, staining the ground beside him. She staggered to his side. His eyes focused on her face as she cradled his head with one hand and lifted his shoulders a little with the other.

"I hesitated—" Quick breaths split each syllable. His lips shivered as if cold.

"Core!" She searched for words, feeling his blood soak her breeches. She moved her hand from his shoulders and pressed it against his ribs. Warm liquid pushed through her fingers. "Core—"

"No—I—want this." His hand groped for hers, pulling it to his chest. Their fingers slicked together. It was hard to keep hold. "I am—not sorry. I—love you—sister—"

Troy could not swallow the burn filling her throat. She opened her mouth, but there was only a sob there. She pressed her lips together and leaned close to his face as his voice began to fade.

"I love—Terra—" Tears rolled from the corners of his eyes, washing trails through grimed skin at his temples. "And you—love him—"

"Core…"

He coughed, and blood trickled from the side of his mouth in a black line. "Imra…watch her…" His body racked with spasm, and then succumbed to the grass.

Troy clenched her teeth hard, squeezing her eyes shut, and curled over him. Her forehead came to rest on his. For a moment, the shouts of men grew distant, fading from her notice. In her mind she saw him young again, vibrant with life. Throwing knives in the copse. Scuffling with Terra. She saw him grinning with bright, sharp excitement, wielding a bundle of sticks as a practice sword. Laughing with his family in their hearthroom.

Now he had saved her life.

"I will never forget." She ground her teeth as tearless sobs jerked from her chest, making her voice uneven. "I will never forget what you've done."

Something unseen, unreal, began to crack in her chest. She was going to shatter from the inside.

Thudding hooves brought her back to the present. Her head snapped up, she tensed to spring to her feet, but it was only D'tanesse and Teyeda riding toward her. They saw her, the dead warrior, and then Core dead in her arms. Their faces fell slack. Both walked their horses toward her, each step taking longer than it should have. One riderless horse paced beside D'tanesse, who held its reins.

There was still the threat of Machaun's warband, milling on the other side of the smoke curtain. There was still the arrowhead in her thigh and the pain shooting from it. Most of all, there was the cracking sensation spreading through her chest, making everything else distant.

"They are rallying already." One of them spoke—she didn't know which. "They'll be on us if we stay another moment. We must go."

Troy knew they must go. She knew she must stand, must mount and ride away. If she stayed, she was dead also. "Where is Terra?"

D'tanesse answered her. His eyes were too much to look at. They spoke too much, while his mouth only said, "Llynx…he fell. I saw him go down and tried to reach him, but the stampede went over…"

Her body pounded in time to the throbbing wound in her thigh. She drew Core's body close against her.

D'tanesse dismounted and came over to her. The grass crushed beneath D'tanesse's shoes as he stopped beside her, and then he was kneeling. His hand found her shoulder. It was trembling, persistent. His lips moved in her peripheral vision. She felt his breath, but his voice was only a resonance in her ear. Core's cooling weight left her hands. His head drifted to one side, resting on the ground. A tangle of auburn hair slid across his closed eyes.

D'tanesse's lips were moving again, and he lifted her bodily to her feet. Then her own legs were dragging her toward Teyeda and the waiting horses. Blood ran down her leg with each step and pooled in her boot. D'tanesse maintained his arm across her shoulders. Keeping her upright. Pressing her forward. Her eyes burned in her skull, radiating heat into her head and face.

It means nothing without him here. It all comes to nothing.

"He lived for you, and that means everything."

She heard D'tanesse's words this time, answering her. She didn't remember speaking.

Laic loomed before her. Her hands reached, gathering coarse black mane. D'tanesse pushed from below and she swung up onto Laic's hot, damp back. His ribs expanded against her throbbing legs with deep breaths.

You have not won, Machaun. You will never win.

She looked back at the fleeing shadows in the camp, cloaked by darkness and turgid air.

D'tanesse mounted his horse beside her.

I am not afraid of you. Come to me, follow and see. I am not afraid of you.

The phrase stuck in her mind. *I am not afraid...I am not afraid of you..I am not—*

D'tanesse slapped Laic's hindquarters, and Laic broke into a jog, following Teyeda who was already riding up the trail that cut across the first mountain face. Laic's body rolled beneath her smoothly, carrying her with him.

I am not afraid of you.

Her own voice lingered, almost an echo behind her, and only then did she realize she was shouting.

Chapter Thirty-Seven

Two dreams chased each other, scintillating before the eye of Terra's mind. One was like a daydream. He sat on the side of a hill looking into the deserted camp. The grass was trampled flat, except for a thin line here or there that had somehow escaped obliteration. He watched two young people, a man and woman, sitting close together. She cradled him in her arms. The young man looked horribly beaten, bloody on every part of his body. The young woman caressed him, rocking him like a child. Her hair was a tangled net falling on either side of her face, resting on her shoulders and brushing his torn cheek with each minute shift of her body. She rocked back and forth, then side to side.

"Could this be what you want?" he asked.

His companion, someone sitting beside him but whom he could not see, answered, "My will is for other things."

"Mine too," Terra said.

"Our will made known makes it breakable. The unknown cannot be undone."

* * * *

The second dream was filled with the dull hum of his failing mind and watery, bleary images.

An arrowhead dangled above him, swinging on the end of a scarlet thread. The thread wound around a woman's neck. Her hair was as light as the haze enveloping both of them. It brushed his cheek as she leaned over him, rocking him back and forth, side to side. Her hand was cool against his skin when she lifted his head. He tried to say her name, but could not form the word.

Imra smiled faintly.

* * * *

"Troy is gone." Terra pulled his knees toward his chest. His bare feet rested in trampled yellow grass.

It was the peaceful dream again.

He and his companion observed the scene below quietly, talking without turning their eyes from it.

"She is going through the mountains, yes."

"To Carmul?"

"Yes."

His companion was very calm, making Terra feel calm. Near the young man and woman, two more men lay unmoving. One had curly hair, with a dark, open gash in his side. The other was headless. The woman only paid attention to the one in her arms.

"Will she be alright? Will she live?"

* * * *

In the second dream, his vision clouded and then cleared again when tears overflowed his eyelids. He should have tried harder to help his sister. He could have. All the time she spent alone, grieving alone, and he'd left her to do it. He left her because he couldn't help her, and that…

That thought broke him.

Imra looked into his face. Concerned lines tensed across her forehead. She pressed her cheek against his, comforting silently. Her hands gathered his shoulders with gentle affection.

Terra's words came out finally in broken, breathy puffs. He could not seem to make air stay in his lungs. "I was—the reason she—came back and—I've lost her—"

Imra rocked him gently. Tears dropped from her eyes and splashed, burning, onto his cheek.

* * * *

"My breath is here, but the place is your domain," said his companion. "Life can be given and it can be taken away. That is the choice of man."

"Will you help?" Terra continued to watch the young woman cradling the young man.

"Yes."

* * * *

He wanted to say so many things. *Watch over her,* Siegra had told him. *Watch over our queen.*

He had lost her twice now. In the end Troy loved him. That was his victory. So futile, lost as soon as found.

"I couldn't—help." His words choked in his throat. "Couldn't even—"

A faint rush of wind pushed past them, bending what was left of the standing grasses.

Imra's lips brushed his ear as she whispered with a voice long dormant. "Sometimes…you cannot."

Pain consumed Terra. He couldn't breathe.

* * * *

"So you are for us." Terra felt a small satisfaction at this. It just went to show D'tanesse did not know everything, after all.

"I am always."

"Why let this happen? If you could help, why not sooner? It might have been avoided."

His companion never moved, but when he answered his voice had somehow changed. It was less the voice of a man and more an essence of weight and presence.

"Life must be created, but also maintained. I keep the agreement I make because I am the agreement."

"But how can you suffer such injustice? I don't understand."

"Do you truly know what justice is? Don't you know love must be chosen, or it is no love at all?"

The young man lay still in the woman's arms. A rumbling sound entered the valley, the noise of many riders. Terra watched them appear over the crest of the ridge. Their faces flashed in the glow of sun diffused by smoke. Their cloaks were soiled but whole. Beneath the dark cast the original colors showed: deep blue, dusk red and pine green.

"If Troy L'abri Glor asks, I take action. My choice is to let her choose."

The riders drifted over the ridge down into the ravine where the young woman sat with the dying young man. Two men rode ahead of the assembly—one dark skinned with black curls and the other pale, wider in the shoulders with straight brown hair bound at his thick neck.

"I will not waste your sacrifices, nor will I fail to help when you ask of me," his companion continued. "This is always so. Your strength is not enough. I give you some of mine."

A hand rested on Terra's shoulder and warmth seeped from it into him. It was not a dry heat. Not a heat from the outside, scorching skin and flesh to ash. It was warm like the comfort of hot stew, of intimate laughter before a bright hearth, or stepping into a warm room out of freezing cold, running into welcome arms. It filled Terra to his toes, like wine stretching a wineskin. It overflowed to his thoughts, his breath. It was ending his life, and beginning it, ending and beginning again.

"I will not abandon you, Terra of Kcen."

The dreams ended.

* * * *

Water touched Terra's lips, spilling onto his tongue. It tasted of leather. He swallowed, desperate for its cool comfort to be in his body. He opened his eyes and light flooded in. An arrowhead dangled above him swinging on the end of a scarlet thread.

Real.

Terra closed his eyes. It was still there when he reopened them. The thread wound about a young woman's neck. Her hair was lighter than the smoke haze above her, diffused by midday. It brushed his cheek as she leaned over him, dank but cool against his skin when she lifted his head with one hand. Her cheeks shone wet, scored with dark smudges. Terra tried to say her name, but could not form the words.

Nearby, he could hear voices. Boots trudged and scuffed around them, walking about. Neither the voices nor footsteps sounded angry or panicked, but that meant little to Terra just now. All that concerned him was the face above him, the very last face he thought he would see…and here she was, with relief shining in her wet gray eyes. One corner of her mouth lifted in the characteristic smile so long hidden, and then her face and head moved out of his field of vision.

More cool water came a moment later, pouring over his arms, his bare stomach, his legs. His skin felt stretched. Water poured over it smoothly, as over river stones. Her palm rubbed away dirt and blood which grated briefly as it ran off him.

When her face reappeared above him he tried once more to speak. This time his voice obeyed. "You're back…"

Imra lifted him again with an arm around his shoulders, supporting his head as she embraced him.

"You too." Her voice cracked from smoke or misuse. Terra didn't care. She spoke.

Sticky moisture welled and overflowed from Terra's eyes. He rested his chin on her thin shoulder and with effort lifted one arm to hug her.

She rocked him gently. Their heads and hair and fingers tangled together as the embrace tightened and their chests heaved in hard, silent emotion. Drops of water lingering on his skin soaked into the threads of her faded dress and her dress gave up bits of its grime to smear on his skin.

Later she would tell him how she followed Troy from Kcen across the plains and hills to Machaun's camp. Her mind had cleared in spite of the smoke clogging everything else, cleared with distance as she left Kcen behind. She would tell how she found his body in the trampled grass, and at last found her voice when she held him. For now they simply clung to each other in shared tears and reunion.

Gradually he became aware of someone crouching behind Imra, watching his face closely. He blinked several times, bringing the new face into focus. Streaks of ash meandered along the curve of her chin and over round cheeks. Caramel hair escaped the edges of a long, once-red headscarf. Her lips moved, speaking his name.

"Terra. Oh, Terra…"

"Sema?" Of course it could not be, but here she was. A deep blue cloak pocked with tiny burns draped down her front, framing a burnt-orange tunic. She reached out to him, squeezing his arm while she gazed at him with peculiar sadness.

As if that weren't enough shock, Siegra appeared next, crouching beside Sema. She laid her dry, dirty hand over his wet one, gripping so hard his knuckles rubbed against each other.

"You're a sight," she rasped, and shook her head once sharply. Black soot filled the crinkles of skin around her dark eyes and masked her freckles. Her cheeks, merely thin when they left Yettmis, were now obvious depressions on either side of her face. "We ride soon, when Norem and Ivel are back. Can you walk?"

Terra managed to lift his head from Imra's shoulder and nod. He was upright only with her help, and he hadn't yet considered standing, much less walking. He must do both though, or be left behind. And if he stayed here, he would never see Troy again.

Troy.

His memories returned with the force of a nightmare, and he found he could sit on his own. He was struggling to gather his feet under him before he realized it. "Where is Troy?"

Siegra caught one arm, lifting him the rest of the way, and Imra bore him up with his other arm still around her neck.

"Your friend—" Sema glanced at Imra, faltering.

"My sister."

Sema blinked and continued. "—sister indicated she went into the mountains by that trail." She pointed toward it.

"Norem and Ivel went to scout while we…looked after you." Siegra's voice caught strangely, and suddenly she needed to look at anything but

Terra's face. They settled on the trail in question, which began near a fat boulder and disappeared into the tree-covered slope. Terra looked where she did, then turned a questioning look of his own to Sema. Her eyes were soft with pity.

"Terra." She swallowed and could not finish, also turning to look elsewhere. When she moved, Terra saw what lay on the other side of the boulder. Warriors walked up and down, gathering rocks and placing them on a long, growing pile.

Terra's head began to throb.

"We found you by accident, coming from a village a few hours away along the foothills. We came upon this place as you see it. You were near death, and Core…" Her voice thinned then disappeared in Terra's ears.

He forced his legs to move, leaning on Imra and Siegra's arms heavily at first. As they drew near the pile of rocks, he shrugged free of them. He stumbled over knobs of grass and disrupted sod on his own, toward the mound and his brother's body hidden beneath it. Imra and Siegra stayed close on either side of him. Sema came a few steps behind.

The chinking of stones dropping onto the resting place halted as he approached. The sun gleamed sharp and warm through thinning smoke, illuminating each stone and darkening the shadows between each jagged edge.

Terra bent and reached out to the pile. His fingers splayed over the top of the mound, then closed slowly into a fist. His fingernails scraped through a film of ash and choss as his fingers wrapped around one stone. Imra's arm crept across his shoulders and pulled him close against her. Over his closed fist she placed her own hand, wrapping her fingers around his so their hands appeared as one giant fist, enclosing the small grave stone. Terra lifted both their hands and pressed his lips to the back of Imra's gritted knuckles.

Sema, stopping beside them, bowed her head. Tears pattered onto the ground in front of her worn boots. Terra became aware of hands coming to rest on his shoulders, his arms, his back. Maon's voice murmured behind him. Emori closed in beside Siegra with his head uncovered, the wrappings loose about his neck and shoulders. Mikal came in on the other side by Imra, looming a head above them all.

"Your brother was a sincere man." Siegra still did not look at Terra as she spoke, but stared down at the grave and then across it as more men, warriors Terra did not recognize, gathered facing them. On the slope beyond, two riders in gray came out of the trees' cover at a jog.

"Sometimes he cared too much about his siblings." Terra found he could speak easier now, though his throat was still rough. "So much that it blinded him to the struggles of others."

"Cannot fault him for loving deeply." Her mouth tightened, as one of the riders raised his hand to them. "Not when I am guilty of the same."

The riders came closer, and Terra recognized Norem and Ivel, the remaining members of the Watch. Norem hailed them, stopping short of the assembly. He bent his head as he dismounted, saluting the sky with the thick tuft of ropelike hair bound tight back from his face. One of the warriors among those that Terra did not recognize strode to meet them.

Sema touched Terra's elbow. "It is unlikely an enemy will come this way again soon. I can stay behind with you, if you need—"

"Who is that?" Terra nodded at the thick-shouldered warrior talking to Norem and Ivel.

"That is Kilar," she said quietly. "The chieftain of Daehexa, where I was born. He met us before we even reached the village."

"He had anticipated trouble for some time," Siegra put in, "and had prepared his people well. We rode on to the next village without stopping, and Kilar joined us later with any warriors he could gather. We were making our way to Klenit on the other side of this mountain."

"Come with me." Terra made his way around Core's grave to where Kilar was speaking with Norem and Ivel.

"This trail is the most direct route through the mountains, besides the Aigroe pass to the west," Maon added, walking behind him, "which Estimal and his warhost now occupy."

Terra nodded, but his focus and words were for the chieftain. Kilar stopped speaking to Norem and turned as Terra stopped beside him.

"Lord Kilar. Machaun is after Troy at this moment. She is the queen of Cathylon, and of the Seawolves, and she wields the Otnas. We must follow them and stop him." He was aware that there was a better way to preface these facts, but not a quicker one. Time was all that mattered.

Kilar examined Terra, looking him up and down as he spoke. Terra made his expression as earnest as possible. If standing on tiptoes would have lent his words influence, he would have done it.

"Why do I sense—" Kilar rubbed his eye, flush from smoke around a pale blue iris "—that if your gaze were an arrow, I would be pinned to the man behind me?"

"If we do not help her, Klenit will be lost. All of Cathylon will be lost. We must go after her. And she is the Deliv—"

"Yes, I am aware." Kilar did not smile but his voice hinted amusement. He nodded with raised brow to Sema before asking Terra, "What is your name?"

"Terra of Kcen."

"And of the Watch, Lord Kilar," Siegra said, close beside Terra's shoulder. Terra did not remember being followed, but her presence was nonetheless appreciated.

"I am glad you are better, Terra of Kcen and the Watch. Your wounds when we first happened upon you looked fatal."

"Well enough," Terra began, glancing down, and quickly lost his words. His breeches were sheared below the knees and his tunic rent with gashes, but his skin was whole. Bruised, and a little muddy, but whole.

"Your companion must be an excellent healer."

Imra shook her head and kept shaking it when Terra replied eventually, "Yes, she…has always been good with remedies."

Kilar nodded. His pale blue eyes moved to the other members of the Watch standing around Terra, then to Sema. He rubbed his beard with a gloved hand. "Norem tells me we are several hours behind Troy."

Norem fidgeted with the reins in his hand, looking from Siegra to Terra, then back to Siegra. Another time Terra would have looked back to Siegra to see what look she was giving Norem, but Kilar's words superseded any other curiosity.

"That trail opens out on the far side of the mountains. Klenit is to the west and the ruins of Carmul on the nearer eastern side. Both Machaun riding after Troy and Estimal riding to Klenit will first have to enter the valley between the pass and Carmul. If we can reach her in time, we may be able to keep her from riding into the maw of a warhost. One way or another, we must go now and quickly."

His warriors took the statement as command and went for their horses, as did most of the Watch. Terra, Maon and Sema stayed beside Kilar. Imra still held Terra's hand on his other side. Siegra stayed also, in case anything important was about to be planned.

"Troy held her own well enough when I knew her," said Kilar, "but every power has its limit. This chase will end one way or another, hard or harder. She must not make her stand alone."

"I will do whatever you need," Terra told him.

"I know." Kilar's raw glance was tinged with desperation held under strict control. "I am counting on it."

Chapter Thirty-Eight

They stopped only to rest and tend Troy's leg. The trail zigzagged first through close ranks of pine trees, then over the first ridge before descending into a ravine.

D'tanesse led them through the center of it until they came to an aged pine, thick and knobbed at the bottom. Troy sat at the base of the pine, back pressed against the deep ridges of bark, shoulders weighted by Teyeda's wide hands, while D'tanesse worked the arrowhead out of her flesh. He spread the edges of the wound open, grasping the splintered tip of the shaft with his fingers.

Troy punched back against the trunk with her shoulders and head. White bursts of light crowned her vision.

"Llynx, control it. Teyeda, stop her moving."

Teyeda leaned on her shoulders, and the bark bit into her skin on the other side. Her left heel protested, scraping lines through the layer of pine needles and tiny flowers.

"Teyeda! Speak to her, or something."

"I don't know what to say!"

D'tanesse pulled at the shaft, and the arrowhead dragged after. Troy's hands seized at her sides, cracking fistfuls of needles. Saliva bubbled between her clenched teeth, and a prolonged shriek boiled in her throat. Teyeda grabbed for her hands and opened them with his. Shards of dry needles sprinkled to the ground. Her fingers clawed into the backs of his hands.

D'tanesse muttered and pulled again. Troy arched her head back and forced her legs still, clamping her jaw shut. Tears escaped her eyes and coursed in tandem down her cheeks, mingling with saliva in the corners of her mouth.

"Teyeda, I can't do it all myself! Say anything, whatever comes to mind!"

Teyeda began to speak to her, and her mind latched onto the sound of his voice to escape her body's pain. "He saved our lives, Llynx. Stared right at Machaun and told him you knew what he would do all along. If you kill us, he said, you will lose any chance of meeting her on your own terms. He was strong for you. Be strong now."

"He deserved better—"

"Machaun fears you more than anyone now."

Her words were groaned from the pit of her stomach between gasps. "I treated him terribly—couldn't even let him keep his promise—"

"He never held it against you. He loved you."

"I killed him!" Another sharp groan, as pain seared into her hip and knee.

"We all killed him!" D'tanesse snapped, glaring at his own fingertips buried in her flesh. "Stay still!"

Teyeda sighed, holding her hands down at her sides. His voice remained low and constant beside her ear. "You loved him. That was all he wanted."

The arrowhead came free. New, clean pain rushed into her leg. Troy's head dropped forward onto Teyeda's shoulder and he settled an arm across her back. "He made Machaun believe—he made all of us believe you have a plan, some ultimatum. Let us make his effort count."

D'tanesse packed the cavity left by the arrow with clean leaves and bound it with strips cut from his breeches. Teyeda let her rest against him, brushing her palms clear and pulling out the needles that burrowed into her skin when she'd grabbed them. Eventually he pulled gently away from her.

"What am I now?" she whispered, bowing her head. "What am I doing?" Her tears dripped down onto her tunic, then on D'tanesse's hand as he reached for her. Blood and water mingled—her blood—on his skin, in the dark all seeming the same. D'tanesse pressed her shoulder. She reached for him as sobs shook her again, and he cried with her, their mingled regrets accepted and understood.

Teyeda returned with the horses, speaking a quiet, "Llynx," to remind them of the situation. A sword belt was buckled around his waist, the weapon that had belonged to the warrior who killed Core. He saw her looking at it and stepped back, shifting to remove it from her line of vision. Troy understood why he would take it—any weapon right now was better than none. In his place she would have taken it also, but she looked away regardless.

She wiped her face, finally controlling herself, and they walked her to Laic. Pain throbbed in her throat as she settled on his back. She buckled forward, gagging into his mane. D'tanesse swung up behind her and wrapped his arm securely around her waist, and they moved on. Teyeda led D'tanesse's roan mount ahead of them, guided by the thin trail meandering through the mountains.

Sunlight painted the peaks above them as the sun rose, then dappled pine boughs at midday.

"The air is clearer here. And cooler," Teyeda observed at one point, when they sat to rest beside a trickling stream.

Troy cupped water over her thigh, sitting with her leg extended over a dark, rock shelf jutting above the stream.

"At least breathing is no longer among our afflictions." D'tanesse squeezed water from her discarded, blood-soaked bandage, strips of sullied white cloth. Rose-colored dribbles ran out between his fingers. He rinsed and squeezed until only the bandages were bloodstained and the escaping dribbles were clear. The water blushed pink also after touching Troy's outer thigh. She stared at it: the red edges of her skin looked like a slack mouth and the inside a raw, toothless maw.

D'tanesse caught her hands as she continued to splash automatic douses of water over her thigh. "It will have to do." He sprinkled a small amount of white powder along the line of her wound, then pulled two gray stones from an oblong pocket and held them, each in one hand, over the line.

Teyeda held down her ankles. "Try not to scream. They might be close enough to hear."

"She screamed enough right outside their camp." D'tanesse cracked the stones against each other.

The powder flashed blue-white as sparks fell on it. Smoke curled up in small clouds and quickly dissipated. Troy groaned, stiffening with both hands pressing her hips. Her head slumped forward.

"At least your pain will be a burn now, not infection—"

Her knuckles clipped his jaw and he jerked back. She then spun to the side, heaving bile into the trickling water. She had insisted on closing the wound this way after she realized she was trailing blood. D'tanesse agreed it would be prudent, as they didn't have time to care for it properly. Once the bitter nausea subsided and she could think again, Troy was not sorry. The pain was distracting but now she could make it useful. It would keep her awake, and the black scar would remind her of things she did not want to forget. She needed that pain to think of, or else she had only the cold ache settling in her core.

They slept briefly, and were moving again before the sky darkened.

A full moon silvered clusters of leaves overhead when they rounded the final mountain before the coast. The ground sloped away evenly toward a wall of yet more trees. Moonlight glowed over a clearing of wild flowers on long stems and soft, short grass. Troy was riding on her own now, bent forward and using Laic's withers for balance, but independent nonetheless.

Teyeda and D'tanesse rode just behind her. They muttered back and forth on occasion, and though Troy could hear them she did not care to include herself.

"We should try to cheer her." This, from D'tanesse. He had made little fuss over his own wound the past two days, however it must still be aching.

"What do you suggest?" Teyeda also suffered in silence. Though his bruises might not be as grievous in depth, they all but covered his body. There was nothing to do except keep riding, so they did.

"I was hoping you had an idea."

Troy stared ahead at Laic's ears, listening to the four-count of his steps until they reached the far edge of the clearing. A large flat rock lay at the base of the treeline, as good a place as any to stop, she felt. Teyeda and D'tanesse stopped beside her and waited for her to say something.

She stared at the trees and then down at the flat rock. A silver mist seeped along the ground behind them, flowing around it.

"Should we rest?" D'tanesse took conversation upon himself, solely. "Yes, we must. It's not very far from here. In daylight we might glimpse the water here and there through these trees." He dismounted. "Doesn't it smell like the sea? Yes, I believe it does…"

Teyeda dismounted and offered his hand to help her dismount. As she shifted to one side, a burning cramp seized her entire leg from hip to heel. She grimaced and shook her head.

"If I get down, I won't get back up."

"We will help you. If you don't move it occasionally it will grow too stiff. You must walk a little."

Still shaking her head, Troy allowed him to help her down. D'tanesse appeared on her other side, and they walked along the treeline. On their right were the trees and dense shadows; on their left, a moon-silvered field. Faint purples and yellows showed up in the faint glow, bobbing on long stalks as they passed.

"Klenit is only hours away." D'tanesse clutched her wrist, circling her arm around his neck. "If we don't rest again we should reach it by morning."

Across the clearing, the other line of trees observed their progress. Silence gathered itself for breaking.

"Turn back." Troy twisted against their arms. "This is far enough."

"We have at least a few minutes. We would hear them before they burst upon us." D'tanesse began, but Teyeda was already doing as told.

"I'll walk behind the horses, but we should not stop."

"You are not well," he began another protest.

"None of us are well," she returned, "and we'll be even worse if Machaun catches us now. The Otnas is right there, and he needs no proficiency with elaa to use it as a blade. We cannot stop until we reach Klenit."

"How far behind is he?" Teyeda divided his attention between the far trees tucked against the backdrop of the sloping mountains and the Otnas lying across the travel roll on Laic's back.

"Not very far, I'm sure," sighed D'tanesse. "He has a larger group and will move slower but Machaun has lost control of his prey and that knowledge will spur him on."

Teyeda's mouth tightened. One half of his stern profile was dampened by a slanted shadow curving over his blunted chin.

Troy raised her head. "Teyeda."

His mouth tightened further, becoming a thin slash.

"It's not about protecting me anymore."

"It has always been about that."

"Then go to Klenit. Take the Otnas. Bring them to help us. That is the only way we will survive this night."

"But you will need it."

"I need the Esobir in Klenit to see it. You are the strongest of us, and you have the best chance of reaching Klenit in the shortest time." Troy retracted her arm from around his shoulders, spreading her feet and forcing them to bear her weight.

Teyeda protested as she took the Otnas in its baldric and fastened the leather strap across his chest. D'tanesse was—for once—silent.

"The sooner you take it to them, the sooner they will know I have sent you, and they will return with you as fast as possible." She placed a hand on either shoulder and met his gaze steadily. "We will ride behind you. Fare well."

His mouth remained tight, but his eyes were dry as he inclined his head. "And you."

"There is somewhere we can hide if we cannot make it to Klenit," said D'tanesse. "When we come out of the forest there will be a cliff beside the ruins of Carmul, and a cave beneath the cliff. We will meet you there."

Chapter Thirty-Nine

Troy waited until Teyeda mounted and entered the trees before shifting her feet. As she did, her right leg buckled and she sagged against D'tanesse.

He supported her weight with a quiet grunt. "I thought you said you would kill Machaun, next time you see him."

"Machaun doesn't know how easily he can be undone by the Otnas. I do, and I am the one who wills it to work."

He kept his face forward and drew a slow breath. "I do not... disagree..."

"I will use it against him if I have no other choice. I would rather kill him with an object he understands."

His arm around her tightened.

She shifted, turning to look at it. "You still have trinkets in those pockets?"

"Oh. Yes." He shrugged his other shoulder and walked her toward the remaining horses. "But the most dangerous ones have all been used."

Troy forced herself to turn her back to the clearing, focusing instead on the trees they were about to enter. "Let's walk a little farther. My leg does feel better."

He held the reins in one hand. Laic and the roan mare trailed behind them as they entered the last flat stretch of forest separating them from the coast.

"Do you still carry that ocean jar?"

"Right here." He tapped his waist with his knuckle. The end of the reins brushed the red-brown bloodstain that had dried in a long blotch on the side of his coat.

Troy glanced at it and then looked ahead again, scanning the shrouded ground before placing her feet. Her left ankle still ached, but the pain was a trifle compared to her left thigh. "Did you make it?"

"It was a gift." He also kept his eyes forward.

"Who gave it to you?"

He took several steps in silence, also staring at the ground.

"When I met you in Camil Askanda, in the tunnel," she continued, pretending to ignore his non-answer, "was when I first heard it. It bothered me because it reminded me of a dream I often have of drowning."

He swung the reins gently, back and forth, and shrugged on one side again. "So it was not...elaa that bothered you. It was the sound of water."

"I hate it."

"It's the sound of the ocean. You'll hear it once we get out of the trees."

Troy was not sure she wanted to dwell on that yet. "We should ride again."

D'tanesse helped her onto Laic, then mounted and took the lead. The hours toiled along with them.

The forest stretched on, fading from stark pillar trunks to thin black lines a little farther in the distance, and then into shadow. At first the trunks clustered thick around the narrow trail. As they plodded on, these thinned and the ground was patched with moonlight. Birdsong floated down on the heavy air, endeavoring to speed daybreak. The air whispered above them, echoing with news of the expanse beyond. It filled Troy's ears with a smooth hiss, broken only by the sounds of horses, the occasional voices of birds and her own breathing.

Her head dropped forward, tugging on her shoulders to follow. She brought it up, sucking in a sharp breath and blinking hard. The short grasses sighed as she passed over them, softly constant. Mist blanketed her skin and her head tugged again on her shoulders.

Quiet, rolling surges of sound filled her ears, curling up and over, brushing beneath her and then covering her.

Now she was under water and could not lift her head. Black liquid and silver foam covered her eyes, rushing into her nose and mouth. Bubbles of sound trickled through the rushing, sucking liquid: many voices shouting somewhere above her. She heard her own struggle to rise: lurching, coughing, vomiting water into water and sucking more in again. Her lungs were filled with it. She fell deeper, even as she twisted to find air above the surface—

Pain exploded in her head and shoulder as she hit the ground. She gasped, pulling hard with her lungs. Air rushed in. Laic stood beside her, having stopped as soon as she slipped off. For a moment she could only breathe, staring up at a dark gray sky through green branches and listening to D'tanesse call her name as he turned back to help her.

Images floated on currents of shadow, some real and some left over from her dreams. The trees—those were real. D'tanesse lurching to a stop and dropping down beside her was real. Laic was real. If she knew anything by now, she knew the smell and form of her horse. Cool particles of mist close to the ground rubbed on her cheeks and neck, curling around her and the bases of the tree trunks some yards away. The moon gleamed, partially hidden behind a starburst of pine needles as it sank westward, on her left.

Troy sat up and turned to face D'tanesse. He stared past her at the trees behind. His lower lip was folded beneath the white line of his teeth. His hand wandered over his jacket, patting the myriad pockets embedded in the stained fabric. His eyes flicked down, saw her, and his wandering hand pointed.

She looked, and this time she saw them. A flash of pale fetlock, a flicker of hoof. Horsemen were taking up position, flanking them, closing in. The sight of four-sided spearheads standing at attention on the ends of their shafts brought her to her feet.

"Get on your horse, Llynx." D'tanesse stood and mounted between one breath and the next. He pulled a tear-shaped stone from one pocket and dropped it into the mist, holding the thin leather string in one hand while he guided his mount between Troy and the nearest horsemen.

Troy backed up to Laic, rubbing her arm with one hand and reaching for her dagger with the other. The warriors circled around, facing them.

D'tanesse swung the stone at first vertically, and then as the mist began to cling to it, horizontally, above his head. The mist rolled upward in a lazy wave, circling around him and Troy. It obscured the warriors gathering around them, then the outside world was lost as more mist was pulled into the swirling cloud.

D'tanesse hollered for her to get on her horse, pumping his arm wildly about his head. Troy finally moved, tearing her eyes from the enclosing wall of water, and stumbled to Laic to catch his bridle. Laic trembled and jerked his head toward the sky. Troy understood his near panic—the air fairly crackled with energy and it was growing hard to breathe. She looked again at the thickening wall of mist. A shadow, barely a line at first, followed the path of the stone on its tether. Gradually the line grew wider, expanding, bleeding through the dense mist, which melted into horizontal rain.

"D'tanesse!"

"Be ready to follow me!"

Troy reached for Laic's mane to swing herself up, and doubled over as the whole right side of her body contracted with tearing pain. The maelstrom began to thrum, creating its own rhythm as it gained momentum.

The blurred figures on the other side of the wall moved at once, and spearheads penetrated the swirling water. They spun like matchsticks and spewed away, some landing harmless inside and some flying back toward the throwers.

"D'tanesse!"

Next came a body.

The warrior dove in headfirst. Troy saw his light hair, his bare shoulders and leather tunic emerge, and then she was running. Her legs swept through the grass as she sprinted toward him on the balls of her feet. Her thigh sang a high note of agony. The thick air raked through her open mouth, slamming her lungs full. Her chest clenched.

They collided. She slammed him backward into the swirling wall, leading with her left shoulder. His body sheared a brief path for them which closed on her feet as she passed through the water after him. They burst out almost as soon as he had gone in. A chill shower of water hit Troy's face and eyes, but she did not need to see—only breathe. Drops rolled from her forehead and nose over her cheeks and were forgotten.

A hand grabbed her wrist and jerked her upright. Her right shoulder gave a watery snap, and she bellowed a scream. The hand jerked again, and another clamped her jaw, bringing her head up. She blinked hard and glimpsed Machaun's wide, ruddy face. She went for her dagger. He dropped her and planted a kick in her ribs, sending her spinning. She landed hard on her back. Water gushed through her clothes. Pine needles poked against her neck and ears.

Troy tucked her legs, preparing to kick out as Machaun came at her. A tear-shaped stone bounced off his cheek. He flinched, glancing at the projectile as it fell point down near his boots.

Troy scrambled backwards, abandoning her first plan in favor of escaping what would follow the stone. A second later, sheets of water pummeled over Machaun as the maelstrom uncoiled. It beat him backward into the ground, into quick-forming mud, following the path of the waterstone.

Troy pushed to her feet, using one hand to steady herself. Her right arm would not respond.

"Llynx!" D'tanesse was beside her then, pulling her upright. The ground seemed to tilt as her legs buckled. He picked her up bodily and pushed her onto the roan mare's back.

"Laic—I can ride—"

He jumped up behind her and kicked hard. The poor mare jumped forward, desperate to escape the phenomena she'd been trapped in a moment ago.

Troy twisted around to see behind them. Machaun rose out of the sodden mess, dripping water from every point and orifice. He shouted for a horse.

D'tanesse banded his arm around her, trapping her own useless arm against her side and crushing her to him. "You are deranged! That water could have killed you!"

"How far to Klenit?" was her answer.

"Not close enough! Carmul lies ahead—what is left of it."

Through the trunks ahead was a sparkling, writhing blackness beyond a gray-green expanse of flat ground. The warriors fanned out behind them, pulling closer. D'tanesse kicked the mare steadily, in case that would make her go any faster. They burst leaping from the treeline in a flurry of pine needles. D'tanesse bent his head close to Troy's as they ripped through the last branches that snapped and fell in their wake. They galloped along the edge of a plateau that crossed open land toward a line of black water on the gray horizon. To their right the plateau stepped, dipping down to a second level of flat grassy ground. Ahead, the upper plane ended as cliffs above the water. The lower plane was separated from the water by a ribbon of gray sand.

D'tanesse flung an arm to their right, at the lower plane. "There, Carmul!"

Troy only glimpsed it—ruined buildings in a sprawling half-circle that stopped before the beach, clustered around the Hall that was a roofless rectangle of jagged walls—before Machaun's warriors broke through the treeline, racing after them.

D'tanesse turned to look with her, and his arm jerked tighter around her waist. "Get us out of the open! Go downhill and left on the beach, there's a cave at the base of the cliffs!" Suddenly he pointed again, still shouting. "Teyeda! It's Teyeda! He is coming—look there!"

Troy followed the line his arm made and sat up straighter. A cluster of new riders galloped past the ruins toward them. Their robes flapped and surged about their bodies, crouched on their mounts' backs, and each held a long staff out at their side, except the lead rider who had no cloak or staff. The handle and curved handguards of a sword floated above his left shoulder.

D'tanesse whooped, his voice cracking. "Teyeda! He reached them! To us, Klenit Esobir, to us!"

Troy looked back again at Machaun's warriors and grunted disbelief through clenched teeth. "They're slowing. They're turning away!"

In the ashen light, Machaun and his warriors were plainly discernible, swinging left, away from them on the plateau. When she saw who they rode to join, her body went cold, and then numb. Estimal Glor's warhost covered the plateau, moving toward them. In the early gray light, still a mile or two in the distance, they were a mass of shapes, bristling along the front with upright spears.

"D'tanesse!" Troy leaned forward and hissed close to the roan mare's flattened ears. The mare pressed them against her skull and redoubled her speed. Troy guided her rightward down the incline. D'tanesse clung to her with both arms around her waist, his torso pressed against her back.

Teyeda and the robed Esobir met them halfway down the slope, splitting to surround them, some leading the way, some circling to ride behind.

They angled toward the beach where land met water. Grass became wet sand that dampened running sound. They turned left, galloping between cliffs and long, curling waves hemming the strand. Carmul's ruins were behind them now, the plateau high overhead.

Nausea shot through Troy's stomach like a misplaced heartbeat. Suddenly D'tanesse's arm was the only thing keeping her upright. She couldn't force the sounds away, the rushing crashes and swelling roars. Salt foam hissed as it died on jagged rocks jutting out of the deeper water.

They rode about one hundred yards then turned left again, into a cavern at the base of the cliff where they all halted. Inside, the noise of the ocean echoed all the more. They were surrounded by darkness and slick wet shelves of rock, glistening faintly whenever light reflected in.

Chapter Forty

Troy did not struggle when D'tanesse pulled her from the saddle. She was a deadweight against him, sinking to her knees in a shallow puddle of water. At the mouth of the cave a flame sparked to life at the end of a stick, illuminating the space somewhat more. The Esobir from Klenit spread themselves out to guard the opening, while three or four consulted with each other as they drew nearer to Troy.

"They haven't followed us."

"No need. There's no place to get away from them…"

The water was warming against her skin. If she moved it would turn cold and sloppy on the knees of her breeches. Troy raised her eyes and counted the men Teyeda had brought. Seventeen. They may have been a match for a small band of warriors, but not the warhost Estimal had succeeded in gathering.

"We are not going to run." She silenced their conversation as it began. Their disadvantage was not a surprise, and it did not change what must be done. "Not only is it impossible, but it would leave Klenit completely defenseless."

Four Esobir pushed closer, dark eyes in thin faces examining her where she knelt in the saltwater puddle. One in the center passed the lighted branch to one of his companions.

"I know you." He continued to advance when the others halted.

Troy eyed the speaker sharply, finally recognizing him, but he was addressing D'tanesse. The man had no beard, and held a short staff in one hand, pockmarked and scarred from repeated deflecting and striking. "We—a few of us met you when you came to Klenit the night Carmul was attacked. My name is Andres."

"I remember you." D'tanesse nodded, staying where he knelt beside Troy. His hands were both support and a weight holding Troy back. As if she could lunge at anyone now and hope to do damage.

"We are far from safe here." She grunted, clutching her limp arm against her body. "Send scouts along the beach. Tell me if the warhost is sending anyone to us, messenger or executioner."

Teyeda knelt on her other side. She grimaced, biting back a yelp as his fingers probed the swelling joint.

"If you have khoni, or anything for pain, I would appreciate it."

Andres snagged the elbow of the man who was turning to leave at

Troy's first command and spoke low into his ear. The man nodded and went to the mouth of the cave, while the remaining two and Andres remained, watching her. "I thought you might return to us one day with the Otnas, but I did not imagine it would be this way," he said.

"Soon after we left you, Machaun was after us," Troy answered. "My companion Mytch died protecting me in a skirmish, and I was taken to Camil Askanda where I met D'tanesse. When I finally reached Yettmis, Yessac insisted I keep the Otnas with me."

"Are you the Deliverer, then?"

"She is," D'tanesse said for her. "Though a little worse for wear at the moment."

Troy shot him through with a hard glance as Teyeda lifted her injured arm.

D'tanesse looked at Teyeda, then pressed on. "She is a warrior, and Esobir and a Seawolf. In fact, she is their queen."

"I am not—aah!"

Teyeda thrust her shoulder into place as she was distracted, and words fled.

D'tanesse left her side briefly, seizing the excuse of greeting the tall leader of the Klenit Esobir and escape any violent reaction from Troy when her strength returned.

"Andres, we thank you for coming." He extended his hand.

Andres took it, shaking his head. "There are barely fifty Esobir in Klenit. It will only take the warhost a few hours, if that, to tire of waiting for us to surrender and come to flush us out. I'm afraid we don't have much time to come up with a plan of action."

Troy stared at the waves crooking toward her while she came to terms with his news. The mouth of the cave was an instant from devouring her; the back of it felt like a hollow throat stretching into infinite danger. Her vision was suddenly obscured by a blue robe and Andres' face as he knelt before her. His features were like his staff: Weather-worn, etched by exposure to wind and water. His eyes were mixed shades of gray, same as the color worn by members of the Watch. She looked down at his open hand and saw he offered a palm full of heart-shaped leaves. Khoni. She took several, grinding them between her molars to release the blessed juices.

He peered closely at her. "I thought, when we first met, you looked like a Seawolf I once knew, named Natug. She was also Esobir. She taught me and most of the others here the way."

She swallowed. "I am called Troy—"

"Among other things," D'tanesse put in.

She shot him a cutting glance. “I am a Seawolf, as he said, but my name and my childhood are lost to me.”

Andres inclined his head, understanding. “May I see your mark?” He tapped the back of his own neck and then nodded at her again.

Her wooden fingers fumbled with the laces binding the cuff around her neck. It dangled, pinched between her thumb and first finger, when she stood and turned her back to him. Teyeda supported her with one thick arm around her waist, but the khoni was already beginning to work.

Salt fumes stifled her nose and mouth. Troy stared into the cave’s hollow throat, surrounded by the furious echoes of thrumming water that nearly drowned out the murmurs of shock from the men behind her.

It was all familiar. The echoes of waves. The salt smell. Even the cave itself. She knew this place. She had seen it before.

“I think I can tell you your name.” Andres had suffered a change of countenance when she shuffled back around to face him. The fine lines engrained around his mouth and eyes became more stark as they tightened. “You, my dear Lady, are the true High Ruler. The only one of your unique blood.”

“I think you are mistaken.” Troy would have rubbed her suddenly aching temple if they hadn’t all been staring at her. She’d come to this cave once before, but for what?

“There is no mistaking the mark,” Andres continued, reverent. He stayed kneeling, looking up at her. “Among the Seawolves, only royalty are marked with the circled seastar, which you are. Natug, the queen of the Seawolves, had one daughter with L’estim Glor. That daughter was you.”

Troy began to protest again, but the robed men—all of them—were already dropping to their knees, framed by vague white curls of ocean crashing beyond the darkened cave mouth.

The waves distracted her again and she stared past the men, tugged from the moment by their nagging familiarity. There it was, just outside, a looming tangible memory. Her trachea began to burn.

“When D’tanesse came to us, Carmul was already burning. We all thought, except for D’tanesse, that you were dead with the rest.” Andres bowed his head. “Forgive us, L’abri Glor…”

L’abri. Forgive me, L’abri. Forgive me.

Those three words she would never forget, spoken by D’tanesse in another cave. The sound of waves had also been in that cave, and a fainter smell of salt from the ocean jar.

The ocean jar.

L’abri.

I am L'abri.

The dream that had been plaguing her came rushing back, breaking over her while she was still awake. This time, instead of glimpses, she saw it all.

Chapter Forty-One

Troy

It begins in the cave.

I run there as fast as I can. Coarse sand flies up behind me, a miniature wake—

No. It begins before the cave.

I am digging my heels in as I am dragged. Two dark lines stress the beach, marking our progress toward Inatru warriors waiting by a wagon cart.

His hand is in my hair, pulling it and me. My fists beat at his hand and arm, my fingers dig at his flesh, but he does not let go.

I am screaming.

He killed my mother. My home is burning, and my father with it.

I am screaming for help.

I am tearing free. Running.

The cave is ahead. The cave where we always go to share secrets, build fires to roast fish and warm ourselves. The cave where my mother helped me capture the sound of the ocean in a jar made of elaa.

Coarse sand flies up behind me, a miniature wake. I run to the cave, crying out for D'tanesse. The cave is empty.

My foot strikes a rock, and I bruise my elbows falling. Outside, the shouting of warriors grows louder.

Now at the cave entrance stands my uncle, framed by white curls of ocean crashing in the dark beyond.

He drags me to the water. The salt waves burn my eyes and sting places on my skull where hair used to be.

He subdues me with his knee along my spine, his palm cupping the back of my head. My whole body is under water.

I hear my own struggle to rise. Voices above me, muffled.

I remember my mother's words: do not fear the water…

I cannot breathe.

* * * *

The leather cuff slipped from Troy's fingers and landed with a wet thump in the sand.

"Let me go." Her voice strained from a constricted throat. Teyeda released her. She stepped past Andres and the other Esobir. Their upturned faces were blurs on the edge of awareness, watching her walk to the entrance of the cave. Little stones rocked beneath her boots, a quiet chorus undermining the noise of the waves. She stepped through the ragged rock arch into waxing gray light. A sluggish wind pulled at her clothes, further cooling the wet patches on her knees, but she was numb to discomfort.

A twisted line of sea grass drowned in white foam stretched before her along the sand, ejected from the deep by the constant waves. She turned away from the sight, her eyes sweeping toward the growing eastern light. The cliff wall on her left and the ocean on her right made a long corridor. Seagulls splashed in silver pools of water scattered across the rocky gray shore.

She flinched at a light touch on her elbow. D'tanesse stood beside her, studying the rocky sand at their feet. Teyeda, Andres and the other Esobir assembled behind them at a respectful distance.

"I told them about your memory."

She raised a hand to her face. Tears slipped from her eyes. They hit her fingers, leaving warm trails down her knuckles. "That jar…your gift. I gave it to you."

D'tanesse raised his head, drawing a deep breath. His chest expanded, drawing his thin shoulders back, then collapsed again with a shaking sigh.

Like dawn breaking quietly over the hushed world to shed light on the sleeping, the dreaded question broke its barrier, drawing the space closed between them.

"What happened to me?"

His hand found her shoulder, light and trembling.

Her eyes searched the line of fading stars along the horizon, afraid to watch his face as he told her.

He told her everything.

* * * *

"There is a message from Estimal Glor."

Andres stood a few feet behind them, holding a curled square yellow parchment. "We are out of time, I'm afraid. The king is calling for our immediate surrender, and will spare some of our lives if we give him the Otnas and the book of Esobir."

Troy turned her back to the water and stared up at the cliff while she listened. The chossy white-blue wall loomed, seeming to lean above them. An overhanging fringe of long grass was visible along the very top.

"He still thinks we have the book," she rasped, then coughed to clear her throat. Andres and D'tanesse pretended not to see the last tears clinging to her face. "And we know for sure he does not have Sema, or he would have made her life part of the bargain."

The parchment rustled as D'tanesse took it from Andres to read for himself. "Whether we have it or not they intend to kill us." His thoughts were not with his words at that moment. He sounded more relieved than disturbed.

Troy continued her study of the cliff. Estimal's behavior toward her in Camil Askanda, all of his strange instigated debates that felt pointed at someone besides herself, now began to make sense. They were pointed at someone else—someone he knew and she did not. That person, L'abri, was fully capable of ending his reign with her right of heritage, with the Otnas, and with the influence of knowledge from the book of Esobir. That was destroyed of course, but Estimal did not know it.

Troy could not deny anything D'tanesse had just told her, but neither could she say to herself or anyone that it felt real. She was just as empty of her own memory—save for the one muddled flashback of nearly drowning—as she was of real food. Yet, she could not say hunger proved the nonexistence of meat. In fact, her craving only proved its existence and its necessity.

Her stomach pinched, and she made herself stop thinking about it in those terms.

"You still have the Otnas." Andres moved to stand facing both of them, rubbing his hands up and down the top third of his staff. "Considering what it is, the king and even his host cannot stand against you."

Troy lowered her eyes to study his face, then raised them again to the cliff. "And what should I do with it? Massacre them all? Obliterate the common people with the warriors? Even the warriors are not all evil. Two men have brought us to this, not an entire host."

"Those men command the host." Andres nodded, conceding her point while countering it. "If we had time for any other plan, I would follow it. If there were any other way to end this purge and restore peace certainly we should do that, but there is not. Now I have given my counsel, and I submit to you. Whatever you say will be done."

They waited, watching her, for her next words. A watery light reflected in Andres' eyes, making them like polished stones. This man, who hardly knew her, now trusted her with his life.

D'tanesse touched her arm. "We will need khoni to sustain more action without any rest."

"Take what I have left." Andres produced a small beaded bag from inside his robe and placed it in her hand. "Whatever your plan, we will back you. You are our queen and always have been."

Troy opened it and pulled out two heart-shaped leaves. She remembered Terra, and anguish struggled to surface. She closed her fingers over the leaves and turned toward the water. "Send a return message to the king. Tell Estimal that I—that L'abri will meet him. Tell him I will bring the Otnas and the book."

* * * *

Terra stood among the trees, squinting through the gray light to glimpse the assembled warhost. They appeared as a mass of standing shapes at this distance, a wall of men. There were more than he had ever seen, even on the crowded streets of Camil Askanda. Between the tree trunks he could make out spears standing tall here and there. The column followed the treeline to the west, stretching along it and out of sight. The head of the column ended about thirty yards to Terra's right.

Maon and Kilar stood beside him inside a muddy circle of earth. Next to the circle was a deep rut with streaks around it as if someone had struggled out. The ground ahead was gorged with running tracks heading out of the trees. There had been a struggle here, likely between Troy and Machaun. The only consolation here for Terra was the lack of bodies. Troy must be alive, but where? The warhost was waiting, not charging ahead, so she must either be nearby or captive.

"They are still coming through the Aigroe pass in the west, I'm sure," murmured Kilar. His blue eyes were bright beneath his pinched brow.

"We cannot face anything that big, even if most are untrained," Maon said, also speaking quietly. "They would crush us with sheer numbers."

Terra glanced over his shoulder. The rest of their company—the Watch, Sema and Imra, and Kilar's warriors—waited a short distance behind in seven rows of eight on their horses, where their movements would not attract attention. Siegra was walking down the front line, giving instructions in a low voice. Terra couldn't make out her words. Her hands alternated positions, first loose at her sides and then resting on the black heads of the axes hanging from her belt. She stopped at the near end of the front, where the Watch sat upon their horses. Her upturned gaze lingered on each of them: Mikal, Emori, Ivel and Norem. They nodded as she spoke and drew their cowls up. Norem's grin shone white in the pallor of dawn before the gray cloth hid his face. Whatever the situation, the Watch would ride out first to Troy's side, to guard or do battle.

Siegra mounted her horse and Mikal handed her the reins to Terra's mount. Siegra turned, scanning the area, and found Terra with Kilar and Maon. She nodded to him and then to his horse. When it was time, Terra would ride with the Watch. He nodded back, and Siegra pulled her cowl up, facing the treeline with the Watch and the other warriors.

Imra and Sema were the only ones dismounted, as they would not be fighting. They bent over a thicket of blackberry shrubs at the far end of the line of warriors, piling fruit in Sema's cloak.

Terra's stomach was shrunken, impervious to any sensation but anxiety. If Machaun had caught Troy, by now she would be facing the king. By now she might be dead. But why would the warhost still stand waiting if she were?

He moved forward, walking carefully. Troy was somewhere, and to help her he had to know where.

Maon caught Terra's arm, halting him before he crossed the distance through the trees right into the warhost's ranks.

Terra stared stiffly ahead. "We can't help her unless we know what's happened to her."

"Let him go," Kilar said to Maon. "You and I will scout ahead beyond the front lines. We may see something from there."

Maon's grip relaxed slowly. Terra finally looked at him, fixing the man's eyes and face in his memory. "I must do what I can," he said.

Maon let him go. "Fare well."

"And you." Terra moved forward. He stepped quietly, walking westward parallel to the warhost, screened by the trees between. The men faced eastward, many shifting in place, uncertain. Terra could sympathize. Right now he felt anything but certain, but he was desperate and that made him bold.

He stopped with his back against a wide, straight trunk, and looked back the way he'd come. Maon and Kilar were outlines in the weak light, moving away from him. Maon melded with the gray dawn, shifting through the shadows. Kilar's warriors could just be seen, dim figures far back from the treeline. They were a warband, fifty strong, but Terra thought of them as individuals. Kilar had trained them as Troy trained the Watch; they were able to use several weapons instead of one, and all could think for themselves. And all of them were here, ready to help Troy.

Terra turned toward the warhost again and scanned the column. The nearest men were twenty yards distant. The trunks clustered between him and them made a clear view difficult. One of those men could tell him about Troy's whereabouts. Any of them could raise the alarm once he showed himself, or once he started talking, and then his advantage would be gone. Probably along with his life.

It was a necessary risk.

He untied his hip quiver and left the tree, approaching the nearest part of the column at an angle. When he came close enough to see their faces, he refastened the quiver, fumbling with the laces more than necessary. He recalled his confusion, lost in Camil Askanda, and put the emotion on his face as if he had left the line earlier and, now returning, couldn't remember his place. One of the men in a faded tunic, its color and substance leeched by hours working in the sun, gestured to him. A few others watched but many ignored him, keeping their attention forward. Terra hurried to stand beside him.

"Don't go so far out to relieve yourself next time," the man said, shifting to give Terra room to stand in line. "You'll get lost in the trees and mist."

"I almost fell asleep," Terra said with contrived guilt. "I'm used to hard work, but this march has been brutal."

The man shifted his hands along his spear. They were tanned, parched and dry. Soot filled the thick creases at his knuckles. His nails were short and broken along the edges, outlined with black.

"We'll be going home soon enough, or what's left of it. The king is about to get what he's after."

Terra's mouth dried instantly. "Does he…have her then? The…one he's hunting?"

"Not yet. Last word from the front was he sent her a message demanding her surrender. She's hiding in a cave or some crevice on the beach. She has nowhere to go. She'll surrender, or he'll send his warriors to drag her out."

"He doesn't seem to need us so much." Terra stretched up on his toes to see around those standing in front of him.

The man eyed Terra sideways, through a dingy fall of auburn hair thinned with age. "What village are you from?"

"Kcen."

He didn't answer immediately. "The forest?"

"Yes."

"It's gone now?"

"It's been gone a long time."

The man shook his head in sympathy. "Those Seawolves…"

"It wasn't the Seawolves. It was Machaun, the king's second in command, three years ago."

The man stared full at him. “That was when the Seawolves began raiding. Why would Machaun be with them?”

Terra’s heart began to pound. He opened his mouth to speak, then thought better of it and stayed silent. Better to let the man question on his own. He would believe his own conclusions over what Terra, a stranger, might tell him. Besides, there was not much time for discussion.

“Machaun and the king said they’re protecting Cathylon from the Seawolves,” the man said at last, contemplative.

“Then why take all the Seawolves to their city, instead of making them go back to their own island? If they attacked at all. I have my doubts. And the king isn’t protecting Cathylon anymore. He’s destroying it.”

Heads began to turn at those words. Other men were listening. Terra forced his voice steady and stepped away from the column. “I cannot follow such a man. A king, a leader, serves the people, not his own desires. I will fight for Cathylon, but I will not help him fight for himself.”

More heads were turning, and the men began muttering amongst themselves. Terra turned away and walked back into the forest. When he was far enough into the trees to be mostly hidden, he ran back to Kilar and Maon to give the news.

Chapter Forty-Two

As the first real light broke over the edge of the sky, Troy L'abri Glor and nineteen Esobir rode to meet the warhost. They came, mounted, over the rise from the beach, solid shapes cutting through a diffuse veil of white mist.

Troy appeared first, riding Laic. She held the Otnas in her right hand with the blade angled toward the ground. D'tanesse came up next on her right, carrying her short bow. His open coat framed his chest, bare save for a line of dirty bandages swathing his middle. Troy's leather quiver showed on his right thigh when the lower edge of his coat curled open. Teyeda was next, on Troy's left, impervious to his fatigue and limbs spotted with bruises. The Inatru sword hung heavy from his side in its weathered sheath.

Seventeen more Esobir spread out behind them, their mounts at first jogging then walking as they came over the hill crest beside the cliff. Their clean blue robes flagged and rippled over their horses' hindquarters, and each man's staff stood upright clenched in one hand.

Every back was straight, every head raised as the group advanced steadily toward the warhost. Their eyes were shadowed, their mouths closed above tight jaws.

Troy raised her eyes to the jagged fingers of mountains poking up behind the wall of pine trees she and D'tanesse had fled from less than two hours ago. She raised her eyes higher to the heaps of smoke pushing above the mountains, tainting the silken sea mist. The Otnas emitted a constant subdued shiver, warming her fingers. Elaa, protect us from our enemies…

D'tanesse uttered a low whistle beside her. "Not only a murderer but a thief. He's stolen most of the men alive in Cathylon."

Laic slowed and pointed his broad ears, arching his neck toward the sight as if in agreement. The host facing them sprawled like a spillage of water, filling the valley from the trees to the cliffs. The front rank was all Inatru warriors in bronze-colored leather, each with a four-bladed spear. They stood seven deep across the plateau from the trees to the cliffs.

Andres came alongside them, reluctant to bring his mount to a full stop. Small breaths of wind tugged at his thin forelock while he studied what lay before them. Finally he breathed deeply. "With such a force behind them, Estimal Glor and Machaun won't be motivated to conference with us."

Troy nudged Laic with her left heel and he picked up his pace. Her right leg and shoulder tinged only vaguely now, thanks to the khoni from Andres. The effects would wear off all too soon, though. "No matter what happens, stay near me. If I fall, take the Otnas and get it away. If you cannot get away, bury it in the sea, as far out as you can. They must not possess it."

Andres murmured a promise, then added, "This challenge won't sit well with them, if it sits at all."

"It won't, but I mean to fight them, not the whole host."

"There is only one reason the host would not fight, not counting the Inatru."

"That reason is why I am making the challenge," she said. "You follow me because you know the truth. They follow Estimal because they must."

Teyeda growled a phrase as the ranks parted in the center, emitting Estimal Glor and Machaun. Conversation gave way to a focus of aggression which tightened like a bowstring as Troy and her companions drew closer. The two men strode on foot to meet their enemies. Estimal's stocky sloped shoulders were garnished with a bright clean cloak the color of cherry wine. His beard was brushed and his skin just washed. He carried an Inatru spear, knocking the butt on the ground with every other step. Machaun's clothes were not as fresh—his travel-stained breeches and leather vest were coated in soot—but he had washed. He carried a spear as well as a sword. Both men stalked to a halt only ten yards from the front line.

"They expect us to dismount and lose our last advantage." Now it was Andres' turn to growl. He lifted the reins in tightened fists, a gesture of disgust.

A fragment of words, a prayer learned years ago in Yettmis, had been repeating in Troy's mind. At the sight of Machaun, blind fury welled up and her heart pulsed into her throat. She muttered the words aloud, proving to her fury and her fear what control she had over both.

"Elaa protect us from our enemies. Let our swords never falter, deliver us from harm…"

D'tanesse heard this and looked full at her. His mouth opened, then closed in a miraculous stay of opinion. A thought flashed through her mind—if only she'd tried this years ago to shut him up—but there was no time for indulgence. "Forgive the blood we shed, for life is precious."

"Elaa, protect us from our enemies. Let our courage never falter…" He echoed the prayer. Then Andres took it up, and then the Esobir riding in a half-ring behind them were all quietly reciting.

"Let our courage never falter…"

"Elaa protect us from our enemies…"

"Forgive the blood we shed…"

"Elaa protect us…"

They stopped close together before the two leaders of Cathylon. Troy's shadow was a dark shape chased by the strengthening light onto Estimal's legs and wide chest. Other faint shadows, cast by those around her, stretched toward the front line.

"Did you really find more men to die for you?" Machaun rested his spear on the ground and leaned on it. "I thought by now they would know better."

"Murder is an easy solution for those who can't handle their own relatives." D'tanesse looked above Machaun's head as he spoke, as if offering the time of day rather than a retort.

"You talk bold enough, perched there on a horse," Machaun snapped.

"And you, backed by a thousand men."

Troy hadn't tried to estimate, but she hoped it was far less than a thousand. "I warn you," she said as Machaun began to lift his spear, "that you are watched. If you make a move against us before I say what I have come for, those who watch you will put an arrow in your eye."

"The only thing I want to hear from you," Estimal snarled as Machaun's movement stalled, "is whether you will hand over the book and the sword before a whipping, or after one."

Troy's eyes slanted toward him. "You already did that, once."

The king clenched his teeth, so hard his cheeks trembled. "This time, you will not survive it."

"I believe you." Troy raised her voice, directing it past the king to the assembled mass. "And I challenge you now for the rule of Cathylon."

A shudder of wind moved around them, pushing the king's cloak across the bulk of his chest. He narrowed his stare at her face as she dismounted, while his knuckles blanched around his spear.

Troy landed carefully with most of her weight on her left leg and stepped toward him holding the Otnas out at her side, meeting his stare. D'tanesse raised his voice to be heard by the warriors looking on, continuing where she had ended.

"We call you to account, Estimal Glor, for the murder of your brother, L'estim Glor the High King; of Natug, queen of the Seawolves and Cathylon; of Natami, your wife—"

"There was no death by my hands that was undeserved! The woman was undermining our sacred practices!" Estimal took a step forward, shouting up at his son.

D'tanesse's voice shook, but he continued. "—your wife and my mother, who—"

"They were all against me!" Estimal's rage compelled him forward. Machaun stole a glance at the treeline, then caught the king's arm to stay him. Troy remained where she stood, watching their faces.

"—who was with child!" D'tanesse's cry was keening.

Estimal's breath cut short. His eyes slammed wide open, showing their whites.

"She waited for your return, so she could tell you. Instead you plotted treason and fed her poison!"

"Silence!" Estimal jerked free of Machaun and thrust a demanding finger at D'tanesse.

"I was silent once, and my silence helped you do all this. Moreover you repeat your crime, destroying the homes and trades of the people you lead, driven to purge what you call evil. They suffer because you fear her!" D'tanesse flung his arm out at Troy. His blazing shout severed for a moment every other sound, expanding overhead to be heard by the front ranks of the warriors and the villagers behind them. "They must rebuild what you tear down in this selfish, pointless hunt! I declaim you, Estimal Glor! You are not fit to serve Cathylon. You have lost your right to lead the people!"

These last words hit the king like physical blows. With a rising scream, he drew back his spear to throw it. The shaft was struck hard in the next instant near its head, so hard it was knocked from Estimal's raised hand and flopped onto the grass. He stumbled back, staring at the arrow quivering in the shaft, then turned to see who had fired it.

Troy only let herself look for a moment. It was long enough to recognize gray shapes emerging from the trees, cantering toward them: Mikal's long body leaning forward over his horse's neck as it ran; Maon, whose very shape she could tell at a glance; Siegra, with a graceful woman's form, but deadly; all of them came sweeping along the edge of the plateau, leaving the trees behind. All but one wore a gray cowl. Her eyes passed over him before comprehension registered. The Watch only numbered six. Now they had a seventh.

It was too late to look again.

They came to a stop behind Machaun and Estimal. Their figures were now black and charcoal blurs to Troy's eyes, which fixed upon Estimal and Machaun. No doubt each of the Watch had their bow in hand, with arrow set to string.

The king, crimson faced, held out his hand. Machaun unsheathed his sword, handing it over for the king's use. He also stared at Troy, glowering, but a ring of white showed around his mouth.

"Troy—" Teyeda began. The note in his voice thrilled and terrified her. That seventh rider…

"Tell them to stay back," she said quickly. "I have challenged this man for the rule of Cathylon."

"We are ready," Maon called from somewhere on her right. "We are with you and guard you."

Siegra barked a command, and the Watch turned their horses in a row to face the warhost. Their arms lifted, arrows set.

The Esobir dismounted and walked ahead, stopping several yards out with their staves held upright and diagonal in front of them. They set their feet, a line of seventeen men between the Watch and the warhost.

"This is no challenge," Estimal snarled. "It is an execution. I was prepared to spare some of these men in exchange for the book and the sword. That was the agreement!"

"I did bring the Otnas. As for the book…" Troy reached for her belt where Andres' beaded pouch hung ready. She had filled it with scrapings from the extinguished torches before leaving the cave.

Estimal and Machaun fixed their attention on it, their expressions for a moment double portraits of relief and greed.

"The book was hidden in a stable in Kcen," she said, loosening the strings and holding the pouch up before them. "Which Machaun burned to the ground. This is what the book is now." She turned the pouch, pouring out a stream of ash. "I have lived with that knowledge through all this dark time, a torture I cannot express. Here ends the darkness. Welcome to the morning."

Two sets of eyes swelled in their sockets, following the colorless remains sprinkling onto the grass.

Chapter Forty-Three

Her own eyes at last, at the worst possible moment, betrayed her. Her focus shifted from Estimal's coal eyes and hooked nose to the mounted figure just behind him.

It could not be…but it was.

It was Terra's pale hair, Terra's shoulders lined with tense muscles from partly drawing his bow. He turned his head and looked back at her. There were his livid, brown eyes. His stubbled jaw. His face was faintly bruised, but nothing compared to what it was the last time she saw him.

The last time she saw him…

Her lips parted, slack.

Ash, falling from the mouth of the beaded pouch, continued to wisp away in bits and vanish.

Terra…

An arm flashed up, rising between them. Troy remembered slowly.

Estimal.

Sword.

Move.

His sword came down and she jerked back, blocking with a desperate upward swipe.

Machaun lifted his spear and screamed, "Forward! Surround! Surround!"

The Watch released their arrows.

Troy took rapid steps backward. Estimal moved in, swinging his blade up. She anticipated and parried the stroke. Her right arm was sluggish as she whipped the Otnas around at his side. He sidestepped. Jabbed at her ribs. She continued the spin and blocked again with an upstroke, coming face to face with him. He rocked backward, thrusting his hilt over and down, connecting with her right shoulder. Troy reeled away, listing to one side.

Machaun was there, the star point on the end of his spear shooting toward her face. Troy whipped her head back, arching to escape it. Teyeda rode up from behind and dove from his saddle onto Machaun's shoulders. They went down together, arms and fists heaving. Teyeda's horse turned and galloped from the plateau, down the incline toward Carmul.

Troy turned to face Estimal as he moved in again, swinging down at her skull. She raised the Otnas with her left hand. Blades clashed. His pushed against hers and her arm gave way. His blade rushed down. She dropped to her knees and rolled aside.

* * * *

The Inatru advanced behind lowered spears. The Watch sent arrows into the rush as fast as they could draw. Along the front line, warriors jerked and crumpled as arrows pummeled them, and those behind stepped over their bodies. Terra sat on his horse between Emori and Norem, launching arrows at an alternate rhythm to theirs. His neck ached to turn and look for Troy. He couldn't hear anything above the growing roar of men charging, but not all of the warhost followed the Inatru. Perhaps his words earlier had made some difference. Or perhaps it was D'tanesse's words about Estimal's treachery. Yet, the Inatru alone were too many for the Watch to keep at bay, even with arrows.

The Esobir were the only reason they had not been overwhelmed already. They were seventeen in all, standing an arm's length apart. Each heaved his staff like a headless ax, slamming the blunt tips on the ground. Lines of sod swelled from the points of contact, speeding into the ranks of Inatru like miniature earthquakes. The advancing spearsmen wavered like a sheet shaken in the wind. The Esobir swung their staves up and down, up and down. More warriors stepped over those who fell, slowly gaining ground.

* * * *

Steadily, Estimal beat Troy back. She forced her legs to move, her left arm to compensate for her right's weakness. She felt pain as a distant ache in her thigh and shoulder. Sparks of white floated on her vision. The Otnas throbbed in her hand. It seemed eager to break out in power at her will. She resisted, focusing with each swing, willing it to be only a blade. Slowly, Estimal worked her backward toward the cliff edge.

* * * *

Warriors closed in on either side of the Watch like giant pincers. Spears edged closer. The Esobir spread out, maintaining a half circle around the Watch. The grass in front of them was obliterated by long streaks of dirt. Dust rose in clouds each time the Esobir hit their staves against the ground.

Terra shot constantly, every arrow bringing down a warrior. Every warrior was replaced by two more. He was almost out of arrows.

D'tanesse was out already. He threw down his bow and pulled a long leather strap from one of his pockets. He dipped into another pocket, dropped a rock into the sling, and whipped the stone into the front ranks. The rock sank into a warrior's eye, and the man went over backward.

"Arrow in the left eye, a rock in the right!" sang D'tanesse. His laugh was half scream as he hurled another stone.

"Ready to melee!" Siegra yelled, somewhere to Terra's right. "Stand ready!"

Inatru pressed in from both sides, stretching around their flanks to close them in. A spear flew through rising dust and landed in an Esobir's chest. He went down, dropping his staff, grasping the spear as he died.

"Ready melee! Readaaaayy!" Siegra shouldered her bow and stepped her mount forward, brandishing both axes.

The Inatru pushed forward, spears hovering above the ground, ready to jab and puncture. A warrior in front rushed forward and, as the Esobir nearest him swung down with his staff, hurled his spear. A line of tremoring earth snaked between the warrior's feet, throwing him backward, while the spear soared over and sank into the Esobir's skull. Four-bladed spears began flying in earnest then, and the space around Terra burst into a frenzy of screaming and madness. Siegra twisted to avoid one spear and whipped down with a hatchet, cleaving a near warrior's forehead. Blood cascaded over his nose and open mouth. She wrenched the hatchet free and her mount sprang forward as the warrior dropped, stepping into the space before another spear could fill it. Norem was close behind her, howling as he swung his sword into the thick of bodies closing in on the left. The ground pulsed, tremoring as the Esobir struck it again.

Spears shot forward and two more Esobir collapsed, blue robes billowing in the dust as their bodies hit the ground. A knot of warriors rushed forward through the gap, stumbling across quaking ground and leaping over the fallen Esobir. They burst through the line of Esobir and then the Watch. Emori and Mikal were pushed right, separated from the rest of the Watch with D'tanesse. Emori, in front of the other two, was quickly surrounded. He hacked wildly at the hands pulling him down. Blood mist turned the dust red around him. His horse took a spear in the chest and screamed, then sank writhing. Mikal and D'tanesse stood close together, Mikal hacking with his sword and D'tanesse flailing with his loaded sling, beating at the warriors surrounding Emori.

Terra kicked his horse and dodged to the left as the group of warriors charged past. A spear cut toward his head and he rolled to one side out of his saddle, landing hard on broken ground beside a fallen Inatru warrior. He slipped his bow over his head, secure on his back, then grabbed the dead man's spear, cradling it in one arm and scrambling backward.

Maon appeared behind him. He grabbed Terra's other arm and hauled him upright, then was moving again, running toward Machaun. Machaun stood panting over Teyeda, holding the sword Terra had seen on Teyeda's hip before the fighting began. It gleamed red. Teyeda lay still on his side, his face a mask of blood. Beyond Machaun, Troy and Estimal clashed swords where the plateau cut off against a brightening sky.

Siegra and Norem surged forward to reach Emori but were pushed back from the tight knot of Inatru. Emori disappeared under a circle of warriors, their spears rising and falling.

Terra raised his spear, rushed up beside Siegra and stabbed the point down at the cluster of warriors, thrusting with his arms raised high. It went into one man's back, sliding through flesh, cracking bone. The pierced warrior gave an animal howl. Terra yanked back and stabbed again. Screams rose over the battlefield, like dogs baying or wolves enraged, snarling as they died. Beyond the Inatru warriors the main body of the warhost was unmoving, not fighting but not helping either.

One of the Esobir raised his staff with a shout and swung down, this time aiming not for the ground but for the Inatru warrior rushing at him. The staff hit the warrior's chest, staving it in like a rotten log. Blood rose instead of dust, lingering in the air as the warrior dropped. The Esobir struck out again at a thrusting spear, and the haft shattered, splinters exploding into the faces and flesh of the unlucky Inatru nearby.

Ivel dipped in and out of sight among the stream of warriors pushing past the Esobir, now spinning with sword outstretched to sever a warrior's head, now jumping up behind a spearsman, arms wrapped around the man's shoulders, stabbing between his ribs. Blood spattered his cowl and dripped from his forearms where spears had grazed them.

The Inatru on one side were forcing them backward, toward the cliff, and the ones who had broken through curved to either side, hemming them in. Siegra and Norem made a triangle with Terra, shoulders almost touching, and they began to rotate as they fought, slowly forcing their backward march into a diagonal one toward Mikal and D'tanesse.

Out of the trees burst horsemen at full charge, led by Kilar. The warriors nearest the trees turned to meet them too late. Kilar and fifty warriors rode over them, plowing a swath through the Inatru toward the Watch and the remaining Esobir. Kilar's sword flashed on either side, dipping into the writhing mass of footmen, flinging red spray into the air. His warriors came behind him, leaving a path as they plunged forward.

Norem and Siegra jostled on either side of Terra, forcing their way to

Mikal and D'tanesse. Between thrusts and staggering steps sideways, Terra looked out and glimpsed Maon beyond the thinning line of surrounding warriors. He was struggling with Machaun for control of a knife, grappling on the ground. Troy was beyond them, fending off Estimal's blows with her sword in one hand.

The Inatru's forces were separated, most caught between Kilar's fifty and the standing warhost. As Kilar was recognized, a shout rose among the men in the warhost who watched the battle. Some began to use their own weapons, common spears and staves, attacking the Inatru warriors on one side as Kilar assaulted them on the other. At first it was only a few—those from Daehexa who knew Kilar—but others joined those few, and then more with the others while the shouting spread:

Kilar of Daehexa fights for Cathylon! For Cathylon! Down with Estimal Glor!

Still in rotating formation with Siegra and Norem, Terra turned until the clash and roar of the warhost was on his left, the trees behind, and he was again facing the cliffs. Warriors pressed in and he pushed out, lashing, flicking with his spear at their faces, plunging the star-shaped head through their throats or bellies when they flinched back. Beyond them, Machaun strode toward Troy and Estimal, stooping to pick up Teyeda's sword again. Maon lay on his back, clutching the hilt of the knife in his stomach. A long blade chopped into the haft below Terra's spearhead. Terra shoved forward with both arms, pushing hard at the sword's owner. The shaft cracked and broke off in the warrior's chest. Terra ran forward, running over him and through the line of warriors between him and the cliffs. Machaun was straight ahead, closer to Troy.

Troy's back was to him. She slammed her sword against Estimal's, hammering him backward with fast, desperate strokes. Machaun was yards behind her, raising his sword. Terra swung out as hard as he could with the broken spear. The splintered end caught Machaun across the ear and he stumbled sideways, reeling. Terra swung again, still running. The shaft slammed down and Machaun's hand jerked, dropping the sword as his wrist snapped.

Troy faltered at the edge of the cliff, her strokes slower and slower. Estimal went on the attack, stepping to her as she blocked, then curving his blade down at her side. She pivoted, struggling to block again. Her right hand went slack, leaving her with one hand to wield the sword.

Terra tore his bow over his head. He had saved one arrow. Now he whipped it to the string while he screamed, "Use your sword, Troy! Use it!"

Estimal hit at her again. Her parry deflected his blade but hers dipped and slammed down, wedged at an angle in the grass. Troy fell onto one knee.

"Use it!" Terra screamed, jerking the string back to his ear. "Use the Otnas!"

The arrow jumped from the string.

Troy bowed her head. Her lips moved, the words imperceptible. A new tremble shook the ground as a fault line ripped from the Otnas past Estimal's feet, diagonal to the edge of the cliff.

Estimal jolted, the arrow wedged into his neck, then staggered forward. Troy braced her left hand on the ground beside her hip and kicked out, hooking her left heel around his knee, jerking to collapse it. The Otnas trembled between them in its sheath of ground. A slice of grass disappeared, sinking out of sight as it broke away. Estimal pitched backward, flailing with his arms, over the new edge. Troy pulled the Otnas out of the grass and dragged herself backward, struggling away from the edge.

Machaun tackled Terra, shoulder slamming into ribs. His fist crashed into Terra's cheek, and blood filled his mouth. Terra banged his own fist against the bloody mess of Machaun's ear, once, twice—

Machaun's elbow came down like a spike on Terra's skull, and for a moment Terra floated, numb, in a cloud of white stars. The Esobir staves continued to boom and crash, sounding far away. His body swam in numbing whiteness, then pain brought him crashing back.

Machaun was on his feet, almost to Troy, who slowly raised her head, starting to stand. Chunks of sod and white choss sank out of sight behind her, leaving a cloud of dust to mark their former place.

A few Inatru, those who were nearest, broke off fighting and ran to join Machaun, responding to his bellowing call. Siegra and Norem were in formation with Mikal now, surrounded but pressing the attack. Ivel appeared beside them, a constant flow of strikes, and the triangle became a square. Kilar and his growing ranks were turning the battle in their favor, the warhost surging forward to swallow the main body of Inatru warriors. D'tanesse had one of the Esobir staves and was bashing his way through knots of warriors toward the cliff and Troy.

Terra could not get up fast enough.

Troy found her feet and straightened. Machaun was there to meet her. His kick caught her beneath the jaw. Her head snapped back and her body followed. Machaun grabbed the Otnas as it dropped from her hand. Her body arched backward, her heels scraping the sheer edge of the cliff, slipping on exposed roots. Her left arm cast out to catch herself as she went over, but grasped nothing.

Machaun stepped up to the edge holding the Otnas, watching her fall.

Terra did not make it to the edge, where a fresh line of dirt marked the falling place, a curved chunk torn from the cliff. As he lurched forward, he was grabbed from behind by the warriors running to join Machaun. D'tanesse, also running to the cliff edge where Machaun stood alone, reached it in time to be hit from behind and thrown onto his stomach. He screamed, scrabbling for rocks, for the Esobir staff which they kicked away, for fallen spears, dirt, anything to throw at his attackers. A line of blood smeared his lips, and a thick streak of red stained his ribs and smeared down one side of his breeches.

Machaun turned from the cliff and saw them. He looked beyond and saw the battle turning against the Inatru. "Bring them down to the beach," he said, pointing the Otnas at Terra and D'tanesse. His other hand was useless, twisted at the end of his swollen wrist. "All of you, come with me."

Terra thrashed, kicked, bit at the warrior grabbing him. He latched onto the man's hand as the man began to drag him down. His teeth severed skin and tendon. Blood tang pooled on his tongue and the hand relented. Terra wriggled free and dashed down the incline after Machaun, who was already at beach level and striding around the high corner made by the edge of the plateau. Terra flew after him, just ahead of the warriors, veering left when he came to the beach. The cliffs stretched to the west, hulking along the sand. On the plateau, the battle still roared and echoed overhead, but Terra didn't care. Machaun walked along the beach at the base of the cliffs, toward a heap of grassy rubble smoldering in its own dust on the dry sand. Troy lay on her back on top of it, bleeding from her mouth and ears.

Terra's feet skimmed the ground, but he was not fast enough. He pushed his chest forward, stumbled top-heavy and sprawled, skidding on his stomach. Sand crept into his mouth, struck his cheeks and ears. He picked himself up to run again.

Machaun stepped onto the hill of rubble, lifting the sword with its point above Troy's body.

Terra screamed and lunged against the hands clamping down on his arms. His legs scrabbled in the sand, running in place as he screamed. D'tanesse landed on his face beside him, not screaming but writhing like a snake, lashing about until he was heaved upright by two warriors who knelt on his legs and wrenched his arms back. Machaun's shoulders lifted, his arms raising above his head with the Otnas, and then swiftly sank down, stabbing the blade through Troy's chest.

Terra continued to scream. He continued to struggle, bucking against the arms clutching him. A spear haft caught him in the mouth, finally cutting the scream short.

Machaun straightened, lingered for a moment looking down at her, then descended the hill of rubble still holding the Otnas, walking toward Terra and D'tanesse. Blood ran from the blade in streaks, collecting on the tip to drop in a spotty line behind him—the blood of the queen of Cathylon.

Chapter Forty-Four

Troy

I fell.

The edge of the cliff shrank up and away, while the wall of blue-gray stone rose, sweeping by in a blur of velocity. Only the top of the cliff several yards down and in each direction was affected. That much, at least, went as I had hoped. Estimal Glor fell to his death below me, which was half the battle won.

Platforms of stone jutted out stair-like from the cliff face. Estimal had been flung out far enough to miss them. I hit many on the way down. One shelf caught most of my weight before it cracked and plummeted with me.

At some point between falling and hitting, falling and hitting again, my mind and body separated. I watched my body twisting, arms and legs hapless threads swinging limp and useless. Blood smeared some of the rock shelves and tiny sprays misted the air, falling slowly after me.

I hit the heap of rock rubble and crunched, slapping down on it with a deep thud. It was strange to hover over my own body, staring down at my eyes, which stared sightless up. Machaun came around the bend where the cliff sloped down to meet the beach. He walked to the place where my body lay and stared at it as well.

Terra came next, struggling to reach me, heedless of the warriors pushing him down in the sand. His expression was of one trapped in a nightmare, and I was on the other side of his nightmare, invisible. He was forced to kneel, his arms restrained behind his back. His chest swelled and he screamed with contorted sobs, “Elaa! Elaaaa!”

I could only watch.

It was strange to see myself bleed but feel nothing.

Then whiteness rolled in, a glowing fog from the horizon that closed around me. I waited, suspended over my body and staring into the white, trying to see if the figure emerging toward me was Terra.

It was a woman.

It was my mother.

One moment, my memory was nothing, some silent nightmare in the dark. The next moment, I knew her voice, her name, and she was lifting her arms to embrace me.

I smelled her—rose and salt essence from the soap she used to wash with and the sea that she loved so much. I pressed my fingers into her shoulders and back. I rested my chin in the silken hollow of her neck and my face brushed against the coarse web of her black hair.

"L'abri," she said. "My little lioness."

Lioness. Oh, Elaa. I remember.

I began to speak, but my heart cracked and memories spilled their color into the fog of light, painting it with scenes I had lived before and now remembered living. I lifted my eyes, looking past her shoulder at these memories, and saw what I never wanted to see again. I saw that night. The night she died.

"I don't know what happened in that room," D'tanesse had told me not so long ago. "When I got there, your mother was dead and you were gone."

I knew what happened.

I watched it.

* * * *

My mother stumbles into the medicine room. I am a little girl of twelve being carried, clinging to her neck. My mother digs frantically through the jars lining stone shelves along the wall. Pottery shatters on black and white square tiles. My mother is breathing in ragged gasps, having as much trouble staying conscious as I. We are fading. I open my eyes and see over my mother's shoulder. A purple cloth ripples to the ground from its overturned box. Blue pearls dance and skip over the shadowy tiles below. The ground is rising fast.

We thump down on the tiles together. My mother's hands twitch as she pushes small blue-black pellets into my mouth between my chattering teeth. When I begin to vomit, she holds me up, kneeling behind me with trembling arms around my shoulders. We convulse together on the floor among shards of pottery while my mother's body absorbs its poison and my body rejects it.

I look up from the spreading puddle of vomit between my knees. My uncle is standing in the doorway. My hand freezes in the act of rubbing a stream of bile from my chin. My mother's body shakes against my back. Her flesh is clammy. Cold seeps into my shoulders and back where my mother presses against me. I reach up, finding my mother's head, and pull it gently toward my shoulder, protective. Her breath puffs against my neck, jerked in and out of her mouth by failing lungs. A stream of liquid dribbles over my shoulder and slides down my chest and stomach, cold beneath my dress.

"It's alright," I whisper, turning a little to touch my forehead to her damp temple. "I'm going to live."

Her eyes only bore upward, staring at Estimal as he steps forward. I have no weapons at hand, nothing within reach except my own blue-flecked vomit. It smells sour and earthy, choking the air above it.

Estimal looks at this, then at me, a little girl bowed beneath her mother's dying weight. My mother did not trust him with the deep knowledge, this much I know. I am never to tell him about the Agreement, or that the Otnas has already been passed to me, or where they sent it. My mother's arms tighten, locking around my upper arms so they are pinned to my side. A last tight embrace. It feels good, secure and affectionate.

If only I weren't now trapped with my mother's body so cold against me.

"It will be over in a moment," Estimal says. He picks up a knife from the shelf, a thin tool used for slicing seeds and paring fruit.

"You have no place here." My stare digs a relentless path through him. My hands stray to the floor, fingers searching for one thing I can reach. "I am not afraid of you."

My mother shakes a final time, then goes still. I am alone now with my uncle, who seems to gain courage and steps close to reach us.

I raise my hand, dripping cloudy bile, and thrust it at his face, fingers like claws. He jerks away as my vomit stings his eyes, then with a roar and redoubled violence his hands shoot for my neck. I curl over my knees and he grabs my mother's body instead as she goes over with me. He yanks her up as I wriggle away on my stomach. I slip beneath the table and scramble to my knees.

My uncle rises, holding my mother by her hair at the back of her neck. Her head is dropped back, exposing the pale tracheal curve. He places the knife against it, looks over at me and slides the blade through. Her skin and cartilage splits open, oozing red at the edges.

I am suddenly on my feet, both hands gripping the edge of the table between us. Estimal drops her body as he stands, now facing me. There are candles on the table, lighted. Stacks of gauze. Clay pots filled with leaves and powders. The flames twist on their wicks, flickered by an unseen breeze.

A scream explodes from my mouth as my whole body heaves, lifting the table on one side, overturning it. "I am not afraid of you!"

I am vaulting over the upended table, landing amidst shattered pottery and the rolling, lighted candles. We crash together, a struggle of fists, little and large. I will not be subdued. He catches my arms, and I pummel him with my knees, my feet, my thighs. I slam my head over and over against his chest, his chin, his neck. Our struggle lasts until he drags me out of the room, out of the Hall to the beach.

He finally subdues me beneath the waves with his knee along my spine, his palm cupping the back of my head. My whole body is under water.

I hear my own struggle to rise. Voices above me, muffled.

I remember my mother's words: do not fear the water…

I cannot breathe.

* * * *

When the memory ended I was standing on my own. My mother was gone. A shadow, the outline of a woman, now faced me, nebulous except for a sense of familiarity. A voice spoke, but was drowned by the sound of my own weeping. The shadow came toward me and a silver light bloomed in its center, where a heart would be if it had a physical body.

The shadow did have a body, I realized, and I knew the shadow's name. She was L'abri, and her heart was the sheath of a sword. A heart of stone, but living, illuminating; a deadly force against its opposite.

The voice, however, did not come from the shadow. It came from around us and between us. It was a voice, yet it was not a voice at all. I heard words, but their sound was like nothing I have heard from the mouth of man.

"I have always known you, though you forgot me. Our agreement stands, if you choose it."

The bright fog rolled back, and now I could see along the glistening shore between land and water, the Place Between.

"I will make you live. Live, and protect your people. Fear not. Yes?"

I wanted to see my mother's face again, just once. To remember our lives before I became such a wretched shell, wandering in the dark to forget. I have wanted many things, many good things, but they were selfish to pursue.

I do not live for the dead. I live for the living.

The shadow nodded.

I reached for the light.

Chapter Forty-Five

Terra spat blood on the sand in front of him and blinked hard. Tears washed grit from his eyes, clearing his vision. Machaun walked toward him. The waves, far to Terra's right, heaved and wept in their bed. He began screaming again. The scream cut his throat. He could feel it bleed. The cliffs on his left absorbed the sound. No one would know how he tried to save her. The battle was ending. Machaun would be defeated when the warhost finally came for him, but he had already stolen the victory.

Terra kept screaming. "Elaa!"

Machaun was almost to him, about to stand over him with the Otnas, to kill him and then D'tanesse with it. Terra would gladly tear free and rush at him, rush to his death fighting this monster.

"Elaa! Elaaaaaa!"

The sky suddenly felt very close, sinking toward Terra's head. The ocean quieted.

The waves became a flat line of still, gray water. Machaun's eyes burned into Terra, but he slowed. The line of water sped forward, covering the beach. It sped over the sand, glossing it blue-gray, a mirror of the looming sky.

The Otnas changed shape in Machaun's hand.

Terra saw it flicker: there and gone, back and now different. The same way it had in the storm of black rain.

Machaun didn't seem to notice it. The warriors holding Terra only reacted to the water, quieting as it had, all heads turning from Machaun to the rising tide, then back to Machaun. Not even D'tanesse seemed to see the white cord, brimming with light, that hung in Machaun's fist. The thread did not drag; it was suspended above ground, the other end stretching behind him in a line to the rubble hill.

Terra stopped struggling, and in mid-shout his voice died away, and he stared past Machaun, beyond him to the figure rising to her feet. The other end of the Otnas traveled to the top of the mound and disappeared in Troy's chest. She stood with her feet braced apart, looking down at Machaun, at the warriors, at Terra and D'tanesse. Terra's breath raked through his open mouth, fire-hot in his throat.

D'tanesse stared at her, then tipped his face to the sky and began to laugh.

Water rushed past the tideline. It swirled against the base of the mound where Troy stood and pushed against the feet of the nearest warriors. It stayed there, and more sheets of water followed the first, making a deeper mirror that bulged toward the beach.

White light pooled around the thread in Troy's chest then spilled over, blooming into a thousand filigree tendrils which spread like a spiderweb over her torso. The threads shone through her clothes, stark white, like a garment intricately lacing down her abdomen and over her hips. Other threads spread over her arms and legs, overwhelming the scars as if they didn't exist. The white veins reached into her feet and sank into the dirt, winding over chunks of rock and packed earth until the heap was covered in a mass of gleaming white. Serene, she descended the mound, and the mass moved beneath her, fibrous like grassroots. It stranded into the water that lapped against her left foot and floated beside her, a web of white veins.

As she approached Machaun she began to speak. Her clear words soared above the water's noise. "The Otnas does not belong to you, Machaun of Camil Askanda."

Machaun jerked around, his sword arm snapping up out of reflex. Terra wondered if he saw the white threads covering her body, or if he saw only her. Machaun's weight was forward. He was about to rush her.

White streaks raced across the sand, dipping over tiny indents toward the group of men gathering themselves for the final onslaught. The hands gripping Terra's arms disappeared and he scooted back from the rising water, hands and feet churning beneath him.

"You are dead." Machaun made the words a command and promise, lifting his closed fist as if it were still around a sword hilt. The Inatru pointed their spears at Troy.

"You do not understand Otnas." Troy also lifted her hand. Along the beach, the line of water began to mound on itself forming a gray-green hump, a growing hill of saltwater looped with white veins. "Call your men from their slaughter."

Machaun raised his arm higher, not seeing a thread pulsing in his own hand, but a weapon he was about to use. All around Terra spears were leveled, pointing at Troy's approach. Terra flinched at a new hand on his shoulder. D'tanesse had worked his way beside him.

"You have proved unfit to serve this domain, and your place is forfeit," she addressed Machaun a last time, and then to the warriors behind him said, "If you lay down your weapons I will spare you, but if you continue you will become nothing. As you were made so you can be unmade. You are warned."

They broke into motion at the same time: Machaun leading his warriors' charge, Troy forward, the Otnas unfurling in Machaun's hand, the water gushing onto the beach, and Terra and D'tanesse scrambling toward the cliff, out of the way.

Machaun was the first to die.

The Otnas bloomed inside his lifted fist. Tendrils unfurled from the center, crawling between his fingers, through his knuckles. The next instant, his arm dissipated. His body followed, melting into a mist of red droplets in mid-step. White curls swept through his evaporating shape.

The hill of water split as it rolled forward, and became two curled fists that smashed down on the group of warriors, obliterating from all sides. Like spillage from a bucket the edges of the water spread, speeding out in every direction while the center roiled violently.

Terra turned and scrambled over the sand, further away from the rising water, stumbling to his feet. The sky still pressed down, seeming about to meet the rising water and smother them. He reeled; white clouded his vision. D'tanesse caught him by the arm and pulled him forward. Water slopped against legs. A cold shower of foam soaked his back, his shoulders, his neck, and he could breathe again. His skin began to burn where the water touched open cuts. He found his feet and bounded to the base of the cliff. D'tanesse smacked into the white wall of rock with his arms and hands thrown open in a desperate embrace. The water chased them, rippling as if it were contained by invisible walls, suspended on the beach instead of its natural bed. They both turned to face the ocean, pressing their backs to the solid rock, sinking to their ankles in the sand while the water rose almost to their knees.

Troy stood alone in waist-deep water. The Otnas stretched out from her chest and spread through the water, tangling with legs, feet, and broken spear shafts that tumbled in the boiling surge. White foam blushed red. Then the limbs vanished, and the vibrant tendrils receded back into one thick thread. The thread then returned to her, coiling around her right arm. The other end crowned her head, settling above her eyebrows, tucking into itself above her neck.

Terra and D'tanesse pushed backward, clutching at outcroppings and making themselves as flat as possible against the cliff. Water pulled hard against their legs as the ocean sucked itself back into its proper bed. Troy raised her hand to her chest as the water surged past her. Two waves rose like arms, surrounding her, and she went under.

* * * *

The dream came like a gift offered in silence, saying all that was needed.

She floated on her back. The sun was a hot blanket over her front, and her father's hands were beneath her in the cool water. His dark beard ringed his smile as he looked down at her. His eyes were circles of brown, beaming more than his smile...

There was her mother, sweeping across the beach in her divided skirts. Her hair gleamed as the sunlight struck it, flowing over her sculpted shoulders, pulled back from her smooth temples...

They were together again.

Troy's body floated limp, laid out as if sleeping, and slowly descended in the water.

She traced her mother's tattoo, the circled star smooth on her skin beneath wisps of her long hair... She was between them, an arm around each neck, pressing her lips to their cheeks, trapped in the circle of their arms, hearing their voices as if for the first time. But their lips and cheeks and voices had always been there...

Her body continued to sink. The sword of elaa stone lay angled across her torso.

They romped in the valley, chasing each other barefoot. The long grasses brushed their ankles and arches, clinging to their heels, staining them green. They took trips to the cool pine forests that nestled the feet of the mountains, and ate beneath the sun-silvered boughs. They caught silver fishes with their feet soaking in the playful lapping waves...

She dreamed feasts in the great Hall, sitting at long tables between white scalloped pillars, while tall arched windows let the sea wind breathe over them. She dreamed of D'tanesse, of sitting on his lap at the table, stealing food from his plate and drumming her tiny bare heels into his shins. She dreamed nights beside the circle hearth pit, wrapped in a wool blanket with D'tanesse, sharing sweet hot roasted grain while Natami told them stories...

Her body came to rest on the sand, rocking in the quieting currents. Her hair floated like seaweed around her face.

She dreamed beautiful people who carried water and herded sheep and cut the stones that built Carmul. She dreamed of the children racing along the streets and narrows. Every piece of the dream fitted together in a span of days and weeks and years, of seasons shifting hot, warm, cool, hot again. She dreamed them all: all of their bright smiles, their warm breath, their open soft hands...

Her eyes opened. Above her wavered a bright water ceiling.

I live...

Her lungs swelled, aching to burst. She lifted her hand, stretching for the surface.

I live for the living.

A shadow, the shape of a man, flew overhead, flickering into the light. It hung for a heartbeat over the water, then crashed in. His splash obliterated the sky as he came down to her, propelling with both arms. His hair, a long black tail, streamed out behind him.

He grabbed her reaching hand, fingers slipping in the water and sliding over her wrist, and they went up together. The sword rocked upright as she rose, then sank down again. It came to rest in the thick sand, standing with its point buried in it.

Troy's lungs burned for air. She pressed her eyes and mouth closed, thrashing beside him.

She remembered lying on her back in long grasses, counting shapes in bright clouds…

She remembered. Everything.

Her head broke the surface, and her mouth sprang open gasping and choking. The water rolled and peaked, pushing at her from three directions at once. D'tanesse wrapped a bare arm around her shoulders, holding her up. She found her feet, and moments later they were standing chest deep in water.

She walked with him, staggering through the push and shove of the waves. His arm stayed around her shoulders and arm, his fingers clenching her hand. Her toes dug into the sand underwater, and pushed forward again.

Forward, toward Terra.

He thrashed through and leaped over little swells to reach her. White, salty spray gushed between them, and then they came together. Arms and elbows twined around necks, holding tight. Their fingers tunneled through wet hair, clenching and unclenching while their shoulders shook with weeping.

Tears mingled as the three clutched each other, their heads pressed close together, standing up to their knees in the gray-blue swells, and the sun shot solid bars of light through the mist around them.

Epilogue

Sema

Carmul is rebuilt.

We sit around the circle hearth pit on the portico of the Great Hall: Imra, Siegra, Norem, Ivel, Mikal and I, eating sweet, roasted grain that is almost too hot. It burns my tongue. We drink mint tea spiced with caddy, the first of Imra's many discoveries since before she became Esobir.

We have met in Carmul in celebration of L'eran's fifth Eulba. He is the first son of Troy L'abri Glor and Terra of Kcen. Troy is the High Ruler of Cathylon and Terra commands the Watch. He prefers that we not call him a king, though he is one by marriage. Some of us are meant to sit in thrones, and some to stand behind them. Terra is like me in that way.

L'eran runs to his mother as she comes out of the Hall with D'tanesse, and she kneels to embrace him. Her hair falls long over her shoulders, softening but not quite hiding the scars lacing her olive skin. She swings L'eran into the air, laughing with him. Her fingertips are stained with ink, and D'tanesse's fingernails are black with it. Now that the restoration of Cathylon is coming to an end, we have begun to record our history as the first Esobir did, writing down events as they happen for those who come after us.

Siegra and Norem sit close together on the circular bench, across from me. The hearth pit is between us, and its orange heat makes their forms ripple. Their own firstborn will arrive soon. Siegra is happy but also impatient to return to her students, the newest members of the Watch. They were carefully chosen by herself with help from the others: five Seawolves from among the former captives in Camil Askanda who stayed behind when most of their people returned to their island, Seya Wul. Carmi, Maon's daughter, is one of Siegra's students.

Maon is revered as a hero by his people and the Esobir. A formation of standing stones were raised on the plateau, monuments to him and others who were dear to us, who gave their lives protecting Cathylon's true High Ruler, or whose lives were taken while Estimal Glor hunted for her. Each stone is covered in names. Maon and Emori of the Seawolves, Teyeda of the Esobir, Core of Kcen, Mytch of the Inatru, Remus and Melaine of Daehexa, and many others. The four stones are covered in a clear green glaze made with elaa so that the names etched on them will never be erased. They stand at the four points of direction, north, south, east and west. They are the heroes of Cathylon.

Troy L'abri joins us at the fireside, sitting on the bench near me where she can see the tops of the stones visible on the crest of the plateau in the west. The setting sun floods the space between them with blood-orange beams that stretch down to us and touch the dome ceiling of the portico.

L'eran squirms in his mother's lap, rubbing his pale hair on her jade green dress, and she lets him down. He sees his father coming from the beach. Terra has been walking with Raelcun and Andres, who are visiting from their villages, Yettmis and Klenit. Terra sees his son and runs to meet him, arms wide. The sunset wraps them in light, catching the sand particles tossed by L'eran's bare feet as Terra spins with him. The light thins, and shadows deepen.

Troy L'abri is arguing with D'tanesse about whether or not the Inatru should be forced to give over their book. They are subdued by L'eran's laughter as he and Terra join us, followed by Raelcun and Andres. The discussion is set aside for the time being.

Ivel helps Imra serve the last of the roasted grain, as usual saying little, but there are many thoughts in his dark eyes—especially when they meet hers, and she smiles.

D'tanesse is singing now. L'eran is trying to sing with him, a little voice fading out, but in key with the stronger, older one. Their song goes past the scalloped pillars circling the portico and up into the night.

The stars are coming out, glimmering white in the fading blue. They feel very close.

About The Author

Jinn Nelson lives in Waukesha, WI with her husband and three cats. She is an avid reader and writer, particularly reading Celtic mythology and writing adventure fantasy. In addition to writing, she enjoys knitting, rock climbing, loose-leaf tea, zombies, dancing, Scotland, and the Internet.

CPSIA information can be obtained at www.ICGtesting.com
Printed in the USA
LVOW050830050812

292936LV00002B/6/P